I0720281

ALMOST A REMEMBRANCE

Almost a Remembrance

EDDY KNIGHT

Waterlinewords

Copyright © 2024 by Eddy Knight

All rights reserved. No part of this book may be reproduced in any manner whatsoever without written permission except in the case of brief quotations embodied in critical articles and reviews.

First Printing, 2024

AUTHOR'S NOTE

POETRY SHOULD SURPRISE BY A FINE EXCESS...AND
APPEAR ALMOST A REMEMBRANCE.

JOHN KEATS

This is predominately a work of fiction, but also partly memoir. I do not like the term autofiction, coined nearly fifty years ago, as the form long predates it. I much prefer quoting one of my heroes in calling it 'almost a remembrance'. Hopefully the reader will neither wonder nor care what was real and what was invented, but should they do so, it is best to consider that anything which seems particularly fanciful most likely happened.

EDDY KNIGHT

Also by Eddy Knight
A Short Walk to the Sea - Fifteen Short Stories.

For Justene; my helpmeet, my lover and my muse.

With thanks to

Dave Walker, the archivist at the Royal Borough of Kensington and Chelsea (who is not a huge Scotsman) for providing me with photographs of the Electric Cinema, Portobello Road.

Cousin Susan Knight for research and information about our transported ancestor – William Langbridge.

~ 1 ~

1972

It was late, three o'clock in the morning, when Jonno got the black taxi to drop him on the far side of the park opposite his London flat. He'd watched the grass being cut earlier, and now he stumbled along the path and collapsed onto a bench while inhaling great lungsful. It was his favourite smell, one he often tried to capture in a poem, always failing.

He had taken Susie to the Roundhouse to see the Titus Groans. Henry, the lead guitarist, sang a few of Jonno's lyrics, so he was hoping that on their first night out together Susie would be impressed. It seemed she was. She invited him in when they got back to her place, in one of the red-brick mansion blocks near Battersea Park. Unfortunately her three flatmates were there; hairy, hippie Scotsmen to a man. Instead of diplomatically retiring to their rooms, they sat around, smoking joints and talking, like self-appointed chaperones, protecting their waif-like countrywoman from the wiles of a devious Sassenach. After a couple of hours, despairing of spending time with her alone, he caught the cab home.

So, now he was sitting on a bench with the whole evening going round and round in his brain; the music, the noise and the smell of the crowd, a combination of sweat and patchouli oil. He pictured Susie holding her arms up as she turned and turned, the way her red-gold tresses spun out as she twirled and shook her head, and how he moved around her in attempted syncopation.

She had baked some wicked hash cookies for them to eat beforehand, and he was still completely off his face.

Most of all, he remembered the kiss. As he was leaving, the pair of them finally alone in the hall, he placed a tentative hand on her left shoulder, then reached up and stroked her cheek, before burying his hand in the abundance of her hair and kissing her on the lips. Their mouths opened in unison and their tongues commenced an ancient dance.

He should have invited her back to his place, but it was too dangerous. He had agreed not to break his and Steve's policy of total secrecy. Not until the heat died down. Which, considering Doctor Ritchie's phone call that morning, didn't sound to be happening any time soon. So when they parted, he didn't give her his phone number. Which he could see she was expecting, and now felt hurt. With his brain still addled he couldn't explain, just mumbled, "I'll give you a ring." Which sounded pathetic even to him, as he stumbled away from her door.

He so wanted Susie to become his lover. As he sat on the bench he ached with disappointment, but after this mess it seemed unlikely. At best she might become a friend, once he was able to explain. But it is hard to recover from a hurt sustained before a relationship has even begun. With a sigh he stood up and moved towards the flat. There was a crack, as if someone stood on a twig. Jonno turned sharply but couldn't see anyone. Besides, he was almost home so perhaps there was no real cause for alarm.

Which was wrong, as it happened.

Just in case there *was* some mugger out there he decided not to bother going around to the side entrance, but use the front door. There was a connecting door from the end of the hall into their flat, past the back of the staircase.

The twig snapping worried him, so he peered out around the front door as he closed it. There was nothing to see, but something felt wrong. Rather than turning on the light he retrieved the zippo from his pocket and, like some private-eye from an American film, flipped the lid up with his thumb and then rotated the wheel in one motion. Holding the lighter high he advanced down the hall while distorted shadows danced across the walls around him, flickering at the edges of sight.

As he passed the cellar door behind the staircase, he thought he smelt the air stale with ancient coal-dust, escaping around its warped, ill-fitting jambs. But no, it was just a sensory memory of its claustrophobic atmosphere. He'd been down there recently, burying something in the earth.

Down there with a shovel, amongst the cobwebs and the gloom, with the massive weight of a Victorian tenement bearing down upon him, feeling he had stepped back into a more gothic world. He merely lacked a gabardine cape and a guttering candle in a leaded lamp to be a character out of Poe or Robert Louis Stevenson. A body snatcher, or worse.

A sudden change of genre. When he reached the end of the hall, he saw the door of his flat was merely pulled to, not firmly shut. It wasn't him. However stoned he'd been he would never have left it like that. And Steve was down in Brighton. So why was the fucking door open?

All thoughts of dank graveyards instantly evaporated.

From the cowboy boots on his feet with the steer's-head stitching, up through his Levi's to the pearl-buttoned denim shirt and the fur-lined, white goat-skin coat, he was instantly all Butch Cassidy and the Sundance Kid. If he'd had a pistol, he would have drawn it. Instead he kicked the door open as he shouted out, "Who the fuck's in there?"

The light clicked on.

"Come on in Jonno. You don't mind if I call you Jonno do you? Come along in. We've been waiting for you. For rather a long time, actually."

The room was full of men, six or seven of them at least, and they were all staring in his direction. It was not a welcoming stare. Jonno turned, to see an enormous figure coming down the hall behind him.

"Don't bother, Jonno," said the man on the sofa who first addressed him. "Frankie there has been sitting up on the landing for a good few hours now and I dare say he's not in a mood to be particularly gentle, are you Frankie?"

"Certainly not, boss," the looming figure intoned.

"I thought as much. Oh, and I should tell you he spends his weekends playing for London Irish. Now, why don't you take a seat and I'll introduce myself?"

With a flourish of his right hand he indicated the armchair across the coffee table from him. As he sat, Jonno took stock of the few articles piled on the mirrored surface; his notebooks full of occasional observations and scraps of poetry, the hinged wooden box with the lid open displaying neat bundles of banknotes, the chillum, the ashtray, somewhat overflowing with dog-ends and roaches, and the little round Japanese lacquered box which contained a small lump of gold seal Paki black. Also there was his passport and the diary which served as a private phone book. It looked like its pages had been ripped out and then stuffed back between the covers somewhat haphazardly. The man on the sofa caught his gaze.

"Sorry about that. The police wanted to copy the numbers."

"You're not the police?"

"Goodness me, no," and he gave a mock shudder before indicating a group standing around the kitchen door where one of them was saying into a walkie-talkie,

"OK., good job, you can stand down, get back to the station, warm up and get a brew on. We'll bring him along in a bit."

"They are," the man on the sofa said with such a disparaging tone that he earned himself a filthy look from the one with the radio.

"So who...?"

"...the fuck are we, as you so eloquently put it? You may call me Robert. I am a Senior Investigations Officer with Her Majesty's Customs and Excise and these are most of my team," indicating the burly Frankie and three other men standing behind the sofa. "Andy is back at H.Q. getting some well-earned rest. We have been working on your case for over a week now and most of us have not had a great deal of sleep. So I would strongly recommend you don't give us any shit. As customs officers, we have an open warrant to enter any premises in the country that we fancy, as long as we take some police along to make sure we don't get up to anything...nefarious, shall we say? Which is a little unfortunate for you, considering the contents of that lovely little Japanese box. I have no interest whatsoever in your recreational pursuits. I am only concerned with your smuggling activities. Our friends over there, on the other hand, are very interested in every little thing they can find, and since we have all been sitting here for several hours awaiting your return, they have had quite a good look around. By the way, the note on your back door 'back in five minutes' was that some kind of a fucking joke?"

"What? No. It's been there for days. A plumber came round to fix one of the sinks. I forgot to take it down."

"I do so wish that you had. I can assure you it has pissed all of us off for a terribly long time. So I'd advise you to go easy with the cops, do whatever they tell you. We, of course, are perfect gentlemen but they...well you never know do you?" This earned him more filthy looks from Mr. Walkie-Talkie, and from his minions. Big Frankie turned in their direction and stroked his bristly chin as if sizing up an opposition scrum.

God, he was winding them up. Jonno wished he would stop. Ten big men having a punch-up in his living room was going to destroy the place.

"So, having found you in possession of an illegal substance they are going to arrest you. You will be their guest for what remains of the night, and in the morning they will take you to the magistrates' court to get you bound over. I'm terribly sorry about all that rigmarole. Personally, I would prefer to whisk you away right now and get on with our job, but you might as well start getting used to the ins and outs of our glorious legal system. Over the next few weeks you are going to get somewhat intimately acquainted with it. Next few years, perhaps I should say. Once they have finished with you someone will come and drive you back to our headquarters for a bit of a chat. Then we'll lay the more serious, smuggling charges. Ok? You understand?"

Jonno wasn't 'Ok' in the least, but he nodded because he did understand. Only too well. Robert and his cohort left.

"Arrogant pricks," commented Mr. Walkie-Talkie. One of the coppers bagged the items spread out on the table while Jonno was hustled out of the side door and into the back of an unmarked car. It seemed that more pressure than necessary was exerted on his head, and he recalled Robert's advice not to antagonise the overtired policemen.

After the short drive up to Shepherd's Bush they dragged a drunk out of a stinking cell, took Jonno's leather belt and cowboy boots, handed him a thin blanket and slammed shut the door. Not a chance of sleep. After picking his way around pools of vomit in his socks to use the seat-less toilet, he sat crossed legged on the bare wooden shelf, wrapped the blanket around his shoulders and, like some Hindu mystic longing for Mount Kailash, he entered a dark night of the soul.

For the next few hours Jonno was aware of footsteps outside his cell door and the occasional lifting of the surveillance flap.

"Bloody Norman," he thought, more than once. "This is all that greedy bastard's fault. Swanning around Kenya at Daddy's expense. Decides he wants to make a fortune on the side, doesn't take any risks himself, but goes and lands us right in the shit. And for what? Something we didn't want; at a price we could have paid just down the road. Bastard."

As he sat through the night, crossed legged on the hard wooden bench, with the inadequate blanket draped around his shoulders, the effect of Susie's killer cookies gradually wearing off, his thoughts turned inwards. Greedy he'd called Norman. But what of himself? Was he so very different? Norman had spotted a business opportunity and taken it. The availability of a particular product in a foreign country, knowledge of that product's ready market, and an acquaintanceship with two middle-men capable of its distribution. All he needed to do was package it up and ship it. Which is where it all fell apart. Jonno had tried to stop it, but knew that should it have arrived safely they would have moved it on. Quickly, as a job lot. Paul would have taken it off their hands, not at the price Norman wanted but that would have been his problem.

All up ten kilos of cocaine. Two kilos of it coming to them. Christ, what was that worth. Even at the slimmest of profit margins they would have made a bundle selling it to Kiwi Paul. Or they could have held on to it, sold it off in individual grams. Most of the dealers they knew would have taken a few for the kudos, to demonstrate how cool they were to their own customers. An underground loss leader, like in a supermarket. Two thousand grams. How long would it take to shift two thousand grams?

It would have been bloody dangerous, but with just a few quid mark up on a gram they could each have bought a house. Is that what he'd turned into? A businessman. Like the bloke who'd opened a record shop up in Notting Hill. Pete and he had called in there a couple of years back when they were looking for a flat. The guy running it came across as a fully paid-up member of the alternative society, with his bean bags to sit in and his offers of vegetarian food, while customers stuck on headphones and listened to the stock of Virgin Records and Tapes. But where was his head at really?

Jonno was forced to consider that rather than undermining straight society, he had become one more cog in the capitalist system. Made him wonder if the dream of a truly alternative culture was even possible. Just because their trade was underground, it didn't make it righteous. He'd been amused by the shonky, wide-boy character Walker in *Dad's Army* with his unobtainable stockings and his under-the-counter meats. Milo Minderbinder in *Catch-22* had made him laugh out loud. But Harry Lime in *The Third Man* was probably closer to the truth. The black market was capitalism run riot, gone red in tooth and claw. The romantic outlaw image peddled by Hollywood was alluring, but in reality, most of the Billy the Kids and the Clyde Barrows of the world were just ignorant, vicious thugs.

He'd been lured down a false track. One which had led to this; shivering in the dark on a hard wooden bench in a vomit-reeking cell, and the prospect of several years in prison. God knows what it would do to him. And for what? To become an entrepreneur? He might just as well have gone to business school if that was what he'd wanted. He didn't. It wasn't.

None of this was how he'd started out. He'd drifted into it. Back then it had just been fun.

~ 2 ~

1968

Three buses turned in off the Lewes Road. They pulled up outside the Union building of Basil Spence's brutalist Sussex University campus. Students dressed in an assortment of warm clothes clambered aboard. Some carried flags rolled up around wooden poles. Jonno Tremaine recognised two banner-carrying men as Trotskyites from the debates he'd attended in Union Hall. They carried their rolled-up banner up the steps and caused the driver to duck as they manoeuvred it around to lie it on the gangway floor. The blond guy two seats back from the front surreptitiously stuck out his foot to trip one of them up. Jonno knew him as a fervent Maoist. As the Trotskyite stumbled there was a chorus of laughter from the anarchists sprawling at the back of the bus, but when the driver tried to prevent another giant sign being carried aboard the whole passenger contingent united to howl down his objections.

There had been arguments about tactics for the forth-coming demonstration. Should they follow the organisers' line about non-violence generating maximum public support, causing politicians to re-evaluate their support for the American position? Or was this doomed from the start? Was change dependent upon direct action? Should they break away from the proscribed route and attempt an assault on the embassy? It had failed in March. This time were they more prepared, more determined?

The debates lasted for three days. Jonno amongst the crowd at every session, adding his voice to the shouts of approval for a particularly stirring orator, or to the howls of derision at a dunderhead. He felt himself standing on the edge of history. Taking part, feeling liberated and alive.

The nightly portrayal of the latest massive destruction visited upon North Vietnamese rice farmers and their Southern cousins, had sparked heated dissent between him and his father. The peasants' only wish, as far as Jonno could make out, was to free themselves from their corrupt overlords, and the blood-thirsty foreigners who, for reasons of their own, propped up their invidious regime.

Later, when evidence of the My Lai massacre was bruited abroad, Jonno's father flatly refused to accept that American soldiers were capable of such an atrocity; could massacre 500 unarmed civilians in a drug-fuelled frenzy of blood-lust. However, he condoned the carpet-bombing wreaking mayhem and misery on the population of that benighted country. Along with most of his contemporaries, he accepted the theory of falling dominos, and believed America to have some God given right to stem the southern flow of such a devious 'yellow peril.'

As the coach pulled away Jonno turned to look at the woman sitting next to him. He wondered what his father would make of her, with her short black hair, her jeans, her red neckerchief, and her industrial strength donkey-jacket with the black plastic panel covering her shoulder blades. Probably make some comment about her looking like one of McAlpine's navvies fresh from laying concrete on a motorway. She must have felt his scrutiny because she twisted her head and looked him up and down.

"If I were you, I'd get rid of the scarf, comrade," she told him.

It was a long woollen job, similar to the one worn by David Warner when playing Hamlet a few years previously. The day after a stunned Jonno had witnessed his electrifying performance on their black and white television set, he had asked his mother to knit him something similar. In alternating sections of black and red, he had worn it nearly every day since arriving at university. Because of the colours he was assumed to be an anarchist, which he thought he probably was. He certainly didn't ascribe to any of the more rigid ideologies paraded about the place. He hadn't read any of the works of Karl Marx, as most of his fellow students appeared to have done. He had seen all of the brothers' movies however, and laughed at every one.

"Why would I want to do that?"

"Too easy for the cops to grab hold of it. They get you in a stranglehold with that and you're fucked."

She had a cockney accent. Jonno wasn't used to girls swearing and was a little shocked, although he wasn't going to show it.

"What about your red one?"

"Too small. Besides it's soaked in lemon juice."

"I thought that was your perfume I could smell."

"You think I'm a perfume wearer, do you?"

"No, of course not, not to demonstrations anyway. What's it for then."

"Tear gas. In case the bastards use it. I can pull it up over my face, the lemon juice neutralises the chemicals. Supposed to anyway. We might find out later. I've got a couple of spares in my pocket, want one?"

"No. Thanks all the same. I think I'll be alright."

"Suit yourself comrade," and she turned away to look out the window.

Just outside of Crawley the cops were waiting for them. The bus was pulled over and the students made to get out. They searched the vehicle thoroughly before turning their attention to the passengers, forcing them against the side of the bus and patting them down, presumably in a hunt for weapons. The hold-up was not unexpected. It appeared the establishment believed the propaganda peddled by their media baron friends. The gutter-press had been emphasising the possibility of violence at the peace march for weeks, no doubt attempting to boost their circulation figures. When the cops started asking for lunch boxes the situation lurched towards the outrageously surreal.

Jonno, obeying some atavistic notion about coach journeys and day-trips, had provided himself with a couple of sandwiches and a hard-boiled egg in a plain brown paper-bag. When the egg was discovered, the constable searching quickly stepped back and shouted for his sergeant. He peered into the bag Jonno was holding, and in an unconscious parody of *Dixon of Dock Green* said "Hello, hello, hello, what's all this then?"

"It's a hard-boiled egg."

"It *looks* like a hard-boiled egg; I'll give you that much."

"It *is* a hard-boiled egg. Feel it, go on."

"Oh no, son. You're not getting me that easily. Prove it."

"What?"

"You heard me. Prove it. Go on, take it over there, away from my constables, and crack it open."

"But it's my lunch."

"If you refuse to crack it open, I'll arrest you right now for carrying an offensive weapon."

"A hard-boiled egg? I know some people don't like them but they're hardly offensive. If it was raw rather than hard-boiled, I could understand why you might think..."

"Saunders, cuff him."

"Alright, alright, I'll do it."

"If it is what you say, you can have an early lunch. Otherwise, sunshine, you're fucking nicked. Go on, right over there, crack it on the curb. Everyone else, stand well back."

The crowd of onlookers, both students and coppers alike, huddled back against the side of the bus as Jonno walked away and, bemused, bent down to the edge of the granite curb. Against this he cracked the egg which he had boiled for the exact number of minutes his mother had stipulated, insisting that he master all manner of the cooking of eggs, as well as the frying of bacon, before she would allow him to leave home for the purpose of studying Literature. There was an expectant hush, before a collective sigh of disappointment as Jonno stood, peeling bits of eggshell off the pristine, glistening white oval. Then, looking the sergeant square in the face he raised it to his mouth and bit it in half.

"Satisfied?" he asked once he had chewed it enough to swallow.

"Sorry son, I didn't mean to ruin your lunch. I'm partial to an egg meself. It's just some bloody reporter from the Daily Mail told the powers that be, some of your lot were planning to blow some eggs, and fill the empty shells with acid. So we've got strict orders to check."

"You have got to be joking!" An expostulation from amongst the crowd of students.

"Shut your mouth, sunshine. We're just doing our job," said the red-faced sergeant as he pulled himself upright, to frown in the general direction the comment had come from.

"This is pure bloody Gilbert and Sullivan." Jonno recognised the speaker as Steve, one of the members of the drama society he had nearly joined on enrolment day.

"On your way then. Go on, get out of it. Go and have your bloody peace march."

As they trooped back onto the bus Steve led a number of his fellow thespians in a rousing chorus of 'A Policeman's Lot is not an 'Appy One' from *The Pirates of Penzance.* The rest of them fell about laughing and grinning at the discomforted constables through the bus windows. As Jonno sank into his seat his companion turned and congratulated him on showing the police up to be the ignorant tools of state suppression.

"That's taking it a bit far," said Steve, leaning across the aisle from the neighbouring seat. "You want to watch out for Harriet there, don't let her get you into trouble. It was one of her mates threw the tin of red paint at the American ambassador last semester."

"Bloody pacifist," she retorted. "Direct action is the only way to achieve significant change. Oh no, here we bloody go. Aunty Andrew wants a word."

This last was in response to one of the students at the front of the bus who had risen to his feet and was winding himself up to address the passengers.

"Comrades," he began, holding up his arms to gain their attention. "In the light of that little incident, which demonstrated the level of paranoia the government is labouring under, I wish to remind you of our purpose here today. The whole idea has always been that this should be a peaceful demonstration. The media has, and probably always will, demonised us as a bunch of unruly left-wing radicals bent on nothing more than destruction."

"Too bloody right," Harriet shouted out. "You can't make an omelette..."

Andrew ignored her and carried on. "Whatever your personal feelings, this is not the time to give in to them. We of the Vietnam Solidarity Campaign, have organised this march in order to demonstrate that an overwhelming mass of ordinary British citizens object to our government supporting the actions of the imperialist American forces, in their attempt to crush the glorious revolution of the heroic Vietnamese peoples. If we resort to violence we will be playing right into the establishment's hands. They will dismiss us as a bunch of long-haired ne'er-do-wells. If we can galvanise a hundred thousand people to march through London peacefully then it won't be so easy for them. Even the media, after their concerted campaign of vilification, will not be able to ignore a hundred thousand voices raised in opposition. So, we have organised numerous marshals to keep the march on track, to keep us to the specified route the cops have sanctioned, thereby avoiding direct confrontation. A wide number of differing political factions have joined together to promote this demonstration and we welcome you all and thank you for joining with us. All I am asking is that all of you obey the marshals so we may make the point which we are all agreed upon. America Out – Victory to the NLF!"

This last delivered in a shout and with a raised fist which the majority of passengers took up and chanted back at him again and again.

While he was talking George, a part-time theatre technician for Brighton Combination, stood and popped up one of the Perspex roof ventilators, withdrew a roll of gaffer tape from his greatcoat pocket and proceeded to secure the posts of two NLF flags so that they surmounted the coach at forty-five-degree angles. Jonno looked up and saw one of them through the clear Perspex streaming out gloriously in their slip-stream.

Harriet, sitting to Jonno's right, was unimpressed by Andrew's diatribe. Almost under her breath, Jonno made out the single word she uttered – "tosser."

Steve, across his aisle to the left, was dismissive. "It's bollocks that the media won't be able to ignore us. If we get a hundred thousand turn-out they'll say it was thirty thousand. Maybe less. They daren't frighten people over their corn flakes in the morning, or they might buy a different paper."

Harriet joined in, "I'm sick of those bloody International Marxist Group wimps spouting their hundred-year-old philosophy. They do nothing but sit around and talk. You know where Saint Karl thought revolution and the overthrow of capitalism was going to occur first?" She asked Jonno.

"No. Where?"

"Here. In dear old Britain. He said it would be an advanced industrial country with a working class which would 'inevitably' rise up and throw off its shackles. That's a laugh. The Romans knew. Bread and circuses win out every fucking time. Our workers are too busy watching Match of the Day, filling in their football pools, and dreaming of holidays in Torremolinos. Where it did happen was Russia, China, Cuba, and now in Vietnam. Peasant economies all of them. People have to be angry to rise up. Be ground down, suffering."

"I guess you're right."

"Know the likeliest place for a revolution to break out in Britain?"

"Where?"

"Northern Ireland."

"Why there?"

"Because the Catholics are treated like peasants by the Protestant majority. They have no rights and a shit-load of discrimination. It's already starting, did you see the news a couple of weeks ago when the cops broke up a civil rights march in Londonderry?"

"I don't watch the telly these days."

"They busted the head of a Westminster politician. That's a stupid move for a start. They attacked women and children with batons and water cannon. No one's going to stand that for too long. They'll fight back. You watch, if we do have a revolution, that's where it'll start."

Soon the bus was pulling through the suburbs of South London. There was an atmosphere of rising excitement amongst the passengers, a shared anticipation of the approach to a great event. Jonno was far from immune. He welcomed the feverish agitation, felt his lungs expanding in his chest and sat up straighter in his seat, eager for whatever might occur.

The bus finally stopped and the cohort of rebellious youth disembarked. The other two buses were there, also in the process of disgorging the Sussex contingent. People shouted greetings to compatriots who had travelled in the other coaches, stood and stretched out cramped backs, unfurled their flags, and raised high placards and banners. Other coaches from differing universities, art schools and technical colleges were also disembarking their passengers. Jonno stared in amazement as a group of nurses, resplendent in starched uniforms, stepped onto the pavement and formed a phalanx at the behest of their matron, eager to join the growing crowd.

Andrew, the orator from Jonno's coach, organised their three groups into one, and positioned the two banner bearers at either side, flanking him and a couple of other student union officials. Under the blazon of Sussex University they led off, heading towards a bridge over the Thames and forward into central London.

Jonno found himself marching between his two new acquaintances, Harriet and Steve. He took them to be second year students, veterans of the protest movement which had spread, like a forest fire in a drought, right across Europe in the spring, which he could only gaze at on television. Now, finally, he was here, in the thick and throb of it all, marching to add his voice to the disgust felt at the machinations of the political establishment. Hopefully to contribute, in however small a way, to the dismantling and final passing of the old order.

He raised himself to his full six-foot height and turned to survey the crowd. He thought of the expression 'a sea of faces.' Well, this was a veritable flood, an ocean, biblical in proportions. Carrying banners, waving flags, and chanting, chanting, as if by noise alone, like Joshua and the children of Israel circling Jericho, as if just by shouting their great shouts the walls of this intransigent city might similarly be brought crashing down.

Jonno was new to London, and as the tide of students and other protestors passed over the great river he was struck by the grandeur of a building on the far bank. "Somerset House," said Harriet, noticing the direction of his gaze. "We're all in there" she added, referring to the government records of births, deaths and marriages, "Fascist regimes always pride themselves on getting the paperwork right."

The crowd took up the whole width of the bridge, its length so vast that Jonno couldn't see the start of it. His view of the classical edifice was occasionally interrupted by the jostling of banners, and the waving and flapping of flags; red over blue with a central golden star, the emblem of the National Liberation Front, the proud symbol of the Viet-Cong. "It looks like the storming of the Winter Palace," he remarked to his neighbour, thinking of the Evreinov film.

"October's always been a good month for a revolution," came her reply.

Their section of the crowd moved off the bridge and eventually turned left into the Strand. They filled the street of tall buildings elevated at either side, whose solid facades echoed all around, throwing back the chant being raised – "Ho, Ho, Ho Chi Minh," changing occasionally to, "Hey, hey, LBJ, how many kids have you killed today?" The girl by his side pointed at an alleyway coming up on their left. "The Savoy Hotel," Harriet said, "that's where all the rich Americans stay when they come over here. If we wanted to do something really symbolic, we should go in there and trash the place."

"How come?"

"Don't recognise the name, eh? It's built on the site of John of Gaunt's old Savoy Palace."

"Oh God," interjected Steve, "On the corner. The Savoy Theatre. That's where all the G and S musicals were first staged."

"Fuck off Steve. Who gives a shit about bloody Gilbert and Sullivan?"

"So? The Savoy Palace?" Jonno enquired as they marched past the alleyway which led to an opulent-looking hotel in front of which stood a top-hatted and uniformed man all garlanded about with gold braid. He was watching the passing parade with an expression on his face as if he were sucking on a particularly astringent lemon.

"Wat Tyler? The Peasants Revolt?" Harriet turned an enquiring face back to Jonno. "Don't you know your history?"

"Not that bit obviously. What happened?"

"It was one of the peasants' main targets. They blamed old John for imposing the poll tax on them, so they broke into his Palace and trashed it. It was the richest house in England at the time but they didn't steal a single thing. They declared themselves Zealots for Truth and Justice, not thieves and robbers. So instead, they burned the tapestries, broke up the precious metalwork, used mattocks and hammers to crush gems into dust, and destroyed all of the duke's records and papers. What they couldn't rip up or smash they threw into the river. Then they burnt the place down."

"Christ, they must have been bloody angry."

"They had good reason. They were slaves trying to throw off their shackles."

"What happened?"

"What do you think? It was the fourteenth century. Huge repression, torture, executions, heads on spikes, all that. But it was a start. The overlords never slept quite so soundly in their beds afterwards."

"How come you know all this?" he asked her.

"Always been fascinated by insurrections. Protest's got a long and glorious history in England. Don't know much, do you? I thought you were studying history, I seen you around the place now and then."

"I go to the odd lecture out of interest. But I'm doing English and American Lit."

"Oh, one of the scribbling classes like Steve there. Going to write a book someday, are you?"

"Maybe. I hope so. Perhaps one day I'll write about this."

"If you do, bloody well get it right. Don't ponce about with all that literary turns of phrase bollocks."

"God, Harriet," interjected Steve, "there has to be some place for creation after you and your mates have overthrown the system, otherwise what's the point?"

"Bloody poets," she expostulated.

"Unacknowledged legislators of the world."

"Bollocks. Shelley was probably trying to persuade some impressionable young woman to drop her drawers when he said that."

"Is there no place for romance in your world?" Steve asked her. "After the revolution no singing and dancing, no literature, no art?"

"Of course there will be. But making the revolution comes first. Idealists and romantic dreamers just get in the fucking way. What happens afterwards will take care of itself."

She was so vehement, so dismissive that Jonno wondered if there was some personal history between her and Steve. He lost interest in their dispute as their section of the crowd finally poured into Trafalgar Square.

After a cursory glance at the grey neo-classical relics from a monumental age, his whole attention was focussed on the colour and movement swirling around the lions at the base of Nelson's Column. This was the present; this was where he lived.

There were thousands of people crowding into the square and more arriving every minute. They were pouring in from every direction and brandishing all manner of flags and banners. Jonno could make out one proclaiming the presence of the Hackney Young Liberals not ten yards away from that of the Fulham Young Communists. He saw a multitude of different styles of dress, from long-haired students in duffle coats like himself, to middle-aged men wearing suits and trilby hats. Girls in mini-skirts and boots, stood alongside women in twin-sets, tweeds and court shoes. Vicars rubbed their peace-loving shoulders with Maoist agitators bent on destruction. Old-school CND members, veterans of many an Aldermaston march, linked arms with dope-smoking anarchists young enough to be their grandchildren.

It was time to move on. The square was filled to capacity and hundreds more were attempting to march into it. The organisers had underestimated when they envisioned a hundred thousand people turning out. Such was the disgust felt by a population treated nightly to graphic depictions of military violence. It was a fair way through central London to Hyde Park and it would take an age for this many people to arrive at their destination to hear the speeches.

"Bugger the speeches," Harriet shouted in his ear, above the general tumult. "What good have speeches ever done? With this many people now is the time for action. Are you coming with us?"

"With who?"

"With all the other militants and troublemakers," Steve shouted from his other side. "Don't do it. Stay with the proper march. It'll be safer for one thing."

"Safer!" Harriet spat out contemptuously. "If you want to write about this you need to be where the action is, not limping along to bloody Speakers' Corner."

"We should stick to the agreed route. Demonstrate to the media that the peace movement is disciplined, not just a bunch of left-wing fanatics." Steve insisted.

"Fuck the bloody media. Look Jonno, if you want to waste your time listening to a lot of crappy old-fashioned rhetoric and holding hands while singing 'We shall over-come' then stick with Steve. If you're keen to at least *try* to achieve something, want to join the real struggle for change, then come with me. We need to get up the front when the march moves off. That's where the comrades are going to be, and we aint going to no sodding park for no fucking picnic."

Whatever the argument amongst the organisers at the base of Nelson's Column, a section of the crowd settled it by moving off. Relieved to be underway at last, the rest of the protestors crammed into the square prepared to follow on behind the avant-garde.

Harriet and Jonno manoeuvred around the southern edge of the giant crowd, working their way towards the front. They passed the bronze equestrian statue of Charles 1st, the only English monarch ever executed by order of a revolutionary parliament. Jonno turned to speak to Steve but he was lost in the multitude of faces jostling about in the square. Harriet linked her arm through his so that they not become separated as they pushed, shoved and threaded their way towards the front.

Finally she was satisfied they were far enough forward amongst her like-minded comrades. Everyone was linking arms with their flanking neighbours and falling into step. The chanting throng stretched from side to side of the wide thoroughfares they passed along, hemmed in between cliff-like buildings, resembling the canyons funnelling an army in one of the Biblical epics Jonno saw as a child.

Finally they were marching up Park Lane, Hyde Park to their left and Speakers' Corner in sight up ahead. There the marchers ignored the marshals and swung right into Grosvenor Street, across which a thin line of police was strung. This was quickly swept aside by the crush of some few thousand militant students, who made their rapid way towards the square. Jonno felt a surge of emotion, just making it to the grass outside the American Embassy tasted like victory. He turned and looked back, expecting to see the rest of the marchers piling in behind them. They weren't.

Instead hundreds more policemen were emerging from buildings and alleyways where they had been hiding, to re-inforce and seal off the entrance to Grosvenor Street. The marchers left outside were being harangued by the official marshals to leave them, to carry on to the park. After some consternation the main body of the march did so. A few frustrated demonstrators hung back, appealing to the pass-ing crowd, trying to gather enough numbers to attempt an attack on the greatly reinforced police line, but they shortly realised that forcing such a breach was impossible. They argued with the marshals directing the march on its pre-ordained way but were informed that violence was childish and served no purpose. "But our mates in there are about to be massacred," they shouted, to which the reply came, "Well they shouldn't have gone in there then, should they?"

Jonno realised it must have been a set-up all along. In order to be allowed their march the traditional left-wing organisers must have colluded with the cops. Allow the militants to get up to the front, make it easy for them to get into the square, siphon them off, seal them off, and then deal with them in there. And deal with them the police had every intention of doing. They were servants of the government, and the government, albeit socialist in theory, gave tacit support to the American adventure in Vietnam. It stopped short of sending troops but declared itself to be in moral agreement. The aim of the protestors was to convince the government to withdraw this support, as they saw isolating America as the likeliest way to end the carnage inflicted on the Vietnamese people. In between these two positions stood the police, who mostly just hated students.

Their feelings were reciprocated. The five or six thousand students and other militant intellectuals who made it into the square mostly hated the police, at whose hands many of them had suffered previously. As they gathered on the grassy square and faced the embassy, they also faced about one thousand police, standing five deep in a wide row before them. Big, beefy men, whose imposing regulation height was increased a good six inches by their tall helmets, and who, once they linked arms, formed an impregnable blue wall easily capable of withstanding assault by a motley collection of undernourished, weedy-looking students. The whole set-up smacked of a well-planned military strategy. Behind the coppers, numerous vehicles, paddy wagons and the like, were drawn up nose to tail directly in front of the embassy, providing a final physical obstacle should the line be broken. In a corridor between them and the disciplined constables, senior officers carrying megaphones strode about, barking orders.

Jonno looked up at roof of the multi-windowed embassy. There a giant, gilded bald-headed eagle squatted, stretching its wings out some thirty-five feet from one wing-tip to the other like the evil steed of one of Tolkien's Ringwraiths. Its cruelly curved beak seemingly ready to snatch up any malefactor which caught its roaming, baleful eye. Nearly everyone he knew had read *The Lord of the Rings* the previous summer. Jonno imagined he was not alone in relating the current position to that of an assault on Mordor. This illusion was further strengthened by the sound of oncoming horses' hooves. These were not fictive, however, were in fact very real and heading straight towards him.

After a brief triumphant moment the students gathered themselves together and advanced on the massed policemen, shouting slogans, waving flags and finally, as they closed, pushing and shoving. Fists flew from both sides, an occasional blue-uniformed five-man snatch squad would rush into the crowd to grab hold of a perceived ring leader, or rescue one of their number who had waded too far into the melee. Banners became weapons but were rendered ineffective by the press of numbers. Stones and clods of earth were thrown, shouts, cries, incredible noise and then, above all this, the sound of massed hooves.

The police lines parted in several places and through these gaps poured giant horses. Their mounted officers lost no time in laying about themselves with the long batons with which they were armed. Heads were cracked. Blood was spilled. The crowd was angered exponentially. No longer was this a game, nor yet some fictive adventure. The wooden banner support poles came into their own at last as a policeman was knocked off of his horse, to be kicked severely by those who had suffered his indiscriminate lashings out. A snatch-squad beat and punched their way to where he had fallen, lifted him up and helped him re-mount.

Smoke drifted across the square. Beside him, Harriet shouted "tear gas" as she pulled her scarf up over her nose. She was wrong; it was a flare thrown by someone from their side. It seemed many were prepared for serious confrontation. Some were wearing crash helmets. To his left a man threw marbles under an oncoming horse's hooves. They failed to bring down horse and rider, uselessly pressed into soft earth. He was instantly laid low by a severe blow between the shoulder blades.

The great, grey descendent of a war-horse turned in their direction. Harriet, distracted for a moment, reaching into her donkey jacket to get a lemon-drenched scarf for Jonno, received a glancing blow to her temple. It dropped her to the ground, falling between the horse's legs. Discomforted, the huge beast reared up on its hind legs. Terrified it was going to bring its steel-shod hooves down onto Harriet's unprotected head, Jonno reached in beneath the impending weight of the descending colossus, grabbed at the hem of her jacket, and dragged her out of the way.

The horse charged off, its mount flailing indiscriminately about himself with his long baton. A century before it would have been a sabre with its blade sharpened to a lethal edge. Even now it was serious enough when brought down upon the vulnerable heads crowded beneath him. Jonno helped a dazed Harriet to her feet, looked around and dragged her over to one of the trees, whose low hanging branches provided shelter from further onslaught by the mounted police. He took the scarf she had been attempting to offer him and used it to staunch the flow of blood which ran down the side of her face.

"You ok?" he shouted above the tumult.

"Yeh. I think. Bit groggy. Head fucking hurts."

"Let's get out of here."

"No, we can't let them win."

Jonno looked around at the melee. Which, in places, looked to have descended to the level of Saturday night punch-ups. In effect it was a gradual pushing back of the disorganised militants by a disciplined force of constabulary. There was no serious defence against the baton wielding mounted coppers who cut swathes through the angry jostling crowd. This eased the pressure on the advancing line of their colleagues and now more protestors were being sought out by the snatch squads, lifted from their feet and hauled back behind police lines, there to be flung into the back of Black Mariahs.

"They are winning. Have won. Don't be stupid."

Jonno looked back towards the embassy where he'd caught a glimpse of something glittering in a window. It was a U.S. marine. A marine with an M16. Each of the first-floor windows were similarly occupied. He shuddered at the thought of the bloodbath which would have ensued, had the protestors managed to reach the building. He didn't doubt that the marines would protect what was considered their home soil with ultimate force. Senior police officers must have understood it too, and there was no way they could allow for it to happen. Hence the brutal tactics employed. Jonno saw a double irony, for the police were in fact protecting the militants. On the other hand, should some of them have broken through and been shot, the protestors might have achieved their aim of fundamentally breaking the British-American détente.

"Politics" he said to himself, grimacing, as if the very word left a dirty taste in his mouth. He was drained. The day started with him being filled with excitement and the enthusiasm of youth. It had seemed so easy. If they all stood together then society must change. Now he knew better. They might have the numbers but the others had the guns, and they wouldn't hesitate to use them. What had they been thinking? Had the naiveté of the previous year's 'summer of love' infected them? Had they really believed that, armed with nothing more than a clutch of simplistic mantras, they could cause entrenched capitalist interests to crumble and wither away? Or, like children on bonfire night, been over-excited by the fireworks of the spring-time Parisian street-fights they'd eagerly watched on their televisions? Been so encouraged by the student riots across Europe and America, they hadn't considered that occupying a university was a relatively easy task? That changing the world might be a tad more difficult? Well, this was patently not the way to do it.

"Come on," he said to Harriet whom he'd propped up against the trunk of the tree. "Your head's bleeding, you've probably got concussion so you're not thinking straight. I reckon our point's been made but there's no way we're going to win this one. Look around you, the cops will have cleared the square in twenty minutes, so why bother? Another crack on the head will probably give you brain damage. Or do you want to be arrested?"

"God no."

"Then come with me. I'm leaving. I don't know where the fuck I am but I'm not staying here." He wrapped an arm around her and dragged her stumbling body across a rapidly diminishing vacant section of the square, to disappear up one of the side streets and back into the centre of London.

~ 3 ~

1972

A bang on the cell door. He must have fallen asleep, lain down on the hardwood bench at some point during the night. All his joints ached, his knees particularly, which, since he always slept on his front, had been pressed into the unresisting wood.

"Stand away from the door!"

Was that a joke? He wasn't going to stand anywhere; seized up muscles and compromised joints wouldn't let him. But the man outside kept waiting, so, slowly and painfully, Jonno swung his legs around and pulled himself upright. The door swung back and a constable entered. He was young, about the same age as Jonno, with very short blond hair and a sympathetic look on his face. He was not one of the policemen who'd been in his room the previous night.

"Fancy a mug of tea?"

"Oh God, yes please. What time is it?"

"Eight. You're in court at ten. The van'll be here for you at 9.30. You can have a bit of a wash in our bog if you want, but I'll have to come with you – make sure you don't try to escape – or slit your wrists."

"I'm hardly likely…"

"It's been known. First timer aint yuh?"

"Yes."

"They're the ones we have to watch."

After a swift wash he was escorted back to the cell where a mug of industrial- strength tea was waiting for him. His throat was so dry that swallowing was difficult, but he forced it down, not knowing where the next one might be coming from. He was taken out into the carpark at the rear of the station where a white van was pulled up, engine running. Inside another copper ushered him into one of the tiny cells, three to each side of the central gangway. The door was locked behind him and he sat on the hard chair and watched through the wire mesh as his gaoler walked towards the front and pulled down a folding seat for himself. From this position he could keep his eye on all of his charges, locked into their individual compartments. No one spoke. To Jonno's left was a tiny window, six inches wide and three high, armoured glass reinforced with wire. The van pulled out and Jonno stared out at the passing buildings. His stomach lurched as he realised they were driving down his street, passing his very own flat. He wondered whether he would ever see it again, what might happen to all of their stuff, and whether anyone had been down into the cellar.

The journey wasn't long. Soon he was in a holding cell with four others. There was a smell of stale sweat. He wondered if it was coming from him. The bloke with greasy long hair sitting next to him looked him up and down and asked, "What are you up for? Drugs, is it?"

Jonno could only nod, the power of speech having left him. He was scared. He had never contemplated being seen by others as just one amongst a group of criminals. The whole thing was just a bit of fun, an elaborate game that he and Steve had played. Played and, it now appeared, lost.

"Derek," his neighbour said and held out his hand to shake. "Burglary. Second offence. Don't fancy me chances much. Your first?"

"Yes," Jonno said, astonished at how high his voice sounded.

"You'll be right, long as it wasn't much. I've been up in front of this one before.

He's pretty lenient on first timers. 'Course if you was dealing it'd be another matter."

He fixed Jonno with a quizzical gaze.

The temptation to spill his guts was overwhelming, frightened and lonely as he was, and thankful for such a seemingly sympathetic ear. He wanted to admit to his misdemeanours, and get some advice about what he might expect. More than anything he wanted to know about the cellar, but he dare not mention its contents to Derek. He could be a stool-pigeon, trying to prize information out of him that he could trade for a reduction in his sentence. He was probably being paranoid, but all he knew came from fiction he had read, films he'd seen; crime novels and war stories portraying interrogation tactics. He managed to restrain himself.

He felt himself reduced to schoolboy status, waiting in trepidation outside the headmaster's office with its oaken door at the top of dark stairs.

When finally he was called up into the courtroom the resemblance to school was something of a relief. The dark oak panelling, the silence of the dock and the magisterial presence on the raised dais were all recognizable. He wasn't expected to offer an explanation or any kind of defence. He just let them get on with it. He was accused of being in possession of a couple of grams of hashish to which he pleaded guilty. The police prosecutor then asked that he be bound over for a month.

"A bit extreme for a couple of grams, isn't it?" the magistrate asked.

"Investigations by H.M. Customs are ongoing your honour, and I believe that other charges will shortly be laid."

"Is there any suggestion of a risk of flight?"

"The defendant has surrendered his passport."

"In that case I will impose a fine of twenty-five pounds for possession, and bind you over on your own recognisance to report at your nearest police station every Friday for a month or until this matter is cleared up. Do you have anything to say?"

What could he say? They took him out and he paid his fine on the spot. His wallet and the contents of his pockets were returned to him at the station. Not the items that had been on his coffee table however; not his poetry notebook, not the little Japanese lacquered box which contained their personal stash, not their diary with its phone numbers transcribed into a fairly simple code, the pages of which they had torn apart to copy, and not, most importantly, the old hinged wooden box which contained five bundles of ten-pound notes, held together in hundreds by rubber bands.

Frankie, the rugby player from the previous night, was waiting for him in the vestibule and led him outside to an unmarked car. They got in the back while another man drove them across London to an area unfamiliar to Jonno, but which he surmised to be in the vicinity of the City.

They pulled up outside a modern seven storey office block with a row of shops at ground level facing the street. Mostly these were travel agents Jonno noticed, and he wondered if this was deliberate, whether they might be part of some elaborate front. "Now I really am becoming paranoid," he thought. But when he was escorted around the side of the building to a nondescript glass door, then held up at a desk while the uniformed officer behind the counter pinned a plastic disc to his jersey, telling him to wear it at all times, he wasn't so sure. As they moved towards the lifts it felt like he'd stepped into an episode of *The Man from Uncle*. Until then, Napoleon Solo and Ilya Kuryakin were the only people Jonno knew of so adorned with identity tags, as they entered their headquarters.

Out of the lift on the fifth floor he was shown into an open plan office and made to sit in a chair.

"The boss'll be with you when he's ready," he was told.

The way he was left, solitary and unguarded, like an inconvenient parcel its recipient could not be bothered to unwrap at present, served to bring home how supremely confident they were that they had him. How convinced they were that when he left this building, he was going nowhere else but to a gaol, there to remain for a very long time. No passing Go, and certainly not collecting any £200. Since talking to Robert, the previous night, his world was utterly changed. His head was still spinning.

He sat in an office chair, kicking his heels, trying not to think too much. Five desks, each with trays stacked one on top of the other overflowing with loose papers at one end and a giant grey IBM electric typewriter at the other. He'd heard about these new Selectrix machines. They were supposed to have something like a metal golf ball with all the characters raised up on it, which would spin around at a rate of knots, altering the angle of its declension as it went. They sure as hell put his little Olivetti travel typewriter with its torn green plastic carry case to shame. He moved over to the one on the nearest desk and looked at the silver ball. He found the button which turned it on. The machine hummed enticingly. One of the trays contained blank paper. He wound a sheet onto the platen and tried to think of something so he could watch the ball spinning. He had just managed "Help. I have been kidnapped and am being held against my..." when the door opened and Frankie shouted "Stop that!"

Not wishing to be handcuffed, he did. "Sorry," he said, "Just, you know, checking out the modern technology. Poets have a thing for typewriters."

"Poet my arse. You haven't published anything, we checked. Sit fucking down and don't touch nothing."

"Don't suppose there's a chance of a cup of tea is there?" He regained his seat, trying to show he was not as frightened as he felt. He knew that to have any chance of wriggling out of this predicament, he must appear to be nonchalant, act as if he were innocent.

"Jesus, you've got some front, I'll give you that. Ok, I think Andy's putting the kettle on. I'll see if he'll do you one. Just don't fucking touch anything alright? This oper-ation's been a sodding nightmare, what with all your mates down in Brighton, your flatmate's bloody father and that twat out in Kenya. Christ."

"That's good," Jonno thought as Frankie left the room. He'd gleaned some information. Being an avid reader of the spy novels of Len Deighton and John Le Carre he was aware of the value of information in situations such as this. Now he knew something of what was going on. He could work with it. They had obviously picked up Steve. He never talked much about it, but Jonno knew Steve's father was once a very senior police officer. On retirement he'd been headhunted by the home office for work of an unspecified nature, on the clandestine battlefield that was Northern Ireland. And they obviously knew about Norman out there in Kenya, son of some foreign office official. It seemed the best course of action would be to tell them the truth. Just not all of it.

So when he was finally called in to Robert's office, he was somewhat prepared.

"Do you want us to call anybody for you, tell them where you are? Your parents?"

"God no. The shock would kill my Mum."

"As you wish. But they're bound to find out. The charge we will be bringing against you and your friends will be conspiracy to import a 'class A' drug. Ten kilos of cocaine to be exact. Estimated street value of what, about half a million pounds? You may not know it but the charge of conspiracy is very serious, and carries a much stiffer penalty than mere smuggling. It implies a high level of intelligence. The court usually considers conspirators too dangerous to be left out in society. The Great Train Robbers for example. They got thirty years for being so bloody clever, for nearly getting away with it. And they were just crooks. You boys all had university educations, degrees and so forth. I wouldn't bother trying to ask for leniency."

"Not me. I dropped out."

"Nevertheless, you were smart enough to get in. If anything, dropping out puts you in an even worse light, wasting the taxpayers' money and all that. Frittering away opportunities others would give their eye teeth for. No, I don't think the judge will be sympathetic at all."

"It wasn't a conspiracy."

"Look Jonno, we picked up your flatmate Steve down in Brighton, staying in a house with a number of others, all of whom were sent identical parcels. African drums for God's sake, each packed with a kilo of cocaine. You two might have moved flat before they arrived but still a couple of them were addressed to you up in Archway. Those medical boys in your old flat might be good liars, but I've been in this game a long time. No one fools me. We won't involve them if we don't have to, the country needs doctors after all, but you'd arranged cover, I could smell it. I reckon they were on the blower the minute we left your old place. If necessary, we will pull them in. I don't reckon they'd last five minutes without owning up, do you?"

"They had nothing to do with anything. I'd never met them before they answered our advert. We just wanted to move, and get our bond back with no hassles. We figured medical students would be able to come up with the cash."

"Sounds convincing. I'm sure it's total bollocks, but it sounds convincing. Like I said we won't involve them unless we have to. But we've got you and Steve, Mark and Trevor and his mates down there in Brighton and some more in a share house in Hove. It wouldn't take much to get Norman extradited from Kenya. His dad is an embassy official after all. Most embarrassing, if the order was refused it could lead to an international incident, and then Daddy could kiss his career goodbye. So even without the medical boys we've still got ten of you. That's a conspiracy in anyone's book."

"But we didn't want the bloody stuff. That's why we moved."

"You what?"

"We didn't want it."

"You expect me to believe that? Bullshit. You're a fucking dealer and you didn't want ten kilos of cocaine? Pull the other one."

"No one said anything about being a dealer."

"That's because we're not interested in that side of your business. And if our brothers in arms missed it then the more fool them. There was five hundred quid neatly wrapped in hundreds at your place. What was that for – don't you trust banks?"

"Bloody capitalists. Of course we don't." He'd made no mention of the cellar. Jonno couldn't believe his luck. This man might be skilful at recognising lies, but maybe not so much at detecting misdirection; the magicians' art, susceptible to the method actor's stock in trade; self-belief.

"Banks are taking over the whole world. Soon we won't have wage packets anymore, it'll all be bloody direct debit and what have you, and we'll all have to have one of their bloody little plastic cards. And every transaction we make they'll skim a bit off the top for themselves. All they're interested in is maximising their profits for the benefit of their shareholders. No thank you very much. The French have the right idea, buy gold and stick it under your bloody mattress."

"Too uncomfortable for me. I'm more of a princess and a pea man myself. But each to his own. If you're not a dealer, what *do* you do for a living? Like it or not we live in a capitalist society. You pay rent, you buy food, wear clothes and have a stereo with a very large record collection. All that costs. You used to be a clerk but you chucked it in. So where did the five hundred quid come from?"

"I write songs. It's a cash in hand kind of business."

"That notebook we found. That was song lyrics, was it?"

"Some of them. Poems mostly, but you can turn them into lyrics pretty easily."

"Oh yes? Who for? Anyone I might have heard of?"

Shit, this was putting him on the spot. What if they should check? It seemed they'd delved into his background fairly thoroughly already. He remembered the afternoon he'd spent underground in a dim basement off the King's Road. Henry sang some lines from a couple of his poems the other night. Surely the band would back him up. They were all members of the alternative society, weren't they? As long as they didn't think that he'd dropped them in the shit. They all smoked dope. He had no choice. "The Titus Groans for one. Heard of them?"

"Not my cup of tea. I favour Pinkerton's Colours myself."

Was he taking the piss? This encounter was taking on all the qualities of a high-stakes poker game. Pinkerton's Colours were a crappy mid-sixties pop band whose claim to fame was that it featured some bloke strumming the same chord over and over on an autoharp. One hit wonders who had sunk without trace, except for their drummer who went on to power Judas Priest. Jonno was fifteen when they appeared on Top of the Pops, Robert would have been what? Thirty? Thirty-five? A possible age for someone to favour such a middle of the road outfit he supposed. If you were young, you watched Top of the Pops, but it exposed you to a lot of crap as well as the really good stuff. The chance of seeing Syd Barrett fronting Pink Floyd as they played *Arnold Layne* had made up for an awful lot of teeny bopper bullshit.

But Jonno also knew that Pinkertons was the original American detective agency, famous for hunting down the likes of Jesse James, the Daltons, Butch and Sundance. What was this? Was Robert toying with him, was this a joke, or did he really still like some nondescript band who'd managed one passable hit record some six or seven years ago? No, this man was smarter than that, this whole interrogation was beginning to resemble Porfiry Petrovich's games with Raskolnikov's tortured conscience. Or was Robert trying to disassociate and confuse him like the protagonist of a Franz Kafka novel? Well Jonno wasn't going to fall for it.

"Bunch of tossers, weren't they? A gap-toothed lead singer and a geek with an autoharp strapped to his chest.

An autoharp for God's sake! Reminded me of Children's Hour with Shirley Abicair playing her zither.

"A favourite of my wife's. As was Shirley Abicair if you must know."

"Sorry," he grinned. Let him take it as he may, sorry for insulting them or sorry his wife had such poor taste.

"Song writing must pay extraordinarily well."

"You get a hit on your hands and you can make an absolute fortune in a short space of time. Album tracks don't pay so well unless the L.P. stays in the charts for ages." Does that sound convincing enough, Jonno wondered? He needed to get Robert away from the money. And from the possibility of any further search of the flat.

Crossing the fingers of his left hand in his jeans pocket appeared to do the trick.

"In any case that is not the issue. What's at stake here is the importation by you and your ex-student collaborators down in Brighton of ten kilos of cocaine. It was addressed to your old flat and to people you know in Brighton. And when we raided them who should we find there but your flatmate. So it looks very much like he was your go-between, arranging for collection, and that you would be in charge of distribution with your dealing contacts up here in London. Tell me how that wasn't a conspiracy."

"Look, I don't know those people down in Brighton. They are old mates of Steve's he was at university with. Like I said, I dropped out after a year to get on with my writing. And I've never met Norman, the guy out in Kenya; he was another mate of theirs."

"So are you telling me the conspiracy was between Steve and his old mates? That you were just an innocent bystander who happened to share a flat with him? That's a bit hard to swallow I'm afraid. If I tried it out on Steve, I wonder how he would react."

"No. I'm saying there *was* no conspiracy. We didn't want the bloody stuff."

"Oh sure! Well the fact is you did get it and we got you. End of..."

"We didn't get it. You got it."

"Don't try to be clever, son. Two kilos were sent to you through the mails and we intercepted it. That's all a judge will want to know, before he sends you down. You're look-ing at ten years I shouldn't wonder, going on past experi-ence. Unless you can come up with a better story. Saying you didn't want it isn't going to cut it with anybody."

"It's true though. We really didn't. The fact is he wanted too much money."

"Ok, now we're getting somewhere. You admit you knew it was on the way."

"Of course we did. Like I said, that was why we moved. And what Steve was doing down in Brighton. He was warn-ing them. Telling them to get the hell out. Move."

"Nice try but I don't think it'll fly. How much did he want for it, anyway?"

"Shitloads. It wasn't worth it. Ok, we're into a little bit of dope now and again but we're definitely not into cocaine. It's too expensive and it's too dangerous. It's not worth the risk. And the fact is that if we *were* into it, we could have bought it for pretty much the same price as he was asking just down the road somewhere. So we told him not to send it."

"You what?"

"We told him we didn't want it."

"He's floating about out there in Kenya somewhere. So how did you do that exactly? Ring the embassy and leave a message with his father? Pull the other one."

"Of course not. We sent him a telegram."

"Saying what?"

"We had to disguise it a bit. Do you know your Ernest Hemingway?"

"Some. *For Whom the Bell Tolls.* Right now I can hear it tolling for you."

"Don't send *The Snows of Kilimanjaro.*"

"I beg your pardon?"

"*The Snows of Kilimanjaro*? It's a short story. One of his best. But the meaning would have been pretty clear. Don't send it. We don't want it."

"Do you know when you sent this cryptic and possibly mythic telegram?"

"It was a couple of days before Steve's birthday, so yes, October the 5th."

Robert reached over to the phone on his desk, pressed a button, and spoke into the receiver.

"Andy, you busy? I've got to check on something, could you give young Jonno here the tour?"

A few minutes later the door opened and a young black man with a shaven head came into the room.

"You the bloke as wanted a cup of tea? Better come with me then. Want one boss?"

Robert shook his head and picked up his phone again. Jonno was escorted upstairs to a small kitchen which opened off a room equipped with six single beds.

"You sleep here?" Jonno asked.

"Sometimes, when we're on a case, don't get no time to make it home. Like yours, complicated, looking for you for a week. Lucky you made that phone call to the university. Lucky for us, that is, 's how we got on to you."

Jonno had wondered how they'd found him, imagined that someone down South must have squealed. According to Andy it was the phone call he'd made, trying to alert Steve about the cops visiting their old Archway flat. It turned out the student he'd spoken to pinned the note with his phone number on it to Brian's door. The investigating officers trying to round up the group found it and his fate was sealed.

"Shit," said Jonno, "bloody students."

"Come on, I'll take you 'roun. You're gonna love our rogues' gallery."

So they took their mugs of tea two floors down in the lift and into a room with a couple of big safes along one wall and shelves around the others. There were no windows in this room and Andy turned on an extractor fan as they entered.

"Gets pretty rank in here sometimes. You'll probably 'preciate the smell though."

At any other time he would have, because it was the smell of dope, the warm entrancing odour of hashish. Lots of it. The safes were crammed full of it according to Andy, different samples from countries all over the world; from Africa to South America, the Middle to the Far East, from Hawaii to the Island of Sumatra, and from the flatlands of Australia to the high mountains of Nepal. By this time-of-day Jonno would normally have smoked several joints but after his enforced abstinence and his restless night in a cell he was feeling decidedly seedy.

"Any chance of a look?" he asked. If it smelt like this with the safe doors shut then opening them should give him just the blast he needed.

"Not a shit-show," Andy said, having noticed he was breathing deeply. "'Sides that's not what we're here for. The boss wanted me to show you some of these," indicating the collection of articles stacked on the shelves. "Some of the ways people have tried to smuggle in drugs. What was yours? African drums? Man, how obvious can you get?"

Jonno grimaced, but didn't say anything. This was precisely what he had said to Steve when they were arguing about Norman's little plan.

Andy pulled an umbrella off a shelf. "Load a these sent from Pakistan to an umbrella shop in town, all a them except the top ones jam-packed tight with a beautifully moulded pound weight of government stamped top quality." He turned, "Now this one from Malawi was a really good one." He held up a banana skin. "A huge shipment of bananas, about a quarter of them bound around with a twist of vine and stuffed with an ounce of compressed grass. Must have thought we'd be too scared to search 'cos of the tarantulas an' such. An' this one," indicating a bolt of cloth. "Looked straightforward at first but the dogs sniffed it out. See, each bolt of cloth is wrapped around a board to stop it getting all creased and damaged in transit. So you make hollow boards and Bob's your contraband uncle. African drums Jonno. I mean no fucking chance man. Strickly amateur hour." Jonno nodded his head in agreement. He wondered if the whole thing had been a set up all along. Whether the Kenyan smugglers had picked Norman as a fool, and counted on his amateurishness to divert attention from a more sophisticated shipment of their own.

Jonno was reluctant to return to the open plan office with the desks. He tried to talk Andy into showing him more exhibits because the aroma in the contraband room was beginning to make him feel a whole lot better. He went along with his escort however, because the man's friendliness was also comforting after a long period of hyper-tension, worry and paranoia.

"That your desk?" Jonno pointed to one which was underneath a large poster stuck to the wall.

"Well it sure don't belong to none of the white boys I work with."

It was a full-size poster featuring a black man with an afro haircut, wearing an open necked shirt and laughing. Soledad Brother was written in big white letters, and in smaller black type on red stripes was *The Prison Letters of George Jackson.*

"I read that," Jonno said.

"You bull-shitting me."

"No. After the prison guards shot him last year, I wanted to find out why."

"'Cos he was black and he wouldn't bow down, is why."

"Well, he was a violent man, obviously, but it seems there was plenty of reason for it."

"Being black in America, that plenty reason enough."

"I read Bobby Seale too, *Seize the Time.* Eye-opening stuff."

"A great man, him and Huey starting the Panthers, man those guys were brave. Eldridge too, all of them revolution-ary guys, taking no shit from the man, they sure turned the world aroun." Now it was Andy's turn to stand nodding his head.

"So what about you? If you think like that, how come you're working in a place like this?"

"I aint a cop. I don't hassle no brothers in the street for no reason. There aint no politics involved, we just bust smugglers."

"You don't think you're supporting the system?"

"Everyone supporting the system man, whether they want to or not. Just being alive you supporting the system, you just got to decide on your relation to it."

"So you reckon your poster..."

"It's an aggravation, yeh? Some of my colleagues are a bit racist. 'Course they are. But we're a team, we get on, took a while for some of them, but now they respect me as a person. So I make it damn clear where I stand and maybe that forces them to do a bit of re-thinking."

"Maybe."

"Yeh, maybe. But what else you going to do? That's how you change stuff. Sure, it takes time, but guns and violence never going to work. Those brothers in America, they just trying to protect themselves, but armed struggle? No chance. It's peoples' minds you got to change. An' you don't do it by wasting them."

"Working from the inside, like you? Doesn't that make you part of the problem?"

"I aint no Uncle Tom, if that's what you thinking. I say my piece, I stand up for my ideas, yeh and if I have to, I fight for them. But what's the alternative? What you doing to make a change? Reading books? Good for you, maybe it's a start, but smuggling in drugs man? Sitting on your arse smoking dope and making a bit of money. Where's the benefit? Plenty of brothers out there dying with a needle sticking out 'a them."

"I don't have anything to do with hard shit."

"Good for you. But where's the soft shit getting anyone? Escaping man, that's all it is. Going inward, turning your back."

Jonno was enjoying this, he liked a good political argument. Even though he had little with which to counter Andy's lived reality, the debate was taking his mind off his own predicament. He was marshalling his thoughts to shape a riposte when the phone rang.

"The boss wants to see you," Andy said as he replaced it, then took him next door. Jonno sat in a chair to face the grim-faced Robert who glared at him across his desk.

"Your mate Steve came up with the same story when he was interrogated down in Brighton."

"Thank God for that."

"I very much doubt He had anything to do with it. I think you're lucky you could remember when you sent your telegram. You *are* guilty. I *know* that you are guilty. No, shut up and listen," he said as Jonno opened his mouth to object.

"I have to admit there might be an element of doubt. Not in my mind, but possibly just enough that a good brief might be able to convince a jury. We have a ninety-five percent success rate on getting convictions, and I don't intend to mess it up over an amateurish operation like yours. We have shut down your little network, we have intercepted a significant amount of cocaine, and the police in Brighton will be prosecuting those whom they also found in possession of large quantities of cannabis. In the light of all that, I am going to say enough is enough, and I am going to let you go. But if you come across my radar at any future time, you'd better believe that I will prosecute you to the limits of my capabilities. Which are significant. Do you understand?"

"Yes. Thank you very much."

"Don't thank me. You're bloody lucky I don't prosecute you for wasting so much of our valuable time. Now, get out. Andy, could you escort our young friend from the building."

Downstairs, he unclipped and passed his badge to the security guard behind the counter. Andy walked him towards the door then stopped and shook his hand.

"Word of advice man, 'afore you go."

"Yeh, what?" Jonno was desperate to get to the other side of the glass door. He was fearful that a couple of beefy men in suits might suddenly appear and shout, "Joking!" Say the whole release thing was a sham, that they had known all along about the contents of his cellar, and were here to re-arrest him. Nevertheless Andy and he had established a relationship of sorts, at a moment when he felt most alone, and he didn't wish to be rude.

"Be careful who your friends are."

"What do you mean?"

"Just what I'm saying. There's some people in the world who believe they can get away with anything, and maybe they can. At the other end there's those who know they never will. And then there's people like you, stuck somewhere in the middle. They likely to get shafted by both."

With that he lifted his arm into the beam of the electronic eye, the door slid back and Jonno was, once again, free.

His first thought was to phone Susie. After this whole ordeal he felt an overwhelming need to talk to her, was desperate for some comfort. But no. He no longer had her number. It was written in code in the notebook that was still in the possession of the police. The customs might have let him go but he was not off the hook yet.

It wasn't until he got home that he pondered on what Andy might have meant about being careful of his friends.

~ 4 ~

1969

Towards the end of Jonno's first year of university he had a problem. He was feeling cramped, hemmed in by the narrow curriculum. He needed to make a decision, and it always took him forever. He would agonise for days, until becoming so sick of the procrastination, he would finally strike out for whatever most appealed at that particular moment.

After several weeks of ruminating on his current dilemma, he faced the fact that he was fundamentally unhappy at university and one day he just walked away. Like Dick Whittington before him, he threw his meagre possessions together and set out for London. Rather than in a handkerchief tied to a stick, his clothes and a few books, winnowed from the pile on his desk, were thrust into a blue holdall whose handles were slung over his left shoulder. With his right hand he carried the green plastic case which housed his Olivetti Dora typewriter. This was his mother's going away present to him the previous year.

As a young woman she'd been employed as a short-hand typist so, as a way of earning a bit of extra money in later life, had bought herself the larger and more robust Olivetti Underwood model. From the age of fifteen Jonno had badgered her to allow him to borrow it occasionally. At first, she denied his wishes, stating, "It's not a toy, Jonathon." But he persisted, and eventually, having come across some of his poems written in biro in one of his school notebooks, she relented. Then, as he was preparing to leave home for the very first time, the little Dora seemed, to both of them, to be the perfect gift.

Although he couldn't touch type as fast as his mother, he progressed to four fingers, with an occasional thumb hitting the space bar. Consequently he had been one of the few undergraduates to submit his assignments neatly printed out, much to the delight of his lecturers. Ok, there was the odd excrescence of Tippex here and there, but these were preferable by far to the numerous smudges and crossings-out which too often besmirched the efforts of his contemporaries, not to mention the illegibility of some of their handwriting.

As he walked off the campus which had been home for almost a year his spirits lifted. It was the fourth of July, summer was upon them, the sun was shining and he was off on an adventure. He thought of his father's letter, sent in immediate response to the one in which Jonno apprised him of his intentions. "You don't want to be a drifter all your life." "Yes, I do," was all of his thought. He certainly didn't wish to get a job in a bank which is what his father advised. 'A good safe job for life' was the very last thing he wanted. If his thoughts ran in that direction, he would have remained at university for another two years, taken his degree, gone on to gain a teaching certificate, and then started the whole cycle all over again, preparing a new batch of schoolchildren for the leavening process of higher education. No, now was the time to shatter the mould, or else be forever imprisoned within the cycle of supply and demand.

He'd not long stood by the side of the road with his thumb out when an old sit-up-and-beg Ford Prefect pulled up, a relic of the days when there was just one colour choice for automobiles; black or black. The current owner had obviously balked at such a limited palette and hand-painted all manner of flowers on the bodywork in a variety of bold colours, and similarly lettered various quotations upon it. With pleasure Jonno recognised a quote from William Blake emblazoned on the passenger door, which the driver flung open for him:

Piping down the valleys wild

Piping songs of pleasant glee.

The driver was as eccentrically dressed as his vehicle was embellished, for he wore a cut away tail-coat over a blue checked flannel shirt and jeans. With his curly blond hair escaping from the confines of a somewhat battered top-hat he bore an uncanny resemblance to Harpo Marx.

"Henry Flagg, at your service," the young man said, "and to what destination might I convey you?"

"I'm trying to make it up to London," Jonno replied.

"The very place we aim at ourselves, Mathilda and I. Not particularly swiftly it has to be said, as the old girl is not as fleet as once she was. Nevertheless, should you be prepared to top up her radiator every twenty minutes or so, from the jerry cans of water sequestered in her boot, then we would be most grateful for a travelling companion."

"Be more than happy to," Jonno said as he climbed inside, to be welcomed by the warm scent of ageing leather as he reached his holdall across onto the back seat and packed it underneath the neck of an electric guitar. This, he noted with some surprise, had its top two strings doubled up after the fashion of a twelve string.

"My own invention," Henry said, noticing Jonno's quizzical look. "Gives me quite a unique sound which, as you might already have ascertained, is a quality I hold most dear. What a boring vale of tears this world would be, should all of its inhabitants wear similar apparel and espouse a common world view? Now then, let us away. Onwards and upwards Mathilda," and he let out the clutch.

The journey took a fair while, since it required two stops to top up the leaky radiator. On the second occasion Henry reached into a bag behind his seat, withdrew a carton of eggs and handed one across.

"What is it with me and eggs on the London Road?" Jonno wondered.

"After you replenish her water crack the egg into the radiator. It sets once she's warmed up again and helps with the old girl's fluid retention."

Conversation was easy between them once Jonno became used to Henry's idiosyncratic style. At some point he asked whether Jonno, "imbibed gaseous substances?" On receiving confirmation Henry indicated that there was a lump of hash in the glove box and requested that Jonno, "Skin us up a little number then, Mathilda hasn't got much in the way of a top speed and I don't want to stop more often than necessary. Be not perturbed, it's only Moroccan, so it won't impair my capabilities. Or not much anyway," he laughed.

Jonno had thought he'd meant cigarettes, and was unused to rolling joints. Nevertheless he had watched numerous of his fellow students doing so, and not wishing to appear naïve, he managed to construct a passable one on the back of a book from his holdall.

From then on, they continued their journey in a most convivial fashion, discussing bands they'd seen, books they'd read, alternative political ideas, films and all manner of topics of joint interest to intelligent young men at the roach-end of the nineteen sixties. At one point Henry said, "Bloody shame about Brian, isn't it?"

"Brian who?"

"Christ, haven't you heard? Brian Jones dematerialised yesterday."

"Shit, I haven't heard any news for weeks. What happened?"

"Drowned in his pool they say. Drug overdose maybe, he was probably off his face."

"Suicide?"

"Could be, since he'd just left the band."

"Is the Stones free concert still on?"

"Hyde Park? Bloody hope so, that's where I'm going. Word is they're going to turn it into a memorial for him. You planning on putting in an attendance?"

"I was going to. Truth is, I don't know anyone in London. I've got some addresses from people at university. I was going to sleep in the park tonight so I'd get a good spot in the morning and then look some of these people up, see if I can crash somewhere for a few days while I look for a place."

"Sleep under the stars? That sounds like a perfect way of celebrating Brian's ascendance to the great beyond. I share a house with some people near Putney, but maybe I'll leave Mathilda there and join you for a bit of a vigil. If you have no objections to company of course."

"More than welcome. I was a bit worried there might be the odd roaming band of skinheads trying to steal my stuff."

"Leave it in Mathilda if you so desire. It'll be safe enough parked in the drive. Someone will be cooking a meal tonight and you'd be welcome to share. Then we could catch a tube."

"Won't your flatmates mind?"

"'Course not. The place is a bit of a commune really."

It was a big old rambling house set back behind some trees on the Upper Richmond Road. Henry was welcomed effusively by three of the residents who were sitting around a huge stripped-pine table in the large kitchen, drinking tea.

Margo was a short, blonde woman dressed in a green and white striped cheesecloth blouse and a paisley patterned cotton skirt which reached to the bracelet around one of her ankles. She jumped up onto her bare feet, causing the bracelet to jingle, and fetched two more mugs from an enormous Welsh dresser to pour them teas from a brown pot. Henry introduced Jonno as, "a peripatetic poet whom I have just liberated from prison, otherwise known as an institute of higher learning." Jonno grinned.

Robert, a sun-tanned young man with flowing brown hair which fell around his shoulders and almost half-way down his back, held out his hand to shake and bade him welcome. Then he returned to the construction of the joint he had been rolling as they entered the room. Jonno could see into the back garden through the French windows and enquired the species of the enormous tree which dominated it. Mulberry, he was informed, particularly good for a midnight crumble when in season. "If the squirrels don't get them all," the other young woman in the room said, whom Jonno learned was called Bea, "Short for Beatrice, but don't you dare."

The joint was smoked, the tea was drunk and conversation flowed smoothly. Jonno learned the house was inhabited by eight young people, each having their own room. Going by the people around the table they were probably all a few years older than his nineteen years. Some were out at work, the others were probably around the place somewhere, he was told.

"Simon will be in his room," said Bea. "He's like a badger, hardly ever seen outside of his lair."

"That's not fair, he goes to work once a week," Margo insisted.

"But usually before the rest of us are up."

"What does he do?" Jonno enquired.

"Lectures in cybernetics, whatever that is, at the local Polytech," said Margo.

"The rest of the time he builds bits of computers in his room. He's a twentieth century alchemist," Robert explained.

"He wouldn't like that. He reckons the rest of us are living in the past, what with our astrology, our meditation and stuff. It's electricity that's going to set us free, according to him," Bea stated.

"Which is why he's here. Brian offered him a room in exchange for re-wiring the house. He's the only one excused from dinner duties. He might be good at fixing the stove but he's got no idea what to do with it. Talking of which, it's my turn tonight. Are you staying for a meal Jonno?" Margo asked.

"If that's alright."

"Of course. If you and Henry are going to sleep in the park, you'll need a good meal inside you. Meanwhile Henry, can you take our guest out into the garden, the cook needs her space to create."

At the rear of the house, to the left of the French windows, was a pergola, whose trellis was all wound about with wisteria. An arbour, Jonno thought, which must have smelled heavenly when in bloom. It was roofed with panes of glass to protect the long refectory table and the ten chairs drawn up to it. Twin day-beds scattered with cushions backed onto the wall of the house, from which one could survey the lawn, its flanking flower beds and the giant mulberry tree which partially obscured a summer house against the far wall.

Robert threw himself onto one of the day-beds and offered the other to Jonno. Henry pulled out a dining chair and began to pick away on the guitar which he had carried out with him. Since it was an electric, solid-bodied instrument, the sound it emanated was muted, a mere tinkling of strings, which suited the peace of the late afternoon. Blackbirds sang and went about the business of feeding their young, busily rooting through the flower beds and casting earth and well-rotted leaf-mould all around them.

Suddenly this suburban idyll was transformed by a banshee wailing crashing down upon them from above. Jonno shot bolt upright and stared wildly about before looking up at the sky. Robert laughed.

"Every ointment has a fly it seems. Ours is the Boeing 707. We're on one of the flight paths to Heathrow. Bloody things. And they're talking about bringing in bigger ones next year. Wide-bodied jobs, which will probably be noisier. There's no point complaining. They tell us the new ones will cut down the number of flights, but that's bollocks, I reckon. It'll just reduce the cost of tickets, so more and more people will fly."

"Jesus, that made me jump. How often do they go over?"

"About every half hour or so. Depends on wind direction. Heathrow's one of the busiest airports in the world," Robert added. "You get used to it after a while. Almost. I suppose it's like living near a railway line but a damn sight noisier. Bloke next door painted FUCK OFF in six-foot-high letters on his roof, before he got arrested."

"What? For public profanity?"

"No. For taking a pot-shot at one of them. Bought a shotgun off a bloke in a pub, got up on the roof and gave one of them both barrels. Stupid bastard. They're far too high for him to do any damage. The cops were round before he even got downstairs. Didn't care about the plane, just wanted to know where he'd got the gun from. Probably been used in a bank job. Gave him a right old grilling."

"What happened to him?"

"Pleaded the noise had driven him mad. Promised he'd sell the place and move to Islington. Got fined and bound over to keep the peace."

The plane gone, Jonno relaxed back onto the day-bed and contemplated his surroundings. He was immensely attracted to the place and the easy-going nature of its inhabitants and quizzed Robert about the whole set-up. One of the residents, Brian, inherited it when his parents were killed in a car crash. Unable to afford its upkeep on his own, he gathered a number of friends and acquaintances to share it and pay rent. Over time some moved out, others moved in and the place developed into a loosely organised commune. They shared the household tasks on a rostered basis and according to their specific aptitudes. Simon, being the most practical, as well as changing fuses was in charge of general maintenance. Pat, who was away at his job up the road at Kew, was in charge of the garden, Margo acted as house mother and was in charge of drawing up duty rosters of necessary tasks. Brian the owner, dealt with finances, paying bills and such. "He's away in Greece for a couple of months with his girlfriend, lucky bastard. The others you'll meet tonight," Robert told him.

"What's your role?"

"Him?" Henry stopped picking and butted into the conversation. "Well, he describes himself as a spiritual advisor, but really he's in charge of procuring illegal substances."

"That's purely secondary, and you well know it. My main task is the maintenance of general equilibrium, which can be a full-time job in a house with eight very different personalities in it, not to mention conflicting star signs."

Bea had mentioned astrology when they'd been in the kitchen. Now Jonno learned it was how Robert and the absent Brian earned their living, casting horoscopes for individuals who answered adverts in various underground magazines such as Oz, International Times and the recently launched Time Out. They supplemented this by writing a weekly horoscope for more mainstream newspapers, under the by-line Azrael.

This news amazed Jonno. He'd not thought about how he was going to earn his own living, merely anticipated that with his rudimentary typing skills he might be able to find employment as a clerk somewhere. Alternative occupations had not really occurred to him, and he wondered if there was some field in which he might be able to commute the products of his imagination into a living wage? It was while pondering this question that he dozed off, lulled by the marijuana and the heat of the late afternoon.

He finally awoke to the sound of a gong emanating from the kitchen.

"Grub's up," said Robert and the three of them trooped inside.

The room was redolent with exotic fragrances. The table held eight plates each heaped with portions of brown rice, an orange concoction of mixed vegetables, with servings of bananas steeped in yoghurt, and a spoonful of what Jonno was later to learn was home-made mango chutney at the side. There was a separate plate holding a mountain of something like giant crisps. He was introduced to Pat, the gardener, who was at the sink scrubbing his finger nails, and to Ben who was dressed in a blue denim suit over an open necked floral shirt. Everyone grabbed a plate, a fork and a couple of the flat crispbreads before moving out to sit at the table in the garden.

Jonno was astounded by the meal and, following Pat's example, lifted the plate and licked up the remaining sauce, which pleased Margo immensely. Curry was not part of his mother's culinary repertoire, consisting mostly of plain English food of the meat and three veg variety. She ventured into kedgeree on the odd occasion, flavouring it with the ready mixed curry powder available in little square tins at the local grocers. Margo created her own mixture of spices from the row of glass jars sitting on a shelf of the dresser, advertising their contents by the range of bright colours from yellow to red and various shades of greenish brown.

They were lit by a gentle twilight by the time the meal was over, although the shadow cast by the mulberry tree lengthened considerably across the grass towards the table. While Robert started to roll an after-dinner joint Jonno collected up the plates and carried them into the kitchen. He was running water into the sink when Bea, following him inside, told him to leave the washing up.

"I'm rostered on for today," she told him. "Besides which, you and Henry better get going soon if you want to find a good spot to doss down in."

Outside someone lit a couple of aromatic candles and the joint was being passed around the table. Jonno was reluctant to leave this haven, but having taken a big toke and handed it on, he said to Henry that perhaps it was time they made a move. The evening was still warm but they accepted Margo's offer of a couple of blankets. Jonno stuffed them into his holdall, having emptied its contents onto the back-seat of Mathilda. Henry rooted around in the boot and found the soft carry-bag for his guitar.

"You're taking it with you?"

"Of course. Henrietta here is my alter ego. She accompanies me on all of my peregrinations. I couldn't leave her behind, especially when we're about to immerse ourselves in music. It wouldn't be fair on her."

Jonno accepted this much in the way that he accepted Henry's idiosyncratic speech. Later, he would be grateful for his new friend's attachment to his instrument.

The light was rapidly dimming by the time they arrived. As they moved through the park towards the stage, they found they were not alone. There were fifty or so people lying on the grass or huddled down in deck chairs, ensuring themselves a good spot for the following day.

"I don't fancy that overmuch," said Henry. "I was envisioning a modicum of peace and quiet. A vigil requires a sense of solitude, don't you agree? Besides which, there could well be security guys along later to chuck everyone out."

"Whatever you think," replied Jonno. "I noticed a couple of ornamental firs back there, the ones whose branches sweep right down to the ground? We could crawl into one. Be like being in a tent."

"Excellent idea, my poetically minded young friend. Arboreal to say the least. I have always felt an affinity with trees."

While the fir they chose was not the most comfortable to lie beneath, the ground being lumpy with roots lying so close to the surface, this was more than made up for by the smell. The weather had been warm for days and the resinous aroma was delicious. Henry sat back against the trunk and unwrapped Henrietta. From the plectrum pocket he also extracted a cigarette packet which proved to contain a number of ready rolled joints.

"Better than a Book at Bedtime," he said as he lit one up.

In between his share of tokes, Jonno began to scrape fallen pine needles together to provide himself a rudimentary mattress. He had never smoked much dope before, and this joint affected him more than any of the others.

"Nepalese temple ball," Henry informed him when asked what it was. "Guaranteed to give you mystical dreams."

Jonno pulled the blankets from his holdall and drew one of them up around himself as he lay back and reviewed the events of the day. He had wanted an adventure and he was definitely experiencing one, filled with the kindness that total strangers had bestowed on him. He loved their amazing house in Putney.

He laughed as he pictured the quirky toilet he visited just before they left. It was the old-fashioned type with a hanging chain and a cast-iron overhead cistern. From this a pipe descended to the back of the bowl. What made it remarkable was that the pipe was wrapped in purple and black snakeskin wallpaper, in contrast to the white of the painted walls. And not only this pipe, but all of them in the little room were similarly covered. One such emerged through the outside wall, angled haphazardly around the tiny room before curving its way up and underneath the sink. Others, thinner, led down from the taps to pierce the wall behind it, and a giant one reared up from the floor, bent over double, before swelling up to form the bowl itself, whose lid was similarly adorned. They looked like different sections of one giant reptile winding in and out of the room. Lifting the lid had seemed like accepting an invitation to piss into the mouth of an anaconda. Not the sort of thing to do while tripping, Jonno imagined, although, as yet, he had no experience of acid.

It reminded him of Bertolt Brecht and the 'alienation effect' they'd learned about in college. This led him to picturing Henry's old Ford Prefect all painted over with flowers, a vehicle transformed into a garden. The quote from William Blake trickled through his mind as he fell asleep to the gentle, un-amplified sibilance of the lightly fingered silver-stringed guitar.

It is amazing how quickly the mind can accommodate any physical reality which might intrude into the dreams of a sleeper. Or perhaps this is a feature restricted to individuals like Jonno, who had been a sleepwalker in childhood. A family joke, which he was never able to dispute, was that at the age of seven he'd thrown off his blankets, left his bedroom for the landing where a lone chest of drawers stood, pulled out the bottom one and urinated into it. This, much to the consternation of his watching mother who, disturbed by the noise, abandoned her own bed but felt unable to interfere in the proceedings, waking a somnambulist being thought to be dangerous.

Whatever the explanation, the dream that Jonno was now inhabiting took a rapid and sudden turn for the worst. One moment he was trekking up towards a mountain pass, a snow-covered cliff-face to his right, a dizzying drop to a far-off ribbon of water to his left, as one of a file of saffron-robed mendicant monks, chanting and waving prayer flags. They were heading for a distant Himalayan shrine to perform some form of ritual puja, when suddenly they were under attack. Faceless mountain men, or possibly the much vaunted and fabled Yetis, outraged at their intrusion, were hurling down rocks at their little procession. One such struck Jonno in his side, he stumbled, lost the path and was soon tumbling headlong towards oblivion in a rushing, snow-fed stream. He grabbed at a tree-root springing from a split in the rock, and jerked awake as a body landed on his legs.

"Fuck!" the body swore as it fell, and then banged its head on solid ground.

Dawn light dimly filtering through the pine needle canopy was enough for Jonno to assess the situation. He scrambled to his feet. There were three of them. The tree root was a leg, whose owner, having kicked him in the ribs, was now groaning and clutching his forehead. Another was bent over the holdall, rummaging through its contents, while the third was aiming to kick Henry in the head. The branches were so low that the stooping antagonist was denied much of a backswing. As the cherry-red, ten-hole Doc Marten's boot which emerged from the elevated turn-up of a jeans leg was making its seemingly slow-motion descent, Jonno shouted, and reached for Henrietta, lying across Henry's lap.

The shout distracted the aggressor. He turned towards Jonno mid-swing and the kick, when it finally connected, had lost a great deal of power. Not to be denied the satisfaction of his adrenaline rush, for a split second he looked back to enjoy the effect of boot upon brain. Jonno picked Henrietta up by the neck and swung the side of the solid body into the looming man's gut, who crumpled with a great outpouring of breath.

Jonno turned to the man rummaging through the holdall and slammed the edge of Henrietta down onto his back, sending him sprawling face-first over the bag and causing him to swallow a mouthful of fallen needles.

"Fucking skinheads! Piss off!" Jonno shouted at them, holding the guitar by the neck and brandishing it at the supine figures as if the metaphorical axe had suddenly been transformed into a real one. He stood, his head crowned with pine-needles amongst the branches, straddling the body of his groaning comrade. Adrenaline pumping, he felt like some berserker from Norse mythology, even Thor himself, hammer in hand, grinning and implacable, standing at the base of Yggdrasil. The three young men, untutored as Jonno in the Icelandic sagas, nevertheless recognised the ferociousness before them and crawled away from the menace of his flashing eyes.

Jonno dropped to Henry's side, still clutching hold of Henrietta in case of renewed attack. There was no blood that he could see, but a lump was appearing on his companion's forehead and the skin around one of his eyes was starting to discolour. Tentatively, Henry felt around his face as he slowly sat up.

"I'd better get you to a hospital," Jonno said.

Henry groggily demurred. "I'll be right, just get me home. Margo will know what to do."

~ 5 ~

1972

Jonno had no idea where he was but was not going back inside to ask for directions. He needed to get as far away as possible and as quickly as he could. He walked south, hopefully heading towards the river, expecting to come across a tube station eventually. He turned around occasionally, frightened that at any moment a heavy hand would land on his shoulder. He lingered in front of shop windows, casting his eyes around to see if he could recognise anyone who might be tailing him. As far as he could tell nobody was. Why would they? They knew where he lived.

At last he came across Tower Hill station, the Tower of London menacing in the distance. It struck him as ironic that on the day of his trial he should be presented with such a view. He quickly dived into the station, relieved to find it was on the District Line, and thus could quickly deliver him close to home.

As the carriage rattled along its subterranean way beneath the heart of the city, he considered his position. Had they really let him go or was this just some elaborate ruse? He took what the customs officer said about not wanting to mess up their conviction rate at face value. They were a government department and, having worked in a bureaucratic institution himself, he knew the importance of statistics. Robert said he knew Jonno was a dealer. There was nothing to stop him phoning the police station he would be reporting to every Friday afternoon for the next month, and dropping a word in their ear. Granted there was obviously no love lost between the two rival forces but still, Jonno's freedom seemed somewhat improbable. He wondered what might be waiting for him when he arrived back home. Another roomful of men in blue perhaps.

Disembarking at West Ken he made his way slowly towards the flat. Walking through the park he tried to see behind every tree. He made his way across the road and down the side street to their private garden entrance. 'Back in Five Minutes' was still pinned to the door.

No one was waiting for him. The place felt different, though. No longer safe. He thought how burglary victims reported feeling violated by the intrusion of strangers. Now he knew what they meant, albeit his interlopers were in pursuit of the law rather than in defiance of it. Even though nothing was broken and no one had crapped on the floor, thank God, it was still a bloody mess. Strangers had rifled through all of their drawers, gone through their pockets, read all of their private correspondence, cast off duvets and turned over mattresses, emptied the cupboards, pulled books out of bookshelves, even investigated the toilet, as its ceramic lid propped against the bathroom wall attested. It wasn't a large flat and according to Robert they had been there for hours. He supposed he should be grateful they hadn't torn things or ripped up the fitted carpet. He made himself a mug of tea and collapsed onto the sofa in the living room.

He stared at the coffee table where his stash should be in its little Japanese box. What he needed was a joint. Should he call someone? No, they could be monitoring his phone. He needed to think, and maybe keeping a clear head was the best option. But he was used to smoking so much on a daily basis that he considered his head clearer when stoned. There was always the cellar. Should he venture down there? What if they came back? But why would they? The customs said they were finished with him. Otherwise why let him go? The cops had arrested, charged and prosecuted him. If he failed to report weekly, they would no doubt be paying a visit, but until then were too busy to bother about him. In their minds he was probably some minor irritant they were happy to pass on to customs to deal with. Thought they had done. Maybe he was safe.

He opened the door into the body of the house and crept down the hallway to listen at the door of the two girls who lived in the front flat. He could hear nothing. It was four o'clock and they should still be at work. Returning, he went through the kitchen and out into the tiny back garden. Propped against the far wall beside the stunted apple tree there was a rusty old shovel which he carried back inside, collecting a torch from one of the drawers the cops had dumped on the floor, as he passed. Going back into the hallway he stopped for a moment and strained his ears for any noises coming from the floors above. He opened the door underneath the back of the staircase. It made no sound. He'd oiled the hinges the last time he'd been down there. He slipped inside, pulled the door closed behind him, then clicked on his torch.

His nostrils twitched as he descended the short flight of bare wooden stairs down to the earthen floor. A sweet aroma of damp and decay rose up to greet him, like the smell from a brown paper bag of rotten apples. To one side lay the remnants of a pile of coal which must have been there for years, ever since the days of the 'pea soupers' and 'great smogs' which eventually caused changes to London's domestic heating regulations.

As quietly as possible he slipped the blade of the shovel under the edge of the coal and lifted off the thin layer he'd scattered there a few days ago, placing it carefully aside. Then another and another until an area of ground was revealed that had obviously been recently disturbed. Digging down into this he unearthed a package wrapped in plastic bin bags and sealed around with gaffer tape. He lifted it from its hole before replacing the earth as best he could, and stamping it down. The scream of the shovel piercing the heap of coal was so loud he only dared scatter one load about the place. He tucked the package under his arm, ascended the stairs again and pressed his ear to the door, listening for any movement. He could tell there was nobody walking on the staircase over his head, and if anyone should be waiting behind the door, well, then the game would be over, wouldn't it? He doused the torch, opened the door and crept back into his flat.

Even though their annex was behind a high garden wall he closed the curtains over the window. He placed the package on the mirror table and retrieved a sharp knife and the scales from the kitchen. He cut through the tape and unwound the black plastic bin liner to reveal eight smaller clear plastic bags, each one containing a silver foil block. He remembered Steve laughing at him as he watched what he had called Jonno's 'fussy' precautions. He'd been trying to prevent any hint of the smell escaping. He wondered if anyone had ventured down into the cellar, whether his fastidious precautions had paid off and prevented disclosure. If so, he was glad they hadn't taken a dog with them, for their noses were reputed to be ten thousand times more sensitive than a human's.

He opened one bag, withdrew the contents and peeled off the foil. An immediate smell pervaded the lounge room. There, like a super family-sized block of the darkest chocolate lay a pound weight of Paki black with the two gold medallions pressed into its surface; the seals that were said to be government stamps confirming it to be of the highest quality.

He brought it to his nose and deeply inhaled, before laying it flat on the table. With the tip of his knife he scored the surface in half lengthways then crossways eight times. Then, as if he were cutting up toffee, he removed one of the sections and placed it on the scales. A perfect ounce, give or take. Paki Black was so easy to deal with, no messy crumbling as with Moroccan, no tough resistance like with hard-pressed Lebanese, no bits falling off like with Afghani or Nepalese, just soft and pliable, easy to cut, with a uniform thickness across its width and down its length. He rewrapped and replaced the rest of the block in its bag and stuck it back down. Got out his lighter and cigarettes, fetched a packet of Rizlas from a drawer in his desk and rolled himself a joint, gratefully sucking the smoke down into his lungs as he sank back into the sofa. His tea was stone cold but he drank it anyway, too stuffed, for the moment, to rise and make another.

He needed a place to hide the gear until they were no longer under suspicion. He remembered Steve taking the piss out of him when he'd first suggested they bury it. If he hadn't insisted, they would have lost the lot. Plus they would have both been inside by now, irrespective of any customs outcome. Whatever Steve might say, it was too dangerous to keep lying around while they chopped it up and sold it on in dribs and drabs. It was fun playing at gangsters but they had come too close to spending a great deal of time at Her Majesty's dis-pleasure. That was never part of Jonno's plan for his future and he was determined to avoid any chance of it eventuating.

He stared at the package on the table. Eight weights, minus the ounce he'd cut off. What was it worth? If they didn't put on much of a mark-up they could get nearly nine hundred pounds for it, about the price of a new small car. Four hundred and fifty each. It would be enough for him. He could split, bury himself back in Cornwall some-where, and start over with a whole new life. Dealing was something he'd drifted into, a way of ensuring a cheap supply of dope while enabling him to avoid a nine to five job. A means of surviving in the alternative society. But to what end? It was supposed to free him up to concentrate on his writing, wasn't it? And what had he written? Bugger all really. A few lyrics, a few crappy poems he hadn't been satisfied with, because, face it, he'd been too out of it most of the time.

He thought of his hero John Keats, a mediocre rhyme-ster who determined to make himself into a great poet. And succeeded, through sheer force of will, through appli-cation to the craft, through concentration and thorough hard work. Could he say the same thing about himself? Of course not. He'd been pissing into the wind, or lying flat on his back like a beetle waving its little legs in the air. Dream-ing. Kidding himself. This whole episode had to be taken as a wake-up call. If he wanted to amount to anything he should be getting on with it, should straighten himself out.

Even as he was thinking these thoughts, he knew it was the dope talking. It was good at engendering self-awareness but hopeless at promoting self-control. It made him lazy. He thought back to the time when Kiwi Paul sold them the opium. He considered himself to be following in the footsteps of Coleridge and the other romantics. He'd chased after visions and the visions had come, but what had they done for him? Sure, he'd made pilgrimage up to Highgate cemetery, had lain amongst the gravestones and breathed intoxicating fumes, had inhabited distorted dreams. But what had he created?

And then it hit him. The perfect hiding place. He rewrapped the whole lot back into the bin liner and taped it down. Took the package up from the coffee table and sniffed at it. Not too bad, but just in case, he got a can of deodorant from the bathroom and gave it a spray, before wrapping it in a pile of dirty clothes and stuffing the lot into his hold-all. Should anyone ask he was taking a load of clothes round to the laundrette. It wouldn't fool a thorough searcher but it would survive a cursory glance.

A walk back to West Kensington, looking as nonchalant as possible, changing at Earl's Court to the Piccadilly line, then again at Leicester Square to the stuffy and dilapidated Northern. How many times had he travelled in these grungy crowded carriages when he'd lived up in Archway? Then, as now, avoiding the glances of his harried fellow-travellers, as they held themselves encased in private worlds. Staring up at adverts for more luxurious life-styles, picturing themselves spread out and oiled upon exotic sands, getting smashed on Pina Coladas or G and Ts at beachside bars.

Stepping out of the tube, he realised the evening was drawing on, so hurried up the hill as quickly as possible. For all of his scoffing at the supernatural he had no desire to be caught in the cemetery after dark. There would no doubt be officials at some point locking the gates. Since his visits of the previous year he'd spent some time researching the place. He was surprised to learn that Coleridge was buried in the aisle of Saint Michael's Church, which was just above the terrace where the pigeon infested mausoleum lay, and where he'd smoked the first of his two opium laden joints. He also heard the rumour that whenever an inmate escaped from nearby psychiatric hospitals the authorities made a bee-line for the ruined burial ground. It seemed the place held a fascination for more than just stoned hippies.

After taking a few wrong turns he managed to retrace his path to the Rossetti family grave, and then to the chest tomb with the smashed in side where he had surprised the vixen with her cubs. He bent down at the broken slab and peered inside to see whether it might in fact house the fox's den. There were no traces of fresh digging in the earth and he could detect no musky animal scent. Also, thankfully, no other smell, the occupant having been interned some hundred years previously. Everything was quiet, except for the lone thrush sitting atop a nearby tree. It had fallen silent at his approach but now resumed its liquid piping to greet the approach of twilight. Convinced he was alone Jonno removed the plastic package from amongst his dirty washing and placed it inside the tomb. He reached inside with both hands, scraped together a little pile of leaves, and covered it up. Then he weighed them down with a few twigs and bits of broken branch that he gathered from around the tomb. Satisfied it was hidden as well as possible, he slung the hold-all over his shoulder and walked away.

He didn't meet another soul until he slipped out of the cemetery, crossed Swain's Lane and made his way onto the path through the manicured lawns of Waterlow Park. There he was wished a hearty 'good evening' by a man wearing a hound's-tooth jacket and a matching flat cap who was taking his red setter for an early evening constitutional. "You have no idea how good," thought Jonno as he returned the greeting.

An hour later he walked back into the flat and threw himself onto the sofa, breathing a great sigh of relief. It was done, the only dope left in the building that could be traced to him was the ounce he had taped inside the toilet cistern before setting out on his journey. It was not particularly safe there but having picked the lid up from the floor and replaced it, he considered it the best option. The cops had already searched there after all. He went to get it now and cut off about a quarter before retaping the rest in its temporary hiding place. Should anyone now call in unexpectedly, unless they mounted another full-scale search, they would just find this lump which he would claim as his personal stash. He'd be busted again of course, but the fine wouldn't be excessive. Besides he needed another joint.

He made some tea, sat back on the sofa with a mug and started to roll one up. Having just torn a piece off his cigarette packet to stuff in the end as a roach he thought he heard footsteps in the hall and then someone opening the cellar door. He jumped up and placed his ear against the door into the hall. There was no doubt, someone was going down the steps to the cellar! Then there was a scuffling noise as if someone was scrabbling around down there.

"Fuck it!" he thought. "The bastards have come back for another bloody go. Someone down the station must have finally realised these old tenements have coal cellars. Well they're too bloody late. And I'm too bloody shagged. If they're going to drag me in again, I'm going to fucking well smoke this first."

So he sat back down, fired up the joint and took in a huge lungful, expelling a thick cloud of smoke into the room. He knew they would be probably be able to smell it through the door when they came back up but he was beyond caring. He slurped down a mouthful of tea, took another enormous toke and sat there waiting for whatever was going to happen next, staring at the door before him. He heard footsteps ascending the cellar steps and approaching. He could sense someone waiting outside the door. He could almost hear them breathing. Almost see them standing there with their ear pressed to the woodwork. After what seemed an eternity he watched the door-handle slowly turn. Nothing happened. Then there was the sound of a key being slowly fed into the lock. Jonno took in another lungful of smoke, which then exploded out of his mouth as the door swung back to reveal Steve standing there, peering into the room.

"Where the fuck is the dope?" he spat out through a jaw clenched tight.

$$\sim 6 \sim$$

1969

Jonno stuffed the blankets into his holdall, along with Henrietta's cover, slung the guitar over his back by the shoulder strap, and helped Henry to his feet. Picking up the holdall and with his other arm clasped around his companion's back, he led them out from the tree and off in the direction from which he could hear early morning traffic.

They stumbled their way onto the Serpentine Bridge. Jonno saw the cross on top of the Albert Memorial glinting in the light of the newly risen sun. It looked wrong somehow, slightly lopsided, as if it had been placed in haste by someone with a fear of heights. Jonno determined to come back another time to have a look at it, and also the circular building on the other side of the road which he assumed was the Albert Hall. Sometimes London seemed full of memorials to dead princes.

"How are you doing?" Jonno asked. Henry was clutching his head as they stumbled along.

"Head's fucking painful. Need to lie down."

"Not yet you can't. You sure you don't want hospital?"

"Positive. Just get me home."

"I'm not sure I can remember how to get to the tube station."

"I've got money. Flag down a cab."

Henry's reversion to plain speaking worried Jonno more than the lump on his forehead and the rapid spread of discolouration around his eye socket.

It was still early in the morning when the black cab delivered them to the house on Upper Richmond Road. Margot was sitting at the kitchen table cradling a steaming mug of tea. Jonno was surprised to see her in the uniform of a registered nurse rather than the Indian print skirt and cheesecloth blouse. She jumped to her feet as they staggered in and helped to guide Henry into a chair.

"What the hell happened?"

"We got set upon. Skinheads. Henry got kicked in the head."

As if to reinforce the point the injured man groaned as he leant forward, placing his elbows on the table, so that he could cradle his head in his hands.

"How about you?"

"Bruised ribs I reckon. Not too bad, but I'm worried about him, he's been pretty incoherent. I wanted to take him to hospital but he wouldn't go. Insisted on coming home."

"Probably a bit concussed. I'll check him out. Can you get some ice out of the fridge? Wrap it in a tea towel. Clean ones in the dresser. Henry...Henry look up, look at me. How many fingers Henry?" She held up three fingers in front of him.

"Three."

"Good. How are you feeling?"

"Head hurts."

"I'll get you some paracetamols. Don't take aspirins whatever you do. One of your pupils is a bit dilated. And it looks like you're going to have a beautiful shiner on one side. Did he throw up at all?" This last to Jonno as he brought over the improvised ice-pack.

"No."

"That's good. Here Henry, this ice will help, hold it up to your temple for a bit. I don't think there's been any serious damage. What you need more than anything is rest. Let's get you up to bed, can you manage the stairs?"

"I'll help him," Jonno said.

"Go behind him if you'd be so kind, but let's see if he can manage on his own and knows where he's going. I'll be along in a minute with some pain killers."

Henry mounted the stairs alright by slowly pulling himself up the mahogany handrail, then turned left into a room on the first-floor landing. Jonno followed him in.

There was a mattress on the floor facing across the room to a large sash window with a view of the mulberry tree. Well-stocked bookcases covered the far wall, while to the right was an antique mahogany chest of drawers and a matching wardrobe with a mirror between its two doors. The floor was mostly bare varnished floorboards, except for a well-worn Persian rug between the bed and the window. An acoustic guitar was propped against the book-case and an open violin case, displaying a highly polished instrument, lay upon a low table on the far side of the bed. Above this table was a copy of the Martin Sharp psyche-delic poster of Bob Dylan which, rather than being pinned or blue-tacked to the wall, was behind glass in a simple black frame. Next to the violin was an empty ash-tray, a small brass incense burner and an open packet of sandal-wood joss sticks. Indeed the whole room was suffused by an aroma of sandalwood but also something else that Jonno couldn't at first place. Gradually he came to realise it was beeswax polish, which no doubt accounted for the lustrous sheen on the bodies of the two instruments and also on the furniture.

Henry slumped into what looked to be a nineteenth century American rocking chair, the type that was all turned spindles and minimally upholstered in chintz. Then he lifted his feet onto a matching footstool.

"Sorry old son, would you mind terribly divesting my somewhat incapacitated self of these glorious boots. I have to admit not feeling up to the operation in my current state, I am struck by the thought that bending over might be a foolish move."

Jonno, much relieved to hear his new friend returning to his usual idiosyncratic speech, willingly bent forward. Clutching the black boots by both toe and Cuban heel, he managed with some degree of effort to slide each one from the confines of Henry's tight denim jeans. He placed them by the foot of the bed where they stood side by side as if waiting for some cartoon character to jump straight into the pair of them, leap onto a horse and ride off into a western sunset.

Margo entered the room, having changed out of her uniform into the same cotton skirt that Jonno had originally seen her in with a plain white cotton blouse. She retained her nurse's manner though, as she shepherded Henry out of his chair and made him lie on top of his quilt. She handed him a couple of tablets and a glass of water, then watched to make sure he swallowed them. She crossed the room and lifted the bottom sash as far up as it would go before drawing across the blue velvet curtains that hung at either side. These were so thick and heavily lined so that all light was excluded from the room except for a glimmer which crept in around the door.

"There," she said. "You should be able to get some sleep now. I'll leave the door ajar, so if you need anything just shout, ok?"

Henry's eyes were closing already and he just managed a grunt of affirmation and a mumbled, "Thanks, both."

"And you'd better come with me," Margo told Jonno. "You probably need some sleep too and I certainly do, I've been on nights all this week. But first I'll take a look at your side."

"I didn't realise you were a nurse. So that was why Henry insisted on coming home."

"He has a pathological fear of institutions. Public school-boys, they all seem to have it."

"I can understand that."

"Don't tell me you're another one. We've got three in this house as it is. Henry and Brian, the owner, were both at Charterhouse, Robert went to Winchester. How about you?"

"Oh, nothing so grand, a direct-grant grammar. Sort of a junior public school, only been around for a hundred years. Winchester's been turning out our lords and masters since the thirteen hundreds."

As they talked, they walked along a landing which led back towards the front of the house and then started to climb a second staircase. Jonno tried not to look at her backside as it swayed from side to side before him, but he fought a losing battle, it was just too enticing, being a couple of feet in front of him.

"What did you think of his room?" Margo asked.

"Hard to place, kind of Spartan with all that bare wood yet opulent at the same time. So clean and neat and pol-ished looking. It wasn't what I was expecting."

"Opulent, that's a good word for Henry. He was brought up in the Far East, when he wasn't at school, which of course he was most of the time. Daddy worked for the

Hong Kong and Shanghai Bank. He's not short of a bob or two. Henry's been looked after by amahs and servants all of his life. Still is really – he pays me to clean his room once a week."

"You're joking."

"Supplements my income. Nurses don't get paid much. I'm glad you noticed how clean and tidy it is. A bit different from mine, as you're about to find out."

So saying she flung open a door to the left at the top of the stairs. Jonno realised they were directly above Henry's room. It wasn't as bad as she had intimated, sure the quilt was thrown back across the mattress on the floor, revealing a wrinkled sheet and a pair of scrunched up pillows. There were clothes scattered about the place, mostly on the over-stuffed armchair and spilling out of a chest of drawers. A wardrobe door hung open and inside Jonno could make out the uniform which Margo must have just hung up. She strode across to the window and raised the sash.

"There, we'll be able to hear Henry if he calls out."

"We?"

"You do want to sleep, don't you? Nothing else is on offer here. I am far too stuffed apart from anything else. I've been working at the old peoples' home since 10 o'clock last night. But if you take off your shirt, I'll look at your side for you. And then we can both lie down and get some kip."

Jonno pulled his tee-shirt up and over his head while Margo walked across to a little sink in the corner of the room and poured him a glass of water. She turned back to him and proffered a hand containing a couple of pain killers.

She lifted her eyebrows as she studied his torso. "Mmm, nice," she said, jokingly. Jonno swallowed the tablets as she reached out and prodded his lower ribs.

"Ouch!" he shouted.

"Sorry, just checking, but that wasn't excruciating, was it?"

"Not terribly, no."

"Good. Now take a really deep breath...ok, any really sharp pain?"

He shook his head.

"Probably no broken ribs then. Like you said, just bruising. You're lucky. Alright, let's get some rest. I sleep on this side so you're welcome to lie on that. It's too hot to get under the quilt anyway. No offence, but my clothes are staying on. And since I have to, I'd be grateful if you'd put your shirt back on.

Margo drew the curtains and the pair of them lay down. These curtains were nothing like the lined and thick velvet ones in Henry's room, just thin green cotton with a small pattern of foliage. It was dim but not impossible to make out the details of the poster on the far wall, which Jonno felt drawn to. A bare-chested Indian man with long hair piled atop his head and cascading down around his shoulders, was sitting cross legged on a tiger skin spread out on the ground. There were mountains in the background. A full moon shone off in the distance although a bright sun shone behind the man's head as if it were a halo. A trident was standing upright beside him and his right arm was balanced on something looking like a turned chair leg with a cross-piece fixed across the top. There was something similar in Margo's room Jonno noticed, leant up against the chest of drawers. He wondered what use she had for a piece of broken furniture. As drowsiness began to overcome him and his eyelids drooped, he thought he saw a cobra winding around the figure's neck and shoulders, and that the tiger's head beneath his crossed legs was staring right out of the poster and laughing at him. The last conscious thought Jonno had before surrendering himself to oblivion was to wonder why the man's skin was blue.

It was midday before he woke again. Margo was reentering the room with a mug of tea in her hand. "Wake up sleepyhead," she said as she put it down beside him.

"How's Henry?"

"He seems fine. Still got a headache of course, and growing a beautiful black eye, but no serious damage as far as I can tell. He'd probably be better off not smoking any dope for a couple of days but I can't see that happening, can you? Not when he's got a couple of gigs coming up."

"Is he in a band?"

"Didn't he tell you? The Titus Groans they call themselves, after some book he said. Can't say I've ever heard of it, but then I'm not a great reader. Anyway, you'd better come downstairs. Henry's up and told everyone all about what happened. We've been having a house meeting and your presence has been requested. So come on, drink your tea and come down."

Ten minutes later, when Jonno entered the kitchen, he found the whole household, apart from the missing Brian, sat around the scrubbed pine table. Robert the astrologer was seated at the head with Margo and Bea to either side of him, the other men further down. The seat at the far end was vacant and Robert indicated that Jonno should take it. He looked around at all of their faces before taking his place. There was a sort of a grim seriousness about all of them that reminded Jonno of being summoned before a prefects' meeting at his old school.

The nervousness Jonno felt was heightened by the fact that his holdall sat in the middle of the table before them all. The top was open and Jonno could see that Margo's blankets had been removed and replaced by his few possessions from the back of Henry's car. Standing beside the holdall was the green plastic case of his typewriter. It looked like he was about to be delivered his marching orders, cast out from the comfort of their metropolitan idyll.

He looked from one face to the other all the way around the table, as if in one of them he might be able to read whatever indiscretion he might have performed. He was nonplussed, he could think of no sin that would justify this level of intense scrutiny. He had spent very few hours in their company. True he'd been pretty stoned the night before, he wasn't used to smoking so much, but as far as he could remember he hadn't done anything unpleasant, such as throwing up or forgetting to flush the toilet.

Finally Margo could hold the stern expression on her face no longer and burst into an uncontrollable fit of giggles. This set the rest of them off one by one.

"God, if you could see your face, it's an absolute picture," Ben broke out.

Simon thrust back his chair and, standing up, leant over, to slap Jonno on the back.

All around the table there was laughter and shouts of congratulations.

"Good for you," said Pat the gardener. "Bloody skinheads deserve a total thrashing, mindless twats."

Jonno felt a little uneasy about the large man's vehemence but was so relieved at finding they were joking with him that he ignored it. Finally Robert called the meeting to order by striking his cigarette lighter against the mug on the table before him.

"Jonno, Henry has told us what happened last night and painted such a vivid picture of you standing over him, like some vengeful colossus, brandishing his beloved Henrietta in the faces of your assailants. He has also explained to us that you are newly arrived in London and have yet to find a place to stay. In light of this, and as some small recompense for protecting our esteemed friend and colleague, and moreover in consideration of the fact that at present we do have a vacant room, it has been unanimously agreed that we would like to extend to you the hospitality of the house. That is until such time that Brian, the missing member of our little community, returns from his Grecian sojourn. What do you say?"

The theatricality of the whole occasion caused Jonno to grin and, in an effort to enter into its spirit he rose from his chair and bowed to left and right. "What can I say? Any supposed heroism on my part I can assure you was purely instinctual and therefore not in the least heroic. Nevertheless I am, as you say, new to the area and find myself both overwhelmed and overjoyed to accept your most generous offer."

"That's settled then," Robert continued. "I propose that I pack a celebratory chillum whilst someone shows Jonno to his new, if temporary, accommodation."

"I'll do it," said Bea, snatching up the typewriter case from the table and leading Jonno, once more with his hold-all slung across his shoulder, out from the kitchen and up to the first-floor landing. She turned down a short passage-way to the right and threw open a door.

"Brian's room," she announced. "The nicest one in the house."

Two things struck Jonno immediately. Firstly the decor. The original plain white walls and ceiling had subsequently been embellished with a profusion of red spots, each about six inches in diameter. It resembled the inside of a fly agaric mushroom, except the colours were reversed. The other, more traditional feature, was a pair of French windows which led out onto a small balcony overlooking the back garden.

"God, it's like being inside Noddy's house," he expostulated.

"I think it was more the caterpillar's from *Alice in Wonderland* that he was aiming for," said Bea. "Look, there's a hookah out here," as she stepped onto the balcony, Jonno following behind.

So there was. A two-foot-high traditional Arabian water pipe stood to one side of an old armchair, which was drawn up to a telescope mounted upon a tripod.

"He's a real star-gazer, Brian. He sits out here toking away on his hubble-bubble in the middle of the night studying the heavens, although he's always complaining about the amount of light pollution. He and Robert are partners in an astrology business. He's the scientific one, he did physics at Cambridge, so he usually casts the horoscopes. Robert read English at Oxford so he writes the interpretations."

"Do you believe in all of this?"

"They've done a chart for all of us. Mine was pretty accurate I thought, although for personal guidance I prefer to use the I Ching. It's more in the moment. What about you?"

"I've never really thought about it."

"You should get Robert to do one for you. Brian's away, but Robert knows all about consulting the ephemera and how to do the casting. Do you know what time you were born?"

"Two o'clock in the morning according to my mum."

"There you are, you obviously know whereabouts and what date, that's all he needs. And we'd all like to see it and hear what he says."

"Really. Why?"

"Because we're a tight-knit little community. We're our own little solar system if you like. Everyone effects everyone else. It's easier to all live together if we know what to expect, what sort of allowances we need to make." So saying she stepped back into the room before leaving Jonno to sort out his few belongings.

He had travelled light. He found enough room in the chest of drawers for his collection of T-shirts. The polo-necked magenta jersey his mother had knitted he folded and placed on its top, deciding to leave his socks and pants in the holdall. He hung his denim jacket and spare jeans over a hanger in the wardrobe, changed out of his suede desert boots and placed them and his flip-flops under the bed. The few books he'd brought from college he piled up on the bed-side table next to the reading lamp. There was a small desk with a wooden chair to one side of the French windows, affording an angled and slightly truncated view of the garden to anyone sitting at it. Having removed his typewriter and a sheaf of papers from the green case, he placed them next to a black Anglepoise lamp on the desk, which he assumed Brian used when drawing up his charts.

Having sorted out his new domicile he threw himself onto the bed, reached for the topmost book from his little pile and opened it to a well-thumbed page.

And other spirits there are standing apart
Upon the forehead of the age to come;
These, these will give the world another heart,
And other pulses. Hear ye not the hum
Of mighty workings? –
Listen awhile ye nations, and be dumb.

Of all the Romantic poets Jonno had studied at school, he held Keats in the highest regard, revered him as a role model. He knew this early poem, about Wordsworth and Leigh Hunt, Keats wrote at the age of twenty-one, having just dropped out of medical school, determined to pursue what he felt to be his true calling as a poet. That he'd evolved from creating relatively pedestrian sonnets to the magnificence of the Ode to a Nightingale and other soaring masterworks in three short years filled Jonno with awe, and contributed to his own decision to leave university.

Keats' story also reminded him of his own mortality. Tuberculosis was no longer such a ubiquitous scourge, but all of his own short life had been lived beneath the shadow of the atomic bomb. He felt his world presided over by jingoistic madmen, revenants from a bygone age, desperately flexing their militaristic muscles to cling on to their powers and privileges. The likelihood of the succession of hot wars in Asia igniting the cold one closer to home, sparking universal conflagration, seemed a distinct possibility. But this time the holocaust was likely to be permanent. The ultimate 'final solution.'

Hope lay, Jonno thought, as he stretched out on his borrowed bed, in such people as inhabited this house, and their attempts to construct some form of an alternative society. People who, as Keats put it, were living 'on the forehead of the age to come' and striving to 'give the world another heart.'

Of course, his father would dismiss it all as a romantic pipe dream, and maybe it was. Pipes did play a large part in it, but what was so bad about dreaming? It was possible that if everyone took to marijuana as much as his new housemates, then a general change in consciousness might be effected.

The protests sweeping through Europe and the Americas the previous year were supressed with tear gas and guns. The Parisian riots led to nothing beyond a few concessions by the universities. Jan Palach and some Buddhist monks had burnt themselves to death for nothing. Institutional racism was thriving in southern Africa. CIA agents were busy installing fascist dictatorships across South America, while the Soviets crushed dissent in Czechoslovakia. Martin Luther King had been assassinated; a student was shot in Berkeley, while the National Guard threatened demonstrators with fixed bayonets. A military junta seized control in Greece, and all the while the carpet bombing of Vietnamese peasants increased. To Jonno an increase of dreaming seemed the only hope.

Jonno had smoked very little hash before being picked up by Henry's motorised garden, and certainly never as much as over the last couple of days. He could feel it affording him a different perspective. As he leaned back on the bed, nursing his bruised ribs, he realised he was not sorry to miss the Rolling Stones concert. He'd experienced enough of huge crowds the previous year when, with some two hundred thousand protestors, he'd marched from Trafalgar Square. Nothing was achieved; the fighting raged on. He wondered if they were playing *Street Fighting Man* at that very moment. It was a great song with all the punch of a revolutionary rabble rouser, but was strangely ambivalent. "But what can a poor man do?" the lyric asked. Was the band helping to create an alternative society or siphoning off the pressure for change, surfing the crest of the zeitgeist and pocketing the proceeds? Perhaps both. Jonno couldn't decide.

Was it just a question of emphasis, or one of art? Currently Jonno was enamoured of an obscure underground group called Pink Floyd, who had released two very idiosyncratic albums; *The Piper at the Gates of Dawn* and *A Saucerful of Secrets,* and recently the soundtrack for a film called *More.* It seemed unthinkable that such an outfit could ever become absorbed into the mainstream world of charts; and top twenties; and the miming required for appearances on television.

Nevertheless he wondered how he would feel if one day they graduated into international best sellers, like the rebellious Rolling Stones had before them. To be art must a creation remain difficult and obscure, or in the coming world would everything be commodified? In Paris the previous year, art had roamed the streets in anger, rocks in hand. Would the marketplace strike back with derision at such innocent naiveté?

The jumble of such thoughts rattling around inside his brain was brought to an abrupt close by the sound of the gong being sounded down in the kitchen. The evening was as balmy as the previous day's, and the household again carried plates laden with food out to the table beneath the wisteria vine. In between mouthfuls of vegetarian lasagne, as cooked by Ben, the talk was of drought, a condition rarely heard of in an English summer. Pat remarked on how much extra watering was being done at Kew in order to keep the more delicate specimens from succumbing to the heat.

"I guess I'll have to up it here if we want a decent crop of mulberries this year. I'll do the same for the vegetable patch, but I won't bother with the lawn. What does anyone think about the flower beds?"

"Oh we've got to have flowers," from Robert.

"I'm not so sure," said Margo. "Isn't that a little anti-social? If it doesn't rain soon, we might end up with standpipes in the streets, like that winter when the pipes froze."

"It'll rain." Robert insisted.

"What say the stars?" Henry enquired.

"By the end of the month, according to the chart I did for July."

"I'll go and consult the I Ching," said Bea, leaving the table.

"You're not a fan?" Jonno asked, when he saw Robert's lips curl into a disparaging smile, as he started to roll an after-dinner joint.

"It's so convoluted. It will provide her with an obscure homily in inscrutable language which she can interpret any way she wants."

"Whereas astrology?" Jonno queried while Robert crumbled the dope onto the tobacco, rolled and licked the papers.

"At least it's scientific," Simon pitched in. "A little anyway. I mean if the gravitational pull of the moon can make whole oceans rise and fall, and cause crazies to howl at midnight, it stands to reason the rest of the planets might have more subtle influences."

"Thanks for your endorsement," said Robert, firing up.

"My pleasure," responded Simon, "although I must warn you that you will soon be out of a job. All that studying star positions and drawing charts and so forth, soon it will all be done by computers in a fraction of the time it takes you two. Someone is bound to upload the ephemeras and write a program one day, and then people will be able to just hit a button and get their own reading."

"I'll be old and retired by then," he said, breathing out a cloud of sweet-smelling smoke, before passing the joint on.

"I wouldn't count on it mate," Simon said as he took it, "Change is happening fast. Computers won't always be massive things that need their own air-conditioned rooms and a platoon of operators."

"Yeh, yeh, I know, you've told us, electricity is going to change the world."

"You'd better believe it," breathing out his own cloud and passing it to Jonno.

"Changing the subject, who's coming to sat-sang tonight?" Margo broke in.

"What's sat-sang?" Jonno asked, passing her the joint.

"It's where they all sit around in a room and listen to an Indian guy rabbit on about meditation."

"You should approve Simon, it's where we get our batteries re-charged," Ben said, gathering up the plates.

"You should come along Jonno," Margo said to him, "See for yourself."

At which point Bea reappeared. "It said to water."

$$\sim 7 \sim$$

1972

"It's ok. I've hidden it." Jonno passed the joint he'd been smoking across to Steve who closed the door and collapsed into the armchair. He took a long drag before leaning back and closing his eyes. He held the smoke in his lungs for as long as possible before breathing it out in an extended sigh.

"God, I needed that. What a bloody disaster."

"You could say that. They let you go then."

"Didn't want to but had to in the end. Didn't have anything to hold me on. Trev took the rap, since he was going to be done for the coke anyway. He said the two weights I took down there were his. Which they were by then, he'd given me the money and he'd started to cut them into ounces. So they busted him for dealing as well. They tried to get him to say he'd just bought them off me, because of the money in my wallet, but he denied it. He's a bloody good mate Trev."

"Yes, well, if he hadn't encouraged Norman to send the stuff in the first place none of us would be in this mess. I thought we'd agreed you were going to talk him out of it."

Steve looked uncomfortable for a moment. The ash from the end of the joint he was holding fell on the floor and he bent down, avoiding Jonno's eyes, and rubbed it into the carpet. After a short while he sat back up, and replied, "I told him *we* didn't want it, like I said, and you'd sent that telegram telling Norman not to bother. But Trev really wanted it, so told Norman to go ahead. I guess Norman just ignored your message."

Jonno harboured a sneaking suspicion that Trev wasn't the only one who'd really wanted it. He remembered how keenly Steve snorted the stuff after Candy's Rainbow deal fell through. How much pressure he'd had to exert on Steve to prevent him snorting the whole quarter ounce.

The speed with which Steve changed the subject increased his suspicions.

"You didn't really know Norman, did you?"

"I didn't know any of them. I dropped out after first year if you remember. Trev, Dave, Norman, all the rest of them, they were your mates not mine. I don't frequent the circles of people who go to parties in Downing Street."

"That's right, I told you about Dave knocking off the Chancellor of the Exchequer's daughter didn't I. Hah! What a laugh that was."

"What, screwing his daughter?"

"No, smoking dope next door to number 10. There's nothing unusual about fucking a Roedean girl."

"Speak for yourself."

"Oh, don't be so bloody proletarian. It doesn't suit you."

"Oh sorry guv. Fancy a cuppa' char your honour?" Jonno ducked and tugged at his forelock before moving into the kitchen to put the kettle on again. Steve came in as he was putting tea-bags into the mugs.

"They didn't search the basement then?"

"No. I told you it would be a good place to stash the stuff. I guess they thought they had me bang to rights. Bloody idiots didn't look down there, thank God. Otherwise I'd have been..."

"Cool. So where is it?"

"Safe. Safe as you can be in a cemetery."

"You what?"

"I needed to get rid of it, didn't I? In case they came back. It was the safest place I could think of."

"You mean you buried it somewhere?"

"More like interred it."

"Don't piss me about. Whereabouts, is it?"

"Up in Highgate. I put it in one of the tombs."

"Which one?"

"I don't know. I couldn't really ask, what with the occupant being a little bit dead."

"Don't fuck around Jonno. Where is it?"

"Don't worry, I'll be able to find it again. It's near Ophelia."

"Who the fuck...?"

"Lizzie Siddal. The model for our old Rosetti poster, and the Millais. I told you I came across her grave when I went up there last year."

"You and your bloody artistic leanings."

"Good job for us I've got them. It's the perfect place to stash the gear. There's no connection to us but easy to find again. And no one else is going to be rooting around in some poor bastard's tomb, are they?"

"Except one of those stupid vampire hunters you told me about."

"I doubt if any of them have been back since they all got busted. The cops scared them right off, and the cemetery people have put in a night-watchman. It's gone back to being a really peaceful place that hardly anyone goes to. Perfect. As long as we don't go at night, we can get it back whenever we want."

Jonno hoped what he was saying was true. He'd worried about the vampire hunters himself, but thought it unlikely that anyone would stumble across the stash. In the end he had decided the risk was worth it, leaving it buried in the cellar was asking for trouble. They couldn't move flats. He was required to remain there for at least the four weeks he needed to report to the police station. The cops might decide on a return visit at any time. The blocks of dope had felt like a weight chained to his ankle, dragging at his footsteps. It might represent the majority of their joint finances, but in reality, he didn't care about that. When compared with the possibility of a few years in goal there was no contest, he would prefer to lose the lot.

One night spent in the cells was more than enough. He thought back to the long night trying to sleep on the bare board, wondering how he had got himself into his precarious position. He didn't think of himself as a criminal, yet the whole experience brought home to him that people would see him as one. If he managed somehow to survive this debacle, he swore he would never willingly put himself back into danger. Not go straight exactly, the fact was he liked smoking the stuff and saw no reason why he shouldn't.

But dealing it was different. He'd thought it a game, but it was one with dire consequences. It was fun taking risks, cocking a snoop at the powers that be, striking a blow at straight society, but for what actual purpose? Self-aggrandisement? Maybe a bit, if he was honest, a feeling of self-importance, of being 'in the know', and a player in the counter-culture. But what it really came down to was barefaced capitalism. In which case he was just as bad as the system he was avowedly attempting to undermine. No, this wasn't for him, and the sooner he extricated himself from the situation he was embroiled in, the better he would feel about himself.

When he tried to explain his thoughts, Steve laughed at him.

"You're such a bloody romantic. Being tortured by your moral conscience, are you? So what are you going to do about it? Go back to getting ten quid a week as an accounts clerk for one of those giant oil companies polluting the planet by drilling holes in the North Sea?"

"Maybe. At least it's honest. I got into this as a way of supporting myself while I got on with my writing. And what have I done? Sod all. All of my time has been eaten up by this bullshit life."

"Yes well, maybe you haven't got it in you. Face it, you're a fucking dreamer, like thousands of other would-be writers."

"Oh, thanks a lot. That's really bloody encouraging."

"I didn't mean..."

"Yes, you did. And maybe you're right. I have been too long dreaming. Time I got on with stuff. If T.S. Eliot could work in a bank and Franz Kafka for an insurance company there's nothing wrong with me being a clerk. I have to support myself somehow, there was a distinct lack of silver spoons handed out in my family. Besides, at the moment we're broke."

"What do you mean?"

"They took our money."

"They did what?"

"They took away my passport, our address book, the Japanese box with our stash, and they confiscated our money."

"Fuck!"

"Oh, and just by the way, unlike you, I got busted."

"They can't do that, surely. Didn't you tell them half of it was mine?"

"What? And admit we were business partners? Hardly. Good job I didn't. The cops assumed we were dealing anyway; they just didn't pursue it because they thought we were being busted for the coke. If customs tell them they've dropped the charges the cops might come back for us. That's why I hid the stuff as soon as I could."

"Shit."

"With a bit of luck customs won't let on. They looked like coming to blows at one point. As it is I've got to report to the cops every Friday for four weeks. Every time I go round there, I'm going to worry they'll lock me up."

"We need to consult a lawyer. There must be some way of getting the bread back."

"For Christ's sake don't stir the pot. It's only money. The rent's paid till the end of the month. We've got a bit of food, and there's the best part of an ounce taped inside the toilet cistern. Haven't you got any cash?"

"I gave the money Trev gave me back to him because he took the rap. I've got a bit in the bank but not much."

"There you go then. We can survive for a few weeks. Let's just leave it and see what happens."

"We should get the gear from Highgate and sell it."

"No way! We shouldn't touch it until this all blows over, if it blows over. The cops are likely to be watching us. Maybe listening to the phone. We go and get it and they'll pounce. If they were pissed off by customs, they'll be double angry with us two."

"You're not going to tell me where it is, are you?"

"I've told you where it is, next to Lizzie Siddal. I can't be more specific; I didn't read the inscription."

"You're holding out on me."

"How can you say that? Look, I was right about burying it in the cellar, wasn't I? And I was right about sending the telegram. The customs bloke said that was why they let us go. Apparently, they can check. Trust me on this one too. We're partners, aren't we?"

"It doesn't feel like it. We've lost our money and you won't tell me where the dope is, it feels like I've been shafted. By you."

"Christ Steve, I've told you where it is, no one's shafting you. If it makes you feel better, we'll go up there tomorrow and I'll show you where it is. We'll just have to make sure we're not followed. All I'm saying is that it's too risky to sell it straight away. If nothing happens for a few weeks we should be safe. Let's leave it where it is until then. Thanks to Trev you didn't even get busted. You were lucky."

"I don't feel lucky."

"Well you should. Do you think your father could've pulled some strings?"

"Nah, not bloody likely. Anyway he's not a cop any longer, just a civil servant working in Ireland."

"Well the customs people know about him. One of them mentioned how he complicated things. Maybe it worked in our favour."

"Doubt it, he'd gladly see me locked up."

"Whatever. Look, after my four weeks is up, hopefully they'll give us our bread back, then we get the dope and sell it or split it between us, and we can move flat or go our separate ways, whatever we want, ok? Right now I'm too bushed to think straight, I didn't get much kip last night. I've got a soft mattress and a continental quilt in there and I'm longing to get reacquainted with them. We can talk this over in the morning."

"You're seriously thinking of packing it all in?"

"Too bloody right. If I manage to get out of this with my freedom intact, I'm never going to tempt fate again."

So saying he left for his bedroom where he threw his clothes on the floor before pulling the quilt up and over his head. He was overtired though, so lay there for a while thinking about Steve, and his lack of sympathy for Jonno's ordeal. All that his so-called partner was concerned about was the loss of their money and the location of the dope. He tossed and turned for a while wondering what their future might bring, before finally succumbing to fitful sleep.

He was wrenched from troubled dreams by an imperious pounding on the door in the garden wall, which was only a few feet from his bedroom window. Hastily pulling on some jeans, he stumbled out through the kitchen into the early morning daylight. When he threw open the garden door, he fully expected to see a collection of plain-clothes and uniformed officers, eager to resume ransacking the place. Instead there was a sole individual, dressed in a tweed jacket over a pair of cavalry twill trousers, with highly polished brown brogues on his feet and a trilby hat on his head. The stranger stood there, surveying him with steel grey eyes which emanated something that felt like contempt.

"Can I help you?" Jonno enquired, feeling suddenly self-conscious of his half-naked torso.

"I doubt it very much. I've come to collect my son." So saying the man shouldered Jonno to one side and marched up the short path and into the flat. Once there he stood looking around the living room and barked out in a voice obviously used to command, "Stephen, show yourself!"

"Christ dad," a muffled voice emanated from Steve's room. Jonno retreated into his own, grabbed a tee-shirt and hunted around for his socks and shoes. From his open door he could see the stern figure of their visitor standing ramrod straight by the side of the glass coffee table, with his head jerking around spasmodically, quickly summing up the place, as if registering its contents and seeking for any potential threat. The man noticed Jonno watching him and his mouth twisted up in a cross between a smile and a grimace.

"Force of habit," he explained. "My job..."

"Which is?" Jonno enquired into the silence after the stranger stopped in mid-sentence.

"None of your business. Just get him, would you? Then we'll be on our way, and I'd be grateful if you never try to get in touch with my son ever again."

As he said this Steve appeared in the living room looking sheepish, as if used to being brow-beaten by an overbearing father.

"Pack your bags, I'm taking you home to your mother. And I've arranged a little job for you."

"Dad, I can't come at the moment. We've got things we have to sort out."

"I'm the one who's been doing the sorting out. You need to be quiet and pack your stuff, or I'll take you as you are."

"But Dad..."

"No buts, just get on with it. I have been flown back from Northern Ireland. I have been informed what you two have been getting up to and at the cost of a great deal of personal embarrassment I have struck a deal with the powers that be. They will leave you alone if you agree to return home and take up a voluntary position in our local prison, running classes for the inmates. That way you will get a taste of the real rewards of a criminal life. You have managed to avoid becoming an inmate yourself merely by the skin of your teeth and I'm determined you should learn the error of your ways. As for you," he turned to Jonno, "I am informed you have been charged and prosecuted. Good. I believe you to have been a malign influence on my son and I assure you that should you try to contact him in the future I will do my utmost to see that further punishment comes your way. Do I make myself clear?"

"Totally."

"But father…"

"Don't you 'father' me. This is not debateable. I'll wait in the car outside. I'll give you half an hour, then we're leaving with or without your stuff, so I suggest you get cracking." So saying he turned and walked out of the flat.

"Jesus!" Jonno exclaimed as soon as he shut the garden door behind him.

"Fuck, fuck, fuck!"

"Are you going to do what he says?"

"What choice do I have?"

"You could try running away. Go through the house and straight out the front. He won't see you until you are half way across the park."

"Maybe not, but he'd find me quick enough. He works for the Home Office. He's got contacts everywhere. No I'll have to do what he says. I'll send you an address where you can contact me. I'll want my share when you sell the gear."

"He said…"

"Don't worry about that. I'll work something out, get a post office box or something. Don't stiff me Jonno, I want my money."

"Sure, of course. But you'd better get on with it. Christ, what about your stereo?"

"I'll get it later. Or you could send me some money for it when you send the other. Take your albums out of the box and I'll take that with me. I'll chuck my clothes into a bag, grab my stuff from the bathroom, get my guitar and I'm gone. The parting of the ways. Fun while it lasted, eh?"

After packing the last of his possessions into his father's car Steve returned and shook Jonno's hand. "Oh, and by the way, sorry," he said in parting.

"For what?" Jonno shouted after him from the kitchen door.

"You'll see," Steve shouted back, and laughed as he slammed the car door. His father accelerated away.

Jonno closed the garden door and went back inside, wondering whether they would ever meet again. He made a cup of tea and poured corn flakes into a bowl from the half empty packet, using up the last of the milk in the process. The flat seemed colder, somehow. When he'd finished his breakfast, he went across to the stereo and put on *More*, still his favourite album, in an attempt to warm the atmosphere a bit. He pulled out the square of silver paper he'd sequestered beneath the sofa cushions the previous night and rolled himself a joint. He was alone now and needed to think.

The first thing was money. His wallet was nearly empty. Paying the fine had seen to that, leaving him with maybe enough to buy a bottle of milk, some cigarettes and another packet of Rizlas. He thought of Freewheeling Franklin in a Furry Freak Brothers cartoon saying, "Dope will carry you through times of no money better than money will carry you through times of no dope." Maybe, but it wasn't particularly nutritious. As he'd told Steve, there was some food in the kitchen but nowhere near enough to last him for four weeks. Besides, he'd go mad being cooped up for a month. If he was in the country, it wouldn't be so bad, but this was London where going out cost.

On the plus side there was no longer any need to keep his whereabouts secret. He could get in touch with Susie again, find out whether she was as interested in him as he hoped. But again, he would need money, for tube fares if nothing else. And flowers, he'd have to take her flowers if he was to apologise for not giving her his phone number. For not getting in touch after what? Christ, was it only a couple of nights ago? Seemed like forever. He started to reach for the phone but stopped himself. Someone might be listening in if they thought deals were being done. He couldn't risk bringing her and her flatmates to the attention of some surreptitious listener. Besides which, he realised again he didn't have her number

He thought of the rest of the ounce taped inside the toilet cistern. He could cut it in half and take it around to sad Dave's, maybe he would buy it. He rushed into the bathroom and lifted off the lid. The ends of the tape flapped uselessly. Bastard!

So that was what Steve's "sorry' was about. As he returned to the sofa Jonno remembered him laughing as he'd said it. He wasn't sorry at all. Triumphant more like. Jonno reflected on the previous night's conversation. There was a moment when Steve seemed uncomfortable. They were talking about the cocaine. Jonno was saying that this whole thing was Trev's fault. Steve had looked shifty, hadn't answered him straight away.

Had Steve told Trev to tell Norman to ignore the telegram? It was distinctly possible now he thought about it. Steve had loved scoring the cocaine when Candy asked if they could supply the band about to play at the Rainbow. How he'd boasted about breaking into 'the big league'. How they could say they were "By appointment to the Stars." When the whole deal went belly up and they were stuck with the stuff, how keenly Steve insisted they keep it. That it improved his own guitar playing.

"Rotten bastard," he thought as he contemplated how Steve had been spirited out of danger by his well-connected father. He remembered the words of the black customs officer as they parted, about there being three kinds of people – that those in the middle get shafted by everyone. It appeared he might have been right.

With nothing to sell, he decided go round to sad Dave's anyway. It was a five-minute walk away, virtually around the corner. Jonno felt bad about not letting Dave know where their new flat was, especially when it was so close. He could see the sense of keeping their location a secret while the threat of an imminent bust was hanging over them, but nevertheless Dave was a good friend. Since the move Jonno had been dreading the embarrassment of running into him in the street. He decided to tidy up the flat to remove any reminder of the cops and then go round and apologise to him, take his remaining quarter ounce and get the bugger stoned by way of atonement.

~ 8 ~

1969

Jonno took up Margo's offer to take him with her to sat-sang, finding himself sitting on a floor cushion in a crowded basement room in Notting Hill. Ben and Robert were already there as well as ten people who were strangers to him. The profusion of cushions were all covered in Indian designs, some of which incorporated tiny circles of mirror glass or more likely thin bits of metal. The sofa was draped with a similarly oriental-looking piece of material, which matched the one pinned up across the window. The light was dim from a purple bulb in the overhead fitting, and the whole room was suffused with the sweet smoke of three jasmine-scented joss sticks burning in a brass holder. Everyone was faced towards a small Indian man dressed in white robes sitting cross legged at one end of the room. He must have been at least fifty, Jonno thought, going by his pinched-looking, lined face, belied by the sparkling of the liveliest brown eyes he had ever seen.

According to Margo this was Guru Charanand, who would be talking about something called Knowledge. Beside him sat a male western acolyte similarly dressed in white who, rather than having a shaved head like his guru, sported incredibly long dark hair which fell across his chest and almost down to his crossed legs. Into one armpit was tucked a T shaped wooden construction similar to the one Jonno had seen in Margo's room, which he was using to lean upon.

"What's that?" He whispered to Margo, sitting beside him.

"It's called a beragon. You can use it to prop yourself up when meditating."

"You need props?"

The guru heard Jonno's question and turned a beatific smile in his direction.

"Everybody uses props of some kind in this world – sex, alcohol, gambling, drugs, television, ceaseless chatter, anything to fill the void inside themselves. Everyone feels a need, has an emptiness lurking at their centre. So they run to anything they can think of to fill the hole. But nothing does, for these are all mere distractions. They might work for a while, for a moment, a week, maybe for a year, but nothing can truly satisfy their longings because these are all external. Just mirages of fulfilment.

The longings come from inside, from the deep place in all of us, that Christians call a soul, and Hindus call the atman. What you call it doesn't matter. It's the same still place that wants to connect with the life force which pervades the universe, to feel in tune with it, plugged in to the cosmic harmony."

Jonno must have made some minute movement as he was about to ask a question, which Margo sensed and gently nudged him in the ribs. The spot was still tender from the kick he'd received in the park, and it brought him up sharply, stifling the query in his throat, and making him understand that it was not a conversation, they were here to listen. The guru continued seamlessly with his sermon.

"To do this you have to go inside. Just as the longing is deep within us, so too is the answer. It is only through the practice of meditation that we can find that still place, can see the divine light that shines there in the darkness, can hear the rhythm of the universe, taste the elixir of life itself. Then all of our questions just fall away. Then you can walk through this world unaffected by trivial distractions. The journey starts with acquiring the knowledge of meditation. And you can practice it anywhere, and at any time. Props are not necessary, but sometimes they are helpful. The beragon we can use to rest our arms on to stop from feeling cramp, but they are just two pieces of wood, they have no spiritual significance, no mystical powers to impart. The only real prop, the only true thing in this world of manifest illusions is the practice of knowledge itself."

He carried on talking in this vein to the roomful of silent, avid listeners for a couple of hours. Jonno was much taken by his use of obscure metaphors to describe the experience of meditation: images of lotus plants which grow out of stagnant mud to raise themselves up to blossom in glorious sunlight. Of grains of sand being irritants within oyster shells, causing pearls to form around them. Everything he said promised a deeper understanding of life was possible, and that daily practice would lead to a state of transcendent bliss.

When they returned home Jonno was filled with questions which he wanted to ask Margo and the others, but they all put him off in order to repair to their rooms and meditate.

There had been a few students at university who were into Transcendental Meditation. Mostly they were shunned by the majority who were more political, but Jonno was interested enough to try and find out more about their practices. They met regularly in the exquisitely designed and mostly under-used circular university chapel. They were closed sessions however, for initiates only. Maximum press coverage was accorded to meditation once pilgrimages to the ashram in India were made by rock music royalty, but the actual process remained shrouded in secrecy.

If you weren't a celebrity you needed to be interviewed, vetted, and then undertake differing courses for which differing amounts of monies were charged. The whole thing reeked of corporate governance, of an American 'New Age' where capitalism reigned supreme.

Jonno was initially suspicious of the diminutive Indian gentleman in Notting Hill because of the long shadow cast by the Maharishi, who had registered the initials TM as a trade mark. Jonno had thought of it as a sort of Mensa for mystics.

In spite of these misgivings Jonno found himself returning several times to the basement flat, with its purple light and its Indian draperies. Often in the company of Margo, who regularly attended sat-sang, before starting her night-shift at the old peoples' home. Other occupants of the Richmond Road house turned up at irregular intervals, except for Simon, the electronic wizard, who insisted he needed no other-worldly experiences since he was obviously already from another planet.

"Yes, and we all know which one," Robert, the astrologer, quipped one evening when they were all sitting outside enjoying the gathering dusk, admiring the half-moon which was just emerging from behind the abundant foliage of the mulberry tree. Even Bea turned up from time to time, her sophisticated little black dress and stockinged legs making a sharp contrast to the jeans, tee-shirts and ankle-length dresses of the more regular attendees. It amused Jonno to see her high-heels amongst the motley collection of sandals, boots and flip-flops that lined the hall-way outside the meeting room. Such casual footwear would hardly be suitable for a croupier in the exclusive gaming club to which she would repair after having, as she put it, 'had her spiritual batteries recharged.' This infrequent service she usually required after having not come home the previous night, straggling in late in the morning, to gulp down paracetamols and coffee, before heading up to her room and the sanctuary of her own bed.

Pat the gardener and Ben the advertising man usually turned up together, often arm in arm. That they felt comfortable to do so was another mark in the little group's favour as far as Jonno was concerned. Even more than Bea's high heels the sight of two men holding hands was a striking visual confirmation that whatever experience was on offer here, it was freely available to anyone, with no exceptions.

And freely available it was; it was no club, there was no joining fee. The knowledge offered was considered to be priceless, and thus came without cost. There were no rules, no oaths of allegiance to be sworn, and no change in lifestyle insisted upon. As far as Jonno could ascertain, the only requirement was once the meditation techniques had been revealed, that they were practiced. Preferably for at least an hour a day, to gain the maximum benefit, although this was merely a guideline. Attendance at sat-sang was entirely voluntary. Some, like Bea, turning up only occasionally, while others, Margo amongst them, frequently enjoyed the companionship of like-minded souls.

Initiation might be freely given, but was not dispensed automatically, only when the guru considered the applicant ready. Jonno was tentative, worried about committing himself to something that might turn out to be a disappointment. So he spent a number of days sounding out various members of the household individually, asking their opinions on his suitability as a candidate.

The majority of respondents were positive but he found his conversation with Ben quite disturbing. He approached him one evening as he sat on the veranda of the weatherboard summer house at the far end of the garden, which he shared with Pat. Ben was the possessor a round, plumpish face which made Jonno think of a country parson, someone contented and well-fed but shy of imposing their beliefs. He turned out to be far from shy in his opinions, however.

"Why read so many books?" the older man asked him, "Your head must be jam-packed full of them."

Jonno had no immediate answer to the question, except for the obvious "because I like reading."

"Other peoples' experiences, other peoples' thoughts. Life lived vicariously. Such a waste of time," Ben said.

"But you did English at Oxford, like Robert. Surely you thought there's a value in studying literature. Didn't you want to become a writer yourself some day?"

"Initially, I suppose I did. But what would be the point? One thing Oxford taught me was that James Joyce has already said it all, with a footnote tacked on by Samuel Beckett. No one else could hope to compete with them, so why bother?"

Jonno was shocked. "It's not a competition though, is it? There have been plenty of good writers since them. And there other paths, different ways. I mean what about

Tolkien? Maybe something that leans a little more towards myth or fantasy might be the way of the future."

"What? Goblins and dragons? Fairy stories for adults? No thank you very much, that's not literature, that's plain escapism. I get enough of that working in advertising. I tell you, some of the best writing being done at the moment is in the service of selling products to people who don't yet know that they want them. There's a challenge for the creative mind. The twenty second sound bite is the literature of the future."

"God. That is such a depressing thought. I can't really believe that. There will always be people that enjoy reading books, surely?"

"Less and less, I surmise, and books will get shorter and shorter. No one's going to be writing a *Brothers Karamazov* in the future. People don't have the attention span any longer. If you were living on an estate, with serfs and servants doing all the work, then you might have the time to read *War and Peace*. Nowadays our pleasures are more fleeting, our gratifications immediate."

"That sounds like a pitch for masturbation as opposed to making love."

"There's nothing wrong with a damn good wank," Ben laughed, and closed the conversation by standing up and going inside his wooden shack.

Jonno thought about the conversation the next day as he was walking across Barnes Common, heading for the dole office. He couldn't believe someone with experience of studying literature at Oxford could be so dismissive of the pleasures of reading. Ok, he had been disaffected with the regimen imposed on him by his university curriculum, but it was because he wanted to read more rather than less. He did want to become a writer, not just of the poems he was currently experimenting with, but full-fledged novels. He was aware it would require a tremendous amount of self-discipline, more than he currently possessed. If meditation was likely to make that even harder, undermining what little self-confidence he could muster and showing up such endeavours to be mere ego-boosting, as Ben implied, then perhaps he would be wiser not to pursue it. Decisions, decisions, there were always decisions. He felt himself in no position to make them.

One thing Ben had said which did hit home, was the need for a job. He couldn't rely on the beneficence of strangers for much longer. He'd been living in the house for more than a couple of weeks now. Ok, the room was vacant but they had been sharing their food as well as their dope with him. Hence his current pilgrimage.

The inside of the dole office was even more depressing than he expected. It was painted a washed-out, mucky colour that he later referred to as 'social security green'. Beige Lino covered the floor, spotted all over with burn marks from hundreds of cigarettes, ground out in defiance of the tubular metal ash-trays. The queues of people lined up in front of the glassed-in counters didn't help either; stale beery breath, stale clothes, stale body odour combined with stale cigarette smoke to create an olfactory atmosphere previously unknown to Jonno. The smell of poverty.

The only splashes of bright colours were from the caftan worn by the only other long-haired young man in the room, who was crammed into and overflowing a narrow vinyl armchair. Astonishment must have shown on Jonno's face because the caftan wearer closed the book he was reading, smiled at what he perceived to be a kindred spirit, and decided to help him out.

"You never signed on before?"

"No," Jonno replied.

"You gotta queue up. Pick who you'd rather stand behind."

"What about you?"

"Nah, I'm waiting for interview. 'S why I brought the book. Always takes forever."

"What are you reading?" Jonno asked.

"The Soft Machine. William Burroughs. You ever read his stuff?"

"No, I can't say I have. Great band though."

"Yeh, not bad. Prefer the Floyd me."

"Me too. Have you heard their latest album *More*? It's brilliant."

"*A Saucerful of Secrets* is my favourite. The name's Pete by the way. I'd advise you to join 'A' queue."

"Why? Is it faster?"

"Nah, but the last bloke in 'B' fucking reeks. He's an alky, and has a nasty habit of shitting himself."

"Oh great. Thanks for the tip."

"You're going to have to toughen up country boy, if you're going to make it in the big city," Pete said.

"What makes you think I'm from the country?"

"Accent. Where do you think I'm from?"

"Liverpool?"

"Close. It's obvious as soon as I open my mouth, isn't it? You sound too posh to come from anywhere north of Watford, but you're not a cockney. I'd say you went to a fairly good school where they steal your native accent, but there's still a residual lilt there, so I'd say West Country – Somerset, Devon, Cornwall, somewhere like that?"

"Yes. Somewhere like that." Jonno wasn't going to admit to his origins. This stranger might be a fellow hippy but he was spot on with his analysis and this put Jonno on his guard. There was a wealth of literature from the sixteenth century onwards about young men moving to the city being gulled out of their fortunes, and young women robbed of their virginities before being put on the game. Jonno didn't have much worth stealing but the recent movie *Midnight Cowboy* put a more contemporary slant on the genre, reinforcing all too clearly that country cousins were still fair game and should keep their wits about them.

"Hey, I'll probably still be here when they've seen to you. Fancy going for a bevy after?" Pete continued.

"Um, not sure. I'm utterly broke."

"And you probably still will be when you're finished here. 'S alright, I can afford to buy you a pint. I got a proposition to put to you."

"Oh yes, and what's that then?" Suspicions mounting by the moment.

"Nothing that you have to worry about. I might like Burroughs, but I'm not *like* Burroughs if you catch my drift."

"So, what is it?"

"I'll tell you later. You'd better get in a queue if you want to get signed on any time today."

The queue he joined moved forward so glacially that it came as a shock to finally find himself in front of the counter, staring at the pursed lips and unforgiving eyes of the woman who had been listening to lies, and assorted tales of woe for the previous six hours. It did him little good. He got himself registered as unemployed, but in the absence of a current rent book he was ineligible to receive housing support payments, and until he could give a permanent address there was nowhere they were prepared to send any dole money. His only option would be to return on a daily basis and spend untold hours queueing up amongst the numerous alcoholics, junkies and assorted derelicts again. Take it or leave it. Jonno left it.

"Well that was a total waste of time," he complained to Pete, who he was surprised to see still waiting for him.

"Yeh, mine too. Don't know why they bother interviewing people."

"So what was this proposition you were going to put to me?" Jonno asked.

"Let's wait until we've washed the taste of despair from our mouths. There's a pub round the corner that pulls a half-decent pint, and the bar-maid's a damned sight more decorative that that sour-faced individual you've just had the misfortune to rub up against. You'd think it was their own personal largesse we were asking them to dispense."

Jonno had never met many northerners before and found it difficult to read his companion. The accent was stock in trade Liverpudlian, as working class as that of the 'bloody leftie scouse git' that Alf Garnett was constantly abusing on television's *Till Death Us Do Part*. Every now and again though, the depths of Pete's vocabulary would surprise him, more so because of its tendency to lurch towards the blatantly, if roughly-hewn, poetic.

The proposition turned out to be a short-term job that Pete had jacked up for the following day.

"Off the cards, of course. Strictly cash in hand. Suits. A bloody great lorry-load of suits straight from our Eastern comrades. They need to be unloaded into a warehouse, so that the labels can be changed and made to sound English, or maybe Italian. What do you say? You look big enough. There's thousands of the bastards and it'd take me a week to unload them all on me own."

"I could be interested. You sure it's legitimate?"

"Of course it's bloody not, that's why it pays so well. I'd do it all myself but one look inside the back of that truck this morning and I told the guy I'd need a mate. Thousands of suits, all encased in plastic, like dead men hanging from these revolving racks stacked floor to ceiling. You finish one rack, you press a button and another one descends, over and over again. I tell you, it's like Dante's bloody inferno in there. Punishment for wife-beaters; the circle of Hell of the cheap Bulgarian suit."

And so it was that in the back of a pantechnicon, amongst a plethora of cheap and shiny suiting, that their friendship was born. It took the pair of them three days to empty the lorry, grasping as many suits as they could manage off the conveyor racks, walking down the ramp and hooking them onto another rack, which they wheeled into a red-brick warehouse. There, in a massive room, numerous head-scarfed and dark-skinned women sat bent over sewing machines, madly stitching new labels onto collars, waist-bands and linings. As soon as they entered the building two men wearing suits identical to the shiny new ones, grabbed them off the rack, removed them from the plastic covers and laid them down in hessian-sided trolleys. The sleeves of their jackets riding up as they moved, exposing enormous gold watch straps matching the numerous oversized rings on their fingers.

Having established that they were both voracious readers, as they lifted suits from the racks, they took turns to shout out the titles of books which particularly impressed them. Jonno found they were on an unequal footing. While he was well grounded in more established writers,

Pete's field of knowledge was much more eclectic, encompassing not only the wilder shores of experimentation, but also more mainstream contemporary practitioners recently translated from a number of European languages. While Jonno was *au fait* with the works of Franz Kafka and Herman Hesse, Pete had also read Robert Musil, and Gunter Grass. Jonno was familiar with Graham Greene and Anthony Burgess, but Pete knew works by B.S. Jonson and Angela Carter, English authors completely unheard of by Jonno. While he knew what he thought of as groundbreaking contemporary American works by J.D. Salinger, Joseph Heller and Norman Mailer, Pete was a fan of John Barth, Kurt Vonnegut and Richard Brautigan. He was also fascinated by the cut-up techniques invented by the seriously 'out-there' William S. Burroughs, and explained to Jonno that he employed them to create his own strange poems from time to time.

After three days of sweating through the acrid stench of warm plastic and dry-cleaning fluid, moving ever further into the darkness of what they called the belly of the whale, their task was completed. By now the pair of them were so syncopated in their thoughts that as they trundled the final rack's worth into the warehouse, they turned to each other and, as one, shouted "The Myth of Sisyphus." That they had both been saving Camus' existential masterpiece for this moment caused them both to howl with laughter. This prompted the owner of the sweat-shop to shake his head, as he withdrew his wallet from the inside pocket of a jacket crafted in Saville Row, and not the back street of some Bulgarian city.

"You both crazy," he said as he handed them each a wodge of notes. "Still, good job boys, see you next time."

"Not if I can help it," Pete said to Jonno as they walked towards the pub on the corner of the street. "Seen enough suits to last me a lifetime. Don't know how people can wear the fucking things."

"We probably just facilitated a thousand weddings."

"God bless them, and all their frenzied nuptials," replied Pete as they took their pints of beer across to one of the dimpled copper-topped tables in the corner.

"God that's good," Jonno said, after taking a huge swallow. "The smell in that truck. The people where I'm staying complained when I got in last night. Made me take a bath, before they'd let me have a toke on a joint."

Pete laughed. They both knew they were partial to the lure of cannabis. After playing their game of book titles, they discovered very similar tastes in music and films. As well as their mutual love of Pink Floyd, they were great fans of Ken Russel's art films on the BBC.

Once his initial thirst was quenched Jonno said, "Shitty as the job was, it's good get some bread. If you've got any other work lined up count me in."

"I won't be around for a few days. Going back up North."

"Coming back?"

"Sure, I've decided I like it down here, even if the beer is shit. That's why I've got to go. I've got some bread in a building society up there which I'll need for the deposit on a flat or a house."

"I need somewhere to live. The bloke whose room I'm crashing in is coming back soon and I'll have to split. Fancy sharing?"

"Sure. I won't be able to afford to rent on me own. If we got a couple of other folk we could afford to get a house. Better than a flat, more private. Cheaper too, when you share the costs."

"Cool. We could put an advert in Time Out or something."

"How do you feel about hitch-hiking?"

"Fine. I spent last summer hitching all around Devon and Cornwall."

"There you go, I knew that's where you were from. Ever been up North?"

"God no. We've got palm trees in Cornwall. Why would I want to visit the frozen North?"

"Broaden your perspective. You can't write anything set in England unless you've seen it from all sides. Down there in the West all you've got is farming, fishing and tourism. Around here it's all business and banking. Up North it's mining or manufacturing. Heavy industry. Very heavy industry. You should see it. It'd open your eyes. I could do with a mate, it's safer hitching in pairs. Only take a couple of days, we can stay at my parents' place. How about it?"

"Sure. Why not? When were you thinking of going?"

"Tomorrow?"

~ 9 ~

1972

Sad Dave wasn't sad anymore. The conflict between Jonno and Pete which had disrupted the Socrates Street house two years previously had shocked him out of his lethargy.

His father had insisted that he train as an accountant, wanting him eventually to join the family firm. So his days were spent wearing a suit over scratchy collars and ties, slogging away amongst dusty ledgers and being polite to businessmen who treated him like a lackey.

In recompense when he got back to Socrates of an evening, he would throw off the straight-jacket and immediately over-indulge in whatever drugs were available. This schizophrenic existence took such a toll on him that the members of the household started to refer to him amongst themselves as 'sad Dave'. He gradually got to such a state that they avoided him as much as possible. Nothing was said but they were all aware the atmosphere lightened each time he sequestered himself in his room to play guitar.

The break-up spurred him into telling his employer to stuff his meagrely paid job. He signed on the dole, chucked his suit into a skip, grew his hair down to his shoulders, found himself a tiny flat on the top floor of a Victorian house in West Kensington and subsequently shacked up with Melanie, a mousy-haired young woman he met in one of the folk clubs he frequented. His income was now even less, but he blossomed, was no longer 'sad' Dave. Rather a young man whom Jonno always found it a delight to visit.

The front door to the dirty London-brick house was always open. As Jonno climbed the numerous flights he was amused by how progressively threadbare the stair carpet became, until he trod the bare boards of the final flight. Probably the steps up to what once had been the servants' quarters had always just been stained. They were certainly well worn. As he ascended, his nostrils were assailed by a mixture of smells, something like burning fat but also a sweeter scent, jasmine perhaps or possibly sandalwood, he was not good at recognising differing types of incense.

There was music floating down too, Jonno recognised it as a record Dave played interminably back in Socrates Street; Al Stewart's Love Chronicles. He and Pete became fed up with hearing it all the time, being much more into the likes of Crosby, Stills, Nash and Young. Now Jonno remembered it nostalgically and was pleased that Dave still enjoyed listening to it.

At the top of the stairs the smell was much stronger, and he turned into the kitchen, to find Dave standing over the stove.

"What the hell are you cooking?" he asked.

The great bear of a man who nearly filled the diminutive space, turned and with a pleased exclamation, threw his arms around Jonno and almost lifted him off of his feet.

"Good to see you man. I'm making candles. Have a look."

Jonno peered into the enormous pan that covered the whole of the stove-top, to see a mass of molten yellow wax, which was the source of both the fatty smell and also of the lighter, sweeter notes.

"Just mixed in some essential oil, jasmine, supposed to be good for meditation. Nice, eh?"

"A bit overpowering to be honest, but I guess it settles down."

"Sure. Gives off this great aroma as the candle burns. Much more subtle then."

"How long have you been doing this?"

"Couple of weeks. I got a commission from one of the head shops up the Portobello Road. I made a few small ones at the start but now I'm onto giants. Those are the moulds, look." Dave turned and indicated a couple of four-inch diameter plastic pipes standing upright, reaching up to hip height. Jonno could see what he assumed to be the ends of wicks, tied around pencils lying across the tops.

"Do you get much for them?" He asked.

"Not enough to be honest. They take a hell of a lot of wax. At the moment I barely cover the costs, but I'll get faster at making them, and once I've established a market, who knows? This pot-full gives me six inches at a time for the two of them. I start off with really strong colours at the bottom then each next load I mix in less colour, so the finished thing is graduated. There's a couple of green ones in the front room. Go and tell me what you think. I'll pour this load then I'll join you. It's a bit dangerous with two of us crammed in here, hot wax burns like a bastard." So saying he rolled up a sleeve of his flannelette shirt to show a livid red wrist. "Got to be careful of the fumes too, since the cooker's gas. That's why all the windows are open."

The front room was small and the ceiling sloped down half-way towards the floor. The dormer window was open and let in not only light but also traffic noise, now that Al Stewart had finished the history of his romances. There was a busted chintz armchair from which stuffing was escaping from one arm. This faced towards the window and the stereo positioned underneath it. The big chipboard speakers at either side were angled to give the chair's occupant the prime listening position. Two tall green candles stood on each of the speaker boxes, giving the whole stereo set up the appearance of some modern-day altar on which records could be placed like votive offerings. On the floor along the right-hand wall was a single mattress covered in Indian fabric which supported a couple of miss-matched cushions. Before it was a coffee table with its legs sawn down so it only stood six inches above the floor. Jonno sat cross-legged on the mattress, took the doings from the pockets of his denim shirt and started to roll a number.

"Nearly finished here. Put another record on," Dave shouted from the kitchen. Jonno leaned over and flipped through the albums leant against the nearest speaker, finally deciding on another old favourite of Dave's, Traffic's *Mr. Fantasy.* The room soon filled with the sound of psychedelic jazz/rock; a wailing saxophone interspersed with tinkling piano rills running up and down Steve Winwood's keyboard, backed up by free-form drumming as the chorus burst out with "Guide your vision to Heaven and Heaven is in your mind." A hippie anthem from 1967 and so fitting, Jonno thought, for Dave out there in his kitchen, attempting to become self-sufficient through the construction of candles.

When he'd worked in the accountant's office Dave frequently came home with one or other hair-brained scheme for making a living. He would enthusiastically throw himself into it for a week or two until it failed to work out and he retreated back into his shell.

"Have I been any different?" Jonno wondered, and as Dave entered the room, he handed him the joint to light. As they passed it backwards and forwards Jonno launched into the story of his last two days.

Dave listened attentively and when it was finished said "And you've been living just around the corner without telling me?"

"Yeh, sorry about that. We decided not to tell anyone until everything blew over. It was supposed to keep us safe. It didn't."

"Just pissed off all your friends who didn't know where you were. Susie was asking after you yesterday."

"What? Scottish Susie? You've seen her?"

"Yes. She was a bit upset. Wanted to know how to get in touch with you."

"Shit. I didn't know you knew her."

"She works with Mel at the travel agents. She's trying to get some bread together for a trip or something. We were talking yesterday, and she told us about this concert she'd been to. Then we realised it was you who took her. You like her?"

"God yes, she's beautiful. And that accent of hers, like a cat purring, it goes right through me."

"Highland Scots, so much softer than Glaswegian, isn't it? You should hear her speaking Gaelic."

"She talks in Gaelic?"

"She can do. She's from the Western Isles. I think they all do up there."

"How come you know all this?"

"Mel and I met her at a folk club a couple of months ago. She sang in Gaelic. It was amazing."

"I really need to go round to her place and apologise. But I've got no money."

"None at all?"

"Absolutely skint." In the course of the afternoon he didn't mention the stash buried in the tomb in Highgate, just the circumstances of the bust, the loss of their money, and Steve's sudden departure.

"Good riddance," Dave said, "I never trusted that guy, he was a bit too up himself for my liking."

"Yes well, he ran off with the last ounce of our dope."

"No surprise there. Anyway, you don't have to go round to Susie's. Most evenings she comes back with Mel for a cup of tea after work. Their office is just up in Shepherd's Bush. You can do your grovelling then. Talking of which, I'd better clean up the kitchen, they'll be back soon. How about rolling another number to greet the workers' return? You know, if you want to get back into her good books again."

"Oh yeh, it's got nothing to do with you wanting another one of course."

"Never entered my head," was Dave's parting shot, as he left to clear away his candle-making apparatus. Shortly Jonno could hear laughter and footsteps coming up the stairs. Dave emerged and stood at the top calling down, "Look who I've found" before ushering the two young women into the room.

"Oh, hi, the disappearing man," Susie said and gave Jonno an embarrassed little smile. Mel was more demonstrative. As he rose from the mattress, she threw her arms around him and gave him a hug, before retreating to the bedroom to change. Dave followed her out, leaving the pair of them alone. An awkward silence ensued as they avoided each other's eyes. A silence which seemed to last interminably until Jonno finally blurted out, "Look, I need to apologise. I really enjoyed your company the other night and I was going to call you the next day but things kind of got in the way."

"Things?"

"Yes, bad things. I'm in a bit of trouble. I've been bending Dave's ear with it all afternoon and he doesn't need to hear again. I don't suppose you fancy coming round to my place, so I can tell you about it."

"It seems a bit rude, running out on them."

"Dave won't mind, and he'll explain it to Mel. I'll leave them the joint I rolled to celebrate your finishing work."

"Is it far?"

"Five-minute walk, just around the corner."

"He said he didn't know where you were."

"He didn't. He does now, I've told him. You'll be quite safe, honest."

She laughed. "I'm not worried, I'm a big girl, and I would like to see where you live. I'll go and say goodbye." There was laughter from the bedroom, followed by Dave coming back with a grin on his face.

"I'll leave you with this," Jonno said, handing him the joint, before Susie stuck her head back around the door.

"Come on then," she said, "let's go."

~ 10 ~

1969

Before hitching up to London Jonno had never lived more than a few miles from the coast, away from the shrieking of gulls, the pervasive smell of salt water.

Now he was once more entering into uncharted territory, heading for what he thought of as 'the frozen north'. He was sitting high up in the cab of a lorry, one half of his buttocks perched on the seat that he shared with the much bulkier Pete, the rest of him crammed side-on into the door. His knees were folded upwards by his holdall and Pete's rucksack which filled the well at their feet. Uncomfortable, but nevertheless excited to have this elevated view of the countryside they moved across, or the steep verges flashing past as they cut through sculpted hills.

His first time travelling on a motorway, the M1, the very name redolent of its importance. Three lanes of traffic on either side, drivers all hammering along, as if to reach their destination was the sole purpose of life. Cars zipping past and flashing their tail lights in thanks to Don, who was signalling with his head-lights when they were safely past. They drove under bridges, they shot across rivers, they carved their way through plantations of trees.

Every now and again, high in the sky, birds of prey with measured flapping wings hung there, as if weightless. Then, decision made, the sudden plunge, the snatch with talons of some hapless creature, whose tremulous movement the eagle-eyed had spotted in the road-side scrub. At other times a flurry of raggedy wings erupting into the air; a black-beaked crow, dragging some shattered road-kill beyond the path of voracious traffic. Jonno was amazed how swiftly the natural world was colonising the new landscape. It was far from being the desert he imagined.

He was content to leave the onus of conversation up to Pete. He knew that the usual price of a lift was the entertainment of the long-haul driver, who otherwise might fall asleep on such a straight and uneventful passage. He was prepared to play his part but he understood so little of what the man said, beyond that he was carrying "a backlood 'a rice pudd'n away up 'ome tae NewCassel." Pete appeared to have no such difficulty, although to Jonno's ears the man's speech bore no resemblance to his friend's Liverpudlian accent.

Lulled by the monotony of the engine which neither sped up nor slowed down, the absence of junctions or roundabouts requiring no changing of gears, the rumbling of giant tyres rolling inexorably along, the gradual exhaustion of fresh air in the cab, and the rise and fall of his companions' hypnotic voices, meant that Jonno was soon asleep.

A change of motion and an alteration in road noise woke him. They were slowing down and pulling off the motorway onto a slip road.

"Where are we?"

"Good thing you're awake. Watford Gap Services. Don's dropping us here. He's carrying on to Leeds and then Newcastle. We've got to change direction, head northwest."

"Aye, you'll be right here bonny lads," Don said. "A'm gonna stop for me snap a bit further along. But you just ask about. Someone'll tak you all the way I wouldn't wonder."

He pulled up by a steel and glass edifice with a gently sloping triangular roof and the two of them jumped down from the cab. Jonno stumbled, his left leg cramped up from being wedged into the door for so long. Pete lifted out their bags, thanked Don and wished him a safe journey.

"Good luck aye. I hope your Mam recovers fine." So saying he engaged the gears and with a hiss and a roar the lorry pulled off, back towards the motorway.

It started to hammer down with rain so Pete ran for the entrance while Jonno hobbled after him as best he could. As soon as they were both inside, he asked, "What was that about your mother?"

Pete waved a ten bob note in the air. "I told him my mother might be dying. Cancer. So I've got to get home to see her. He gave us this to get something to eat."

"But she's not, is she?"

"She might be. That's all I said. She smokes enough fags."

"You lied."

"Jesus Jonno, I told him a story, that's all. I needed to say something. You were no bloody help."

"I couldn't understand a word he said."

"And you think I could? It was hard work; I can tell you. Bloody Geordies. They have a language all of their own. Anyway it got us a feed, so let's go."

Sliding their trays along the long counter they both opted for bacon, eggs and beans on toast accompanied by generous mugs of industrial strength tea, then made their way across to an empty Formica topped table. The vinyl seats facing each other let out contrastingly pitched sighs as they sank into them, due to Pete's greater weight. He raised his mug and clicked it against Jonno's as he toasted the generosity of Northern lorry drivers.

"So why did you tell him I was along?" Jonno asked.

"You're my sister's boyfriend, came to fetch me."

"Oh, thanks a bunch."

"You won't mind that so much when you see her. She's bloody smashing, not a wide load like me. Anyway here we are, Watford Gap, eat, drink and be merry."

Pete appeared to invest this crowded and steamy barn of a motorway cafe with a significance that Jonno couldn't see, so asked him about it. "It's the border," he was informed. They had now left the South. According to Pete once through the Midlands they would be in God's own country. Also it was the late-night hang-out of every traveling band as they made their way around the country, returning home from far-flung gigs.

"The Stones, the Floyd, Hendrix, even the Beatles back when they were touring. They might have sat at this very table, drunk their teas from the self-same mugs. It's historic. Soak up the ambience."

"Ambience my arse. It's a glorified greasy spoon with pretensions of glory."

"The man's got no soul," responded Pete.

While they were eating the rain stopped. Jonno suggested they hang around the lorry park asking if any driver was heading to Liverpool. Instead, Pete led him around to the back of the building where the rubbish bins were. He pulled out a piece of cardboard, and with a marker pen retrieved from his ruck-sack wrote L'POOL in large letters on it.

"I couldn't stand being squashed into another lorry," he said. "That was fine and got us this far but next time I want a bit of comfort."

So they took their sign and walked across to where the slip-road led back out onto the motorway. A number of drivers passed them, either pretending not to see them or grimacing in disgust at their long hair, as they stood with hopeful expressions on their faces. A couple of more sympathetic ones held up the backs of their hands pointing to the right, indicating that they would be turning off soon. Finally, after half an hour of having their hopes alternately raised and dashed, a beaten-up blue Ford Anglia driven by a young man as long-haired as themselves pulled up. Pete opened the passenger door and asked how far the driver was going. In an accent identical to his own he was told, "All the way, man. Get yourselves in."

Pete folded their cardboard sign in two and shoved it underneath the car. He tilted the passenger seat forward for Jonno to climb into the back, then handed him their bags before settling himself into the front.

"Is this an old cop car?" he asked the driver.

"Like from Z-Cars you mean? Nah. It was my old man's. He works at the Halewood plant. Ford gives them cheap deals. He's just upgraded to the new Capri so he passed it on to me. Neat aint it?"

"I've always loved the way the rear window slopes the other way to most cars," Jonno chipped in, intent to take part in the conversation this time. Being so much closer to the road it felt that they were going much faster than the lorry, almost as if it was a sport's car as they zipped in and out of differing lanes of traffic. Since Mark, the driver, had just filled his tank there was no need for them to stop at all, and they made great time. Having learnt from Pete that they were making for Birkenhead he offered to take them all the way to the Pier Head.

Jonno hadn't realised the significance of this until they were climbing out of the car in front of a massive building that could have been built in Moscow during the triumphalist days, shortly after the revolution. The broken frontage sported eight floors of windows and rose sheer straight up to a cornice which was then surmounted by several more levels of a more byzantine appearance. There were domes, arches, stone balustrades and a huge white clock face set into a cathedral-like tower rising even further skywards. The final level was topped by a verdigrised metal sculpture of a giant bird hanging its wings out to dry, as if it were a cormorant flown up to perch there, having risen from the wide brown estuary below.

Jonno was excited to see the river whose name was synonymous with so much early sixties music. He immediately heard an old song rattling around in his head. Although the Beatles had initially made Liverpool famous, it was Gerry and the Pacemakers who were still indissolubly linked to the city. *Ferry cross the Mersey* was still a regular fixture on Radio One four years after release, and their cover version of *You'll Never Walk Alone* was sung by the crowd at the start of every Liverpool football match.

They entered the arched entrance to a corrugated roofed tunnel sloping downwards toward the river. They bought tickets, passed through the turnstile and emerged into the open air to join a crowd standing on a floating pontoon. Short though the voyage might be Jonno looked forward to it. As the ferry came closer, he could make out the name Overchurch painted on its bow. Seagulls screamed and took off from the roof behind them as it pulled alongside and disgorged a number of ill-assorted and badly dressed passengers.

When they boarded Pete quickly sat on one of the wooden slatted benches. Jonno placed his holdall beside Pete's rucksack, and made his way to the bow so he could mark their progress through the murky water. He watched the bow-wave spread as the diesel engines thrust them forward. He could feel them vibrating through the deck beneath his feet and eagerly breathed in the rising smell of ozone. It was a while since he had been on the water. He could see how such a journey, however short, could inspire such a wistful and romantic song.

Disembarking, they climbed another cantilevered tunnel to the Woodside terminal building and dry land.

"From here we walk," said Pete.

They set out along a main road to their left and soon were skirting a ten-foot-high wall which stretched away into the distance. Suddenly they were enveloped in an enormous cloud of flying insects which erupted from behind it, whirled all around them and stretched across the road from one pavement to the other. Jonno was familiar with masses of flying ants all taking to the air at once, but never in such overwhelming numbers. He started to flail his free arm about to keep them off him. Pete burst out into laughter at his antics.

"They're not flies," he shouted above the grinding noise which also came from behind the wall. "It's soot. That's Camell Laird's shipyards over there, they must be burning something off."

Jonno could smell the stink of it now and raised his hand to cover his mouth and nose until they passed through the worst of it.

"Jesus Christ," he expostulated.

"I told you, heavy industry, they built the Ark Royal in there. Dad used to work for them. My brother Michael still does, although probably not for much longer. You get used to it."

"I don't think I ever would."

"No, perhaps not, country-boy. There's no fields with cows and little lambkins gambolling about in them around here."

What there was, as far as Jonno could see, was noise and dirt and diesel fumes from the lorries roaring up and down the road, loaded to the gunnels with steel and timber and gas cylinders and all manner of other cargos, necessary for the giant industrial processes being carried out on the other side of the wall.

They crossed to the other pavement and turned up a side road which led them under a railway bridge and past a row of trees standing sentinel alongside the tracks. Walking on they entered into a maze of streets, all flanked by identical small terraced houses. They turned left, they turned right and each turning revealed yet another street of similar dwellings all crammed together. Even the front doors and windows were painted in the same tones of cream or beige, as if a job-lot of those particular paints had been on offer at some central depot. Occasionally a bright red or a green door stood out, indicating an occupier desperate to demonstrate their individuality.

Beyond that, the architectural features all remained the same. A bay window was situated to the left of every front door, so that a hallway would separate the front room from that of the neighbour's, cutting down any noise which might seep through the walls. On the second floor each house gazed down through two standard sash windows, one directly above the door and the other over the bay. They might have been copied straight from a child's crayon drawing, except that they faced right onto the street; there were no simple front gardens with gates, no giant flowers and no Mums and Dads holding hands.

Occasionally, where another street ran off from the one they were on, a small shop occupied a corner, a greengrocer's maybe or a newsagents. Pete stopped outside one such building bearing a sign on its window picked out in pink swirling art-nouveau lettering. He bent at the knees to peer in underneath the words spelling out The Pink Paradise, before straightening up and turning to Jonno.

"Come in and meet our Kathleen," he said.

Inside there were two middle-aged women draped in pink nylon smocks sitting under cone shaped dryers, the ends of pink curlers peeking out by their ears on either side of their heads. There was a cloying chemical smell about the place mixed with the odour of cheap perfume. Another woman sat in a chair facing a mirror with a much younger woman standing behind her. She was rolling the customer's hair up and clipping it into more pink plastic rollers. Every feature of the room was pink; the walls, the hand-basins, the light fittings, even the lino on the floor. The chair was spread about with a small amount of hair and beside it stood a pink trolley which held pink trays filled with combs, brushes and pairs of scissors, all of them sporting pink handles.

In fact the only thing of any note in the place that wasn't pink was the hairdresser herself who was dressed in a light blue tabard over a cream blouse and a black mini-skirt. Her jet-black hair fell in a bob emphasising the paleness of her face. This was further heightened by the thick black eye-shadow and her long eye lashes caked with black mascara framing her green eyes. All this was revealed by the mirror in front of her seated customer, and Jonno found himself agreeing with Pete's earlier description of her as 'smashing.' She hadn't looked up from her work as the bell above the door tinkled but rather called out "Be with you in a moment Mavis."

The two women with their heads crowned by what looked like the nose cones of rockets both turned towards the door as the two lads marched in and one of them called out, "It isn't Mavis, love." The young woman finished clipping the roll of hair she was working on before turning around. Then she shrieked and ran towards Pete to throw her arms around him.

"You're home," she cried.

"Hi sis," he gently disengaged himself from her. "Don't get too excited, I'm not stopping. Just came to get my savings. Me and Jonno here are going to get a place together."

She turned towards Jonno and held out her hand. He was a little non-plussed by the gesture. It wasn't usual to shake a woman's hand, so he reached forward and, as he had seen in many a foreign film, brought it to his lips to kiss. This caused her to giggle, and the women below the dryers to clap their hands in glee.

"You'll need to watch out for that one Kathleen," one of them said.

"Is he French or what, Petey?" enquired the other.

"What's going on?" the woman in the chair demanded, her view of proceedings having been blocked by Kathleen's back.

"Petey's brought home a red-hot Latin lover Deidre. You'd better watch out love, no woman will be safe in her bed."

"I think you might be alright there Mrs McConaughey," Pete turned to one of the dryer's occupants, "He only goes for blondes or brunettes, he hasn't graduated to blue rinses yet."

"In that case he doesn't know what he's missing, young Peter Kelly. McConaughey is on nights this week, you send him along if he wants a proper education."

Kathleen could see the colour rising in Jonno's cheeks, and turned to say, "You're a bad woman Siobhan McConaughey, look what you've done to the poor lad."

"Given half a chance love, given half of a chance I might be. Little hope of that round here though is there? What with the twitchers standing to attention behind their nets."

Having his blushes pointed out to everyone increased their depth of colour and Jonno ended up staring at the floor. Kathleen turned to her brother.

"Better get on. Liz has got the morning sickness bad today so I'm on my own. You coming to the club tonight?"

"I reckon. What else is there to do round here on a Friday night?"

"I'll see you both later then. And, if you don't mind..." she held out her hand again, this time with the back of it facing towards Jonno, and raised an eyebrow at his hesitation. Twigging what was required of him he once more raised it to his lips. Cheers and wolf whistles from the three seated ladies accompanied their exit from the shop, Jonno's cheeks once more matching the overall colour scheme of the emporium. Further down the street Pete got out a key and let them into number 46.

"Hi Ma!" he shouted as they moved down the hall to the kitchen at the back of the house, which doubled as the living room. It was large enough as the wall from what must once have served as a tiny dining room had been knocked through. As well as a table covered with oil-cloth and surrounded by numerous chairs, there was the stove, the sink and a shelving unit adorned by crockery. To one side there was a sideboard surmounted by family photographs and a framed print of the Madonna. Next to it a television faced towards a busted old armchair in which a big man with powerful-looking arms reclined, his eyes closed and his bald head listing towards his left shoulder. A woman in a floral apron stood washing something in the sink, a cigarette dangling from her lips. As they entered the room she gave a practiced twitch of her head, which flipped a line of ash into a round Bakelite ash tray on the bench beside her. She turned and held a finger to her lips.

"Shush," she whispered, "he's not long dropped off." Then she held out one of her cheeks for the approaching Pete to kiss.

"And who's this then?" she enquired, as she noticed Jonno hovering in the doorway.

"This is Jonno Ma. He's from down south. We're going to be sharing a house together down the smoke. I need to get to the building society in the morning to get my cash for a deposit."

"You're not back to stay then?"

"Just a fleeting visit Ma. We need to get things sorted. Get a roof over our heads. We'll be off again tomorrow. I'll come back up for a couple of days for your birthday though, promise."

"You've not been sleeping rough, have you?"

"Course not, I'm in a hostel. Jonno's crashing at a friend's place but he's got to move out soon. So we thought we'd team up, maybe get a couple of others in to share the rent."

"You be careful. There's some odd sorts about."

"We'll be fine Ma."

"Make sure that you are. And whereabouts are you from Jonno?"

"Cornwall, Mrs. Kelly. And thanks for putting us up for the night."

"You're very welcome. Petey's always been a good judge of character. You're lucky, Michael is staying over at Andy Brown's place tonight. It'll still be a tight squeeze though. Cornwall, eh? That must be nice, what with all the beaches and such."

"Have you been there?"

"Goodness no. The only beach I've ever seen was at Blackpool on our honeymoon. That and the odd day trip with the Women's League. You two go and unpack your gear and I'll put the kettle on in a bit. He'll be waking up soon and wanting a cuppa."

As they passed back down the hall Pete pointed to the front parlour door.

"Mum and Dad sleep in there since the accident. He can't manage the stairs."

"What happened?"

"A load of steel fell on his legs."

The front room upstairs now belonged to Kathleen and sixteen-year-old Rose and they also supervised their youngest brother, four-year-old Thomas. Pete threw open the door of the back bedroom which was filled by a ward-robe, a chest of drawers and an enormous double bed, covered by a patchwork quilt. There were three pillows against the headboard, and above it a cross of plaited straw was pinned to the wall.

"Ever slept three in a bed?" Pete asked.

"Not with two blokes I haven't. Not with two women either, in case you're wondering, although I'd be prepared to give it a go."

"Dream on sunshine. We're lucky that Michael's away tonight, I'm not sure the old bed could survive the four of us. It'll just be you, me and James."

"Um...I usually sleep naked; I don't have any pyjamas."

"That won't matter once we've got a few pints inside of us. Leave your Tee shirt and pants on if you're shy. You won't be cold I can tell you that. I knew this trip was going to be good for you. An education cheaply bought. They didn't teach you stuff like this at your university, I bet."

He thought of his room on campus with its single bed, a bedside table with a lamp, its low-slung armchair, a desk and chair for studying, a bookcase, a fitted wardrobe with shelves and tucked in beside it a stainless-steel sink in front of a half-length mirror. Toilets, baths and showers were just down the hall. It wasn't a big room, about two thirds the size of the room they now stood in, but he was its sole occupant.

There was a lock on the door to ensure total privacy should he wish it. Apart from the cleaning ladies, that is. He didn't even have to undertake that chore, just keep it relatively tidy, so that they could clean his sink, empty his rubbish bin, vacuum his floor, even make his bed on occasion if he'd left it in a mess. He suddenly realised that his life there had been made easy by *servants*. The three young men crammed into this room weren't afforded any such luxury, nor enjoyed any privacy. Jonno could just imagine the arguments and fights there must have been growing up.

Jonno plonked his holdall on the bed then squeezed his way around it to look out of the window at the back. Below was a high walled yard with an outhouse, a concrete coal bunker and a gate leading to a lane which ran past identical yards to either side and behind the backs of the houses opposite. He thought of his room back in Putney with its view of an extensive back garden, with its spreading Mulberry tree, the lush grass bordered by flower beds, the gazebo and its rustic summer house.

"Come on, Mum will be waiting for us to put the kettle on."

Downstairs Pete's father was awake.

"Good God mother, another bloody long-hair in the house. While you're here the two of you should get our Kathleen to give you a decent bloody hair-cut." So saying he stretched out his hand, which Jonno took with trepidation, expecting a bone crushing shaking from calloused fingers. Instead the hand was soft and smooth and he reflected that the man had not been in work for quite a while.

"Leave the boy alone father. He's from the south, it'll be all the fashion down there."

"Aye, like that Mick Jagger and all the rest of them. Not a pansy are you lad?"

"Certainly not."

"Dad!" Pete exclaimed.

"What? I'm only asking."

"Don't mind him Jonno, he's teasing. Fact is he's glad to see a new face around the place," Mrs. Kelly said.

As Jonno turned to her and smiled to indicate that no offense was taken, he was surprised to see that having filled the large brown tea pot with boiling water she was now stirring four heaped teaspoons of sugar into it.

"Course I am, too many women around here most of the time what with Petey gone and his brothers at work all day. Can't get a decent rise out of 'em."

"You just drink your tea Robert Kelly," his wife said as she handed him a mug.

"Your mother tells me you're going to be staying down there Peter," he said.

"That's the plan. For a while at least."

"Not good enough for you round here anymore?"

"It's not that Dad. It's a question of opportunities. Times are changing. I can't see Lairds lasting for much longer now all the ships are built in Japan. What's going to happen to this place once they've closed down?"

"It'll pick up again," Mr. Kelly asserted while they all started drinking their tea.

"Maybe, maybe not. I'm not going to hang around to find out."

"He'd a good job in the library here, Jonno, did he tell you? Nice clean work, pension and everything."

"No, he didn't say," replied Jonno, not wishing to enter into a competition between the two of them.

"I've got to get out while the goings good, Dad. Surely you can see that?"

"Young men got to spread their wings I suppose. I can see that. Just don't forget about us, will you? This will always be your home."

"Course not, Dad. I've already said I'll be back for Mum's birthday. And I'll need a decent pint of beer from time to time. Speaking of which we'd better get going. I promised I'd take Jonno round the club tonight. Don't worry about supper for us Ma, we'll get something out."

"Kathleen's not back yet," Mrs. Kelly said.

"We called in. She's going straight from work. Liz was off sick today so she's been going flat out to get all the old biddies tarted up for their Friday nights."

"Less of the old biddies, thank you very much."

"Sorry Ma. Not you, of course. Come on Jonno, let's go."

"Thanks for the tea, Mrs. Kelly. Mr. Kelly," Jonno said as he stood up from the table.

"Mind you don't make a ruckus falling up the stairs when you get back in boys," a parting shot from Pete's father.

They stepped from the front door onto the pavement and turned left, re-entering the maze of streets. Most of them were straight, either parallel or at right angles to each other, although an occasional one was slightly curved. It didn't take long before Jonno lost his bearings and knew he would never be able to find his way back to the Kelly's house alone. At one point they entered into a back alley, from the other end of which they emerged onto a main road lined with shops. Pete pointed out his old primary school and shortly afterward the library where he'd worked since leaving secondary. The light was beginning to fade and streetlamps started to flicker on, their bulbs burning amber as they warmed.

Eventually they reached a modern building built of concrete rather than the red-brick of most of the others they'd passed. There was an awning over its double glass doors stretching out over the pavement. They pushed their way inside, then through a door to their right, where Jonno found himself standing in a massive barn of a hall. There was grey lino on the floor and the walls were painted cream. Likewise the ceiling, although this was more yellowish from the tobacco smoke of countless patrons. A row of windows down the right-hand side were all covered by venetian blinds which were slanted shut, light being cast by numerous fluorescent tubes slung beneath metal shades.

A red Formica bar ran half way down one wall, from which sprouted a collection of beer engine handles. The shelves behind the counter were backed with mirrors accentuating the colours of various bottles of spirits and those attached upside down to optics. A couple of large men stood behind the bar; the sleeves of their white shirts rolled up to reveal nautical tattoos gracing their forearms.

They were accompanied by a middle-aged woman with a bouffant hairdo wearing a clinging green sequin dress which sparkled beneath the lights, and whose plunging neckline displayed her more than ample bosom. A number of young men wearing shiny suits and lurid ties sat on stools pulled up to the bar, their elbows resting on the counter and their feet perched on a brass rail that ran along above an old grey metal spittoon which looked now to do service as an ashtray. Others stood around them chatting, pint glasses in hand.

Looking past the crowd at the bar Jonno saw a scattering of moquette covered armchairs at the far end of the room. In these, groups of young women were sitting, small glasses of differing shapes placed on little round tables in front of them. He recognised Kathleen and waved. She smiled and waved back before leaning forwards to engage the others in conversation, no doubt explaining who this stranger was. Pete nudged him towards the bar. Some of the crowd parted, giving him enough room to order two pints of Bass.

"Is that you Petey?" the barman enquired as he started to pull their beers.

"Of course it's me Danny. Christ, I haven't been gone that long."

"I didn't recognise you under all that thatch. You're a hippy now, are you?"

"Always have been Danny, you should know that. Ever since they started giving out pot with the Corn Flakes instead of those little plastic divers with the holes in their heads."

"Oh I used to love them," Danny said, placing Pete's pint in front of him. "Put a bit of baking powder in the hole, stick them in a jam-jar and watch them go up and down for hours."

"The submarines were cool too," Jonno said, as he reached for his own pint.

"So who's this then?' Danny asked before turning to Jonno. "You're not from round here, are you?"

"Cornwall, though I grew up in Plymouth. Name's Jonno."

"Guzz! Thought I recognised your accent, not that you've got much of one. I was stationed there for a bit when I was in the service. Hey, Mikey," he shouted to the other barman. "This one's from Guzz! "

"Is that so?" Mikey approached from the other end of the bar. "Many a happy hour I spent down Union Street, enjoying the company of certain athletic young ladies, if you take my meaning."

"Hey, keep it clean you boys." This from the sequined barmaid, who caught the tail end of their conversation as she held a glass up to the optic under a bottle of Gilbey's. She added a scoop of ice, poured in some tonic and added a sliver of lemon from a board beneath the counter, before passing it across to one of the men in suits. He counted some coinage into her hand, and made his way to the far end of the room where he handed it to one of the miniskirted young women. Then he straightaway returned to join in the conversation of his mates.

This first time it perplexed him but over the course of the evening Jonno watched this same procession occur again and again. One after another, a young man would transport a Baby Cham, or a port and lemon, a gin and tonic and on one occasion a barley wine, to the coiffed and much made-up young women sitting around their little tables. Seldom did they linger, a few words might be spoken, a hand might be laid upon a shoulder as if to assert possession, or to affirm the possibility of a more intimate connection sometime later. After a couple of pints Jonno found this pageant amusing.

He turned to Pete to enquire whether tonight was a special occasion of some sort to find his companion drawn into the throng of masculinity at the bar. It appeared he knew a fair number of them, had been at school with several. Once past making their fair share of jokes about hippies, of not being able to tell the difference and so on, they got to reminiscing about their shared pasts, bringing up exploits and practical jokes that it seemed Pete was re-nowned for. Beer after beer was drunk and although Jonno was introduced and included as much as possible in their conversations, he remained an outsider. After a while he grew bored. The muscles of his face began to ache with the effort of maintaining a smile and the appearance of inter-est. As he started to sink his fifth pint of the evening, he looked around to see that one of the chairs at Kathleen's table was now vacant. He had noticed one of the men at the bar supplying her with drinks through the course of the evening but at the moment her glass looked empty. He decided to go and ask if she needed a refill.

"I'm not sure," she said, then "Oh yes, go on, where's the harm? I'll have another G and T thanks very much."

When he returned with her drink there was still an empty chair amongst her coterie of friends.

"Is she coming back?" he asked, indicating the empty chair.

"Liz? No. She's not long pregnant and her barley wine didn't agree with her."

As he sunk into the chair the other three girls at the table burst into fits of giggles.

"That'll teach her," one of them said. "She should have been more careful."

"Doreen, you're drunk." Kathleen said, and frowned at her friend.

"Maybe, but not so drunk that I don't know what my right hand's for. My Mum says you should keep to that until someone puts a ring on the other one."

Having made such a daring statement in the company of an unknown male she looked up at Jonno from beneath her false eyelashes to see what his reaction might be. He realised that all of them around the table were at least a little drunk and that she was trying to embarrass him. He determined not to appear in any way shocked, so he just nodded and chuckled. Seeing that she hadn't succeeded one of the other girls upped the stakes.

"My boyfriend reckons mouths are better," Maddie stated, to be instantly met by shrieks from her friends so she swiftly added "Of course I'd never let him do such a filthy thing."

Jonno could see her cheeks redden even beneath her heavy foundation as she frowned around at her friends, afraid she might have given too much away. To divert attention from herself she turned back to him.

"We've all heard you're an expert with a hand."

This nonplussed him, given the sexual nature of the allusions flying around. The puzzlement on his face amused them all again until Maddie raised the back of her own hand to her lips and made lascivious kissing noises.

"Show us, go on," Doreen said.

"That's not a good idea," Kathleen stated.

"Oh yes, go on, go on," Doreen insisted.

The other three young women at their table all joined in a chorus of "Show us, show us, show, show, show," making quite a ruckus in the process.

In order to shut them up Jonno reached across and grasped Kathleen's hand in his. To amuse them further, and because he was as drunk as they were, he raised an eyebrow and adopted the clichéd facial expression of a Latin lover, something he imagined Rudolph Valentino might have looked like. Thus, leering at her with smouldering eyes, he brought her hand to his lips.

Unfortunately the amount of noise they were all making attracted the attention of the half-cut men at the bar, who up to that point hadn't noticed there was a male sitting amongst their women-folk. A strange male, a long-haired hippy male, dressed in flared jeans with multiple patches, instead of a suit and tie, and a southerner to boot. Not only was he breaking all their conventions of a Friday night at the club by fraternising with their women, but he was actually kissing one of them.

Suddenly, strong hands gripped Jonno's shoulders and pulled him away. The chair pivoted on its back legs and Jonno crashed backwards. His head hit the floor with some force. In the same motion his legs tilted upwards, kicking over the little table and sending both drinks and glasses flying. Shrieks of glee instantly turned to ones of horror as fluids, some ice cold, some warm and sticky, sprayed over skirts, blouses and nylon clad thighs, running down calves and pooling in shoes. Kathleen, unaware until the last moment of her approaching boyfriend, leaped to her feet and slapped him hard across the face.

"What the hell was that for?" he shouted at her.

"You could have killed him," she shouted back.

"I will bloody kill him, No one kisses my girlfriend."

"Too right, Robbie, give him a good kicking," from one of his mates who rushed over.

"We were pissing about. He was just kissing my hand."

"That's right," from Maddie, who'd avoided the worst of the splashing liquid and was enjoying the excitement.

"What the hell difference does that make? You're my bloody fiancé. He was trying it on."

"He was," from one of his other offsiders, "I saw him. Dirty bloody hippies with their free love and everything. He was muscling in."

"Well it's not surprising is it, when you lot leave us on our own all bloody night?" Doreen couldn't help but add her sixpenny worth, which further inflamed tempers, and individual arguments broke out between the various couples all standing around the supine form of Jonno, who was opening his eyes and shaking his head, as he tried to understand what was happening. Pete was crouched beside him asking if he was alright. Kathleen noticed her boyfriend Robbie was swinging his leg back and jumped in front of him.

"No you bloody don't Robert McAllister, not if you know what's good for you. Kissing will be the very last thing you'll be getting from me the night. It was a misunderstanding, now get over it."

"Oh, you're with him now is that it? Sleeping in your house tonight is he? Are you planning on locking your door? Or waiting for him to begin creeping about?"

"You don't trust me is that it? Are you asking for your ring back?"

"He'll be sleeping between me and James, Robbie. There won't be any creeping about," Pete said from the floor.

"No, not if I takes his legs out like your old man."

"You bastard!" Pete shouted, jumped up and threw a punch which Robbie easily parried before clenching his own into a fist to reciprocate.

Seeing this Jonno stumbled to his feet. He was still groggy, but realised that neither he nor Pete were any match for the muscled steel worker, and how vulnerable he was lying within easy reach of the big man's feet. As he rose both Danny and Mikey arrived from behind the bar, each grabbing one of the initial protagonists with an arm draped around their throats.

"Break it up you two. If you've got a problem, take it outside," Danny said. "You've made enough mess as it is, and busted a couple of glasses."

"Should never have let them in," from one of the bystanders. "Thought there was supposed to be a dress code."

"Maybe we shouldn't've. But Petey's been a member since he left school and he's always been a bit weird. And this one's been signed in as his guest, all legit and above board, so he deserves a bit of respect. As far as I can see he wasn't causing any trouble. He just doesn't know the rules. So why don't the pair of you shake hands." So saying Mikey took his arm from around Jonno's throat. Danny similarly released Robbie and Jonno held out his hand towards him.

"No fucking way," Robbie shouted at him.

"Don't worry about it Danny," Pete said. "We'll split. Got to get something to eat anyway."

"I'll pay for the glasses," Jonno offered, studiously avoiding catching Robbie's eyes.

"Don't worry about it son," Danny said. "I broke more than my share when I was down in your neck of the woods. Just leave. And watch yourself, alright? Be careful."

"You alright?" Pete asked as they left the club and the sound of the raised voices still echoing inside. Jonno rubbed the back of his head. "Think so, just a bit stunned that's all."

"There's a chippie round the corner. Fancy a feed?"

"Not sure. After all that beer and then a bang on the head."

"Plate of curry and chips and you'll be fine."

This was a combination unknown to southern chip shops. As they made their way up the road Jonno dipped a couple of chips into the curry sauce swirling around on his paper plate and was immediately sold. They made their way into a small playground and sat on the swings to consume them.

"Christ, I thought you were a goner then. He's a big bloke, that Robbie, and he's got a hell of a temper on him. Kathleen's going to have her work cut out when they get hitched. Still, she's a tough one. Takes after our Mam."

"I hope I didn't get her into any trouble."

"She'll be alright. We'd better watch out though. We'll take a roundabout way home, just in case."

"You think he'll come after us?"

"It's possible. A few more pints and he'll be well pissed. If his mates wind him up enough he'll get violent. Fuck I hate this place. I love it and I hate it at the same time.

That's why I've got to get out. Come on, we'll take the back alleys."

The feed helped to sober the two of them up, but they still stumbled a little as they navigated the darkness of unlit back alleys, occasionally disturbing a courting couple and pausing to peer around corners before criss-crossing the maze of streets. Eventually Jonno sensed a release of tension in the body language of his companion before realising that he was about to let them back into number 46.

~ 11 ~

1972

On the way back to the flat Jonno stepped into a newsagents to buy a bottle of milk while Susie waited outside,
reading the cards in the window. As he came out, she raised
an inquisitive eyebrow as she saw him struggling to slip a
packet of Number 6 cigarettes into the pocket of his jeans.

"Sorry about these," he said, "they're all I can afford at
the moment."

"That's alright, I've got some B & H in my bag if you
want one of those."

"They do make a better class of joint."

"Bigger too," she laughed.

"Nearly there," Jonno said as they turned the corner.
He watched the surprise spread across her face as they left
the fumes of the choked arterial road behind them and, as
if stepping through some secret door, she beheld the Green
stretched out before her. The recently mown grass gently

exhaled fresh scent into the mellowing sunshine of early evening.

"Wow. You live by a park? Can you hear the trees at night when the wind's blowing?"

"Not often. But I do come out and sit under them with a book from time to time. Especially when they've just cut the grass."

"I would too. I love this smell. Can we walk here for a minute?"

"We have to cross it anyway; I live on the other side. God that's so weird. Yesterday I would have said 'we' live on the other side."

"I'm sorry, I didn't realise you were in a relationship, Dave never mentioned it. Have you just split up with someone?"

Jonno was gratified to see that however nonchalantly she tried to frame her question, she still looked disappointed. He hastened to clarify.

"No, no nothing like that. Well, yes, I guess I have, but it was a bloke, a flatmate I mean, someone I thought was a mate, but now it seems he was only a business partner."

Half-way across the Green Susie slumped down at the foot of a birch tree, leant back against its slender trunk, and stared up into its cross-hatched branches as she breathed in the new-mown scent.

"My first boyfriend suffered from hay fever."

Now it was Jonno's turn to react with a twinge of jealousy. "What happened to him?"

"He was from Iceland. He went back home."

Jonno sat down beside her so their shoulders and the length of their upper arms touched. He thought about the kiss they shared as he was leaving her flat in Battersea two nights previously.

"The first, you said. Do you have anyone...at the moment?"

She turned her head to look at him. He could see the laughter in her eyes as she asked, "Now, why would you want to know a thing like that?"

"Oh, no reason. Merely curious," he teased her back.

They both broke up in fits of giggles. Jonno hadn't laughed out loud for two days and now felt energised by it. He jumped up and reached down to help Susie to her feet. Overwhelmed by a sense of liberation, he clasped her in his arms and kissed her on the mouth. Her lips opened in response and their tongues met each other once more.

"Wow," she said, as their faces disengaged. "What brought that on?"

"I've just endured a really bad couple of days and suddenly I feel happy again. I am so glad you're here. I'm sorry if it was a bit of a shock."

"No, really, it was nice. I enjoyed myself the other night, but when you didn't ring..."

"Oh God. I haven't explained that yet, have I? Come on, let's go and I'll tell you all about it."

They went in via the front door. As he unlocked the door at the end of the hall he experienced a brief moment of trepidation, wondering if again he would find a number of strangers waiting to plunge him into another nightmare. Thankfully she was behind him and didn't see the flicker of doubt which spread across his face. The lounge was empty, and he offered her a seat on the sofa while he went into the kitchenette to put the kettle on. She followed him though, surveyed the neatness of the place and asked if she could look around, apologising for her curiosity.

"Sure, knock yourself out. That door leads outside and we have our own private entrance in the garden wall. My room's on the left, Steve's was the one at the back. He left in a hurry this morning, so it could be in a bit of a state."

He was glad he'd tidied the mess left in the wake of the police invasion, before setting out for Dave's place earlier. It didn't take her long, and she soon returned to carry her mug of tea into the lounge before sitting on the couch. Jonno followed, sat beside her and scrounged one of her cigarettes to skin up a joint. As he was doing so, he started to explain the bust and his confrontation with the customs department. Although it had all happened when he'd returned from her place late the other night, it now seemed to have been weeks ago.

"God, you must have been so scared."

"Too bloody right I was, although they weren't nasty guys. It was their politeness that was scary. They were so convinced they had me. At first, anyway. The boss got a bit shitty later when he decided I was more trouble than I was worth. He was still a gentleman though. And the black guy...they were impressive, smart, not like the cops. Funny thing, while I was there part of me was thinking theirs must be a pretty good job."

"No."

"Straight up, I did. It must be exciting, tracking down contraband, a bit of cloak and dagger sort of thing. Not dope of course, but nasty shit; heroin and so on, or diamonds, say. Pitting your wits against smugglers must be kind of fun. Maybe that's why they were nice to me. Two sides of the same coin. Too late now though. Now I've got a record."

"You wouldn't seriously want to do it, would you?"

"Not really. But it's an option I would never have thought of in a million years. Now I find that I might have quite liked it. And it makes me wonder what else is out there I haven't considered."

"Are you turning straight?"

"God no!" Jonno laughed. "The world we live in is so fucked. Besides, I couldn't turn into my parents, I'd rather shoot myself. When I dropped out of university my father wanted me to get a job in a bank. Nice steady job, good for a cheap mortgage, get married, have a couple of kids, end up reading the Daily Telegraph and voting conservative. I'd shrivel up and die."

"What about your mother?"

"I love my mother. She's smarter than she knows. I guess she got some kind of fulfilment out of having me and my brother, but really, being a housewife, how frustrating would that be? She's a smart woman, although she doesn't think so."

"Women of their generation didn't have much option. It's beginning to change but there's still plenty who aren't much more than their husbands' chattels."

"So are you one of those women's libbers the gutter press keep going on about?"

"Of course I am. It's my body, I do what I want with it. No one's going to own me, ever. Do you have a problem with that?"

"Not in the least. You should meet my mother. When I was sixteen, she gave me this book to read she'd got from the library – A Vindication of the Rights of Women by Mary Wollstonecraft. God knows where she'd heard about it, she didn't have much of an education my mum. I think maybe her psychiatrist put her on to it, she suffered a bit from depression, you know. Perhaps he thought it would help."

"Bloody hell. Did it?"

"I don't know. Maybe. You'd have to ask her. A couple of years ago I went back for a week's visit. One night I'd been out with some mates and we'd all been tripping, and I was still a bit spaced out when I got home the next afternoon. There was my mum just sitting in the living room, knitting. Waiting for my dad to come home from work so she could get up and make his tea. It looked so sad, like her whole world revolved around her husband. I know they love each other, and I guess she's happy up to a point, but I'm sure she'd have liked something more. Otherwise why does she suffer from bouts of depression, why read books about Freud and Jung? She must feel some void in her life."

"I'm never going to get like that. That's the trap women fall into, investing all their happiness in another person. You end up being a doormat."

"She's not a doormat. They're...I don't know, used to each other, I guess. They've been together for more than thirty years. Grew up in the depression, got married just before he went off to war, leaving her pregnant with my eldest brother. I can't really imagine what it must have been like. Her wondering if she would ever see him again. And him, six years fighting a war, how would that be? Danger, excitement, boredom, tragedies. He never talks about it. Such a different life. What are your parents like?"

"Have you ever been to the Western Isles?"

"Never been to Scotland at all."

"It's beautiful country, but it's hard, and it makes the people hard, or it can do. The Free Church of Scotland. That's a joke, calling it free. They're an island people and they worship a hard God. A God of retribution, of hellfire and damnation. The sixties hasn't got to Lewis yet, let alone the seventies, I doubt if it ever will. Here, I'll tell you what it's like, you can't read the Sunday papers on a Sunday because you can't buy them. That would be sinful. You have to wait until Monday. Everything except the church shuts down on the Sabbath. My parents are believers. So when I got pregnant, they threw me out. Bringing shame on them, how dare I?"

"God, that's awful." Jonno could see that her normally soft expression had turned harder. He wondered what life would be like in a place with such a small population. Everyone must know everything about everyone else's business. Was she shunned by the entire populace, maybe run off the island? It was not something he felt he could ask. He noticed that although he'd finished rolling the joint some time ago, it was still in his hand. To cover the lengthening hiatus caused by her revelation, he reached into his pocket for his Zippo and quickly fired it up. He took a couple of deep drags before handing it on to her. She hesitated for a moment, staring into his eyes, before taking it from him.

"So, you have a child?"

"No. I don't."

"I'm sorry. I don't mean to pry."

"It's alright. You're easy to talk to. It was the best thing for me to do and I refuse to be ashamed. I had an abortion a couple of years ago. It's why I came down to London."

"Jesus."

"You're not a catholic, are you? You don't hate me now?"

"No I'm not, and no I don't. It's a shock that's all. It must have been bloody awful for you. It makes my problems seem paltry."

They sat in silence for a while, handing the joint backwards and forwards until it was finished and the roach stubbed out in the ash-tray on the mirrored table top. Jonno finally broke it by asking "What about the father?"

"Buggered off back to Iceland."

"Shit."

"No, give him his due, he did ask me to go with him, but Lewis was cold enough...I was young. The pill wasn't available on the island and I was caught. I might have been foolish but I wasn't stupid. I wasn't ready to settle down with someone I hardly knew. I'd thought I loved him but it turned out to be an infatuation with a handsome stranger. He was like a window opened onto the wide world. Showed me how claustrophobic the island was. I don't regret what happened. It was a shitty time for a while, but it forced me to realise that I had to escape, or else get buried up to my neck in a peat bog of drudgery. I left. I'm free."

"Fuck. I am so sorry for you."

"Why? It's nothing to do with you. But I needed to tell you if we're going to get to know each other better. Which I hope we are."

"Me too. You are bloody gorgeous."

"Thank you, kind sir. You're not so bad yourself. So, can we lighten up a bit, now we've got that out of the way? Put a record on. What's your favourite album?"

Jonno went over to the pile of records left by Steve and pulled out *More*.

"This one. Are you into the Floyd?"

"Hell yes. Put it on. Have you ever seen the film? The Electric Cinema in Notting Hill is showing it this week to coincide with the release of La Vallee."

"La Vallee?"

"You know *More* is a film soundtrack, right? Well the same people made another one which has just been released, La Vallee, and the Floyd did the soundtrack again. Except the album for this one's called *Obscured by Clouds*. Came out last week, Hamish bought it straight away and it's brilliant."

"They're such a great band."

"I've never seen the film. We're all going to the Electric at the weekend. If it's your favourite album you should come too."

"Ah, I'd love to, but there's a bit more to my problem than I've told you. The truth is I'm skint."

"That doesn't matter. You took me to see the Titus Groans, I'll take you to the pictures. It's only fair."

"The other guys from your place won't mind? The other night...I was wondering if one of them was..."

"An ex? No, nothing like that. They're my cousins. Hamish took me in when I needed a place to stay. Looked after me when...They're mates."

"That's why they all seemed so protective of you the other night."

"Yeh, they do come on like big brothers from time to time. They were all a bit suspicious when I'd told them I was being taken to a concert by a dope dealer. Sorry about that. If it's any consolation you did pass."

"Oh, so it was a test? I was wondering why they all hung around."

"Hamish particularly wanted to check you out. He does a bit of dealing on the side himself. He's a nice guy, the pair of you should get on. Saturday night, please come."

"Sure, I'd love to, as long as you can afford to take me. Like I said, I'm flat broke. When the cops busted me, they confiscated our cash, all tied up in hundreds by rubber bands. I signed for it when they took me in. They didn't charge me with dealing because they thought the customs were going to, so if they don't come back with a new charge maybe they'll give it back. But that won't be for a few weeks. To be honest I don't know how I'm going to last. Won't even have any of this left by then," as he started to unwrap the square of silver paper again "Oh well, might as well go out with a bang. Fancy another one?"

"If you're going to put *More* on, sure."

"And afterwards, when we get the munchies, I can offer you a plate of beans on toast, with cheese grated on top," he laughed.

"Oh, *gourmet* beans on toast. You certainly know how to treat a girl right."

"It's all I've got to offer..."

"I'm joking, ok? There've been times when...never mind."

Jonno put the record on the turntable and started to skin up another joint.

"Do I make you nervous?" She asked, watching as his fingers stumbled over the making of it.

"To be honest, yes," he said and laughed at his own embarrassment.

"Good," she said and pulled his head round towards hers. "I like that" and she kissed him. Then, when the joint was rolled and they'd passed it back and forwards a couple of times, she took it and placed the lit end in her mouth having first curled back her tongue, then leaned towards his open mouth and, as he sucked in, blew a great cloud of smoke straight down into his lungs. Taking it in his turn he repeated her actions.

"There's something so intimate about a shotgun," she said.

"I once saw some G.I.'s on the television doing it in Vietnam. They packed the breech of a rifle full then blew down it so this huge cloud of smoke erupted straight at the camera. It was such a powerful image but my Dad nearly had apoplexy."

"He's in favour of the war?"

"He was. Like most ex-soldiers. I guess because they supported us against the Nazis, he thought America could do no wrong. Nowadays I think he can see that it's a waste of life. We used to argue about it all the time until one day he picked up a hitch-hiker. We were coming back from the beach and there was this young guy at the side of the road with a flat tire on his push-bike. Dad stopped and offered him a lift into town, tied his bike to the roof. Turned out Wayne, his name was, was American. Told us he was doing a cycle tour of England. So he got in the back with me and we got on so well that in the end we took him home to repair his puncture, and my parents fed him and gave him a bed for the night. Like I say, he was a great guy, we were the same age and we really clicked. Next day he cycled off and we never saw him again. Dad never said anything but I reckon he sussed that Wayne was a draft dodger. And it brought home to him that if our government had been involved then I might have been sent there too. He was twenty-six when he went to war. He sure as hell thought that I was too young at eighteen. After that we didn't argue so much."

"Good for him."

"Yes, he's not a bad bloke really, just a different generation."

"I like the sound of your parents. Where are you from? You mentioned going to a beach."

"Cornwall."

"So you're a Celt too! God Jonno, I have to say that your prospects are getting better and better. You don't sound Cornish though."

"No, I went to the kind of school where they rip off your voice." Then he put on a semblance of a West Country accent and said "If'n they adn't I'd a be talking sommut like this – olright my lover?"

She laughed, then looked into his eyes and in a small voice said, "I could be."

"What?"

"Your lover."

"Have I passed another test?"

"No, the test was by the boys. This is more by way of being an audition. Something of an ongoing process. The next hurdle depends upon the quality of your beans on toast."

"Coming right up, madam!"

Later, after eating somewhat voraciously, and her assurance that his audition was progressing satisfactorily, she asked if she might use the phone to let her flatmates know she was alright.

"Best not," Jonno said. "The cops might be listening, and if Cousin Hamish does sell a bit of dope, it would be best for him not to be connected with me at the moment."

"In that case I'd better be getting back soon."

"There's a phone box up the road. You're more than welcome to stay the night. Only if you want to, of course."

"Down boy," she laughed. "I should bloody well hope I would be welcome. I would probably like that too. However, I've got work in the morning. My boss is enough of a sleaze as it is, I hate to think what remarks he'll be making if I turn up wearing exactly the same clothes as I did today. No, I'd better be getting back in an hour or so."

"I'll walk you to the tube."

"A Celt *and* a perfect gentleman. Some people might think that's a contradiction in terms."

"But not another Celt, surely. Are we not the romantics of the western world?"

"The Italians might dispute that, and the French."

"Oh, a gaggle of Latins. Other than our Breton compatriots, all show and no substance. Lancelot du Lac and all of his superficial ilk have nothing on the geological emotions of Tristan and Iseult, or of Gawain's dalliance with the Green Knight's wife, who incidentally came from your neck of the woods."

"Jonno, you are one very strange human being. Dave told me you were a poet. I don't know about that but you certainly are a story teller. You've told me several in the last couple of hours and now you're delving back into mythology. How the hell did you ever become a dope dealer?"

"Possibly not such a great divide. A purveyor of dreams. The ancient bards, moving from one fireside to another, from one great man's hall to the next, chewing on mushrooms, having visions, and shaping their experiences into stories. Maybe it's the self-same impetus, an interpretation of reality, the soul's hidden joys, its secret fears. Or maybe I'm just completely off my face."

She laughed. "That sounds more like it. So, next Saturday night, eight o'clock at the Electric Cinema, will you remember?"

"Susie, how could I possibly forget?"

"How are you going to get there? I could lend you a couple of quid."

"No, thank you all the same, I have my Celtic pride you know. I can walk there from here. It'll take about twenty minutes."

"And food? I don't want you starving to death before I see you again."

"Have no fear, sweet lady, not only are there more beans in the larder but there are tins of spaghetti as well. I might be somewhat spotty by the weekend but I will be upright, and most probably erect as well."

"Oh, you smooth talker you. You had better be, I have plans, that's all I am prepared to say at this time." At which they both collapsed into fits of giggles.

Recovering first, Jonno forgot his earlier resolve not to reveal the full extent of his predicament. He wanted to be completely honest with her, just as she had been with him.

"This is all so silly," he blurted out. "Up in Highgate cemetery, buried in someone's tomb, I have a whole load of dope stashed, which if I sold it would fetch about nine hundred quid. And here I am, unable to scrounge up the tube fare to Ladbroke Grove."

"Are you serious?" She asked.

"It was buried here in the cellar. I moved it. But it still hangs like a weight around my neck. Or eight weights to be precise."

"Eight pounds! Fuck. Sell it."

"I will, but I can't right now. I daren't bring it back here. They could be pissed off that I fell through the gaps and be watching me still. I just want to get rid of it. Maybe keep a couple of ounces for myself, but shift the rest in one go. So it's not hanging over me like a blood-soaked albatross. Once I've done that my career will be over, and I can return to the semblance of normality. It takes you over Susie; the dealing. It cuts you off from everybody. You become suspicious of your friends. You wonder if they like you because of what you can do for them. It's a dog-eat-dog world, where if you cross someone, they might shop you at any moment, and all the time you are thinking about money; about mark ups, and profits, and stupid percentages. You try to look invisible, be careful not to stick out too much in a crowd, while at the same time you want to enjoy flaunting your credentials, want to play the big man, be the one in the know. It is all such shit, and I am sick of it. Don't get me wrong, it's been fun, but it's not who I am, and I want it to be over. Preferably with me not in gaol."

"You should speak to Hamish at the weekend, he might be able to work something out. Eight pounds is a hell of a lot more than he's ever handled, but he's got contacts, maybe he could shift some of it for you."

"I'll think about it. So, one more for the road?"

"You're a bad man, Jonno."

"I know."

~ 12 ~

1969

Choosing a more scenic route for their return to London proved to be a mistake. Pete wanted to show Jonno that the North of England wasn't all endless back-to-back housing or giant factories and industrial estates. So, rather than taking the ferry back into Liverpool, they headed due south, where Jonno was suitably impressed by Chester's remaining medieval buildings and its ancient Roman walls.

The trouble was that away from the motorway there was little commercial traffic. It being a Saturday, the majority of motorists were out with their families, heading for nearby destinations. Towards the end of the afternoon it started to rain, and drivers were even less inclined to let a couple of drenched, long-haired hippies into their nicely upholstered and cleanly carpeted cars.

The boys were stuck for ages waiting by a turn-off where a farmer let them out of his land-rover. Early evening traffic was almost non-existent and they walked to keep themselves warm. The hedgerows offered minimal protection from the driving rain which gradually built up into a torrential downpour. Luckily, they'd both packed plastic anoraks for their journey but after a few hours of steady rain their calves were soaked and the dampness was seeping up the denim of their jeans. Moreover water was beginning to run down the insides of their orange plastic coverings where condensation was forming. Their only hope was that later there might be people returning home or perhaps driving out to a country pub. Just the thought of coming across such a hostelry kept them trudging on through the dark, imagining pulling chairs up to a roaring log fire, their clothes steaming as they settled back to down pints of beer.

At one point they believed their prayers answered when they spotted a light in the distance. They quickened their pace, anxious to reach it before last orders were called. They came close to tears when they arrived at what turned out to be a concrete bus shelter, incongruously stuck out in the middle of nowhere with a solitary street lamp overhanging it. They had been walking for hours with no bus passing them, but nevertheless Jonno raced over to read the time-table. Underneath it's graffitied plastic covering he managed to make out that there was very little service outside of school hours and none at all at weekends.

Despondent, the two of them decided that since they were out of the rain, this would be their home for the night. They hung their anoraks over one end of the seat to drip onto the floor while Jonno stretched out on the other end with his holdall as a rudimentary pillow. Pete was too large to balance on such a narrow bench and was relegated to a position on the cold concrete. Sleep was a long time coming for the pair of them and fitful when it did arrive. By five o'clock they were so cold that they gave up altogether and sat huddled as close as possible, smoking the last of Jonno's cigarettes and waiting for dawn to arrive. When it finally did, they resumed walking to warm themselves up a little, even if there was little likelihood of traffic so early on a Sunday. At least the rain was stopping and the remaining few clouds glowed, reflecting a glorious rising sun.

They hardly travelled any distance when a miracle occurred. A green Morris Traveller came up behind them and stopped.

"Going far?" a young man in a dark suit and a clerical collar enquired when he leant across and opened the passenger door.

"London," the pair of them almost shouted simultaneously.

"Can't do that I'm afraid," the driver informed them. "I'm due to take a service in Stoke-on-Trent, but you should be able to get a lift from there. I could drop you off near the motorway."

"Oh yes please vicar, or father, or whatever..." Jonno said.

"Just Roger will do. The back doors aren't locked. Sling your bags in and then climb in here," and he pushed the passenger seat forwards for one of them to get into the back seat.

"This is very good of you Roger," said Peter.

"Well it is a Sunday, and I am a Christian, and there is a story about leaving someone at the side of a road, you know. And you both look frozen."

"Oh yes, spent last night on the floor of a bus shelter."

"I'll turn the heater up, although it's not very efficient I'm afraid. And no sermons I promise you, I'm saving that for later. You probably didn't sleep much on your floor. Get some now and I'll wake you up when we're there."

"You really are a Christian," Pete said from the back as he yawned and slumped sideways on the seat.

Having thanked their saviour effusively when he dropped them off near a motorway slip road, they were both feeling much happier after a journey which neither of them witnessed. Soon they were picked up by a succession of vehicles and eventually delivered to Archway tube station. Along the way they discussed their plans. Pete would immediately start looking for a house while Jonno declared that he was going to get himself a job.

"Go to one of those temp agencies, there's plenty of them around," Pete suggested. "Brook Street Bureau has adverts in all the tubes."

"I don't want labouring work."

"There's plenty of office jobs. You can count, can't you? Tell them you can type; they'll snap you up."

"Ok. I told you where I'm staying. Whereabouts are you?"

"Oh I'm around and about, nowhere special. I'll come and get you when I've found somewhere decent."

"Fair enough," said Jonno, and they wished each other well as they parted on the platform at Charing Cross.

Back at the house on Upper Richmond Road he was asked how he had found his expedition to the 'frozen north.' "Educational" was all he could think of to say. None of the housemates talked about their childhoods much. He couldn't picture their mothers spending hours in a kitchen boiling up chicken carcasses and scraps to concoct nourishing soups. Possibly they devoted some of their time to doing 'good works', helping those unfortunate enough to live in more straightened circumstances.

Jonno was grateful for the generosity of his housemates, but was not labouring under any illusions. He was living in a borrowed room, and also on borrowed time. He imagined Brian would be returning soon. Nevertheless, he looked forward to a comfortable night's sleep as he gratefully crawled under the missing man's continental quilt. He was full to the brim with one of Margo's outstanding Indian curries, and had partaken of a couple of the usual postprandial joints which circled the candle-lit table.

It was still warm enough to eat outside in the gazebo but wouldn't be for much longer. Autumn was starting to bite and darkness was falling earlier by the day. He was pretty much flat broke again and was soon going to need some warmer clothes. He wondered how long it would take Pete to find somewhere for them to live, and how much rent he would have to pay. He determined not to bother trying to sign on the dole again. He was going to need a job.

"Sorry to bother you but I've got a bit of a problem," he said to Henry the following morning. He went on to explain that he would shortly be moving into a house with his recent travelling companion.

"That's good to hear my peripatetic friend. As far as I'm concerned you are welcome to grace us with your presence for as long as you wish. Others amongst us have been mooting it abroad that perhaps it might be time you moved on. Not for any personal reasons I assure you, we have all found your company to be perfectly agreeable. I have particularly enjoyed your admirable recitations of some of the cream of English poetry of an evening after dinner. But there will come a time in the not-too-distant future when Brian will wish to reclaim his sleeping quarters."

"That's what I have been thinking, which is why I have to get myself a job as soon as possible."

"Wherein lies the essence of your problem?"

"I was going to sign on at one of the temporary office employment agencies, but I'm flat broke and don't really have anything suitable to wear for an interview."

"Ah yes, I can see your predicament. Jeans, tee-shirt and that sloppy-joe jersey of yours would hardly be considered standard office apparel. It is a quandary that is easily overcome, however. I judge us to be of similar stature and girth and while I favour clothing as casual as yours, I do have some of a more acceptable nature. I can easily lend you a pair of trousers, a couple of shirts and a jacket that should suffice."

"That'd be great Henry, thank you so much."

"You'll need them for longer than just an interview, so you are welcome to inhabit them until you have achieved a position and received your first pay packet."

"You have been so kind, Henry. If there's ever anything I can do…"

"Ah, there might well be a way. From your recitations of Blake, Coleridge, and particularly of Keats, it is obvious that you have an appreciation of the musicality of language. Oft-times I have heard you tapping away on that little typewriter of yours. I am given to understand that sometime in the next year the Titus Groans will be given the opportunity to do some recording. Whilst my fellow band members are getting more and more proficient instrumentally, we will be requiring some decent lyrics. Perhaps you could turn your poetic sensibilities in that direction. I am loth to promise anything as all our decisions are taken collectively, but should you come up with anything we would try it out."

"I'll give it a go."

"When you have settled into your new abode do keep in touch. You should come and sit in on our rehearsals, to gain some understanding of our requirements."

"I'd love too."

So it was in borrowed clothes that Jonno turned up at the Brook Street Bureau the following day. He walked into the centre of town, to husband his remaining cash for whatever travel expenses a job might require. At the Bureau he was asked to fill out an application form by the trendily dressed, bottle-blond receptionist, who invited him to wait on a couch while she took it through to her boss in the back office. He was finally ushered through, to find that the middle-aged woman in twin-set and pearls sitting behind a mahogany desk was unimpressed by his typing proficiency.

"We have plenty of girls for that sort of work," she said. "Without shorthand, manual dexterity at a keyboard is something of a redundant skill. There is plenty of demand for people in other clerical positions, however. Reading through this form I see that you have A Levels and a year of university, so you probably aren't stupid. How are you at maths?"

Feeling a little piqued at her school-teacherish manner Jonno responded defensively.

"I can add and subtract if that's what you mean. Even manage a bit of multiplication and long division. Logarithms are a little beyond me and sines and cosines completely passed me by."

"There's no need to be smart, young man. The basics will be enough. There's an opening for a time clerk at a factory down at Clapham that has just come in. How soon could you start?"

"Tomorrow if need be."

"Excellent. It's temporary, for a four-week period while someone is on sick leave, and at the moment they are desperate. So we will give you a try. If you prove to be satisfactory then we might have something else for you. Angela will provide you with the details on your way out, and explain our terms and conditions. We have a reputation to uphold so don't let me down. Good morning to you."

Morris, Reid and Co was an engineering firm located in a massive Victorian brick building not far from Clapham Common. It took Jonno nearly an hour to get there from Upper Richmond Road, once he walked to the nearest tube in Putney, joined a cramped carriage-full of commuters making their way into the centre of London, and then changed to the Northern line going south. There he entered a carriage that felt as if all of its oxygen had been sucked out of it, leaving nothing but second-hand carbon dioxide and dust. At least on this leg of the journey he was guaranteed of a seat, albeit a slightly grimy one.

Having walked from Clapham North station Jonno found himself before a pair of huge wooden doors, designed to allow for the passage of horses and carts. They were curved at the top to fit beneath a great stone archway, the keystone of which was carved into a human face. It was a smooth, young man's face, possibly that of the founder of the company. It reminded him of Keats' death mask, displayed in the Hampstead Museum to which he had made pilgrimage shortly after arriving in London. It seemed he might be about to enter into a castle, or possibly a prison, as he turned the brass handle of the wicket let into the right-hand door. He found himself in a dimly-lit tunnel which ran between offices to either side, whose waist-high windows revealed a number of people all staring out at him. A middle-aged man in the office to his right rose from a desk and opened the door into the corridor.

"You must be our new temporary time clerk from Mrs. Matheson's."

"Yes. I'm afraid I'm a little late," Jonno said as he caught sight of a large clock affixed to the wall between several racks of slots, bristling with brown cards poking up at slight angles. "I thought I'd left in plenty of time but I didn't realise how long it would take me to get here."

"Not an auspicious start for a time clerk, is it? Never mind, we'll leave that for the moment. Tomorrow you'll know. My name's Hardcastle. I'm the under-manager of staff. Come along into the office, and I'll introduce you."

There were four desks illuminated by overhead fluorescent tubes suspended by chains from the false ceiling, which contrived to give the office a more intimate feeling than the lofty roof of the corridor outside. At two desks young women sat behind industrial typewriters, looking up at him with unconcealed curiosity, even while their fingers continued to manipulate the rows of keys on their machines. Occasionally they reached with unconscious precision to slap at the carriage return levers, shifting their platens to the right before starting a new line.

"This is Carol and Bridget," he was told as each one smiled up at him, before returning their gaze to the hand-written notes and letters that they were transcribing.

"Glad to meet you," he said. "Please call me Jonno."

"We like clerical staff to be little more formal in the office," Hardcastle said. "Here we'll refer to you as Mr. Tremain. It strikes the right tone, I find."

"If you say so," Jonno replied and cast a wry smile in the direction of the two women. Carol, whom Jonno thought to be the oldest, maybe twenty-four or so, lifted her head up and caught his look, before pursing her lips to suppress her own smile in return.

"That will be your desk over there," Hardcastle indicated one of the two desks beside the window onto the corridor. "The other is mine. I have a corresponding one in the office over the way for when I'm over there, which is most of the time at the moment, unfortunately. So I will be relying on you to keep up discipline in this office in my absence. Don't let the girls distract you from your duties."

Jonno thought he could detect the ghost of a snigger which was swiftly suppressed as Hardcastle ploughed on with his description of Jonno's duties. It seemed the firm was working three shifts of fitters, turners and assorted labourers in the factory proper which was through a giant steel roller door at the far end of the corridor. Jonno had never worked in a factory before so the process of clocking on was new to him. Apparently, each man would take his card, feed it into a slot on the clock to stamp the time on it, then place it into the far board, reversing the process as they left. At the end of every shift Jonno's task was to take all of their cards to his desk and record each worker's hours into a ledger, before replacing them. Hardcastle explained how meticulously he should perform this task as it was from this ledger that he would be calculating their wages. He would have to repeat this for each of the three shifts, starting straight away for the night shift which had just clocked off. Not a particularly onerous task he thought as he removed the cards and sat at his desk, opening the ledger.

"Right, got that? Then I'll leave you to get on with it. If you have any problems I'll be in the office just over the way. You can get me on the phone on your desk, I've taped my number to it. We don't allow staff to make outgoing calls and I can see if you do so through the window. From time to time I will be ringing you to come and get correspondence which you will give to the girls to type up. There's a small kitchen through that door where you can eat your lunch, and one of the girls will be making tea and coffee at elevenses and half way through the afternoon. I think that's everything. Do your job and we'll get along. Mess it up and I'll be straight on to the agency to have you removed. Remember this is men's wages we're talking about. Any cock-ups and the shop stewards will be down on me like a ton of bricks."

"Bloody hell," Jonno expostulated once Hardcastle left the office and crossed the corridor to the other office.

"He's not so bad really," Carol said. "I've had worse bosses. He's a stickler for punctuality though, and you being late put his back right up."

"Christ, it was only five minutes."

"He's got this saying 'if you're not five minutes early, then you're late.' He repeated it again this morning when you weren't on time," she added.

"His trouble is he thinks he's still in the army," Bridget said.

"I don't suppose there's any chance of a coffee now?" Jonno asked.

Carol laughed. "None at all, I'm afraid. The rules is the rules, and you can be sure he'll be watching you on your first day. Like Bridget said, he was in the army."

"Well then, I suppose I'd better get on with it. Girls," he added in a mocking tone.

"Don't you start," Carol said. "That's one thing that does annoy me. I'm a married woman for God's sake. And I reckon both of us are older than you."

The day passed, shifts clocked on and off as men dressed in overalls passed by in the corridor outside, many of them staring in through the window. At first Jonno thought that it was at the novelty of a new face behind the glass. Later, when he noticed how studiously the two young women concentrated on their typing as a shift passed by, he realised it was them being stared at, and they knew it. When he returned from collecting the cards Carol confirmed his suspicions.

"It's like working in a bloody fish bowl in here some-times. Like they've never seen a pair of legs before."

"Well they are nice legs," Jonno said. "All four of them," he added.

At first Carol scowled at him, but when she saw his face fall, she burst out in laughter.

"Oh you noticed then, did you? What do you think Bridget? Should we take it as a compliment or not?"

"I'm going too. Let's face it he's been sitting in here all day, keeping quiet as a mouse. I think I'd feel insulted if he hadn't noticed. After all, according to my Bob, they are my best feature. And it's not as if he's been ogling them like that lot outside."

"True. He's behaved like a perfect gentleman. So, we'll forgive him."

"It was meant as a compliment," Jonno said, feeling a blush of embarrassment rising to his cheeks. He was aware that he was being gently mocked by the two of them. Indeed, during the course of the day there'd been a fair amount of banter between the two women, including a number of innuendoes slyly pointed in his direction. Un-used to such a situation, he pretended not to notice. Now, just before the end of their working day, he realised that he would have to make some attempt at retaliation. Otherwise they might think him stand-offish, which could adversely affect the atmosphere in their cramped little office, and make the rest of his temporary employment unpleasant.

He was given an opportunity when, at the end of the day, the two women stood in front of him before pulling on their coats and in turn, each done a little twirl.

"So, who's got the better legs then?" Bridget asked.

"I couldn't possibly tell without seeing a whole lot more of them," he replied, affecting a rueful smile.

"Oh *Mister Tremaine*, and there's me thinking you were a gentleman. I am utterly shocked," said Carol putting on her serious face. After which, laughing, all three of them left the building.

The days passed and it seemed he was fulfilling his role to Hardcastle's satisfaction once he started catching an earlier tube and arriving in plenty of time. Since the ice was broken with the two women at the end of his first day, the atmosphere in their little office became very friendly. They proved most inquisitive about his life at university and before that 'down in the West country,' as they described it. Neither of them had lived anywhere other than in South London, and Devon and Cornwall seemed exotic, a location they could only imagine as possible future holiday destinations. The countryside was an almost mythical place, fascinating but also a little frightening. "So much empty space," one of them said. "Not sure I could stand the quiet," from the other.

On the other hand they were excited by thoughts of the student life, one they imagined consisted of a long round of sex, drugs and wild parties. A life as pictured in the pages of their husbands' Daily Mirrors and Sun newspapers. He tried to disabuse them at first but gave up and instead embellished a few of his own experiences for their delectation. These discussions took place mostly in the tea-room during their lunch breaks. After a couple of days they asked why he never brought anything to eat. He sought to evade their questioning, explaining that he was on a diet. This provoked laughter on their part, so he finally gave up and admitted that he was too broke to afford anything other than tube fares. The next day he found both had brought a couple of extra sandwiches for him. When he tried to refuse, they told him not to be stupid.

"We can't sit here and eat in front of a starving man," Carol told him.

"Besides, you'll need to keep your strength up, for when you get back home to that commune of yours of a night-time," Bridget added, laughing.

Having told them a little of his current living arrangements, their imaginations supplied a much more salacious picture, especially when he admitted the existence of Margo and Bea. No, it was a hippie commune as far as they were concerned, and everyone knew what hippies get up to.

"All that free love," Bridget said with a somewhat jealous twinkle in her eyes.

"It must be terribly wearing," Carol joined in.

He tried to explain there was nothing like that going on between the housemates but they refused to believe him, preferring instead the pictures created in their heads.

They enjoyed trying to embarrass him too much to accept he might be telling the truth. At one point, exasperated by their constant ribbing, he invited the pair of them to come and visit him one Saturday afternoon. He was pretty sure they wouldn't accept but he was surprised by how horrified they were at the thought. On reflection he decided it was not so much a fear of close contact with a bunch of hippies, but rather of having their preconceived notions destroyed. He could also see there was a terror of feeling themselves out of place. He didn't press it, instead allowing them to continue with their ribald banter, and enjoying their gentle mockery of him.

The truth was that he rather liked being on the receiving end of their innuendos just as he liked them personally. He found their daily company pleasurable. So much so that after three weeks he began to regret that their time together was drawing to a close. He was receiving his wages by then and was no longer dependent on their generosity for his lunch. He began to wonder whether he might buy each of them some little present when he left. He couldn't think what however, and one night back at the house he asked Margo for some advice. No one back in Putney expressed much interest in his job once he explained it was 'just clerical work.' Now he explained to Margo just how much he enjoyed the bantering relationship with the two very straight, very ordinary South London women. Since so much of their communication was based on sexual innuendos, he wondered about doing something outrageous, such as buying each of them a pair of knickers. Margo was horrified.

"No, no, that would just be embarrassing. And sleazy. You've only known them for a few weeks. Besides which, it could get them into trouble with their husbands. How people behave at work is usually very different from how they are at home. All you need to do on your last day is take in a beautiful cake, with lots of cream and fancy icing. Even if they're on diets they'll eat it and love you for it. And any left-overs they'll take home to their men."

So that was what he did. On his way in on the last day he first called back into a baker's shop and collected his order. The assistant was a bit surprised when he asked whether it would be possible to give him a second box, but when he explained just who the cake was for it hadn't proved to be a problem.

"I was wondering about the icing," she said as she handed over a second, still folded carton.

There was much excitement in their little office when he walked in, balancing a box tied with ribbon on his up-turned hand.

"Not to be opened until lunch-time," he insisted as the pair of them pounced on it and attempted to pull at the ribbon.

"Oh go on, just a little peek, as the bishop said to the actress," Bridget laughed.

"More likely the actress said to the bishop," Carol joined in.

"No peeking at all from anyone, or I'll be forced to call you Girls, and you'll have to call me Mr. Tremaine for the rest of the day. And you won't like that, will you?"

"Ooh, you're so masterful, *Mr. Tremaine.* Ok, bung it in the fridge," said Bridget.

Jonno enjoyed the atmosphere of anticipation as they all trooped into the little kitchen at lunchtime.

"Who's going to unwrap it then?" Carol asked.

"Well I bought it for both of you so you could each take an end of the bow and pull."

This done Carol lifted up the flap and they both burst out laughing. It was a magnificent cream filled sponge with white icing and green piping around the edge. What caused their merriment was the lettering spelling out My Four Favourite Legs underneath a piped rendition in pink icing of two sets of legs protruding from a pair of blue mini-skirts.

"It's beautiful," Carol expostulated while Bridget leered at him and repeated Dick Emery's catchphrase when dressed in drag for his television show "Ooh, you are awful...but I like you." She then leaned in and planted a large smacking kiss on his cheek.

"Hey, I'm the senior typist, I should have first go," Carol said and to assert her authority she planted one right on his lips. They were all a little embarrassed after this so settled down to fetching plates, cutting the cake and eating their slices with forks. Jonno explained there was another box so that they could each take a half home with them.

"That's really nice of you Jonno. But we should get rid of the legs off the top before we do, just in case," Carol explained.

"Yes, don't want to give my Bob any ideas," Bridget added. "We could polish them off at afternoon tea."

Which they did. Later, as they were preparing to leave, and the two women were placing the remains in their respective boxes, Jonno told them how much he enjoyed working alongside them, and how pleasurable they'd made his first experience of office work.

"There's one thing, before you go, you never did say who's got the better legs," Carol complained. So saying she lifted her skirt almost to the top of her thighs. Bridget did likewise saying, "Go on then, tell us."

For a moment Jonno was dumbfounded at the lascivious sight, so provocatively displayed in the incongruous intimacy of the lunch room. Recovering quickly however, he asked whether they had both gone to Sunday school when little.

"Yes," they replied, looking a little guilty and swiftly dropping their hems back down.

"You'll know the story of the judgement of Solomon then. I'll take a leaf out of his book. I'd choose Carol's left one with Bridget's right, and Bridget's left with Carol's right. How's that?"

"A total cop out," Bridget laughed. "But acceptable," added Carol and she grabbed him by the shoulders and kissed him on the lips again, except this time opening her mouth and dancing her tongue around his for a moment. Not to be outdone Bridget followed suit. Then, as they were leaving the building and saying their final goodbyes Bridget added "Cor, when I get home my Bob won't know what's hit him."

When Jonno arrived back home he found Pete sitting at the kitchen table, sharing a joint with Bea, Margo and Ben. It seemed he was regaling them with tales of their expedition to the north, and Jonno's reactions to the situations he encountered. As he leant back in his chair, he looked up at Jonno through heavy lidded eyes and told him, "I think I found us a place. I'll take you there tomorrow, see if you like it."

"Great," Jonno replied, "I've been earning some bread. So I can afford to pay rent."

"Whereabouts is it?" Margo asked.

"Just off Tooting Broadway," Pete replied. "Nothing as fancy as this place of course, smaller but probably a hell of a lot cheaper."

"Wherever, as long as it's not a complete tip," Jonno said. "It's been great living here. Everyone has been really kind, but it'll be good to have a place to call my own finally." This was in response to Margo's slightly disapproving face he discerned once Pete revealed its whereabouts. 'It's all very well for her,' he thought, 'with her steady job and her room in a mid-Victorian mansion in one of the more salubrious suburbs south of the river.' Then he checked himself. He remembered how kind she was when he helped Henry back to the house. He was just being jealous, he thought to himself, when he contemplated what sort of domicile Pete might have found for them. He was grateful that the other members of the household, when they assembled for the evening meal, accepted Pete's presence amongst them. They were not put off by his broad Liverpudlian accent, nor by his repeated use of expletives when describing his own political and social perspectives. Jonno realised that Pete was attempting to shock them out of what he considered their middle-class complacency. Silently he applauded their refusal to rise to his bait.

One comment did disturb him. When Pete asked whether he could stay the night, Jonno enthusiastically acquiesced, considering this to be one of his last nights under this roof. Having spent a night in Pete's bed, and another with him in a bus shelter, Jonno unreservedly offered him the other half of the mattress in his borrowed room. Later, as he was leaving the kitchen to climb the stairs Ben took him to one side.

"I'm assuming that you know your friend is a rent boy, don't you?" he asked.

"What the hell is a rent boy?" Jonno replied.

"You are such an innocent. You really don't know? It's someone who sleeps with men, for money. A male prostitute in other words."

"You've got to be fucking joking, aren't you?"

"Believe me, he is. And I should know."

"I don't believe you," he answered. "You just don't like him."

Nevertheless, as he undressed that night, he couldn't help himself from making sure that he was facing away from his friend as he dropped his jeans. He cursed himself for the niggling fears that Ben had raised in his mind, but still he kept his underpants on.

~ 13 ~

1972

Jonno had very little idea how long it would take him to walk to Notting Hill. Like everyone else in London, any journey likely to take longer than ten minutes was taken by tube. He searched out his dog-eared A to Z from the bookcase by his bed and placed it in the maroon cotton bag with the Indian embroidery which dangled from his left shoulder. He thought about taking the last of his dope but decided to leave it. His previous date with Susie ended with him being busted. The last thing he needed tonight was to be stopped and searched on the way to see her again. His favourite patched Levis with the velvet gussets he had so painstakingly sewn into the calves were a bit of a give-away, as was the white Afghan coat he wore open over a denim shirt.

It was the middle of October now and it was dark when he set out. As he stepped out of the garden door, by force of habit he turned to look at the spot where Steve's mini was usually parked. It had disappeared a couple of days previously. Presumably not driven by Steve. Surely, he would have knocked on the door, filled Jonno in on what was happening in his life. Unless he was embarrassed about ripping off the remains of their mutual stash from the toilet cistern. No, he would have brazened it out, turned it into a joke. He remembered Steve's father saying he would arrange to have it collected. Would that have been by some Special Branch operative he wondered? Maybe they were holding Steve under some kind of house arrest. No, he was just being melodramatic. Steve's father was just a stern old bastard who brooked no arguments and Steve was obliged to go along with his plans. When he burst in upon them, he had informed Jonno that he wanted no further contact between them. That was just fine as far as Jonno was concerned.

He walked towards Shepherd's Bush, then crossed into Holland Park Avenue, stopping for a moment to admire the architecture of the Royal Crescent behind its semi-circle of grass. The avenue was flanked on both sides by rows of magnificent plane trees in front of the terraces of four storey houses. The nearer he got to Notting Hill he could see the paintwork on these once elegant houses was deteriorating, and evidenced a general lack of maintenance. This was particularly obvious once he turned left out of the avenue and began to walk up Ladbroke Grove, entering into the heart of London's hippiedom.

He had come here once before, shortly after he and Pete arrived back from their trip to the frozen north. They were hoping to find a house to rent somewhere in the area, drawn by its reputation as a hippy mecca. Both of them counted Van Morrison's *Astral Weeks* amongst their favourite L.P.s, and had simultaneously started singing *Slim Slow Slider* as they made their way up Ladbroke Grove. The impossibility of renting a whole house soon became clear, for they were huge and already carved up into numerous flats and bed-sits.

These grand houses were built in an era when families were large, and when nearly half of the working population had been domestic servants. Servants labouring in basement kitchens and sculleries, upstairs lighting and tending fires in the early mornings so that the high-ceilinged living rooms would be warm enough for their employers to enter into. That was once they had bathed in the waters heated for them, and been dressed in the clothes laid out for them. When the servants' working day finally drew to a close, they withdrew to pokey little rooms at the top of the house, which they shared, sometimes two and three to a room, and sometimes to a bed.

The First World War initiated a process of change which was completed by the depredations of the Second. During the course of hostilities servant girls learnt both the joys of manufacturing jobs and the accompanying weekly wage packet. Drab domestic uniforms and 'all-found' were no longer attractive. Moreover returning servicemen and women wanted for themselves the freedoms for which they had fought so hard, and not just for their so-called 'betters'. Without the return of servants the lofty Victorian and Georgian houses, however graceful, became cold and unmanageable.

As the resale value of these properties plummeted unscrupulous developers like Peter Rachman snapped them up to carve the once gracious family homes into rabbit warrens. Large living rooms were partitioned into two- and three-roomed pokey little flats, servants' quarters converted into bed-sitting rooms complete with baby belling stoves and wash-basin sinks, and an inadequate number of bathrooms were shared by who knew how many occupants.

At first these cramped sub-standard flats were let out to new arrivals from the Caribbean, as waves of immigrants came to help in the rebuilding of an economy shattered by war. The bohemian atmosphere thus created meant that when the counter-culture started to flourish in the sixties, it was to find a home in Notting Hill. The houses might be run down, the parks and gardens untended and running wild, but the layout of the area was still beautiful, and strongly appealed to the first generation of 'beautiful people'. Head shops, record stores and second-hand clothes shops started to appear along the Portobello Road, and the weekend market grew from an almost exclusively meat and groceries affair into a collection of much more wide-ranging businesses.

Disappointed in their quest for an unoccupied house big enough for them to establish a commune in, Jonno and Pete made their way into one of the parks, to sit behind a bush and skin up a joint. It was a sunny day and as they lay back on the grass to share it, they realised they were not alone in enjoying the afternoon's warmth in this fashion. There were numerous small knots of people dotted about with much surreptitious passing around of what could have been long and fat, hand rolled cigarettes, were it not for the sweet smells drifting over to them from time to time. Suitably uplifted, the pair of them made their way over to the Portobello Road, where they walked up and down, checking out the numerous items on display. In the Dog Shop they admired the hookahs and various pipes, before Pete bought a chillum and Jonno some extra-large cigarette papers imported from America. On their way back to the tube they called into a record shop called Virgin briefly, entranced by its name. Sunk into beanbags and declining the owner's offer of vegetarian nibbles, Pete decided he should concentrate his search south of the river, where he imagined properties would be smaller and cheaper.

Jonno felt a twinge of anguish as he reached the park where the pair of them had sat and enjoyed that distant afternoon. It was only three years previously but it felt like another lifetime. Before the smack, before the coke, before he was so involved in the business of dealing. He regretted the loss of Pete's friendship. He decided not to walk through the park again, as if to do so might defile the memory of a more benevolent era. He continued up Ladbroke Grove before turning right into Elgin Crescent. Just as he was passing the Duke of Wellington, he was caught short by a large hand which clutched at his shoulder.

"Hey pal, we need to have a few words."

Jonno's guts jumped, thinking his fear was about to be realised. He stopped dead in his tracks. As his adrenaline raced, he wondered whether his anticipated relationship with Susie was merely a chimera. A phantasy destined to be thwarted at every turn by the law's long arms. He turned slowly, but instead of a blue uniform he was confronted by a man of about his own age wearing jeans and a roll-necked jersey under a leather jacket. There was a mass of ginger hair curling around his head and down to his shoulders, which at some indistinguishable point merged with a great shovel of ginger beard. Bright blue eyes glistened beneath two equally rampant eyebrows which made Jonno, in his relief, construct an image of someone peering out at him from behind an orange hedge.

"Fuck, you scared me. Going by your accent you're Hamish, right?"

"Yeh. Sorry about the fright, man. Susie saw you walking past and sent me after you. We're all in the pub. Come and have a drink."

"I, um..."

"Don't have any bread. I know, Susie told us about your troubles. I can stand you a beer alright, I'm thinking.

Besides, it sounds like we might be doing a bit of business together."

"She told you about that, did she?"

"Not in any detail she didn't, but I think I sussed out about your wee problem. You've got something you need to get rid of, am I right? Quite a large wee something."

"Yeh, that's about right."

"Well, I might be able to help there, but we'll talk about that later, if you dinnae mind. Right now I wannae have a word about young Susie. Ye ken she's ma cousin, she's family."

"Aye. Sorry, I mean yes, I'm not taking the piss."

"You'd better not be, feller."

"I can't help it. I think because my own accent was drummed out of me at school, I pick them up at the drop of hat. And you've got a really strong one."

"Aye well, we'll leave that for the now. What I wanted to say was to warn you – don't fucking mess up ma cousin. She might come on all tough, but that's because she's had to handle a shovel load of shit. Inside she's still a fragile wee girlie, and she doesnae need some big city fucking dope dealer having his way wi' her and then dropping her when he's bored. You ken well I'll fucking trash anyone who messes wi' her head."

"Yes, I get the picture. Christ, she told me you and your mates were protective. Now I see what she meant. But you don't have to worry, alright? I think she's...lovely, ok?"

Hamish said nothing, just stood there looking straight at Jonno, as if challenging him to state his intentions.

"Christ, this is weird," Jonno said, embarrassed by the silence. "You're not her father, and I'm not asking for her hand in marriage. She's her own woman and can make her own decisions. I know she's had a hard time and it's good you're looking out for her. But I'm not some wicked, big city lothario, carving notches in my bedpost. I really like her. I can't say I know where this is going, because it hasn't even started yet. I wouldn't deliberately hurt her, but in the end, what goes on between us is none of your fucking business, is it?"

The two of them stood there for what seemed to Jonno to be another several minutes but was probably a few seconds, staring into each other's eyes. Finally Jonno realised that the mouth almost hidden by Hamish's profusion of facial hair was curling up in a smile.

"You're nae some lily-livered poltroon then, are you? Good. So come on, before she comes out here and gives me a complete bollocking for interfering, let's go get that drink."

Inside, the pub was crowded with those street traders whose stalls were packed up after a brisk day's trading. There was much shouting, back-slapping and the swopping of war stories about the success or otherwise of the day's takings as more and more of them trickled in. Susie and two others of her flatmates were sat around a table in the window. Jonno pushed his way towards them through the crowd while Hamish made for the bar to get him a pint.

As he approached, he suddenly felt awkward. Should he kiss her? If she was on her own, he would have. But in front of the others? Would she welcome it, or would she feel he was presuming too much? He didn't want to embarrass her. Or himself for that matter, should she turn her head away. If he just reached out and touched her, on her shoulder for example, would she interpret the action as if he were making some kind of claim on her? She was a feminist; he didn't want to make any gesture she might interpret as him indicating some form of ownership. She had obviously said something to Hamish but he wondered what she might have told her other flatmates. Did they think of him as being her boyfriend or just a fellow Pink Floyd fan invited along on their night out? God, modern life was complicated, or maybe he was just being overly self-conscious.

When he saw her face, his worries vanished. With her red-gold hair, her pale skin and her dancing blue eyes, she just looked so bloody gorgeous sitting there, smiling up at him, that he was entranced by her all over again. The other night she was wearing her office clothes, mini-skirt and boots with a cream-coloured blouse. Tonight she looked like she had just stepped down from a Pre-Raphaelite painting, wearing a tartan cloak over a long flowing dress of purple velvet, which looked designed solely for stroking. He just ached to feel it under his finger-tips. It moulded itself to her figure and stretched high over her chest so that only her collar bones were displayed, those and the sensual hollows of skin behind them. Her neck was encircled by a black satin ribbon attached to which was a circular gold brooch, the setting for a large and many faceted amethyst which echoed the colour of her dress.

"Look at you," he couldn't help himself from blurting out.

"It's not too much, is it?" she asked as she stood up from the table, and threw off the cloak to show him the full effect. "This is my singing dress. I mean the one I perform in at folk clubs."

"No, no, it's a singing dress alright, that's pretty much the perfect description for it."

The two men at the table laughed in agreement and Susie, giving a slight giggle of happiness, clutched at the fur of the two open halves of his coat and drew him towards her, obviously expecting the kiss which he was overjoyed to provide. All of his doubts and feelings of awkwardness were dispelled in an instant, and the two of them were happily sitting side by side by the time Hamish returned from the bar. He passed Jonno a pint and then resumed his seat and lifted his own from the table.

"A toast," he cried. "To the good ship Pink Floyd, and all who sail in her." At which everyone sat around the table raised their glasses and drank.

"Did he give you the first degree out there?" Susie whispered in his ear, loud enough for Hamish to hear.

"As if I would, lassie."

"I knew he would. He just can't help himself. Don't take any notice."

"He's a little hard to ignore," Jonno said.

Angus, one of the other flatmates then piped up with "Och, he's all growl. You dinnae have tae worry unless you see him coming for you wearing his kilt. That's when you'll know you're in trouble. Watch out for the sgian dubh down the socks."

"The what?"

"Dirk to you, Sassenach," Angus translated.

"I'll remember that, thanks," Jonno laughed, before taking a long pull at his beer.

"You're earlier than I thought you'd be," said Susie.

"I didn't know how long it would take me to walk, so I left in plenty of time."

"Keen, were you?" Angus asked, laughing. "For the film, of course."

"Well, err, yes."

"Don't mind them, they're just trying to wind you up," Susie said, frowning around at her flatmates one by one.

"Aye, well you're not alone there, Jonno," Duncan, the other flatmate interjected, ignoring her stare. "Our Susie's been on hot bricks all day. That's why we were so early ourselves. Good excuse for a beer mind."

"At the weekends the Electric's like a private film club, so they never start on time, there's always a few announcements," Susie explained to Jonno. "Even so, drink up boys, we don't want to miss the start."

"Certainly not," Jonno agreed with enthusiasm. "I don't know what comes first because the album might not be in order, but there's bound to be music for the titles."

Glasses were raised, then slapped back onto the table as they all rose at once. They were all avid Pink Floyd fans and were equally keen to get into the theatre, although Susie and Jonno perhaps both felt somewhat keener than the others.

The Electric Cinema really was a most extraordinary building, and Jonno was surprised he hadn't taken more notice of it on his previous visit to Portobello Road. The façade was asymmetrical, as if built in two separate sections, although the whole of the ground floor level seemed constructed out of the same grey limestone blocks, in a neo-classical style. There were a couple of blind arches, like filled-in windows, festoons of carved stone garlands, and a half dozen surface-mounted mock Ionic columns purporting to hold up a triple layered cornice. Above this cornice the difference between the two areas was more pronounced. On the right a flat expanse of concrete curved up into the sky in a gentle, elegant arc, while the smaller, left-hand section was box-shaped, topped off by a dome like a miniature of Saint Paul's. Each of the two upper facades were pierced by a row of sash windows. In the darkness Jonno couldn't decide whether there was a landscape painted around these windows, or if the deteriorating plasterwork was discoloured by giant water stains and mould.

There was no mistaking the paintwork of the foyer however, which was brash in fluorescent reds and oranges. The decorator looked to have been a fan of the cover of Cream's *Disraeli Gears* album. It was an odd space, so garish, with its little angled ticket booth to the left, looking like it had once done service at a funfair. The double doors to the right were leaded above dado height with small panes of glass, as were the side-lights and also the enormous curved fanlight. The whole structure would have looked like the entrance to a nineteenth century alehouse, were it not for its incandescent paintwork.

Having collected their tickets they passed through the double doors into a shabby looking lounge, and from there through curtains into the auditorium proper. Here Jonno stopped dead in his tracks. Suddenly he knew the meaning of the phrase 'faded glory'. However much the place was now referred to as a flea pit, there was no doubt that it had once seen much grander days.

There was a great curved ceiling of a diseased brown colour, which looked rather sticky, as if its sixty years of harbouring cigarette smokers had smeared it with a fly-paper emulsion. Jonno could see that there were numerous plaster embellishments up there but their details were indistinct. The walls had fared better, some attempts at re-decoration had been made and the numerous panels with their surrounding mouldings picked out in contrasting colours of magenta and cream, the whole on a dull green background. For all its diseased and flaking plasterwork there was no denying the architectural grandeur that surrounded the screen, with its flanking pillars surmounted by a curved broken pediment with a globe medallion at its centre. It was so out of keeping with contemporary cinema style. Jonno was used to cinemas where nothing was allowed to distract the eye from what was happening on the screen. Where, as darkness descended, curtains pulled back across a flat blank wall, revealing a window looking deep into a different world, a world of bright lights, full of colour and movement. A world which, although fictive, was so carefully constructed that for the duration of the program it could transport the audience into an alternative reality.

The tawdry magnificence of this antique and overblown façade made Jonno think of Roman coliseums where reality was subsumed by spectacle. Arenas wherein supermen fought for their lives against wild and exotic beasts, while audience members, safely removed from the action, looked down from elevated positions upon the mortal struggle as if they themselves were gods. It made him think of history and of the Victorian celebration of death so recently witnessed in the mausoleums of Highgate cemetery. Of a world where cinema had not long existed, where ornament was stationary and to be observed at leisure, not rushing past at 24 frames per second.

In its heyday it must have regularly seated upwards of five hundred people, but as they walked down the central aisle to join the few scattered groups towards the front, they merely swelled the numbers to about forty. As he passed, Jonno noticed a cat curled up on one of the seats. He wondered whether it had managed to fold it down itself or whether it was a broken one it regularly inhabited. He was reaching out to stroke it when Susie grabbed his arm. "Don't," she said. "It bites."

They shuffled into a row about a third of the way back from the screen, behind and to one side of all of the other movie goers. Their timing proved perfect, for just as Jonno settled in next to Susie the lights began to dim. Hamish, sitting to her left, took a cigarette packet and a lighter from his jeans, before taking what looked to Jonno suspiciously like a joint from the packet and placing it between his lips. He lit it just as the auditorium was plunged into darkness, and he was not alone, as numerous lighters were struck at the same instant.

"Christ," said Jonno, "do people smoke dope in here?"

"Sometimes. Depends on the film. We saw *Zabriskie Point* here a few months ago when the place was packed. Just breathing was enough to get you high."

"I can't afford to get busted again."

She reached for his hand. "You won't be, trust me. Have you got anything on you?"

"No."

"There you are then. If any cops do come just step on it and kick it away if you've got the joint. But it won't happen, just relax." So saying she handed on the joint which

Hamish passed to her. Up on the screen the adverts were over and the credits started to roll over an image of a dark sun seen through clouds casting a ring around it. Jonno inhaled a long drag as the rolling sound of brushed cymbals gradually built up, followed by weird organ noises weaving all around. It was a sound Jonno had listened to countless times since first hearing it three years previously, and he relaxed back into the worn and faded plush of his seat. He blew a great lungful of smoke up into the flickering beams of light which danced through the darkness over-head. He passed back the joint but kept his hand clasping Susie's where it lay on the wooden arm rest between them. On the screen the credits finished and a young man was standing by a road in a torrential downpour, hitching as traffic roared past him. Jonno thought of his journey south with Pete and looked up again into the flickering channels of light. As differing shapes were thrown upon the screen through the smoke that was curling upwards, individual beams moved about, intensified or faded, and seemed to flash off and on. Again, he thought of Pete, and of sitting in the Hayward Art Gallery, trying to watch several screens at once while a multi-layered history of Kinetic Art was played out in front of them.

As this film unfolded, he became more and more dis-satisfied with it. The protagonist arrived in Paris, played poker for money with a complete stranger, lost, yet was let off the debt in what was implied to be some kind of hippie camaraderie. The two of them then went to a party where the stranger ripped off the girl throwing it, while the protagonist fell for her in the kitchen, over the course of the most banal conversation ever to make it to film.

"What the fuck is this shit?" Jonno thought to himself at this point, "some kind of second-hand cinema verité bollocks or what?" The two characters on the screen used the stolen money to buy the plans for a house they then robbed, following which the hero returned the girl's cash, got shown by her how to smoke dope and then slept with her. At this point Jonno considered that he would normally have left the cinema, but stayed not just to hear the intermittent snatches of soundtrack, but mostly because of the young woman sitting to his left, and the warmth of her hand under his.

The film became more interesting when the action moved to Ibiza. The sun came out and the mise en scene improved. Not so the story, however. There was some kind of middle-aged, knife-throwing, ex-Nazi nightclub owner, who was a heroin dealer and had a Svengali-like hold over the girl. The pair of young lovers ripped him off, shacked up in a borrowed house where they smoked lots of dope, before she got him hooked on smack. They dropped some acid to get off it for a while, both got back into it again, and had arguments which lead to her returning to the Nazi, whereupon her lover overdosed and took the one-way trip to oblivion.

Once outside the cinema Jonno wasn't sure what to say when asked whether he'd enjoyed the film. Hamish and the other two men seemed to have been quite excited by it, particularly by the scene of two naked women together on a bed, so he restricted himself to saying that he thought Ibiza looked like a cool place, and that he would have enjoyed it more if the music had been more predominant. When pressed further he admitted to enjoying the acid sequence when the guy was tilting at the windmill, as was portrayed on the cover of the album, but thought that the Don Quixote reference was a rather heavy-handed way of pointing up the overall moral message. They looked at him in confusion for a moment before Angus asked "What message was that then?"

Susie was still holding his hand and frowning up at him. Through the course of the film the guy had slapped the woman's face on three occasions and each time her hand clutched his tightly on the arm rest. He saw the expression on her face and decided that she didn't want him to say too much until the two of them were on their own, and could discuss what they thought without the others looking on. So he made light of it, laughing and saying "Oh fairly obvious I thought - Don't Fuck with Drugs."

They all laughed at this as they were splitting up. The boys were returning to the pub, while Jonno and Susie were heading for the Notting Hill tube station. Hamish was the last to go through the door and just before he did, he turned back and shouted to them, "Of course another moral could be drawn: choose who you sleep with very carefully." At which he laughed, good-naturedly, before disappearing.

~ 14 ~

1970

The 'Happy House' as they called it, was in the middle of a street of identical terraced houses just off Tooting Broadway. It reminded Jonno of Pete's house back in Birkenhead, although these terraces were built of dirty yellow London bricks instead of the northern reds. The complement of two up and two down rooms was the same, with in this case the bathroom at the end of the downstairs hallway, surmounted by the kitchen opening off a half-landing partway up the dog-legged staircase. Similarly there was a bay window to one side of each front door and two windows up above. The window over the kitchen sink overlooked a scrubby back yard, similar to the ones on either side, and across to those at the back of the houses on neighbouring Plato Road. Jonno was pleased their house was in Socrates Street, which he considered to have more libertarian connotations.

As the finder of the property Pete took the larger front room upstairs with its two windows, Jonno contented with the downstairs front with the bay window. This he filled with a desk bought from a local second-hand shop, on which he placed his typewriter, and a little plastic battery-driven stereo with two tinny little speakers. The quality of the sound wasn't up to much, but it was all he could afford. He couldn't live without some kind of a sound system. Now he was earning he could afford to buy L.P. records. He hadn't lived in a house with a television since leaving home and didn't need one now, but music was very important to him. Of course the other thing he could afford, and something which immeasurably enhanced his listening pleasure, was marijuana, hash to be specific, grass being rare in Britain.

Nightly, on returning from the office, he would shrug off his working clothes, pull on jeans, tee-shirt, and one of his mother's hand knitted polo-neck jerseys. Then sit at his desk and roll the first joint of the day while listening to his latest acquisition. By the time the first side was over the joint would be rolled and he'd take it up to the kitchen to make tea for himself and an instant coffee for Pete.

When his employment at Morris and Reid's terminated, he returned to the Bureau and, satisfied with the reference he'd been provided with, they sent him on to a succession of other temporary assignments. During the run up to Christmas these mostly involved shop work, but once the desperate rush was over, he'd gained an ongoing temporary contract with Burmah-Castrol Oil. The firm was preparing to go over to the new-fangled computers to store their records. It was explained to him that before they could do this satisfactorily someone needed to go back through all of their old paper files and sort out any anomalies, of which there were a number. He was given his own office, high up in the multi-storey building on Marylebone Road, with a view over London to the west. While winter held, each late afternoon he watched the sun descend into a brown haze of pollution. It was ironic that his current employer was one of its main contributors.

Once settled in he found the work to be remarkably easy, which caused him to worry that his was a logical and methodical mind, rather than the wild and creative one he would have preferred. One whole wall of his office was taken up by giant grey metal cupboards which overflowed with folders containing the accounts of garages, workshops and engineering firms; all manner of businesses which relied on the firm's lubricating oils. On flimsy sheets of pink paper were the copies of monthly invoices sent out over years, recording the delivery of barrels of oil, as well as the settlements of accounts. All Jonno needed to do was wade through them, company by company and month by month, to pick up possible under- or over-payments for each of those barrels. When he stumbled across an anomaly, he would take the folder upstairs to his manager's office and show him the accounting error, for him to rectify and then get the information loaded into their new database. Every time the manager would be overjoyed and congratulate Jonno on his systematic approach and his diligence.

After a few days of such fulsome praise Jonno realised the work was a complete doddle and he relaxed somewhat, arriving late in the mornings and spending large amounts of time on the telephone. Eventually his tardiness meant he would find a steaming mug of coffee on his desk waiting for him, having missed the tea lady on her morning round.

Gradually others moved into the house with them. Kate took the downstairs room behind Jonno's, having responded to one of the adverts the boys placed in Oz and International Times. When she turned up to look at the place Jonno recognised her from the meditation meetings in the Notting Hill basement. She was the epitome of Hippie chic with her long flowing brown hair, which fell around her shoulders and nearly down to her waist, her equally long flowing skirts and dresses, and her waistcoat of brightly coloured crocheted squares. Jonno was surprised to find that she had never been outside of London. He always considered hippies to be country-loving people, and found it hard to comprehend how a person could reach the age of twenty without experiencing any green spaces larger than an urban park. London was so huge. Much as he was enjoying his current time 'up the smoke', he knew it was a youthful phase for him. That one day he would return to wide-open spaces, to rolling moorland, to woods and fields, to cliffs, and more importantly, to the sea.

A guy called Dave moved into the other upstairs room. He was a trainee accountant who hated his job, and came to be thought of as Sad Dave. He was a big man who always looked about to burst out of his ill-fitting suit. He started to shed his office clothing as soon as he walked through the front door, pulling off his jacket and tie as he mounted the stairs, throwing them into his room from the passageway, as if their very touch contaminated his soul, and kicking off his trousers once he'd closed the door behind him. Once in equally ill-fitting jeans and tee-shirt he would proceed to get off his face as quickly and as much as possible with whatever drugs were available. He would then take up his acoustic guitar and spend an hour or so serenading himself, playing contemporary folk-songs by the likes of Cat Stevens, John Martyn and, his favourite, Al Stewart. Having re-established what he considered his natural persona, he would emerge to make himself a coffee and join in any conversations which might be happening.

The kitchen was where most of the household interaction happened, either there or in Pete's somewhat larger room. Sometimes Jonno would carry his portable stereo up to Pete's and all four of them would sit around, smoking dope, talking and listening to albums. In the course of time other people turned up. Kate was in an intermittent relationship with someone called Paul, who would stay with her for a few days or a week, before disappearing again, no one, not even Kate, really knowing to where. After a few months Ann arrived from the frozen north and moved into

Pete's room, sleeping on a single mattress on the floor. It was unclear whether their relationship was a sexual one, Pete being very cagey on the subject, at times implying that it was, at other times acting as a kind of mentor, sending her out to have 'adventures' and debriefing her on her return. The two of them were very close, and shared secrets.

Sometime later Dave asked if anyone minded if a colleague from his work moved into his room for a while. Martin was an oddball and really didn't fit in. While the rest of them were confirmed dope-smokers Martin was heavily into politics and refrained. He was never seen in anything but his dark suit with a polyester shirt and a remarkably ugly tie. He was a member of the International Marxist Group and was out at political meetings a lot. This was fine with the rest of them, and Dave was quizzed as to how long he was expected to be staying.

"Just until he gets a place of his own," was the answer, so they put up with him but secretly hoped it would be soon.

When not fraternising with the others Jonno would be alone in his room, playing records, reading books and occasionally tapping away on his typewriter, trying to channel his mostly addled thoughts into something resembling verse. He was never very satisfied with his efforts and didn't share them with other members of the household. Pete spent time writing too, and was equally precious with his output. He used biro to write into a succession of notebooks which he stuffed underneath his mattress.

Occasionally Jonno returned to the commune in Putney, to spend a convivial evening catching up with the inmates, but also to score a little dope. Robert was happy to accommodate him from time to time with the odd quid deal, and would return to the privacy of his room to cut a piece off of whatever he was holding. But once Jonno was settled into the Oil Company job with a regular income he started wanting to buy larger amounts, quid deals no longer lasting more than a few days now their own house was filling up. Quarter ounces were more the order of the day and Robert was unwilling to part with such quantities.

"I'm not a dealer Jonno, and I've got no desire to become one. I've got some good contacts from my days at Oxford and I'm happy to supply the other members of this house, but I do it at cost, I don't make any money out of it. We all chip in, so it's communal, like most of the things going on here."

"I understand that. It's what makes this place so cool."

"It wasn't easy, it took a long time before it all settled down. People came and went quite a bit at first. With any group you get personality conflicts, jealousies, all sorts of shit. Unless you are really lucky it'll be the same at your place."

"Christ, I hope not."

"Remember the first day you showed up here. Henry described me as a sort of spiritual advisor."

"I rather think he said you describe yourself as such. He, on the other hand, in his inimitable fashion, described you as a supplier of nefarious substances."

"The point is that they pretty much come down to the same thing. If you want to play a similar role in your place, you're going to need a dealer."

"How do I find one? They can't exactly advertise, can they?"

"No, it's all done through contacts and friends of friends. Tell you what, give me your address and I'll see if one of my guys would be interested. He's a New Zealander called Paul. He usually sells halves or ounces but he might make an exception if you're going to turn into a regular. Which it sounds like you are. Has your place got a phone?"

"No."

"Could be difficult. Tell you what, he's coming round on Saturday night. If you come over, he can meet you and suss you out."

Which was how Jonno first made contact with Kiwi Paul, who gave him the address of his flat in South Kensington which he shared with his girlfriend and his sister. He told Jonno to call in any Friday on his way home from work, should he want anything. Paul reckoned he was always guaranteed to have some kind of hash, and fairly regularly tabs of acid too.

This news was greeted enthusiastically by Pete, who was wondering where he could get hold of some. Jonno wasn't so keen. It wasn't that he believed all of the scare stories promulgated by the sensationalist press; he couldn't see himself getting so out of it he would throw himself off a tall building believing he could fly, but he did worry it might disrupt the artistic impulse he was trying so hard to foster in himself.

"Quite the opposite," Pete assured him. "It'll free you up. Put you in touch with your subconscious. Get a tab and we'll split it in two. You wouldn't want to take it alone anyway, especially not the first time. It's always best to have a tripping partner who can get you out of a bad scene if you start having a bummer. I've done it quite a few times and I'll make sure nothing bad happens to you. Hey, we could go and see a movie. It'd be a good way of easing you into it."

There was a flea-pit cinema just around the corner on the high street, which at night showed Bollywood epics for the local Indian population, but on Saturday afternoons screened more art-house productions. Walking past it one evening, coming home from the tube, Jonno saw it would be showing *Women in Love* at the weekend. They had both seen it on first release but he was keen to see it again.

So, a pilgrimage was arranged. Pete took his responsibility for ensuring Jonno enjoyed a positive experience seriously. He insisted they have a light breakfast so there was no danger of a bloated feeling disturbing them later. Afterwards, in Pete's room, Jonno produced the tab he'd scored from Kiwi Paul the night before.

"He said it was Owsley acid, very pure, about 400 micrograms."

"Shit, that's strong," Pete said. "Still, it'll be good between the two of us. And if it really was cooked by Owsley, it should be really pure. Give us a true Haight-Ashbury experience."

The pill was a rounded oblong a little over half an inch long and a vibrant pink in colour.

"Someone's trying to say this is Strawberry Fields acid. Hell, who knows, maybe it is. Acid itself is colourless so you can make the tabs any colour you want."

"I guess if they'd used purple dye, they'd be selling it as Purple Haze," said Jonno.

"Oh they do. Whatever, this is a good size, much easier to split in half than the green microdots I used to get up home. We'll need the sharpest knife and the marble chopping board Kate uses for her bread making, so we don't miss any crumbs. Why don't you bring up the stereo while I go and get them?"

Pete sat on the edge of his bed with the slab of marble across his knees, placed the knife across the middle of the tablet and began a gentle rocking backwards and forwards motion on the top of it.

"It's really hard," he said. "I think you should cup your hands near each end of it in case shoots across the room."

Pete was right, when it finally broke in half each piece slid across the shiny surface of the grey marble and straight into the safety of Jonno's goalkeeping hands.

"Great, a clean break, no crumbs. Now let's get ourselves a cup of tea, drop this and put some music on while we're waiting. It usually takes about half an hour to start coming on."

The film was scheduled for an afternoon's performance, so they swallowed their tabs at about 1 p.m., then smoked a joint to ease themselves into lift off. As they were starting to fly, they set off up the road. The grimy London brick houses facing their own terrace looked two dimensional to Jonno, as if they were stage sets, façades with no substance. In the high street, giant red buses whizzed past, seemingly at a much greater speeds than usual, while angry little cars blasted their shrieking horns.

People too, looking harried as they hurried past, their faces taking on the characteristics of animals, scavenging creatures mostly, with elongated noses and shifty, darting eyes. Some even appeared to have predators' teeth as they scowled at the two hippies who were stumbling about and getting in their way.

The Indian gentleman in the ticket booth was no better, although his turban did spring an echo of the mystic east into Jonno's consciousness. His frown, as they struggled with their coinage, did not speak of a tranquil mind however. Rather that of a frustrated businessman who is not doing too well, faced with two idiots who couldn't even count their own currency. When they finally settled their transactions and placed the grubby maroon velvet curtains between them and the outside world they began to see why. They weren't anticipating huge crowds for a Saturday matinee, as the film had done the rounds of the major cinemas not so long before. It was an Oscar winner however, and one they thought the best English film for years, so they did expect a dedicated group of aficionados come to sit at the feet of the master. Not the eight or ten lone gentlemen scattered haphazardly throughout an auditorium capable of accommodating five hundred. Jonno reflected that Tooting High Street just wasn't ready for Art-House yet.

Thoroughly under the influence by now, it was impossible to tell how long the insane kaleidoscope of adverts played. Disjointed images flashed through Jonno's mind in an unpleasant confusion of brash colours and over-loud noise. Not knowing what to expect he was particularly worried about seeing hallucinations, of being scared by things not really there, as he occasionally felt on waking from twisted dreams. This was different though. Normal things became more intense, were seen from unusual angles, magnified or diminished as different neural pathways channelled the world into his mind. There was no sense of how long he had been sitting there, probably just a few minutes, although it could easily have been half an hour; things seemed to speed up or slow down at will.

"Shit, these tabs are strong," Pete said, as he leaned over in his seat.

"Mmmmmm," was all Jonno managed to reply. He was busy glancing around at everything in the auditorium, worried that things might start to dematerialise if he didn't keep them in focus. He avoided looking at the screen, whose violent images appeared to be grabbing for him, to suck him through the oblong into a place where he didn't wish to go. He noticed they were the only two patrons who sat next to each other, which struck him as odd, before the opening titles appeared and he turned to observe Lawrence's Edwardian world. There was a brief moment of self-consciousness, as he thought how similar the portrayal of the Brangwen sisters' walk through the dark alleys of their mining town was to his and Pete's progress to the cinema. Their exotically colourful clothes contrasted so starkly to the drab dress of the colliers and their grubby children. Then the girls were standing amongst the graves in a country church-yard, looking on at another contrasting life; the extravagance of an upper-class marriage. Jonno felt himself transported *into* Lawrence's England.

About halfway through the movie he started to feel uncomfortable, particularly around the area of his crotch. At first, he just put it down to the tightness of his purple velvet loon pants, and decided he would have to put up with it. The feeling steadily grew however, until he mentioned it to Pete, who suggested he might be wanting a piss. So, he extricated himself from the worn plush seat and made his way to the front of the auditorium. The door to the gents was right beneath the screen and he felt a tad uncomfortable advertising his need so obviously to the onlookers. Nevertheless, Pete was right, he needed relief, as the seemingly half-hour length of his flow attested. When finally it was over, he re-emerged to find Pete standing guard outside the toilet door waiting for him. "I thought I'd better make sure you were alright," he said as they returned to their seats. Looking up at the screen, Jonno saw they were just coming to the end of the scene where Oliver Reed and Alan Bates wrestle naked like two Greek athletes. He was entranced by the beauty of the flames which danced all over their sweat-soaked bodies, burnished gold by reflected light from the roaring log fire piled high in the ancestral grate.

"Oh my God," he thought, "The entire audience has just watched Pete waiting for me outside a toilet while the most homo-erotic scene in the history of western film played out above our heads."

"Don't worry about it," said Pete, when they finally regained the safety of Socrates Street, made themselves a cup of tea and smoked another joint. "Didn't you notice that the audience were all perverts? I reckon they mistook the title for an offering of a very different kind of fare." At which the pair of them fell about laughing. Over the next few hours, as the effects of the drug gradually wore off, Jonno decided how much he'd thoroughly enjoyed the experience.

Tripping became a regular thing for the two of them, mostly at weekends when the other members of the household were busy doing their own things. There was one incident when they nearly got themselves into trouble.

Martin had been going on for weeks about a forthcoming day of action organised by the Trade Union Movement. The dustmen had been on strike for weeks. The streets were littered with piles of uncollected refuse in plastic bags, many of them split or gnawed open by dogs and rats. Rubbish was being blown all over and there was a putrescent stink about the whole place. Martin was increasingly excited about the possibility of civil unrest, holding forth about an impending revolution. Pete and Jonno were dismissive, leading to a great deal of heated argument. Martin responded by quoting snippets of Karl Marx at them, as usual. They laughed at him as he was setting off for his demonstration, and he responded by telling them that when the revolution finally happened, anarchists like them would be the first to be stood up against a wall, and shot.

"You're dangerous. People like you, with no organisation and no concrete planning, will let the forces of reaction back in."

They dropped some acid and thought no more about it until the lights went out. It was a dingy overcast day and they weren't keen on tripping in the dark. Besides which they were wanting cups of tea. Pete looked into the fusebox while Jonno held a torch for him, all the time picturing his friend disappearing in a puff of blue smoke. Having worked out that the fuses were fine, they decided to go shopping for candles. The shops in the High Street were all in darkness and when they staggered into Woolworths they came across an angry crowd, ten deep, huddled around one of the counters, jostling each other and demanding to be served with candles. The stressed-out sales assistants were rationing them out at two per customer, and after they got theirs the two stoned hippies, who were by now well off their faces, looked at each other, raised clenched fists, and as one shouted "Martin!"

This was *it*. The revolution was happening. They ran from the store full of anarchic zeal. As they made their way back along streets strewn with festering rubbish they passed an abandoned building site, where a JCB was parked up beside a hole in the ground. A grin appeared on Pete's face.

"Let's liberate it," he said and leapt aboard. "We can drive it down the main street and crash it into a bank or something."

Jonno could see Pete was in the middle of some Eisensteinian fantasy, was keen to show that anarchists could strike a blow for the revolution too. Jonno was not so sure. Seizing the time was all very well as a slogan, but he knew they were both shit-faced and that it probably wasn't a good idea. Thankfully Pete had no idea how to start the behemoth, so after jumping around on it for a while desperately looking for a switch, or a key, or any button labelled 'Start', he climbed back down and they went back home, where Jonno boiled a saucepan full of water on the gas stove and made them both a cup of tea. When a crestfallen Martin arrived back later that day they didn't tell him about the adventures of the anarchist chapter of Socrates Street.

They did tell Kate though, who decided she should go to keep an eye on them when they next planned an outdoor adventure under the influence of acid. She had tripped numerous times, before giving it up to devote herself to meditation, and Jonno knew he would feel safer with her as a chaperone.

"There's a Kinetic Art exhibition at the Haywood Gallery," Pete said one evening.

"What's Kinetic Art, when it's at home?" Jonno queried.

"Buggered if I know. Stuff moving, I guess. Let's drop some acid on Saturday, and go and find out."

"You fancy it, Kate?" Jonno asked.

"Art Galleries are boring," she replied. "Where is it?"

"At the South Bank Centre," Pete informed her.

"Right by the river. Tell you what, I'll get you there, then go off for a wander, maybe cross over into town. How long do you think you'll be?" she asked.

"Who knows? Three hours, if it's any good. We could fix a time to meet you afterwards."

"Alright, let's do it, and I'll make sure you get home safely."

Jonno was relieved. He found travelling by tube unpleasant enough when he'd just smoked a couple of joints. The thought of trying to negotiate the underground system while off his face on acid was a daunting one. Pete laughed, but to Jonno the prospect of being cooped up in a carriage crammed full of strangers, whose faces might take on hideous masks at any moment, was not one he relished.

To avoid facing such a transformation the boys dropped their tabs just before leaving the house, Jonno thinking they would arrive at their destination before the full effects kicked in. He was wrong. As soon as they sat down, with Kate between them on the bench seat, the doors slid shut and the whoosh of the train shooting into the tunnel provoked a similar WHOOSH in Jonno's brain. He was launched on an ascending plane as if rocket propelled. He turned to Kate who could see the apprehension in his face so reached out to hold his hand. This was all he needed for his worries to dissipate. Suddenly he felt safe, like a little boy, like Christopher Robin being taken on an outing by Alice, to see the changing of the guards at Buckingham Palace. The A.A. Milne poem reverberated in his head and before he knew it they were getting off the train at Waterloo.

"That was intense," he told the others as they stumbled out into fresh air.

"You alright?" Pete asked.

"I am now, how about you?"

"It was pretty weird. I felt like I was in one of those tubes they used to have in shops to send money along the overhead wires. Every time we pulled into a station; I thought I was going to fall out onto the floor."

The building was all grey concrete and severe geometric lines. Jonno thought of the castles visited on Sunday family drives. Great forbidding structures like Launceston or Restormel, built by the Normans to keep the rebellious Cornish in order. Those were round however, their keeps perforated by arrow slits, and their tops broken up by crenelations. This building was severely stripped back. He could see no windows breaking up the façade, and no decorative embellishments at all. It was a perfect series of sharp right-angles, but it squatted on the earth with the same massive weight, the same brutal mass.

It engendered a sense of trepidation in him, the lack of colour somehow threatening, but they'd come this far and he was not going to let his friend down by refusing to go in. He turned to Kate and gave her a big hug.

"I'll be back here at 3 o'clock. You'll be fine," she said, and made her way towards the river.

"Come on, man," shouted Pete, who was already halfway up the steps.

In contrast to the forbidding exterior the inside was all colour and movement, and not just because of the exhibits. There was quite a crowd buzzing through the honeycomb of different rooms and temporary exhibition spaces. It being a Saturday most people were dressed casually, although there were some people in suits. Others looked more like old-fashioned beatniks in black polo-necked jumpers under elbow-patched sports jackets with drainpipe jeans. Jonno wondered if their pockets contained pipes and tobacco pouches, or maybe packets of Gitanes or Disque Bleu. Others were dressed as colourfully as Pete and himself, in bright paisley shirts and caftans, cheesecloth blouses and long flowing skirts, velvet loons or jeans covered in contrasting patches, dresses in Laura Ashley florals.

One such couple were holding hands and seemed to be staring closely at the wall, their noses almost touching it. Pete moved further off into the complex to explore, but Jonno wanted to know what so intrigued this couple, and stayed behind. They finally broke away, revealing an A3 sized Perspex panel let into the wall. Lit from behind it was gradually changing from one luminous colour to another from the bottom up, but so slowly that it was impossible to tell where red bled into orange and then into yellow, and on throughout the whole spectrum, before starting all over again.

Jonno found himself moving closer and closer to the screen in turn, the colours having some magnetic fascination drawing him in and holding him, for he knew not how long. A number exhibits utilized a similar technique, perhaps were all by the same artist. In another room he came upon what appeared to be two pairs of giant buttocks, a large and a smaller pair, moulded together into one plastic shape, beautifully smooth and rounded, which emerged from the floor. This sculpture was also lit from within and was going through another sequence of neon bright colours. Only this time, instead of drawing him in, as they changed hues the shapes appeared to grow bigger, flowing across the floor towards him, threatening to fill the whole of the little room. They looked more and more like the giant bums of Honeybunch Kaminski or Angel Food

McSpade; Robert Crumb cartoons familiar to him from Oz magazine. They just kept on swelling until he felt the need to retreat before being engulfed.

He came upon Pete in another room, playing with something which resembled a Heath Robinson machine crossed with one of M.C. Escher's impossible labyrinths. He was flicking steel balls down tracks until they knocked into a succession of barriers. This caused drawbridges to fall, which diverted the balls down alternative channels before landing in wheels which spun them off in further directions. They collided at times with other balls, bouncing off each other and bumping into spinning carousels which delivered them to further tracks. Occasionally they fell through holes into mesh baskets, to be lifted by the counter-balance of other balls at different stages of the race, and returned to the top of the slide, where they could start their journeys all over again. The whole thing looked to Jonno like a much more complicated version of one of the toys he had longed for as a child but never received.

Pete was laughing hysterically. There was a crowd standing around him waiting for a turn but none of the art-lovers was brave enough to shoulder the over-weight and crazed-looking hippie out of the way. When he noticed Jonno in the crowd he shouted out to him, "Look, look, a perpetual motion machine. Perpetuum Mobile. They said it was impossible but fuck thermodynamics."

To which one of the bystanders watching over it said, "It's a nice try but yet another glorious failure. You are acting as an energy source by flicking the ball out of the dimple at the top of the run. You can't beat the laws of thermodynamics. I should know, I built it."

At which Pete turned and reached out to shake his hand. "You're right, I was forgetting that. It makes a great toy though. It's bloody brilliant."

"My son thinks so. As would these other people if you gave them half a chance."

Pete turned and noticed the crowd for the first time. "Woops, sorry people, got a bit carried away. Just five more minutes then."

He turned back and flicked another ball down. Jonno was embarrassed by his friend's hogging of the exhibit so moved on into the next section. This room contained an artefact that was definitely scary. Something like a giant condom, standing upright about five feet high, was spinning at high speed in the centre of the room. Its thick plastic flapped madly except in those places where six-inch nails protruded from the demoniacally whirling structure. They looked to Jonno as if they could fly off at any moment, and he visualised a fountain of sharpened metal, whizzing up and around the room to rain down upon the onlookers, transforming them into so many pierced Saint Sebastians. From this room he ran.

He entered a darkened space with a feeling of overwhelming relief, for it proved to be a small cinema, and he sank onto one of its benches. Contained as it was within an art gallery, of course it was not a normal cinema. He realised

this as he looked towards the screen and attempted to deci-
pher what he was seeing. In fact there were eight separate
screens, each about the size of a television, and each showing a different picture in turn. Jonno's eyes leapt from one
screen to another, attempting to bring some kind of logical
connection to this mish-mash of images. Some of them he
seemed to recognise, while others were completely alien.
At first the changes were too quick for him, and merely
produced a sense of vertigo. The rods and cones of his eyes
were transferring more information from retina to optic
nerve, from nerve to thalamus and thence to his visual
cortex, before giving him a chance to understand what he
was seeing. By which time his eyes had flicked to another
screen and a whole new set of information was winging its
chemical/electrical way up the chain of his synapses.

Concentrating as much as his chemically enhanced mind
would allow, he came to see that the pictures were in fact
telling a story. A potted history of 20th century art was being unfolded, leading up to the development of the kinetic
works on display in the gallery behind him. In the spirit of
such an oeuvre, the story was leaping around from screen
to screen, rather than following a logical sequence on each
individual screen. An image at the top left might lead on
to one on the middle of the bottom row, then progress to
another somewhere on the right-hand side. It became a
game for him to try and sort out the various sequences. He
might see a painting by the Russian constructivist Male-
vich which would be supplanted by a Bridget Riley before

a Picasso collage took its place. He recognised mobiles by Alexander Calder, and shots of Duchamp's spinning bicycle wheel mounted upside down on a kitchen stool. He tried to withdraw his concentration from each of the individual screens, in an attempt to understand whatever underlying structure governed the choices of whoever spliced the images together.

After a while he managed to work out the patterns so that he could follow each individual sequence. He came to see that rather than eight separate films being shown concurrently, it was one film being shown eight times but split into different time sequences. So engrossed he became that when Pete arrived to tell him they should leave he had quite happily watched the whole film through on two occasions by shifting his focus from one screen to another. He was fascinated by the idea behind constructing such an art-work, and was wondering whether the technique could be attempted in a piece of literature, in order to overcome the imprisoning constrictions of a linear narrative.

As they descended the steps outside and made their way towards the figure of Kate leaning against the embankment in the distance, he tried to communicate this idea to his companion.

"Sounds a bit like Burroughs' idea of cutting up sentences and splicing them together to make new ones," said Pete.

"A bit, I suppose. But doesn't that depend on happy accidents, trying to reveal some kind of hidden universal mind, like the automatic writing the surrealists played around with. What I am talking about is a novel that leaps backwards and forwards in time, as if two stories are being told at once, but one of them ending where the other begins. Like those symbols of snakes eating their own tails"

"Sounds tricky," said Pete. "If it's too confusing the reader might give up, become bored halfway through."

~ 15 ~

1972

Having said their goodbyes, Jonno and Susie walked arm in arm down the Portobello Road without saying much to each other. When they reached the tube Jonno stopped her.

"Look, my place is not really very far from here, do you mind if we walk?"

She turned to him. "If it's about money I don't mind paying."

"No, it's not that. Or maybe it is a little – I'm not used to having women paying for my nights out."

"Male pride rears its ugly head. I'm working, you're not, so what's the problem?"

"It's not that, honestly. I don't know why I said it. I don't really have nights out with women. The concert the other night was the first time I've taken a woman out for ages. I just want to digest the film a little."

"You didn't enjoy it, did you?"

"The music was great, although it could have been louder, and a bit less in the background. I'm glad I saw it, and thanks for taking me, but no, I didn't really like it. It made me feel a bit depressed and I think it would be good to walk it off."

"Fair enough, let's walk and we can discuss it on the way. I'd like to know what you thought."

He turned and kissed her on the mouth briefly before they set off in the direction of Holland Park.

"We don't really know each other, do we?" he asked.

"No, we don't. And this would be a good way to find out more," she replied and then laughed. "That was the title of the film after all. I had misgivings too."

"When he slapped her," Jonno said.

"Three times," she said. "Totally unnecessary."

"I felt you jump each time."

"He was such a bastard. Alright, she was a bit of a bitch at times, but she was only being her own person, and he was trying to slap her back into line. Assert his dominance."

"Agreed. He was out of his depth so he resorted to force. A common male reaction unfortunately," he admitted.

"Far too bloody common. But that wasn't made you depressed, was it?"

"I didn't like it, I jumped as much as you when he slapped her but no, it fitted with the story the film was telling. It was the whole story I object to. I mean it was crass really wasn't it? Innocent young man falls for a more experienced woman who gets him stoned for what looked like the first time and then has sex with him. Afterwards she lures him away to a magic island in the sun where she gets him so hooked on drugs that he ends up killing himself. There was a bit of an overtone of the Odyssey, and the scene where he's tilting at the windmill referenced Don Quixote, but really it was a story that could have come straight out of The News of The World. A little moral fable, like I said to Angus – don't fuck with drugs."

"Hamish was right too, though – be careful who you sleep with," she added.

"Absolutely."

"So is this what you're doing, trying to be careful?"

"It's a bit late, I reckon. You've got me well and truly hooked, and we haven't even done it yet," he laughed. "Don't listen to me. I was just disappointed the film wasn't better. What I do know is that you are bloody gorgeous and I'm really glad you are coming home with me. That velvet dress of yours is so soft I'm finding it really difficult keeping my hands off you. In fact..." he stopped and swung around to clasp her in his arms, before reaching up to touch her face for a moment and then kissing her full on the lips. She responded by opening her mouth so he thrust his tongue inside and recommenced the age-old dance. She held him against her body and he ran his hands up and down her spine underneath her cloak. The driver of a car speeding down the tree-lined avenue gave a celebratory blast on his Colonel Bogie klaxon which made them jump apart and fall about laughing.

"How much further is it?" she asked, catching hold of his hand.

"Not far. About another five minutes."

"Well we'd better get going then, before I go off the boil."

"Oh. Do you think you might?"

"Not a ghost of a chance," she stated.

When they reached the green, she slipped off her shoes and strode off across the grass, with Jonno following behind.

"Be careful where you put your feet," he advised, "there's plenty of dogs around here, not to mention cats and urban foxes."

"Listen to the romantic poet. The princess would never put her foot into anything so nasty or unbecoming. And if by happenstance she should succumb to such a misadventure, then her knightly paramour would sweep her up into his manly arms and carry her off to his nearby castle, there to lave her feet with unguents. Now come here," as she leaned back against the trunk of a tree, "and enfold me in those aforesaid manly arms."

He gave a low growl before slipping back into his cod west-country accent and saying "You've been reading too many fairy stories m'lady. Don't you know that wolves, vampires and Ringwraith's comes out in the dark?" He leaned forward, grabbed her hips and gave her a pretend bite on the neck, before raising his head and kissing her again.

"Oh, oh, I swoon. Carry me off, fair sir to the safety of yonder castle before I am overcome by my emotions and expire here on the ground," was her response.

"My God, what have you been reading? That wasn't Tolkien."

"After the other night when you were going on about Tristan and Iseult, and how Sir Gawain came from my part of the world, I ducked into the library at lunchtime and got out a book about King Arthur. Impressed?"

"Very."

"Well a girl has to keep up, you know. Do you really get foxes here?"

"I've seen one a couple of times, slinking across the park. I guess they raid people's dustbins."

"Oh, that's not very romantic either. I've never seen a fox; we don't get them on the islands. Perhaps we'd better get indoors."

"Whatever you say m'lady. Would you like me to carry you?"

"I don't think that would be appropriate really, do you? Besides, I'd be afraid you might drop me. And I think you should conserve your strength."

"Whatever for?" he laughed.

"Oh, you never know when you might need it, do you? I wouldn't want to wear you out."

Inside the flat he put the kettle on and retrieved the little silver package from inside the tea caddy, then took it into the lounge where she was sitting on the sofa.

"Would you mind if I rolled it?" she asked as he peeled it open to reveal his remaining square of Paki black.

"No, go ahead."

At that she leaped up and kissed him quickly on the lips before giggling as she held it up in the air and twirled around three times. Now it was Jonno's turn to laugh.

"What?" he asked her.

"It's just you, Jonno. I just can't believe you. You've passed every single test I've set for you, without even realising that I was trying you out."

"Another test? What was this one?" He heard the kettle boiling so went to fix them tea as she shouted her answer through the open doorway.

"It never occurred to you I might not be able to roll a joint. The clan back at the flat never let me roll up. They've got this sort of inbuilt sense that it's man's work. Bloody hippies, they go on about being free all the time but most of them are as sexist as anyone."

"I hadn't thought about it before, but I guess you're right," he said as he carried in two mugs of tea and placed them on a couple of the paperbacks spread across the mirrored table top. "Back when I was living in Putney, I never saw Margo or Bea skin one up when the other blokes were around, but I know they did when they were alone. I walked in on both of them at one time or another. It's weird, isn't it?"

"It's pathetic is what it is. It's like my parents' generation, it's always the man who pours the drinks. No one questions it. It just seems natural to everyone the male is in charge of providing the pleasures, whether it be drugs or alcohol or, God help us, the sex. I mean, why is the guy always on top?"

"Umm, we've got stronger thighs, maybe?" he questioned.

"In short bursts possibly, but I doubt if many men could carry a few extra pounds around for a whole nine months."

"No, you've got me there. But I have to tell you I'm really looking forward to you being on top."

She stopped rolling the joint and reached for the cushion that was behind her, then swung it around in his direction, catching him in the back of the head.

"What was that for?" he enquired.

"You were taking the piss."

"I promise you I wasn't. Look, if I'm perfectly honest, I haven't slept with that many women, and never with one who wanted to be on top. I was just wondering what it would be like."

"Wow, really? That must have been quite difficult to admit. I find it hard to believe, except you seem so honest I have to. I mean you're smart, you're handsome and you're a big-time drug dealer. I would have thought you have a string of conquests behind you. So why not?"

"Don't know. Shy maybe. Smoking too much dope. It makes you second guess yourself all the time, makes you paranoid. I'm not saying that I'm a virgin or anything, but I've never thought of myself as handsome before."

"Really?"

"Really."

"Well let me tell you that you are. And, that as a public service and at great personal cost, I am more than happy to expand your horizons, just as soon as we've smoked this."

She held up the joint that she'd finished rolling, put it in his mouth and lit it. He took in a long drag before handing it back to her.

"Perfectly acceptable," he said, "considering that a woman rolled it."

"I should bloody well hope so," she replied, laughing. "Otherwise you're not getting it back. What record should I put on?"

"Anything except *More*."

"Why not? It's your favourite," she asked as she rifled through his collection, before putting *Déjà Vu* onto the turntable.

"Yes, that's better, much more uplifting altogether," as the strains of Steve Stills acoustic guitar flooded the room.

"Come on," she said. "There's something you're not telling me. It can't just be that you were disappointed with the story. What is it? Is it me? Am I coming on too strong? Are you worried that I am going to be some kind of femme fatale who will lead you away from the paths of righteousness?"

"No, nothing like that."

"You said before that we don't really know each other. Well I was completely upfront with you the other day, I told you my deepest, darkest secret and I have never done that before with anyone that I hardly know. It was bloody difficult, but I did it because I really do like you and I wanted you to really know who I am. I'm not looking for a lifetime commitment here, but for any kind of meaningful relationship we need to be honest with each other, don't you think?"

"Yes, I do."

"So what is it? What are you afraid of? What's your deepest regret?"

"Someone I was really close to turned into a junkie."

"Oh, I am so sorry. So the film reminded you of an old love affair? I can see that must have been really difficult."

"We weren't lovers, at least, I wasn't."

"She loved you but you didn't feel the same? That's got to be really tough."

"It was a bloke."

"Oh shit. Don't tell me you go both ways?"

"I don't. That might have been part of the problem."

"He wanted you but you didn't? So he got himself hooked? That's kind of romantic."

"Tragic maybe. But not romantic, not to me. It's just a stupid bloody waste."

"Do you want to talk about it?"

"Nothing to tell. We were best mates. Soul-mates maybe. I'd never met anyone like him, we connected on so many levels, were interested in the same things, you know; art, literature, all that, films, music, and smoking dope of course. But I guess I'm fairly straight, whereas Pete's right out there, right on the edge. I didn't realise he was gay at first, he said he wasn't when we met. I'm not certain but I reckon he is, and that was partly to blame for our bust-up. Where he came from, it wouldn't have been acceptable, and I guess he'd always had to push against boundaries. So he just kept on pushing. Heroin was just one more boundary that he decided to cross."

"So you needn't feel guilty."

"I don't, not really. I think William Burroughs was more to blame than I was."

"Who's he?"

"An experimental novelist. Very experimental. Wrote a book called *The Naked Lunch.* He's gay and a junkie. Pete was right into him, read everything he wrote and wanted to emulate him, I think. So when heroin became available, he dived right in. But it was disgusting, he was going to destroy himself. I hated it. I didn't know how to stop him and I couldn't bear to watch. So I left."

"You were sharing a place?"

"There were a few of us. It was really great at first, our own little commune. Dave was there too. But when smack arrived it all started to change. Ask Dave about it, he left soon after I did. The whole vibe changed. Smack addicts aren't hippies. They're something else. They give up caring. About anything. Except the next hit. Like I said, tragic."

"Like in the movie," Susie almost whispered.

"Yes, just like in the movie, that last bit where he ODs, that's going to happen to Pete one day. Or he'll throw up in his sleep and drown in his own vomit. So fucking sad."

"I'm sorry I put you through it."

"You weren't to know about Pete, and neither of us knew about the movie. I love the music. I thought it was going to be a celebration of the lifestyle, not some moralistic, cheap bloody fairy tale."

"So how do we get out of this?" she asked.

"Easy. By putting it behind us. You told me yours, now I've told you mine, and I do feel better for it, believe me. So, now we both know, no more big secrets."

"We still have pasts though, don't we?"

"Sure, but they're done. We can't know the future, but the present is looking pretty good to me. My whole life feels like it's balanced on a pivot. Right now, anything could happen. I'm in my flat with a woman whom I really fancy, and she says she fancies me. There's a bed in there that I put a clean sheet and duvet cover on this morning. Why don't you roll another of your female joints and we'll take it to bed with us, have our own little celebration of life. The dress you're wearing is exquisite, but I have to say that ever since I saw you in the pub tonight, I have been wondering what you might look like without it."

Returning into the spirit of their earlier banter she replied with, "And I, for one, feel an overwhelming need to check the manliness of those arms. Not to mention the quality and strength of the thighs."

"May I remind you that certain promises have been made with regards to the expansion of a person's horizons?"

"Oh, sod the bloody joint. We'll take the dope with us. Lead the way, fair sir. I assure you I take my commitment to public service very seriously."

Having entered his bedroom she stood looking about her for a few moments, quickly scanning the bed-side bookshelves, the desk by the window with his little travel typewriter and a mess of papers, the fitted wardrobe with the mirror door, and the double mattress, its duvet covered in a Laura Ashley print of purple birds on a light brown background. The pillows looked plump and inviting.

"This looks really nice," she said. "Clean too. Were you expecting visitors?"

"I was rather. Hoping anyway. And I was a boy scout when I was at school."

"So you've got some condoms stashed by the bed-side?"

He nodded, surprised. It was not what he had been meaning.

"Well, you're not going to need them."

"I can't get over have forthright you are all the time."

"You don't like?"

"I love it. I'm just not used to it. Like I said, I'm not very experienced at talking to women, particularly ones I really fancy. But you make me feel I could tell you anything."

"You can." She turned her back to him. "But now I want you to unzip my dress. There's a little hook at the top," and she pulled her red-gold tresses away from the nape of her neck.

He leaned forward and kissed her neck just above the back of her satin choker, before undoing the clip and very slowly lowering the zip. Inch by inch her back was revealed to him, her shoulder blades and the line of vertebrae between them, which disappeared to form the elegant hollow that curved in to her waist, before swelling again towards the rise of her buttocks. Entranced, he watched her shoulder blades moving as she reached up to unfasten the choker. Her back looked so beautiful to him and he placed his hands upon her shoulders, before stroking them slowly downwards until he reached the edge of the black knickers revealed to him. Then he turned each hand so his fingers faced outwards and they retraced the journey, upwards this time, his thumbs pressing hard onto her spine and his palms massaging the muscles on either side. They rested on each of her shoulder blades for a moment before he rotated his wrists once more so that both sets of finger-tips could trace her vertebrae as he stroked back downwards, pressing his finger-tips deep into the hollow that so fascinated him.

As he moved his hands over her back the sides of her dress gaped ever wider and now, as he moved upwards, he slipped the sleeves off her shoulders and onto her upper arms. She groaned, before moving away from him to slide them down past her wrists, shuffling the dress over her hips, to fall to the floor. She bent to retrieve it and hang it on the back of the chair at his desk. He watched her every move while quickly attempting to divest himself of his own clothes. The shirt gone, he sat on the bed to remove his socks, then stood again to pull down his jeans and pants in one move.

"You have a particularly fine back," he said as he watched her carefully folding her 'singing' dress.

She turned. "And the front?" she enquired.

"Exquisite." He moved to her, bent and kissed each of the nipples on her smallish breasts before wrapping her in his arms and kissing her mouth, using his tongue to part her lips and slip inside. They lay on the bed and hugged and kissed each other again and again and traced their fingers up and down each other's skin. She lifted her hips as he slid the knickers down her legs and off. She threw one of her legs over him so that she straddled his thighs. She looked into his eyes and smiled.

"Now, about that promise," she said, as she reached for his erection before gradually sliding herself down upon it.

Like young and first-time lovers do, they spent most of Sunday in bed, emerging once to have lunch at the local pub, which Susie paid for. They had been learning not only about each other's minds but about their bodies as well. For Jonno it had been quite an education, as Susie had shown him exactly how to pleasure her.

"You don't know much, do you?"

"I didn't have any sisters and I went to an all-male school. My mother might have taught me that women are people too, but I don't think I ever heard her say the word vagina, and there was never any mention of a clitoris. She had a hysterectomy when I was about eight or nine but I was far too young to have any idea what that was about, just that 'Mummy was going into hospital to have her insides fixed.' I thought it was something like the appendix operation I'd had."

"So that's what the scar is."

"Not pretty, is it? You can still see where the stitches were."

"There are worse scars. Not all of them visible. Anyway, you're not alone. There are plenty of men, women too, who don't know about clitorises. Or should that be clitorii Mr. Writer?"

"Don't ask me, I failed Latin 'O' Level. How come women don't know, if you've all got one?"

"Because we don't look, it's 'dirty' down there, and we're taught not to touch. Surely, it's the same for boys, masturbation is a terrible sin."

"Oh yes, there's this cryptic line in *Scouting for Boys*, 'Don't make a mess in your sleeping bag.' It took me quite a while before I realised what Baden-Powell was on about. By which time all the boys in my troupe were wanking on a regular basis. I learned how to do it at a scout camp on the Isle of Wight. Six of us sleeping in a bell-tent. A couple of them were going at it like crazy, so of course all of us were curious and by the time we fell asleep we'd all been introduced to the pleasures of the flesh. Not together, I hasten to add. The Curse of Onan was sinful enough. By the time the camp was over we were all fully paid-up sinners, and more than happy to have had our first nibble at the apple. How did you find out about it?"

"I think we all come across it naturally at some time or other, without really knowing what's going on. I learned about it properly at this consciousness raising group I joined after my abortion. I was in a woman's refuge for a while because my second boyfriend got a bit handy with his fists once I'd told him about it. That's why I told you when we'd just met. To see how you'd react."

"Another test."

"Anyway this woman's group. One day the leader got us all to look at ourselves 'down there' and sort of explained the mechanics of it all. God, it was weird. I was the youngest, and terrified that all the rest of them were rampant lesbians, about to have a go at me. So stupid. Of course they weren't, lesbians would have known all about it already. So we're all sitting around, some married women, some divorced, some of them middle-aged even, and the leader hands out a bunch of mirrors and told us to pull our skirts up and knickers off and have a good long look at ourselves. So embarrassing. But then we all started cracking up as she was explaining all of 'the ins and outs' as she put it. So funny. And of all of us, none of us had ever really looked at ourselves before."

"Bloody hell."

"Have you ever?"

"What, really looked, at a woman's...between a woman's legs? No, I can't say I have. Not intimately. Just worried about, you know, getting the aim right."

"Do you want too?" she enquired, "Or would it gross you out?"

"Um, no, I suppose I should."

"You don't sound overly enthusiastic. You don't have too if you don't want."

"No. I'm just a bit shy, I suppose, nervous maybe. Nobody has 'made me an offer I couldn't refuse' before."

"Well then, welcome to the Susie MacDonald Institute of Higher Learning," she said as she threw back the duvet and opened her legs. Wide. Jonno got between them, his head between her upper thighs, looking up. Susie trailed a finger down and opened the lips of her vagina, before moving further up and stroking herself a little.

Jonno was well outside of his comfort zone by now, gazing upon this previously undiscovered country. Possibly as some kind of defence mechanism he did as he always did with new experiences, and related it back to something he'd read. He was as turned on now as when he'd encountered *Lady Chatterley's Lover* at the age of sixteen. He thought of the scene where Mellors was threading violets, or maybe it was forget-me-nots into Lady Constance's pubic hair. He started to blow on the moisture he could see seeping onto the lips in front of him. Susie groaned, and then in a tremulous voice which he could only just hear said,

"If you used your tongue just now, I would probably go off like a cross between a Catherine Wheel and a Jumping Jack."

So he did, and so did she, thrashing about and squeezing his head between her thighs. When her convulsions quieted, he moved up and entered her once again. Susie started to moan in a language that he didn't understand but imagined to be Gaelic. He might not have known the words but passion's tongue is universal and shortly he joined the conversation.

~ 16 ~

1971

The last of Burmah-Castrol's files were reconciled and Jonno's temporary employment came to a close. Instead, he secured a permanent position in the research grants section of Imperial College. This made scoring easier since Kiwi Paul's South Kensington flat was just a few streets away. Sometimes Jonno called round there in his lunch break, which made for an interesting afternoon. It also improved his take home pay, not having to give a cut to an agency. This meant he could afford to buy in larger quantities. As favours he even began to sell on a little to friends.

Time passed, and the house settled. Kate finally succumbed to Jonno's attempts at seduction, but more as a reward for his persistence than because she was overwhelmed by desire. Indeed, the more she meditated the more desire slipped away from her. Jonno enjoyed a blissful week returning from work each evening to share her body and her bed, but at the end of it she brought their intimacy to a close, and he returned to his own room. For some time she'd been contemplating relocating to an ashram in India, to sit at the feet of a master reputed to be little more than a child, and sex with Jonno was too much of a complication.

Pete was still signing on the dole but seemed to have grown more affluent than before. Ann still occupied a mattress on the floor of his room. Dave's guitar playing improved. Martin moved on, once Pete freaked him out.

They were all relieved when Martin departed, although Jonno felt sick about how Pete engineered it. By now even Dave thought his work colleague was a self-righteous prig, and agreed that if not a Marxist he would probably have been the elder of some joyless, fundamentalist sect.

One day, unknown to anyone else, Pete slipped a quarter tab of acid into the mug of tea he gave to Martin who, a little later, began to feel slightly odd and lay down on Ann's mattress. He was still there when Jonno came home and took his stereo upstairs to play Pete his latest acquisition. *An Electric Storm* by White Noise was an obscure, heavy duty psychedelic album he'd heard John Peel play on the radio. The band were three experimental sound engineers who created it using numerous overdubs on basic tape recorders. One of them, Delia Derbyshire, worked at the BBC radiophonic workshop and had created the alien-sounding Doctor Who theme, based on Ron Grainer's music. *An Electric Storm* was considerably more confronting.

Martin weathered the first side of the album reasonably well, but when Jonno flipped it over doubts began to assail, and then to undermine him. There were only two tracks. The first, *Visitation*, was an eerie looping of gothic voices; a mish-mash of a screaming motor-cycle crash, a crying girl-friend, and the rider's mournful voice supposedly reaching out to her from beyond the grave. By the end of the track Martin was sweating from every pore. The final track finished him off. He was completely psychically unprepared for the demonic frenzy of *Black Mass: An Electric Storm in Hell*. He fled the room, and then the house, with sad Dave running after him to make sure he didn't do himself a damage leaping about amongst the traffic. Martin never returned. Dave took his stuff to work the following Monday and the doors of Socrates Street were never darkened by him again.

After the incident Jonno didn't spend so much time in Pete's company. He decided he'd dropped enough acid. It had graphically demonstrated to him that so-called reality was constructed by habits of thinking, and that there was a whole other way of perceiving the world. But, in the wake of Martin's similar, if unkindly forced epiphany, he came to see the drug as potentially dangerous to his psyche. He was still aspiring to become a poet, and worried about the effect chemicals might be having.

It certainly wasn't helping his powers of description. After the euphoria of the first few trips, attempts to put into words exactly what he experienced failed miserably. A transcendental experience is just that; it rises above the quotidian world, of which language is not only a constituent part, but fundamentally its creator.

To Jonno's mind the poet's job was rendering the ineffable into words capable of being appreciated by others. To be able to reach into the fountainhead of poetic experience by merely swallowing a pill was beginning to seem like cheating.

The decision to stop exacerbated a widening rift with Pete, who was disappointed to be losing his partner in chemical adventuring. It was a path he was determined to continue journeying down himself and tried his hardest to convince Jonno to accompany him. When unsuccessful he became bitter.

"You're just a hopeless bloody romantic," Pete called him, flatly refusing to listen to Jonno's attempts to explain his decision and walking away from him.

"So what if I am," an angered Jonno shouted after his departing back. "At least I'm trying to create something worthwhile, not just lying around all day on the dole, thinking great thoughts but doing nothing with them."

Since Jonno had started dealing dope in his small, part-time way, he was beginning to feel a little resentful of Pete happily smoking a substantial amount of his profits without offering anything by way of contribution. He went into the business as a way of subsidising his own consumption of hashish, and also as a favour to a number of the friends he was making beyond the confines of the little house. The south London two-up and two-down terrace was beginning to feel increasingly claustrophobic. He was also pissed off he was the only occupant who spent any time trying to keep the place clean and tidy. He particularly resented Pete's suggestion he was becoming bourgeois.

The stately, if somewhat faded grandeur of Kiwi Paul's flat, with its high ceilings, Georgian windows and large, white and airy rooms increasingly appealed to him. He didn't consider himself bourgeois, merely objected to living in the increasing squalor he saw around him. Moreover his daily commute to and from South Kensington was beginning to feel onerous, and the dingy carriages of the Northern line left him feeling exhausted and dirty when he returned home of an evening.

Jonno was spending more time around at Kiwi Paul's, and at weekends would often visit the commune in Putney. Now he'd secured his own supply of dope he was no longer sponging, but rather was able to repay the kindness shown him when he first arrived in London. The peaceful atmosphere pervading their house was in sharp contrast to the growing tension he felt at his own place. Margo in particular welcomed him with open arms and persuaded him to return occasionally to the Notting Hill basement to listen to sat-sang. Although he was in no way likely to become a convert like Kate, who was usually there in preparation for her impending departure to India, spending time amongst people with spiritual aspirations made him feel more at ease with himself.

It was also good to reacquaint himself with Henry, whose band was going from strength to strength. They were on the verge of signing a recording contract and were busily trying to get material together. Henry reiterated his invitation for Jonno to sit in on some of their rehearsals, and consider writing them some lyrics.

A further break with Pete occurred one Saturday morning after a strange man knocked on their door. Jonno was lying on his bed, reading Herman Hesse's *The Glass Bead Game.* He was a big fan of Hesse's work and had been so excited to return home the previous evening with a newly purchased copy of the author's masterwork. He made elaborate preparations for what he proposed to be an uninterrupted Friday evening of reading. Having placed the book on his desk he changed clothes, made himself a mug of tea, rolled and lit himself a joint and put Neil Young on his stereo before opening the fly leaf.

Unfortunately he overdid the strength of the joint. By the time he reached the bottom of the first page, he realised he hadn't taken in a single one of the words dancing about on the paper. He tried again with the same result. "Bugger" he thought to himself "so much for building up expectations." He closed the book and gazed at the cover, a stylized portrait of six scribes sitting at a desk in a medieval scriptorium. Frustrated, he went to see if Kate wanted company on her now nightly trip to Notting Hill.

The following morning he refrained from smoking a joint on awakening, but rather settled down for an extended communion with one of his current favourite authors. He was well into the second chapter when the knock came. At first, he ignored it, but when it became clear he was alone in the house, he arose to answer the repeated knocking. A small man with a squashed in face and very little neck stood there wearing a brown coat which looked to be made out of some kind of imitation animal skin.

"Is this where Peter Kelly lives?" he asked.

"Yes, but he's not in at the moment. Can I help you?"

"Are you Jonno?"

"Yes, why?"

"Peter has told me you are a good friend of his. I've got a package for him. It's the latest piece of his that I've published, plus a little something by way of payment. Can you see he gets it?" So saying the squat little man reached inside his coat and withdrew a largish envelope which was tucked into the waistband of his trousers.

"Sure," Jonno said and took it, anxious to get rid of the unpleasant looking stranger and get back to Herman. Once back in his room he was overcome by curiosity. He was used to catching Pete scribbling away into a note book, only to see him burying it quickly under his bedclothes. Whenever he asked what he was working on he was always given evasive answers.

"Oh, just some notes I've been jotting down. Nothing serious. Sort of cut-up experiments, like William Burroughs'."

Jonno couldn't resist. If Pete was getting stuff published, he wanted to see it. The envelope wasn't sealed and he up-ended it over his desk. The small magazine which fell out was about the same size as the literary journals that Jonno regularly borrowed from the library. There was nothing literary about this one, however. Under the title *True Confessions* there was a pen and ink drawing of a woman in torn underwear, her wrists tied to a brass bedstead, being approached by a couple of shadowy figures. The five stories listed on the contents page were all credited with women's names. He assumed Petra Kelly to be Pete, so turned to that one. A folded square of paper fell out. Jonno sat at his desk and started to read the story. It was written from a young woman's point of view about accepting a lift home from her teacher training college by a group of male students. She was squeezed in between two of them on the back seat of the car. She was wearing a mini skirt which gradually rode up through the friction of her neighbours' thighs. The men started laughing and joking, making sexual innuendos and trying to get her to join in with some sexual 'horseplay', as they described it. The man in the front seat turned around and thrust his hand up between her thighs. When she resisted their molestation, they became more forceful, until finally they drove to a park where they raped her. What particularly sickened Jonno was the woman's guilty admission once it was all over and they had left, that secretly she had been turned on by the whole experience.

"Jesus, Pete!" he exclaimed aloud as he shut the magazine in disgust.

Jonno unfolded the square of paper to find it contained a small amount of an off-white powder. So this was the bloke's 'little something', presumably either cocaine or heroin, Jonno didn't know which, never having seen either before. He replaced it next to the story and put the magazine back into the envelope. If this was what his friend was into now, he didn't want any part of it, and determined to have it out with him as soon as he returned.

He didn't get the chance, however. Pete and Ann came rushing into the house, laughing uproariously. They slammed shut the front door, as if being pursued by all the hounds of hell, and fell upon Jonno's bed, wheezing and trying to catch their breaths, before bursting out into another fit of giggles.

"Fuck, that was funny," Pete said once finally catching his breath.

"It nearly wasn't," Ann corrected him.

"No, it nearly wasn't," he agreed. "And now we've lost the damn card so we won't be able to do it again."

"I could apply for another one."

"You probably should, otherwise they might suspect you. But we shouldn't try it again for a long time."

"What are you two on about?" Jonno asked.

Apparently, Ann had applied for, and been granted one of the new bankcards which allowed for a £50 withdrawal at any of her bank's branches. She then phoned to report her card stolen, while Pete travelled from branch to branch to make withdrawals. It worked twice. On the third occasion the teller took the card and said he would have to check something. Stoned, Pete knew he was in danger, and would happily have cancelled the transaction and asked for the card back, but realised how stupid this would sound. He waited for what seemed like an eternity for the teller to return. Reflected in the security screen he saw a man closing in on him from behind. Guessing he was a security guard Pete swiftly elbowed him in the stomach, then whipped around and threw an uppercut into the bent over man's jaw. He raced out of the bank, and met up with Ann around the corner. Then they pretty much ran all the way home, and were now laughing themselves silly re-living the whole affair.

Jonno was not so amused. Although he held no brief for the bank, reputed to have close links with the white supremacist regimes of South Africa and Rhodesia, he frowned on Pete's use of violence. He was seeing a new side to the young carefree hippie with whom he'd travelled to the north of England. He was turning harder, becoming more self-centred and Jonno didn't like it. Martin being spiked with acid he thought a really underhanded action. Now this. He decided that rather than confronting him with the magazine he would wait to see what Pete said about it.

Which, as it turned out, was nothing. Jonno picked the envelope off his desk and held it out.

"Some bloke brought this around for you," he said.

"Did you open it?" Pete asked.

"Of course not," Jonno lied.

"Good," was all Pete said, and pulling Ann to her feet added, "Come on princess, let's go see what the nice man has given us, and leave the closet intellectual to his new book."

Jonno didn't take kindly to being referred to as a closet intellectual but said nothing which might prolong their stay. He listened as their footsteps climbed the stairs, and wondered what they were about to get up to with the packet of off-white powder. If it was what he thought, he considered it might be time for him to be moving on.

~ 17 ~

1972

When Susie turned up at Jonno's flat the following Friday after work, she carried a small suitcase. He jumped when he heard the knocking at the garden door, even though he was expecting her. He'd not long returned from the police station, signing his name in the ledger that a doleful sergeant slapped down in front of him. All that week he'd been worrying about being visited by the drug squad, thinking by now they might have learned he was off the customs department's hook. He was hyper-aware of any movements in the rest of the house. Footsteps on the stairs, or the front door opening and closing had him carrying the dwindling remains of his quarter ounce into the toilet to stand over the bowl until the noises ceased.

Much as the pair of them were tempted to ring each other up every day of the previous week, they had decided not to risk it. Mid way through the week they shared a few hours together round at Dave and Mel's place, but the embarrassment they both felt at their frustrations made for a tense evening. Any new couple needs to spend time alone together before they become comfortable in the company of others.

After that stilted atmosphere Jonno was apprehensive about how they would be together over this, their second weekend together. He shouldn't have worried. Susie strode into his bedroom, flung open her suitcase and carefully withdrew the purple velvet dress folded inside it. She doubled up a couple of his shirts and used the emptied hanger. She turned to him,

"I hope you don't mind. I've got a gig tomorrow night and I didn't want to have to go home for it."

"Of course not." Jonno, having been on tenterhooks all day waiting for her arrival, was hardly likely to object to her invading his privacy. "Please, help yourself to anything you need."

"I thought you might say that," she laughed, and began to unbutton her blouse. He moved towards her. "But not you, right now. This is not an invitation. I've been sitting in a sweaty office all day, being leered at by my creepy boss who, when he saw the suitcase, kept making remarks about going to Brighton for a dirty weekend. Like it was an invitation. I need to step into your shower and wash his glances off me. Then I'll need a cup of tea and a joint if you've managed to save any, and then we can talk. I come bearing messages from the Hairy One. And this..." as she reached into the suitcase and handed him an envelope.

"What's this?"

"Hamish said it was a deposit. To show good faith. Mind you, if the gear's all gone, he'll have it back, thank you very much."

"Fair enough," Jonno said as he ripped open the envelope and counted one hundred pounds in ten-pound notes.

"He said he'd be able to shift one of your weights on his own. The others might take a bit longer, but he'll ask around."

"That's fine. It's good of him to help out like this. He's not going to be keeping it all at your place, is he?"

"I have no idea. Nor do I wish to."

"Sorry, force of habit, I guess. I shouldn't pry. Whatever he does is fine by me, just as long as they can't be traced back to me. Or to you, that's what I worry about."

"You don't understand about Scottish clans either, do you? The boys would never let that happen. Now, stand aside, kind sir, and allow the lady some private time."

Jonno made the tea and was half-way through rolling a joint when she joined him on the couch in his living room, having changed from her work gear into jeans over which she had donned one of his denim shirts.

"You don't mind, do you?"

"Listen, woman, going on past experiences I don't think I'm going to mind anything you do. Plus the shirt is going to smell of you which will help me get through next week, if I don't get to see you again for a while."

"Yes, last week was difficult, wasn't it? We should talk about it later. But first, fire that up while I choose some music."

So, to the strains of Carlos Santana's wailing guitar they proceeded to get stoned, which led to a prolonged bout of tongue dancing. As he started to reach for the pearl buttons on the shirt, she stopped him.

"Down boy, time for that later. So, what's the plan?"

"That *was* the plan. But there's always plan B. I'm nothing if not flexible. I've been living off beans on toast for long enough. How about we take some of my new found wealth around to the Indian restaurant and have ourselves a slap-up dinner. You do like curries, don't you?"

"Love them. And I'm starving, I only had a sandwich for lunch. Then we could come back and, if you played your cards right, I might just let you re-instate plan A."

"I'll try hard not to bolt my food."

While sitting at a table in the Taj Mahal, with its red flock wallpaper, it's almost luminous painting of Krishna serenading the cowherd maidens, and a recording of Ravi Shankar playing a raga softly in the background, they discussed their plans for the weekend.

"I'll have to go up to Highgate cemetery, grab the gear and take it round to Hamish. You're welcome to come with me, but if you'd rather not I'll understand."

"Oh a cemetery, you do know how to treat a girl right."

"You might like it, it's a pretty amazing place."

"Only joking. Of course I'll come with you. Besides, I want to see the look on Hamish's face when you deliver it. I don't suppose he's ever seen so much..." here she lowered her voice to a whisper, "dope in one place before. We'll have to come back to your place for tea because I've got a gig at the folk club and I'll need to change. Are you going to come and watch me? Dave and Mel will be there."

"Of course I'm going to come."

By this time the waiter started delivering bowls of food to their table, as well as plates of poppadums, dishes of raitas and a couple of glasses of lager. Conversation ceased as Jonno devoured the first full meal he had eaten all week. Susie was not exactly picking at her food either, and when they finally cleared every plate and bowl on the table, satiated, they left the restaurant and staggered back to his flat to indulge themselves in further pleasures of the flesh.

The following morning, bright and early, saw the two of them walking hand in hand towards the tube station, Jonno with his trusty old holdall slung over one shoulder which again was packed with some of his dirty laundry. Just over an hour later they stood outside the gate at the top of Swain's Lane. Jonno lifted the latch and they made their way inside. Almost at once what little traffic noise they'd previously heard seemed absorbed by the high walls. Were it not for the profusion of cracked and tottering gravestones, they would have thought themselves walking through some enchanted forest. Angels peered out at them from behind ivy draped tree-trunks. Their footfalls were muted by a carpet of fallen leaves which lay rotting on the ground. Shortly they came upon a fork in the path where Susie stopped and looked all about herself at the rampant greenery, and at the abundance of broken and lichen covered statuary.

"Last night when you were telling me about the grave you needed to find you said I looked a bit like Lizzie Siddal," she said.

"Just a little. It's your hair, it's the same colour and almost as long. Your mouth is different though, wider. In the paintings her mouth always looks a little pinched. Your nose is fuller too."

"Are you saying that I've got a big nose?" She punched his arm lightly.

Jonno laughed, "No, not at all, I love your nose, hers always looks too sharp to me."

"I'm a little sensitive about my nose."

"It's a lovely nose. And your face is beautiful. You are beautiful, like she was, but in a different way. Your cheekbones are similar and the colour of your hair, that's all I was saying."

"Good. But this place is creepy enough as it is. It's lovely and peaceful, but it's creepy. I don't think I ought to see her grave."

"Fair enough. Just go for a walk around, it's a fascinating place. You'll be alright on your own, won't you? If you need me just shout, I'm bound to hear it. Tell you what, if you go up that way, you'll find this amazing ring of catacombs with an enormous cedar of Lebanon on the top. I won't be long, then I'll come up there and find you, alright?"

"Sure. It's not I'm scared of ghosts or anything, it just feels so weird." He held her face in his hands for a moment before kissing her, and then moving off down the left-hand path.

It was less than a fortnight since his last surreptitious visit. Nevertheless it took him some time to locate the Rossetti family plot, since it was a little off one of the paths. He was looking for a particular ash tree that he'd made note of as a marker. The trouble was that there were so many of them and several times he mistook one for another. Finally he came upon the one he was seeking and he stepped into the undergrowth, being careful not to step on some long-dead occupant's final resting place. He recognised the headstone of Rossetti's father Gabriele, sur-mounted by a four-leaved clover which was inscribed with the three intertwined letters IHS. To the right of the plot was the chest tomb that he had once lain upon to indulge himself in fanciful dreams.

He knelt down and reached into its shattered side, hastily scraping away at the pile of twigs and leaves which covered his contraband package. For one horrible moment he thought it was no longer there, but more debris had blown in and covered it more deeply. Shortly his fingers felt the black plastic wrapping and he withdrew the parcel and stuffed it below the clothes in his holdall. Footsteps passed nearby on the path. He held his breath and stayed ducked down until they moved further off.

Once they had gone, he stood and retraced his way back up the rise, towards the Egyptian Avenue and the Circle of Lebanon with its ring of vaults. There, sitting on the flight of steps which led up to the catacombs above, he found Susie, humming a tune to herself.

"Just warming up my voice," she said, "even the acoustic here is weird. Can we get out of here now?"

Jonno patted the side of his holdall, "Sure, let's go."

As she was standing, she said, "A funny thing happened. This bloke came across me sitting here and looked at me really strangely. Like he was shocked to see me. He scared me to be honest. I remember you telling me about nutters coming here when they escaped. I was just about to shout for you but he sort of blinked and seemed to relax and asked me where Lizzie Siddal was buried."

"Really. What did you say?"

"I asked him who Lizzie Siddal was."

"'Oh, just some woman,' he said and walked off."

"What did he look like?"

"About your age, tall, quite good looking, with dark curly hair."

"Steve! Searching for it. I told him I was going to leave it here for a month, until I'm off the hook with the cops."

"Why did he stare at me like that?"

Jonno laughed. "He knows what she looks like. We had a print of Rossetti's *Beata Beatrix* in our old flat. He's looking for her grave, and suddenly there you are, looking a bit like her. You probably freaked him out. Serve him right. If he's looking for it, he must be planning to rip me off."

"Half of it's his, isn't it?"

"Yes, but only half. If he'd come round to the flat, I would have told him we're moving it to a safer place. Brought him along. But no, he's looking for it on his own. Not content with the ounce he took, now he's trying to get hold of the lot. Once I've sold it, I was planning on sending him the money. Now I'm not so sure. If he comes round, I'll give him his share. If he doesn't, I'll think about it. Right, let's get out of here as quick as we can, I'd rather not run into him. I don't trust him anymore."

So, they crept down the steps, stopped at the overgrown entrance to the Egyptian Avenue, where Susie went out first to check that Steve wasn't coming up one of the paths. Then they swiftly made their way out of the cemetery and back up to the village. It wasn't until they were safely sitting in a half-empty carriage with the holdall under his feet that Jonno felt the muscles of his back and shoulders relax. He was still a little on edge, not because of Steve, but in case he was still under police surveillance. Being found with the holdall's contents would have guaranteed serious prison time.

At the mansion flat in Battersea he was still anxious, worried about Susie and her Scottish flatmates. For the boys, on the other hand, it was party time. They all crowded into the kitchen to watch him unwrapping the parcel. None of them had seen so much dope in one place before. Jonno tore open the black plastic wrapping and laid the eight slabs on the table. He picked one up and handed it to Hamish.

"That's yours, man, at cost for the hundred you gave me. Normally we'd sell them on at one-twenty, but because of what you're doing..."

"No, that's fair enough, I'll make plenty at that rate."

Jonno peeled the foil off another slab, and asked for a kitchen knife and their scales as he revealed the block he had previously cut an ounce from. He cut off another ounce.

"That'll last me for a while," he said. "Now, who wants to skin up," and he offered the little block to Susie.

"No, I'm not partaking, I need to save my voice for tonight."

"Wow, you're really serious, aren't you?"

"Singing is what I do and who I am. Hot smoke can mess up your vocal folds."

"It doesn't harm my fiddle playing," said Duncan as he pulled a packet of Rizlas from his jeans.

"It improves my bodhran playing," added Angus, "gets the rhythm going fine."

"Are you all in the band?"

"We are the band, man, didn't she tell you? Except for Hamish, he's the roadie."

"I'm the manager, thank you Angus. They wouldn't trust me with their instruments anyway."

"Cool, I'm looking forward to tonight." Jonno returned to the scales and cut off a further two-ounce block before re-wrapping the rest in its foil. "So that block is now three quarters. Have you got any kitchen foil so I can wrap up these two?"

Once he'd done that, he stacked it all up.

"So, Hamish, apart from yours, six- and three-quarter weights, for you to stash, if you don't mind keeping them for a while."

"No problem."

"Do you mind my asking where you'll put them? I think it's too dangerous keeping them here. If the cops have been watching me, they'll know about Susie soon enough, if they don't already."

"I'll archive them," he said as re-wrapped the foil slabs in the plastic and then stuffed the parcel into a small back-pack with a little Scottish flag stitched to the back pocket.

"What?"

"At the Royal Borough of Kensington and Chelsea. I'm the archivist. There's plenty of places down in the vaults I can hide them. Nobody else has access, and if anyone did accidently come across them, they'll recognise my bag and leave it alone.

"That's so good, under council protection."

"I'll be awa' now just as soon as we've smoked yon wee joint. I'll deal with mine later."

"I was thinking, if you can move them on that'd be great, but don't worry too much about it. In a couple of weeks I can go round to some of my contacts and off-load them. There'll be a few people hanging out and wondering what's happened to us. I don't want to do it right now in case my old partner has been in touch with some of them. I'm really not sure where his head's at."

"Nah, that's cool man. I will if I can, otherwise they'll be safe enough. I'll see you at the club later."

"Can we go now?" asked Susie. "You don't need to smoke that do you? I'll need something to eat and then I'll get ready."

"Certainly, my lady."

~ 18 ~

1971

The Titus Groans were going to rehearse in the basement of a shop in the King's Road. As he was walking towards it one Saturday morning Jonno was taking in the fashions displayed in the multitude of trendy little shops. This was his first-time treading Chelsea's renowned pavements. It came to him that having lived in the metropolis for over a year now, there was still so much to be explored. He should get out more, expand his horizons beyond the brick terraces of South London. Any move would cost money, but what with his job and a little dealing on the side, he figured he could afford it.

While he was thinking this, he stopped outside one of the boutiques and stared at an Afghan coat draped on a mannequin in the window. 'Why not' he thought to himself. He always loved the look of the brown Afghan coats with the embroidered yellow stitching worn by so many hippies, both men and women. He'd shivered through most of the previous winter when outdoors, and autumn was fast approaching. Besides, this was no ordinary Afghan. The leather on the outside was pure white, and rather than falling shapelessly, this coat was gathered at the waist. It looked to be created out of a number of goatskins for the thick curls of fur on the inside were of differing colours, some off-white and some a deep brown. It looked like a coat fit for a rock star.

He had more than a fortnight's wages in the back pocket of his jeans. He wasn't leaving any money lying around in his room since discovering the suspicious powder in Pete's book. He didn't know much about junkies but the common wisdom was you couldn't trust them. He hadn't noticed Pete slipping that low yet, but the discovery of the pornographic story, hearing about the bank scam and witnessing the spiking of Martin had all made him distrustful. Which he didn't like.

Jonno walked into the shop and asked to try it on. The fur was so thick it necessitated taking his woollen jersey off to fit into it. This wasn't a problem because inside it was so warm. When he saw himself in the full-length mirror, he knew he needed to buy it. With the fur collar turned up around his shoulder length hair, the white suede of the goat skin open over his denim shirt with the pearl buttons and his patched Levis, he did indeed look like a rock star. It cost more than he had ever spent on an item of clothing before, indeed on his whole wardrobe, but he was making a statement. To himself, if to no one else. He was not some mundane dweller of a dingy South London room, not some underground man heading nowhere. He was a poet, walking the streets of Chelsea as if he belonged, about to sit in on a rehearsal of a friend's group shortly to be making records, possibly using his lyrics. With his jersey in a carry bag he felt like he was bouncing on the soles of his feet as he crossed the road and walked into the Chelsea Potter.

Henry was sitting at one of the round oak tables towards the back of the pub, deep in conversation with four other men. His back was to the door so he didn't notice Jonno's approach. One man, who looked vaguely familiar, saw him coming and jumped up out of his seat.

"Whoo-hoo, look at you," he said, and stretched out his hand for Jonno to shake. Henry turned and introduced the man as Steve, a friend of their bass player David.

"You don't remember me, do you? Amazing coat by the way. You look like you've come a long way since you were carrying hard-boiled eggs to an anti-Vietnam demo In Hyde Park."

"Steve? The guy who was into Gilbert and Sullivan?"

"I've moved on a bit since then too." He broke into a chorus of *a policeman's lot is not an 'appy one.* "Remember that?"

"I do, yes. It really pissed them off. I never got to Hyde Park though. Ended up in Grosvenor Square nearly getting the shit kicked out of me."

"I warned you about sticking with Harriet."

"She nearly got her skull cracked open."

"So she told me. And about your gallant recue."

"You've seen her?"

"Not since graduation. Sit down, I'll get you a pint."

While he was at the bar Henry introduced him to the other men at the table, who turned out to be the other members of the Titus Groans.

"Is Steve in the band?" Jonno asked.

"No, he's just a mate," David said. "Bit of a pain really, he'd be a groupie if he was a woman."

"That's a tad unfair," Henry responded. "Stephen is more like our number one fan. Insists on coming to each of our rehearsals and accompanies us to whatever manky club we might be lucky enough to get a gig in. I believe he anticipates a great future for us in the music industry and wants to be in a position to be able to say 'I knew them when' sort of thing."

"Like I said, a groupie."

"Actually I believe he's manoeuvring for a position as our manager. Sees himself as a latter-day Andrew Loog Oldham. I hate to disabuse him but under no circumstances will that ever be coming to pass. Anyway chaps, Jonno here is a weaver of poetic flights of fancy, and I requested his presence amongst us this afternoon to see if he might feel up to the task of supplying us with a few lyrics."

Jonno turned to the others around the table. "I'm not a musician, and I'm not really sure how song writing works. So when Henry asked me to write some stuff I thought I'd better come along first and see if I got any ideas."

"It also appears from what Stephen was relating just before that Jonno has a history of rescuing innocents labouring under a certain amount of duress. I know that to be true in my own case so I am keen to hear about this Harriet character."

Jonno was dismissive, but Steve, on returning from the bar, settled into his chair and in response to Henry's request began to relate what Harriet had told him about Jonno plucking her out from under a horse's hooves in Grosvenor Square. After which Henry embarrassed Jonno further by retailing an account of their skirmish with the three skinheads amongst the branches of a tree in Hyde Park. When he finished, he mentioned that the rehearsal time they were booked for was about to commence and they should get going.

The basement was dark, with the walls, floor and ceiling all painted black and the thin window under the pavement above blocked out with plywood. Under the paint, by way of soundproofing, egg cartons had been glued over everything save the floor. As the band members moved about, setting up the drum kit, throwing a multitude of switches, plugging cords into amplifiers and adjusting microphone stands, Jonno and Steve sat on a couple of wooden chairs, catching up on everything that had happened to each of them since the demonstration some three years previously. Steve finished university with a minor second, which he said was fair enough considering how little work he'd done. He remained for a while in a shared house in

Brighton before deciding to move up to London, where he was staying with an aunt in Hampstead.

"Bit of a drag but ok until I find a place." As he was talking Steve moved his chair to one of the speaker boxes and started to roll a joint on top of it.

"How about you?" he asked, "Where are you living?"

"Down in Tooting with a couple of mates," Jonno replied.

"Nasty. I could never live south of the river," Steve stated.

"Henry's place in Putney's alright."

"Yes, well, Putney, Richmond, Barnes all that, it's different, isn't it? I mean it's almost in the country. But Tooting, yuck."

"It is a bit grotty; I'll grant you. Actually I have been wondering if it's time to be moving on."

"Oh, yes? I'll be looking for a flatmate when I get a place. Are you working? Could you afford to go halves on somewhere decent? I'm not talking a palace or anything, but certainly not a shit-hole. Just somewhere nice and private in a reasonable area."

"Private?"

"Somewhere where no one cares what you get up to." Steve lit his joint and after a few drags passed it to Jonno, with an enquiring look on his face.

Jonno took a few tokes on it before walking over and handing it to Henry. When he got back to his chair he asked "So, what do you get up to?"

"Oh, nothing serious," Steve replied. The practiced way that Jonno had inhaled the joint had obviously not escaped his notice. That, and the fact that he was a friend of Henry's must have given him the confidence to say, "Just, you know, I deal a little bit of dope from time to time. Wouldn't be a problem, would it?"

"Funny you should say that," Jonno replied, "I do a little myself. And what with that and my job I should be able to go halves on a decent place."

"Cool, we could even go into business together. We should keep in touch; I'll give you my aunt's number."

While they were talking the boys finished sorting out their gear, and once the drummer stubbed out the roach he'd been finishing and hit the rim of the snare with three introductory taps, the Titus Groans launched into one of their numbers.

In the cramped little basement it was incredibly loud. Henry did sing a few lines but mostly it was 'ums and aahs' a bit like scat singing, with the odd word thrown in here and there. Nothing struck Jonno as being anything he could put words to. Mostly it was fast and furious, with a lot of scowling attitude. He was surprised. Knowing Henry, he was expecting something more lyrical, more along the lines of Fairport Convention rather than this King Crimson-like spaced out hard rock. Nevertheless he enjoyed the pumping rhythms, the howling guitar work and he was particularly impressed by the drummer, who seemed to be driving the whole thing along with a technique that made him think more of jazz than rock and roll.

"So what do you think?" Henry asked, when their set was over.

"Bloody great," he answered. "But I'm not sure how I could fit anything of mine into it. Song writing has got to be a whole different thing. Tell you what, why don't I drop some of my poems around to your place, then you could decide whether you can do anything with them."

"Fair enough, as long as you don't mind my playing around with them a bit. Some people get a bit precious about their work."

"No, that'd be fine. It'll just be jottings really, a few lines here and there. I'm still learning, haven't written anything I'm really proud of yet."

As the band was packing up their gear Steve gave Jonno a piece of paper with his aunt's phone number on it.

"Think about it, but don't take too long, I'm really going to have to move out of her place soon."

Jonno assured him he would, and decided that when he got home, he'd have a heart to heart with Pete.

He had been worried by the bankcard business, thinking it might bring the cops down on them. If they searched the place now, they would come across an ounce of dope all cut up into quid deals and a further quarter ounce in a desk drawer. He'd yet to mention it, but felt sickened by the exploitation stories it appeared Pete was now writing. He was also dismayed at the thought of what the powder stuck into the magazine might be. Smoking dope was one thing, dropping acid was eye-opening and fun while it lasted, but a passing phase as far as he was concerned. But smack, if that was what it was, smack was a whole new ball game, and one which he wanted nothing whatsoever to do with. He needed to find out if it was a one-off thing, just another of Pete's William Burroughs experiments, or whether his friend was becoming a junkie.

He had his answer when he got back to Socrates Street. His stereo was missing, and music was booming down from the room above. He didn't mind Pete borrowing it from time to time, but he wasn't too keen on him going into his room when he wasn't in. He wondered what else he might have helped himself to. He checked his drawer to find one of his deals missing and climbed the stairs to have it out with him. He was unprepared for the sight which greeted him.

There were four people sitting on the two mattresses, Pete, Ann and a couple of unshaven guys with greasy hair who were new to him. There was a smog of sweet smoke in the room mixed with the cloying smell of burning candle wax. Pete was holding a teaspoon over the flame while one of the strangers sat beside him, a syringe in his hand, needle poised to suck up the bubbling fluid.

"Hi Jonno," Pete enunciated slowly, as if from a far-away place. "This is Brian and that's Gilbert, two new friends of ours. Take a seat man, come and join us."

"No fucking way," Jonno said, turned and quickly left the room and then the house. He walked to the phone box at the end of the street.

~ 19 ~

1972

Jonno felt so proud to be walking into the Feathers with Susie on his arm. She was unquestionably the most striking woman in the pub, with her red-gold hair falling in waves down past her shoulders. The tartan cloak was slung around her shoulders, fastened by the amethyst brooch in its gold setting, glinting in the overhead lights. The skirt of her purple dress could be glimpsed with each step and she moved with such assurance that she appeared to Jonno like some kind of highland princess, come to receive tribute from her clan members. As they moved behind the crowd of patrons standing at the bar, and passed the benches of drinkers ranged around the walls, the noise of conversation dropped. He could see heads turning to watch their progress towards the staircase at the far end of the room. The murmuring resumed once they were half way up the gently curving flight of steps.

When they reached the top, he was about to push open the door for her when she placed a hand on his arm to stop him.

"Thank you for coming in with me tonight. I was so scared."

"You're kidding."

"No. Crowds of people. When they go quiet like that, I always think they're about to turn on me, tell me I have no place being here. I usually arrive with the boys surrounding me so I don't have to see their faces."

"Jesus! How do you manage to stand on a stage and sing then?"

"Oh, the singing's different, it's like I'm in a different place, you'll see. Besides, up here it's a folk club, they're my people, they want to hear me. But down there, I know it's stupid, I'm sure they are all fine and I know no one's going to hurt me, but they still frighten me."

"Shit," Jonno said and gathered her into his arms. He leaned down and kissed her, before saying, "I never realised. When you said you were driven off the island; it must have really hurt."

"Sticks and stones, you know that saying? It's not true. They didn't actually throw rocks, but it sure as hell felt like it."

"Just because you got pregnant?"

"Because I was a *sinner*. I had transgressed God's laws."

"But that's not in the ten..."

"Doesn't matter. God forgot."

"How can He do that if He's omniscient?"

"The fathers of the church, and I do mean fathers, consider it their duty to help Him out. To remind Him, and also of course us lowly mortals, that the road to hell lies between a woman's legs. Didn't you see it the other day?"

"That's so fucking twisted."

"That's a good word," she laughed. "I agree, it's just every now and again it's hard to forget all the Sunday school bullshit. So, now you know, I might look invincible sometimes but it's pretty much an act."

"Hamish said something along those lines before we went to see *More*."

"He's a good bloke Hamish, and he's more perceptive than he makes out. Angus, Duncan and I all take the piss out of him from time to time, but really he's the smart one. So let's go and see if he's here yet."

The Feathers was an 18th century coaching inn, built for travellers newly arrived in London, or as a departure point for those journeying further afield. But then, having suffered damage during the blitz, and no longer requiring numerous rooms for overnight guests, the upper floor had been converted into one large space suitable for wedding receptions, or more sombre occasions. Sometime in the sixties the landlord had decided to cash in on the folk revival boom, and instigated a weekly Saturday night folk club. It quickly caught on with the local population and many an aspiring musician cut their teeth playing Upstairs at the Feathers.

At a much smaller folk club Jonno's old housemate Dave had first met Melanie, or Mel as she preferred to be called, to avoid confusion with the American singer. She was in a duo with her then boyfriend and Dave had found them very impressive. He told Jonno that on leaving the club he'd come across the pair of them having a full-on argument in the alley around the side of the building. He didn't know what caused it but as their voices rose to screaming point, he was thinking about stepping in when the guy slapped her face, hard. That was enough for Dave, who, being a big man, had no trouble encouraging the angry man to "fuck off", as Dave suggested.

The argument turned out to mark the end of the couple's relationship, both professionally and more personally. Within a month Mel moved into the attic flat, which finally lifted any residual cloud of sadness still lingering around Dave. They were good for each other. At first, after the break-up, Mel was too nervous to contemplate performing again. Dave was spending time busking in tube station corridors but had never played on a stage before. Mel insisted he was good enough and Dave agreed to give it a go as long as she sang with him. So after a few weeks of practicing, they began to spend their weekends doing the rounds of the smaller clubs, playing at first for free.

After a while the two of them graduated to becoming early evening regulars at the much larger Feathers, singing cover versions of Al Stewart songs, interspersed with the odd Leonard Cohen or Judy Collins number. It was here they first saw Susie and her cousins perform, and been blown away by them. Mel and Susie became friends, finding they shared experience of violent boyfriends. When a job came up at the travel agent where Mel worked Susie had leapt at the opportunity.

The place was packed, maybe a hundred animated punters all crammed together under a low flying cloud of tobacco smoke. Jonno could just make out Dave's head rising above those crowded around a collection of tables, all facing towards the stage. There was plenty of noise and movement as people shouted greetings to each other while making their way to and from the bar at the back of the hall. Jonno steered Susie towards Dave's table where they found him sitting with Mel, as well as Angus, Hamish and Duncan. Ever the gentleman, Dave stood to collect a couple of more chairs from the stacks leant against one of the walls. Jonno looked at Hamish and raised an eyebrow. Hamish nodded, "It's as safe as the bank of Scotland, man." Jonno leaned down and shook his hand as Dave returned with the chairs.

"There you go," Dave said, "Now the star attraction has arrived the evening can begin."

Jonno turned his quizzical gaze from Hamish to him.

"The headline act mate, didn't she tell you?" Dave asked. "Of course no one, apart from these three, understands a single word she's singing, but somehow it doesn't seem to matter."

"We all get the feeling," Mel agreed.

"So are you two going to be on tonight?" Jonno asked her. "I haven't heard Dave play for over a year. I'm imagining he's improved a bit. At least I hope so."

"Out of sight man. Once I'd dropped that stupid bloody job. And got out of Socrates Street before it turned really sour. Amazing how much time you can spend practising when you're trying to impress someone."

"Well, it worked," Mel said as she lifted a half pint of cider from the table and clicked it against Dave's pint glass. "You'll be able to judge for yourself in a minute. That's Chris up there at the mike, and we're first up."

Dave was right, his playing had vastly improved. Jonno found Mel's voice at first a little thin and reedy, and not really up to the Joni Mitchell song they led off with. It improved on the next song, when she alternated the vocals with Dave, giving a rendition of Fairport's *Meet on the Ledge* from a few years ago; a song more than familiar to British folk fans. The whole audience enthusiastically joined in the several choruses, as they belted out their desires to be reunited with their friends and lovers at life's end.

When the applause finally died down Mel, after grinning broadly at their success, moved closer to the microphone and in a soft voice said,

"I really hope that lyric is true. There are some people I am more than happy to forget, but not my friends. I cannot imagine a greater pleasure than to meet up with all of them again, whenever the time comes that we finally do fall off the ledge. Talking of which I want to dedicate my favourite

Fairport Convention song to someone who has, in a fairly short time, become my best friend."

For this number Dave moved from his previous enthusiastic strumming to a more considered and complicated finger-picking style to accompany Mel on Sandy Denny's brilliant *Who Knows Where the Time Goes*. Jonno had always been a fan of Fairport and this was one of his all-time favourite songs. The first few lines paint a picture of birds who have clustered together in autumn, now embarking on the great flight south, leaving the singer wondering how they could know that it's time to be gone. As Mel tentatively launched herself into the lyric Jonno had a moment of doubt, worried that again she might not be up to it. But by the time she reached the first chorus her voice had strengthened, and all of his misgivings were dispelled. Goosebumps rose on his arms, as did the hairs on the back of his head. He was not alone. Complete silence fell in the hall, even the people standing at the bar stopped and turned while the staff momentarily ceased pulling pints. The chorus over, it sounded like Mel poured the whole of her soul into the second verse, the one which talks of her fickle friends departing from deserted shores. The great melancholy beauty of the verse reached deep into his Celtic soul, which was why Jonno loved it so much. He gave himself up to the atmosphere of love and loss and abandonment, which was why he missed the frown on Susie's face, did not see her sudden look of anguish.

When the song finished Mel leant over and kissed Dave, who had been sitting on a stool while he played, then grinned around the room as she received the audience's rapturous applause. As she stepped off the stage she looked sheepishly towards the table where Susie was sitting, before approaching and regaining her seat.

"You weren't kidding Dave, and Mel, that was fabulous. Let me buy you both another drink." Jonno stood and moved towards the bar, missing the looks passing between the two women.

When he returned with the drinks the evening continued with a number of different soloists and combos taking to the stage, performing a mixture of well-known covers interspersed with a few original numbers. Eventually the MC took to the microphone again. "A sincere vote of thanks to everyone who has played and sung here tonight, but now it's the time you have all been waiting for, as we welcome back our friends from across the border." He moved three chairs close together at the back of the stage and then placed the microphone stand right at the front.

"Come on boys, it's time to shine," Susie said as she stood from the table. "And Dave, please don't put your guitar away just yet. I'm thinking I'm going to need your help a bit later."

Once the three of them were seated, with Susie in the middle, Angus led off with a rhythm he spanked out on the stretched skin of his bodhran with the double ended wooden bone in his fist, swivelling his wrist around with amazing agility. Then Duncan tucked his fiddle under his chin, raised his bow and began, lightly at first, to join him in what Jonno assumed was a reel. Gradually the strength of his playing increased. Susie was sitting totally still between them with her eyes closed. After a while Jonno noticed her feet began tapping along to the rhythm until eventually she unfasted the broach, threw off her cloak, stood and started to dance around the stage. The full skirt of the purple dress flew out and up around her calves as she twirled, twisted and turned, her arms lifted and rotating in counterpoint to the frenzied movements of her legs and feet. Her eyes were still closed, and Jonno worried that she might dance herself right off the boards, but she appeared to have some innate knowledge of the space available for her crazed gyrations. All the while she seemed to be looking inwards, conjuring up some internal vision that the music was creating for her. Finally the three of them stopped dead as one. She opened her eyes, to look out at the crowd, as if becoming aware of her surroundings for the first time. She bowed in turn to each of her cousins and then out to the audience who by now were all clapping madly. "Thank you," she said, moving towards the microphone, "and now for a wee bit of singing."

With the boys playing behind her she launched into a song incomprehensible to Jonno, and presumably to most of the others in the room, in such a soft and lilting voice that it didn't in the least matter. They were each taken on a journey to a place inside themselves where they could imagine whatever they liked. To some it was a place where waves rose and fell, where sea birds called out to one another, and where high winds blew. Others were taken to memories of their childhoods, to family holidays perhaps, to vanished love affairs or to vanquished aspirations. Song followed song, melding seamlessly into one another. Some were mournful, those ones seeming to speak of love and of loss, others more exultant, as if celebrating a bountiful harvest, of burgeoning fishing nets, and of a lover returned from the sea. Members of the crowd sometimes sat with their eyes closed to summon whatever pictures occurred to them, while at other times they watched her swaying body as she moved in tune with the music.

After one particularly mournful lament she stopped and held herself still for a few moments. The crowd too held its collective breath before interpreting this as the end of the concert and gave her a deafening round of applause. She held out her hands to quieten them however.

"That song is so sad and I don't want to leave you all on a downbeat. So, Dave could you bring up your guitar now please. Don't worry, you know this tune, I've heard you playing it. I need to explain something."

As Dave moved onto the stage and took over her vacant seat, she carried on talking.

"I only ever sing in my own language but tonight I'm going to make an exception. The thing is, it seems I have fallen in love."

This was greeted by a fair amount of whistling, applause and cat-calls.

"Wonderful as falling in love feels, it can sometimes be inconvenient. My paramour, for want of a better word, is sitting in here with us and has no idea what I'm talking about, but I think he might have been getting a bit of the picture earlier on. When we get home tonight things could get really tough, so I thought I'd finish by singing one of his favourite songs, in the hope he will realise that I really have come to love him. This is a song from a film we saw a couple of weeks ago, not a very good film but a great soundtrack, and for me the prelude to one of the best nights of my life; one that, whatever happens now, I shall always treasure. I can only hope that he might feel the same. While it's not really a folk song it could be and I think most of you will be familiar with Pink Floyd's *Cymbaline* from the album *More*."

She was right, most people did know the song, if not the verses certainly the few words of the chorus, and when their time came around nearly a hundred voices joined in to sing that it was "high time," which, for a number of them, it probably was.

Not for Jonno though, who scowled at Mel. "It's her you were singing about before, wasn't it? She's leaving me."

Hamish leaned across. "She's leaving all of us, pal."

"What? God, she's not sick, is she? She's not dying?"

"No, no, nothing like that. Dinnae fash yourself, man."

Jonno turned to Mel again.

"Please, don't ask me?" she begged him. "God. I didn't realise she hadn't...Please...Let her tell you herself."

Jonno jumped up from his seat. "No. 'Please wake me' – what has this all been about? Tell me!" he shouted at her, but she looked away from him. He turned towards the stage and watched as Susie walked down through the crowd, bending to left and to right, accepting plaudits from members of the audience, but all the time looking towards Jonno, her face creased by worry.

By the time she reached Jonno he was as immobile and stony faced as an Easter Island statue. He was beyond words. She reached a tentative hand up from within her tartan cloak and gently stroked his cheek.

"Please, will you take me back to your home, and let me explain. I meant everything that I said up there, but I've only just tonight realised how unfairly I've treated you. I didn't mean to be unkind to you, honestly."

Jonno turned and strode towards the door without saying farewell to anyone at the table. When he reached it, he flung it open, then turned to look back in her direction. His mouth twisted up into a wry, lop-sided smile, as if he knew the scene he was creating, and was embarrassed by it. Seeing this, Susie flew across the room towards him.

~ 20 ~

1971-1972

Jonno seemed fated to remain travelling to work inside the well-worn rolling stock of the Northern Line. The new pad was up towards the other end of the track. He still needed to make one change, this time at Leicester Square to move over to the Piccadilly Line. Having lived in London for a few years by now, much of the initial excitement had worn off. Nevertheless childhood years of playing Monopoly meant that such names were invested with a romanticism unattached to Tooting Broadway. A frisson of trepidation too, since the yellow topped properties were adjacent to the corner where the man in blue stood, blowing into his whistle. The corner from whence you were sent directly to gaol, you did not pass Go, and you did not collect £200. When Steve took him to see what he thought, the irony of this had not been obvious.

"This place is amazing; how did you find it?" Jonno asked.

"My old man. I guess he's still got loads of contacts from his old job."

"Which was?"

"Copper."

"You're having me on."

"I kid you not. A very senior copper. Remember Softly, Softly, the series which took over from Z Cars?"

"Of course."

"The chief superintendent in that, Barlow, was modelled on the old bastard. The producer and the actor Stratford Johns used to take him out to dinner, copy his mannerisms and stuff."

"Fuck. So he's retired now, is he?"

"Yes, he packed it in a few years ago. Now he's a civil servant. Works for the Home Office over in Northern Ireland. He must have asked around some of his old mates when I told him I was looking for a flat, because he came up with this place almost straight away. I reckon it's pretty much perfect, don't you? It's a bit out of the way, I know, but I guess that's why the rent's so low. That and the shop down below."

The property was originally built as a mews cottage sometime in the 19th century. What was once a coachhouse and stable now served as a little general stores cum newsagent. There was a separate cream painted door to one side which led out the back to a ground-floor kitchen and bathroom, and beyond to a fairly extensive garden, with a tatty lawn. This was sheltered on two sides by the high brick walls of warehouses, and behind a couple of nondescript shrubs and a struggling apple tree was a wall separating them from houses in the next street. At one side of the kitchen a staircase went up to the living room which ran the whole width of the building, off which were two bedrooms and a largish boxroom all directly over the shop.

"The pub over the road is Irish so there might be a bit of noisy folk music at the weekends, but it wouldn't bother me."

"Me neither. And having a shop downstairs means we'll never run out of milk," Jonno laughed.

"So, what do you think?" Steve asked.

"I think I want to move in. How soon can we do it?"

"As soon as we pay the bond according to my dad. Next weekend if you can raise your half straightaway."

"Not a problem."

"Need a hand moving?"

"I'll want to bring my desk."

"Would it fit in the back of a minivan?"

"Not sure."

"I'll come round on Saturday. If it doesn't, we can tie it on the roof."

Jonno determined that in the new place it would be different. They were strangers not mates. At university their paths had barely crossed, merely shared a coach ride to London once, where they'd gone their separate ways. After seeing him at the Groans' rehearsal Jonno imagined his musical tastes must have broadened quite a lot. He hoped so anyway, he was not interested in opera himself, even less so in operetta.

It turned out he needn't have worried. It seemed Steve's fascination with Gilbert and Sullivan was merely a hangover from membership of his school's choral society. Nowadays he was as tuned in to contemporary music as Jonno. Indeed one of the great plusses of the new place was Steve's state of the art stereo, with its massive speaker cabinets constructed out of thick chipboard. These were placed on the far side of the low wooden coffee table in the living room, facing towards the sofa and the two flanking armchairs, one of which Jonno would collapse into on his nightly return from Imperial College.

In the first few days, if Steve was at home, there would often be a joint already rolled waiting on the table shortly to be accompanied by a mug of tea, for which Jonno was extremely grateful. The pair of them would sit, smoking, drinking tea and listening to music, and discuss the possibility of merging their dealing endeavours into a partnership. While it appeared Steve knew many more contacts to sell to, particularly down in Brighton, Jonno knew the more reliable supplier in Kiwi Paul. Many of Steve's contemporaries had stayed on in Brighton after graduating and were keen to supply the enormous market their alma mater represented. Their only problem was getting hold of enough of the stuff. It was with this in mind, Steve told Jonno, that he'd moved up to London.

Jonno's situation was almost the opposite. Having a few customers interested in scoring fairly small amounts on a regular basis, meant Jonno usually bought a quarter of a weight at a time. Kiwi Paul was intimating that he was moving further up the supply chain, and wanted to sell in much larger quantities. In fact he only remained selling to Jonno for old time's sake, and because he worked just around the corner from the South Kensington flat. This was apparently about to change. Paul reckoned too many people knew where he lived these days, and for safety's sake decided to relocate. He was thinking about shedding his smaller customers, Jonno included.

"How about if I bought in larger quantities?" Jonno asked him, "Say a weight at a time?"

"That would be fine," Paul replied after Jonno told him of the new partnership arrangements he was making with Steve. "I'll not tell you where I'm moving though, I'm keeping it a secret from everybody except very close contacts. At this level you have to be really careful, the risks get magnified as do the consequences of being busted. No one's even going to get my phone number. I'm going to be ringing round, say on a weekly basis, to see if anyone wants anything, and then I'll do deliveries. It's the best way to keep myself safe, I reckon."

"Good job my new place has a phone then. It's a bit of a hike up to Archway from here though."

"Nice try," Paul laughed, "But I won't be coming from here, will I? Anyway I don't mind the travel if you're going to be buying in more bulk. I'll be glad to keep you on, you're a nice bloke, you're not away with the fairies like some of them, and you're trustworthy. That's worth a lot in this game."

So the partnership between Jonno and Steve was formed. At first, they both kicked in £50 and bought a weight of Paki black which Paul delivered up to Archway. On his first visit to their new flat he also brought a present, the poster of Rossetti's *Beata Beatrix*, which he unrolled on their coffee table.

"Jonno always used to stare at it when he came round to my old place in South Ken," Paul explained to Steve. "My new place is more modern and it doesn't really go, so I thought he might want it."

"I do, I've loved that painting ever since I first saw it. Thanks so much man."

"You ought to go and visit her. She's just up the road, buried somewhere in Highgate Cemetery," Paul informed him.

"Really? I'll do that one day."

"Oh yuck," said Steve. "Graveyards? Not my idea of fun."

"I'll put it in my room if you're not keen, Steve."

"No, no, let's have it in here," he said. "It'll look great up on the wall between the speakers. She looks like she's having some kind of mystical revelation with her eyes closed like that. Or is she just off her face?"

"Maybe both. It's Lizzie Siddal, she's the artist's wife. I looked her up," Jonno said. "She was addicted to opium.

She'd been dead for a year when Rossetti painted it. The opium killed her, poor woman."

"She's beautiful."

"Isn't she just?" Jonno agreed. "I guess Rossetti was saying something about the transitoriness of life, what with the sundial there, and those ghostly figures in the background. Or maybe something about drugs; those are opium poppies in the dove's mouth. Perhaps it's about drugs and death."

"Speaking of drugs..." Kiwi Paul said, producing their weight of Paki black from the leather satchel lying next to him on the sofa.

"Brilliant," said Steve as he started counting out ten-pound notes onto the table in front of him.

"Fancy a cup of tea?" Jonno enquired as Paul, with a sense of urgency, took the money and folded it into one of the satchel's pockets.

"Nah, right now I've got to move on, places to be, people to see, deals to be done. Next time maybe. How long before you'll be wanting more, do you reckon?"

"Not sure," Steve said, "depends. Couple of weeks maybe."

"Fair enough, I'll give you a ring in a fortnight, then. A pleasure doing business," he said as he shook Steve's hand. Jonno followed him downstairs and saw him to the door. "Really cool place you've found here," he said as he was leaving. "Having a shop out front is damn good cover, no one's attention is drawn to a bit of coming and going."

It turned out this was the first of many visits Kiwi Paul was to make to their flat, gradually transporting larger and larger quantities of dope, with greater and greater frequency. For their business thrived. It was risky, word of mouth was getting around, which brought in new customers, but also increased opportunities for discovery by the constabulary. Steve was doing runs down to Brighton in his minivan, but now people from other universities and from shared households around town would occasionally turn up, having heard from a friend of a friend, a whisper on the alternative society's grapevine, that here was a place where dope could be bought in quantities larger than an ounce or two.

For the first few months Jonno kept turning up to work in the offices of Imperial College, but as their business grew, he saw less and less point in subjecting himself to the rigours of tube travel. There was now more money coming in than ever before. Their rent was ridiculously cheap, they took it in turns to cook fairly basic meals, they rarely went out of a night-time, their social life revolving around people turning up to score, or fellow dealers dropping in for chats, and their dope was effectively free. They could easily cut tiny, almost unnoticeable amounts off the numerous weights passing through their hands, using the incredibly accurate set of scales bought from a specialist shop, whose pan would crash down with only a couple of cigarette papers placed on it.

Apart from food and cigarettes bought from the shop beneath them and the rolling papers from one a little further afield, Jonno's only real expenditure was on books and records. So there came a time when he could no longer be bothered getting up early in the morning, fighting his way through the fog left over from the previous night's indulgence.

He told himself he was now in a position to stay at home and concentrate on his writing, give himself the freedom to let his creative impulses have free reign. His desk was set up in his bedroom, but it was hardly used as these days he preferred to lounge around in the living room, with his legs up on the sofa, scribbling away with a biro into a notebook. He attempted some lyrics for the Titus Groans but they didn't come to much. All he managed were some meandering poems that really went nowhere, which Henry plundered for the odd image here and there. The fact was he and Steve were now smoking dope from when they got up at midday until they fell into their beds at two and three o'clock in the morning, spending most of the intervening hours reading and listening to their extensive record collections.

The boys were moving up the supply chain in the wake of Kiwi Paul, who was making contact with people closer to importers. This meant he was coming across a greater variety of the hash being smuggled into the country. Occasionally he was able to offer special deals to favoured customers. One such was the strongest grass Jonno and Steve had ever smoked, which supposedly came from Brazil, and rendered them pretty much helpless for hours. Another time it was a quarter ounce of the legendary Maui-Wowie, so beloved of West Coast musicians like the Grateful Dead and Jefferson Airplane. Such exemplary treats only came in small quantities, never got down to street level, but were shared around amongst the dealing fraternity.

It was by means of these channels that Jonno received the raw opium which led to his discovery of Lizzie Siddal's grave.

One day Kiwi Paul turned up at the Archway flat with the weights they had ordered and asked if they wanted a few grams of something special. Opium was a rarity, and this was all he could spare them, but if they wanted to try it they were welcome, at a price. Of course they said yes, and asked how best to take it.

"You could score a proper opium pipe in antique shop, but it'd cost a bit. You could swallow some but it probably tastes like shit and you might throw it up again. It's really pliable, so you can pinch a bit off and roll it out into a long thin sausage then lay that on the tobacco in a joint. The best way, since there's two of you, would be to hot-knife it."

"What's that?"

"It's how we smoke buds of grass back in NZ," he sounded enthusiastic at the memory. "I'll show you if you like, you've got a gas cooker but you'll need an empty beer can. They all trooped downstairs to the kitchen. "And we'll need a knife. An ordinary desert one will do as long as it's got a bone or wooden handle, all metal ones burn your fucking fingers."

Under instruction from Paul, Steve took their sharpest kitchen knife and began cutting the bottom off an empty can of Double Diamond he found in their bin. Jonno lit one of the gas burners and rummaged in the drawer for a suitable bone-handled knife. Paul slid its blade under the cooker's trivet so that the end could heat up while he unwrapped the ball of opium. He pinched a small piece off with his thumb nail. When the can was ready, he told Jonno to pull the knife from the flame.

"Back home we use two knives, get the tips red hot then burn a bud of grass between them. Opium's more subtle though, you don't want to burn it, just heat it up until it smokes like crazy. So Jonno, hold the blade horizontal and when you're ready drop this little bit on it higher up where it's still bloody warm but not red-hot. Steve holds the bottom of the can over it and sucks like fuck through the hole on the top. Simple but effective."

So Steve got the first hit, and then Jonno when they swapped implements. They offered the can to Paul who laughed.

"No thanks boys. I'd love to, but I've got to drive, and believe me after a couple of hits you can't. All those cats in the nineteenth century with their laudanum and stuff must have been right off their faces. Enjoy," he said as he walked down the passage to their front door. He offered a last piece of advice to Jonno before leaving, "I wouldn't be doing it during the day when the shop here is open. The smell is really strong, not to mention overpowering." He laughed again as he walked away.

When he was gone, they each took another hit before climbing back upstairs. Jonno did manage to put the Dead's *American Beauty* on the stereo before collapsing into an armchair, Steve having already stretched out on the couch. The music sounded fantastic, and soon led to them spinning little stories inside their heads, fantasies really. Neither of them could muster enough energy to get up and turn the album over for quite a while.

After this first session they were wary not only of its addictive reputation but also of the lethargy it engendered. Hash got you high. Opium *drugged* you.

Nevertheless Jonno gradually became entranced by the idea of trying it again. Kiwi Paul's mention of nineteenth century imbibers struck a chord. All of the Romantic poets he had studied for his English 'A' Level were well-known partakers, including his hero Keats. Besides which, he had been enamoured of the addicted Lizzie Siddal from the very first time he saw *Beata Beatrix* hanging in Paul's South Kensington flat. The Millais painting of her as Ophelia was now pinned up in Jonno's room.

He came across an article in the local paper about people breaking into Highgate cemetery to track down vampires. Bloody idiots. He thought a belief in undead creatures roaming the earth to suck blood from nubile virgins totally ridiculous. Erotic phantasies engendered in the minds of repressed and frustrated individuals seemed much more plausible.

What did grab his attention was the article's description of the cemetery itself. He knew Karl Marx was buried up there but it seemed this was an older section, a Victorian extravaganza fallen into ruin and overgrown. Apparently, its mausoleums and catacombs had attracted a crowd of crucifix wearing, garlic draped and stake-wielding idiots who scaled the walls one night. The police were called to eject them, tampering with internments having remained an offence since the days of the so-called 'Resurrection Men', who supplied fresh cadavers to medical schools.

Jonno thought such a place sounded an ideal setting for the consumption of the drug so enamoured of his nineteenth century idols. He rolled himself a couple of joints, each with a thinly rolled snake of the oleaginous substance inside, and set off on the bus up to Highgate Village.

Near the top of Swain's Lane he came across a pair of wrought iron gates suspended between brick pillars which he recognised from the photo in the paper. He was worried that after the reported fracas they might have been locked, but the ornate handle turned and lifted the latch. The rusty metal shrieked in protest, but he managed to push the gate open.

The atmosphere behind the imposing spike-topped gates and the high crumbling brick walls far exceeded his expectations. He could see why vampire-hunters would be attracted to the place, quite apart from any reports of late-night spectral encounters outside in the lane. Originally it was laid out with the geometric fastidiousness which Victorians deemed appropriate for dealings with their dear departed. It had been neglected now for decades, enabling a wild, unruly nature to claim it as its own. Headstones were forced up by tree roots to totter about at crazy angles. Some were clasped in such a tight embrace by ivy's wandering tendrils that whole sections had shattered and broken off. Young trees shouldered flat-laid slabs aside, as they thrust upwards through such abundantly fertilised soil, their decomposing fallen leaves obscuring whatever epitaphs were chiselled into once polished surfaces.

Turning right at a fork in the path Jonno discovered an elaborate archway, which looked like an abandoned part of a film set. Something which could have done for *Exodus*, *The Ten Commandments* or any number of once fashionable biblical epics. Just visible through a profusion of creepers and overhanging ferns were two pairs of bulbous lotus columns holding up a coved pediment over what looked to be the mouth of a tunnel. To each side an accompanying obelisk reared up, overtopping the shrubs and saplings which crowded about the entrance.

Passing through he found himself in an overgrown alley, so dark it seemed he might have been underground, flanked on either side by vaults carved into the hillside. Most of them were sealed shut by rusting wrought-iron doors, and each embellished with an inverted flaming torch. Some doors were busted open or wrenched off their hinges and he couldn't resist peering into their dark interiors. In the gloom he could just see honeycombs of stone shelves which supported the coffins and urns of numerous family members.

After sloping gently upwards for a hundred feet the alley opened up into a circular avenue of further vaults, those spaced around the inside having Egyptian style flat-topped pediments while those facing them on the outer ring were more Roman in style, surmounted by triangular ones. Again a number of these vaults had been divested of their double wrought-iron doors, either through age but more likely by human interference Jonno thought, as he recalled the vampire hunting story which drew him there in the first place.

Looking up through the confusion of brambles overhanging this circle of catacombs he saw what looked like a neglected Buddhist or Hindu temple, although this seemed unlikely, as the tapering stone spire which roofed it was surmounted by a Christian cross. Jonno ascended a moss-covered flight of stone steps to a level terrace, from where he could peer in through the wrought iron lattice which sealed its doorway.

Inside, against its far wall, he could just make out an angel carved out of marble, but so discoloured by bird droppings, that it was impossible to see what it clasped in its arms as it rose above a huge pile of decomposing pigeon shit. This must have accumulated over decades, and gave off an acrid stink which so gripped at his throat that he reeled backwards. He walked away, to a place where he could admire the enormous cedar tree growing from the top of the ring of Egyptian vaults below. He sank down on the scant and weed infested grass, withdrew an opium laden joint from his cigarette packet and fired it up.

It was warm, the sun shone down on him and he was sorely tempted to lie back and surrender himself to any dreams and visions which might be conjured in the recesses of his brain. He resisted however. The whole purpose of his current enterprise was an exploration of these exotic surroundings, not to give himself up to sleep. With an effort of will he roused himself, descended once more to the ring of catacombs, traversed the subterranean alley and emerged through the Egyptian gateway.

In a way it was like being back in the country again, a feeling of peace so pervaded the atmosphere, such as he'd not experienced since leaving his West Country home. For all that he was in London, no noise of traffic penetrated the dense vegetation run riot behind the crumbling walls. All he could hear was bird-song and the rustling of the wind disturbing the leaves of the crowding saplings and trees. He struck off down a path overhung with ash trees, from behind which marble angels stared out at him, sometimes in sorrow, sometimes, it seemed, in peace. The whole area was so redolent with growth, so fecund in the face of death, that the very air itself seemed green. Occasionally this was broken up into camouflage patterns by splashes of golden sunlight percolating through the foliage, lighting a profusion of air-borne motes which danced in and out of arboreal shadows.

As he made his way along narrow paths and through dense shrubbery, he was amazed at the variety of memorials erected over the burial plots of the loved and lost, and of once-famous celebrities, now long forgotten. As well as those angels observing his progress there were others laid down upon marble slabs as if in eternal sleep. There were crosses galore and draped and broken columns, chest tombs and raised sarcophagi, and the occasional family mausoleum built like a miniature Palladian mansion. All of these interspersed by shrubs and crawled across by rampant ivy.

At one point he was astonished to come across the burial place of a menagerist who had a full-sized stone lion sleeping on top of his tomb. There was another surmounted by a half-sized marble grand piano, with its lid tilted open. Jonno pondered whether the sculptor imagined that in the dark of night the occupant below might rise up to practice on the stone keyboard. He was almost brought to tears by the tomb of Thomas Sayers, whose head was carved in relief over an accompanying life-sized sculpture of his favourite dog, which lay with the most mournful expression on its face and its head drooping down upon its paws.

As he picked his way through the undergrowth, he startled a vixen which was sitting on a broken tomb with one of its sides smashed in. She was watching over two cubs play-fighting in and out of more busted memorials and, on his intrusion, gave a short bark before all three disappeared into the trees. Jonno was becoming overwhelmed, the strength in his legs was sapping, and he was looking for a place to sit when he recognised a name. On an upright headstone were carved the words Gabriele Rossetti, and below them his wife Frances Mary. There was a smaller footstone with the name of their son William chiselled into it and between the two a small slab inscribed with the name of their daughter Christina and also of Elizabeth Eleanor, wife of their eldest son Dante Gabriel. He had come across the final resting place of the model for *Beata Beatrix*.

Jonno took her proximity as some kind of sign, although he wasn't sure of what. He sat on the chest tomb with the smashed in side, lit up his remaining opium charged joint and contemplated her grave. She had overdosed on laudanum, possibly on purpose, or maybe by accident like the misadventure she represented in Millais' painting. Was the universe communicating with him, Jonno wondered, was finding her quiet resting place some kind of a warning? Each time he exhaled he blew the heavy smoke in her direction before laying back and falling into a reverie of his own.

As the opium drew him deeper and deeper, he found himself inhabiting the old Ken Russel television film of her lover, and later husband, Dante Gabriel Rossetti. It was incredibly confusing. He could see it all before him, as if on a screen, and yet it seemed that he was living it too, sometimes occupying a role, as the scenes became jump-cuts from one to another, and conflicting emotions crashed through him. He was heartbroken at her death and guilt-ridden by his infidelities. He wound his solitary book of poems into the luxuriance of her red-gold hair, burying it in the coffin alongside her. Swinburne appeared and persuaded him to get it back. He was dazzled by flashes of light. Black-clad figures danced past flames leaping from an enormous bonfire, which spat sparks up into the darkness of night. The coffin was exhumed. The lid broken open. A white gloved hand reached in, retrieving the volume from amongst the hair which had continued to grow and wind about the fleshless skull. The jaw cracked open and shrieked at the violation.

Jonno jerked awake. A fox-cub had run across his feet and the vixen barked a reprimand close to his ear. He was grateful to have been aroused from this daytime nightmare, and determined he should heed the message it seemed the universe was vouchsafing. He would curtail his flirtation with the poppy's tears.

The following day he returned with the small amount of opium left, scratched a shallow depression in the soil to one side of Lizzie's grave and buried it there, to leach down to her over the years as if in a gesture of thanks.

~ 21 ~

1972

The journey home was painful for both of them. At the tube, Jonno steered them into one of the smoking carriages, pulled out his cigarettes and offered her one. They sat side by side in silence, surrounded by strangers, puffing away and occasionally slipping each other a sideways glance. For all of the carriage's stuffy warmth they both were frigid, frozen.

As they made for the escalator, Jonno ensured that he preceded her, sparing himself the sight of her body in such close proximity. As they ascended into the night he determinedly didn't look round. The fact was he didn't know what on earth he could say. He was afraid that if he did start talking, he would blurt out something irrevocably hurtful, something he would be ashamed of later. Or he might break down, which would be equally embarrassing. So they walked the streets, still not talking, still locked inside their own worlds. Jonno felt himself encased within an armour of politeness as he unlocked the garden gate and held the back door open for her to enter.

When they were finally standing face to face in the kitchen, he realised the silence was no longer tenable.

"So, were you ever going to tell me, or were you planning on just disappearing one day?"

"I know you're angry, but please, if this has to be the end, can we try not to destroy the memory. Of course I was going to tell you. It just never seemed to be the right moment. It was selfish of me, I know. I was enjoying myself so much being with you, I didn't want to destroy it."

"I enjoyed it too. Too much, it seems."

"Don't say that, please. These last three weeks have been the happiest I've felt for years. If you want them to end, can we at least do it as friends?"

"I don't, I didn't want them to end, but I'm not the one going away."

"I am so tired. Could we, maybe sit down, to talk about this?"

"Of course, please," Jonno said, pulling one of the wooden chairs out from under the narrow formica-topped kitchen table. "I think I'm going to need some tea. Do you fancy a cup?"

"Please."

While he busied himself putting on the kettle, finding mugs and tea bags, he realised the pointlessness of his anger. With his back turned to her, he felt it leaking away from him, to be replaced by a profound sadness.

He remembered Hamish outside the pub in Notting Hill; saying she might appear to be really tough most of the time, inside she was still fragile. Indeed, she had confessed as much just before they entered the hall at the folk club. And yet, after Mel nearly let the cat out of the bag, she still stood in front of a room full of strangers and proclaimed her love for him. How much courage had that taken?

When he turned, mugs in hand, he looked down at her perched upon the edge of the chair. The abundance of her hair flowed around such an apprehensive face which was tilted up towards him. Wrapped tightly as she was in her tartan shawl, and with the fullness of the purple dress flowing about and over her knees, she reminded him of a little girl. For a brief moment he pictured her as one of Tenniel's illustrations for *Alice in Wonderland*, an innocent lost in a confusing world, and his heart went out to her.

He placed the mugs on the table, pulled out the other chair and sat facing her.

"So, tell me, whereabouts are you going?"

"Australia."

"Why, for God's sake?"

"Because it's warm? Because the sun shines there?"

"Now you're taking the piss."

"No, I'm sorry, but I'm not. It's just hard to put into English. Because it's about feelings. Ever since...well I've told you most of the things...ever since my parents threw me out, I've felt kind of frozen, inside. The only real thing I've been able to hang onto was my singing, everything else..."

"...That doesn't make me feel too good, Susie."

"Until you came along, I was going to say. But I've been like this for years. And we've known each other for what? Three weeks. Three and a half."

"Does time matter?"

"But it's all arranged, don't you see? I've been working towards this for months, nearly a year. I met this Aussie girl when I was in the refuge, Mandy. Her bloke was trying to put her on the game. Eventually she ran away. After a couple of months she'd straightened her head out and she went back home. We kept in touch and she kept telling me to go over, start a new life. Land of opportunity, all that. It's why I took the job working for a travel agent. So I could get a cheap ticket. I've been there six months and I've nearly got it saved. And then you came along."

"Did you mean it?"

"What?"

"Falling in love."

"I kept trying to put you off. I thought if you really knew about me, my past and everything, you wouldn't want me. Not permanently."

"So they weren't really tests."

"Well yes, except I was expecting you to fail them, sort of. It's hard to explain, it wasn't clear-cut. I mean I was really enjoying your company. You are a great bloke and I hadn't been with anybody for over a year, but you were safe. I could be with you because there was an end-point, I was going to leave. I wouldn't get involved, no complications, no chance of getting hurt. We'd just have a good time together for a little while, go to a few concerts maybe, see a few films, smoke a bit of dope, enjoy some uncomplicated sex, and then..."

"And then?"

"And then, goodbye."

"So that's what this is?"

"I really don't want it to be. Yes, I meant what I said. I fell in love. But I am still going to go. I have to. It could be a huge mistake but I've made them before. Staying could easily be a bigger one. I don't know you. You don't know me. Not really. We like each other very much. I call it love. But how long would it last? Long enough that I wouldn't regret making the biggest mistake of my life? Yet again. I can't afford to take the risk. I have to look after myself."

"Yes, I can see that. I guess I'm the one being selfish."

"You bastard," she shot him a filthy look, before breaking up into laughter when she saw the confused expression on his face.

"What?" Jonno asked.

"How dare you be so understanding? You're doing it again. Passing tests you're supposed to fail."

"That's too bloody deep for me. Do you fancy a joint?" Jonno asked as he pulled a square of silver paper from one of his socks.

"I thought you'd never ask. Of course I bloody do. It's been a really long day, it seems like weeks since we were up in Highgate, I've bared my soul on stage in front of strangers, and I'm emotionally overwrought and exhausted. So yes, I want a joint, and after we've smoked it, if you don't hate me now, do you think you could take me to bed? I not promising anything mind, as soon as I lie down, I'm going to blow out like a candle. You could probably have your wicked way with me, although I'd prefer you didn't."

Horrified, Jonno blurted out, "Just holding you and listening to you breathing will be enough, for tonight."

They continued to sit at the kitchen table while Jonno rolled a joint, which they shared companionably as they drank their mugs of tea. When it was finished, Susie tried unsuccessfully to stifle a yawn, and Jonno realised how dog-tired and wrung out they both were. He stretched out his hand to her as he rose, which she clasped. When they were both standing, he threw his other arm around her waist and hugged her as he kissed the top of her head. He then led her through the darkened lounge, before relinquishing her hand as he leaned down to put on his bedside lamp.

The pair of them divested themselves of their clothes as quickly as possible, Jonno dropping his on the floor beside the bed, Susie careful to hang up her purple dress. Then gratefully they crawled underneath the quilt from either side, met in the middle of the mattress, kissed and immediately fell asleep. Jonno unable, as he had thought, to remain awake long enough to hear the gentle rise and fall of his companion's breathing.

In the dim light of early morning he awoke to find Susie lying beside him, propped up on one elbow, watching him.

"What?" he asked, as he struggled to re-orientate himself from the distant realm of his dreams.

"Nothing," she replied. "Just capturing memories, I guess. Do you know you talk in your sleep sometimes?"

"No. What did I say?"

"Oh nothing that made much sense. It was just weird, funny, I think you were telling me not to put the cat out. Did you have a cat?"

"When I was little, we did. Marnie was beautiful, tortoiseshell, she got run over in the end."

"I'm sorry. You must have been dreaming about her."

"No, I was dreaming about you." He reached out and pulled her in towards him. "And about doing something like this," as he stroked his hand up and down her spine, feeling for each of her vertebrae.

"Don't put the cat out?" she queried.

"Wouldn't dream of it," he replied as his hand moved further down to stroke across her buttocks, before moving between her legs.

Afterwards, they both fell back to sleep again. Somewhat later, Jonno woke to the sound of running water coming from the bathroom. When he pulled open one of his drawers to get some clean underpants, he got the first surprise of his morning. While not being particularly fastidious in the way of folding his clothes he was not this messy. Pants, socks and Tee shirts were all scrunched up together. It seemed someone had been rummaging about in there, and he didn't think it was Susie. He hurriedly dressed as he looked through the other drawers, and then around the rest of the room. Someone had searched the place. Too tired to notice the previous night, he now saw his typewriter was sitting at an awkward angle on his desk. Pulling out the desk drawers confirmed their contents too had been disturbed.

His immediate thought was that the police had paid another visit while they were at the folk club. Perhaps their warrant was yet to expire; he had no real idea how such things worked. He moved into the living room, and it was there he realised who the visitor must have been. The turntable and amplifier were missing. As Susie was coming out of the bathroom, he rushed past her and lifted the lid of the cistern.

"Bastard!" he shouted.

"What?" Susie, who at first had thought him bursting for a piss, turned to watch from the doorway when she heard him lifting the lid off the cistern.

"Stevie. He's bloody done it again."

"What do you mean?"

"He's been here. While we were out last night, he's turned the place over. He's still got a key. Maybe he was watching us. He's taken the two ounces I hid in the toilet while you were getting changed yesterday. Like I said up in Highgate, he's looking for our stash. He thinks I'm keeping it all for myself. He must have hoped that I'd brought it here. I guess he was sending me a message."

"Why not just get in touch?"

"He doesn't trust me. And he's taking what he can. He's taken the stereo, which is fine because it was his. He must have thought the speakers were too heavy or looked too suspect in the middle of the night. He's taken most of my records too. *More* has gone."

"Why would he do that?"

"Because he knows it's my favourite album. His father is giving him a hard time, so he wants to give me one."

"Would he get violent?"

"I wouldn't have thought so, but then I never really knew him. Maybe. Depends on how pissed off he is, what's happening in his life now. His Dad was going to make him work in a prison. Maybe this wasn't him. Maybe he gave his key to someone inside due for release. Get one of the crims to do this. I suppose we could be in some kind of danger."

"Jesus."

"He loved the coke. Maybe he got addicted. In which case anything could happen."

"I think you should come home with me. Share my room for a while."

"Until you split?"

"Oh God, I don't know. Yes, why not? I need you to be safe. I can't leave, wondering about you. Stay with me until then?"

"You are still going to leave though, aren't you?"

"Yes, it will be really painful, but I'm still going to go, I have to. For the sake of my mental health."

"I'm not sure my mental health would be able to cope with staying at your place, wondering all the time if you were going to disappear."

"I wouldn't just walk out. I'll give you plenty of warning. Once I've bought my ticket I'll know when I'm going."

"What about the boys? Your place is crowded as it is."

"One more won't hurt. They'll understand. They like you. Maybe you could take over my room when I've gone. You won't be keeping this place on, will you?"

"No, I couldn't afford it on my own when I stop dealing."

"You are giving it up then?"

"For sure. I don't know what I am going to do. Get myself some kind of job, I guess. I won't say dealing wasn't fun, but it's too distracting, I haven't written a poem for months. Maybe I'll try writing a book, I've had plenty of unusual experiences these last few years."

"You should. You're always telling stories."

"Not necessarily ones that people will want to hear. Someone once told me that James Joyce has already said everything."

"Rubbish. Nobody has said everything. Everyone has a different story to tell. I've never read any James Joyce, I don't even know who he is, or was, but I'd read something you wrote."

"Would you?"

"Of course I bloody would. Why have you got so little self-confidence?"

"When you've read as many great writers as I have it seems arrogant to believe you could be on the same level."

"So don't try. Be on your own level, write your own stuff. People still read. Writers still write. It's silly being daunted by the past. It's past. Be in the present. Write about it."

"You are so good for me. I'm going to be devastated but yes, I'll come and stay with you until you go."

"So come on, pack what you really need and let's go before some heavy turns up to do us over."

It didn't take long to pack. He managed to cram some of his clothes in with Susie's in her suitcase, some into a plastic bag he found in the kitchen and the rest into the battered holdall which had accompanied him on all of his travels over the last few years. He said a reluctant farewell to the desk, but had no problem leaving behind the drawers full of papers and bits of half-written poems he'd scribbled down. He left the remainder of the records, Steve's speakers, and the very expensive set of scales along with everything else in the kitchen. With a bit of a wrench he decided he didn't need his collection of books, merely stuffing his dog-eared copy of the poems of John Keats down into one side of the hold-all. Susie picked up her suit-case, Jonno slung the holdall over one shoulder and with the plastic bag in one hand and the typewriter case in the other, together they exited through the hall door. They stopped in the porch, and he looked out over the green.

"I'm going to miss this place," he said. "It's the most expensive flat I've ever lived in. But it's a pad for a dope dealer, not for a starving artist. Oh well, back to the garret where I belong."

"Hey, our place isn't that bad."

"Only joking. Ok, 'lead on McDuff.'"

"The name's MacDonald."

"I know, I know. It's a miss-quote from Macbeth."

"Jesus, I can see having you around is going to be an education. First, I had to check out Arthurian legends, now I'm going to have to bone up on Shakespeare."

So saying she raced across the road and into the park. Jonno followed more slowly. Trying not to alarm her, he surreptitiously cast his eyes all around, but couldn't see anyone who looked out of place. Nevertheless every time they passed a shop window on their way to the tube, Jonno slowed his pace a little, and gazed at their reflections. The last thing he wanted was to be followed, either by Steve or by whoever he might have employed to keep an eye on him. He decided it was taking paranoia too far to think the cops might still be interested in his movements, but it was worth taking precautions. There was still one week to go before signing on for the last time at the local police station.

$$\sim 22 \sim$$

1972

It was also through Kiwi Paul they had their first brush with cocaine, thanks to a request from Candy Mellon. Candy first arrived in the company of Ken, one of their regular customers, who was picking up a weight. He should have known better than to bring her as by now there were strict rules about who was allowed to know about their business. Candy was American and, as Ken said when he later phoned to apologise for his indiscretion, she was entirely trustworthy, but very pushy. She was not long in the country, and intent on wasting no time in making her way around the scene in London. By implication the boys understood she was doing this by way of various beds, including, currently, Ken's.

This was confirmed when a few days later she turned up late one night, unaccompanied, and made it clear she wished to stay. What she didn't make quite so clear, was with which one of them. Jonno quickly fathomed she wasn't choosy, that either one of them would do, or should they be keen, both of them together. He had only slept with one woman since the previous year but however horny smoking dope made him, he couldn't bring himself to countenance such an impersonal connection. Still less did he fancy being three in a bed with another bloke. He recognised the hypocrisy of this when he realised that if the offer was made by two women things would have been quite different. He smiled as he thought this to himself, then yawned, stated his need for an early night and took himself off to his bed, alone.

He was first up the next day, shortly to be joined by Candy in the kitchen, who was wearing one of Steve's shirts. She expressed her horror at finding her only option was instant coffee.

"I'll never understand you limey guys," she said as she was pouring hot water over the fine brown powder at the bottom of a mug. "The rest of the whole fucking world drinks real coffee, made out of real ground-up beans for breakfast. Whereas you guys, pour water over shrivelled-up leaves for God's sake, or else this powdered shit which bears as much relationship to coffee as crap does to chocolate."

"You could try drinking tea without milk. With a drop of lemon juice? Some people swear by it. Especially Earl Grey."

"Is that the one with the oil in it? Never tasted anything so disgusting. Like urine in a cup."

"I don't think you're going to enjoy England, are you?"

"Don't get me wrong, there are compensations. I am having one hell of a time. Your guy's accents are just so fucking cute. Are you sure you don't want some of this?" So saying she lifted the hem of Steve's shirt to reveal the black lace briefs she was wearing."

"It's a little early in the day for me, thanks all the same."

"Your loss buster," as she carried her mug back upstairs. A little over half an hour later, now fully dressed, she passed back through the living room where Jonno was sitting. Before descending she bent over the back of his armchair and kissed the top of his head. Steve appeared, looking somewhat rumpled, and made for the stairs mumbling "Tea, coffee, sustenance," as if he were recovering from a long-distance hike on Dartmoor.

"Candy called," Jonno announced a week later one lunchtime when Steve emerged from his room, having spent an hour practicing on his new, hand-made acoustic guitar. "She wants to know if we can supply a quarter ounce of coke and a couple of ounces of grass."

"What does she want with a quarter ounce of coke, and how the hell can she afford it?"

"It's not for her, she's with a band. Groupieing, I guess."

"Candy?" Steve was incredulous.

"So she said."

"Which band?"

"The one we're going to see at the Rainbow next week."

"You're shitting me! Manassas? Steve Stills? Never."

"That's what she said."

It did seem unlikely. Although not unattractive Candy wouldn't have seemed ideal groupie material for one of the hottest American acts currently touring Europe.

"Maybe it's a wind-up, some game she's playing, trying to get back at me for turning her down," Jonno said before having another thought. "Of course it could be worse, like some kind of trap. I mean we know nothing about her, do we? Perhaps she's got herself into trouble with immigration and she's struck a deal. We shouldn't touch it with industrial-strength rubber gloves."

"No, she wouldn't. We gave her a good time the other night. At least I did. Think about it. Stills is here with his new band. He's going to want some gear isn't he, for recreation purposes? He can hardly bring it with him, not with his reputation. Customs will be going through their gear with X-ray specs. Candy's American too, maybe they go back, maybe they're family friends or something, or she knows someone else in the band."

"I guess you could be right," Jonno said. "I didn't commit us to anything, just told her we'd find out. I'll ask Paul when he rings tomorrow. Let's face it when we see them, we do want them to be on top form, not strung out and needing."

"We'd need to be bloody careful. It's dangerous shit. It's not just a few months, possession of coke is more like a few years. And dealing it...who knows? A couple of young, middle-class, long-haired guys in gaol, have you got any idea? We'd never sit down again." With that Steve started to roll his first joint of the day.

Jonno blinked. He'd never really considered what prison might be like. What he was doing was more by way of a romantic adventure. In the circles they frequented they were outlaws rather than criminals. Butch Cassidy and the Sundance Kid maybe, certainly not Ronnie and Reggie Kray. Most contemporary films glorified outlaws as heroes. Bonnie and Clyde, Easy Rider. But he wasn't stupid, given his father's old occupation he knew Steve would have a clearer idea of the reality of prison. His was a different kind of revolution.

The joint was fired up and passed slowly backwards and forwards while they listened to one side of the double album that the band was here to promote. West coast American country rock with the emphasis more on rock than on country. The influence was plain though, the sweet sound of the mandolin underscoring the lead's blistering guitar, while the bass relentlessly pumped them all forward with a jazz/funk energy.

"Ok," Steve said, after some thought, "Let's face it, it would be a gas to get it for them, sort of like being 'By Appointment to the Queen' on the marmalade jars. The grass could be more difficult than the coke."

"It's the bass player wants the grass. Candy said the black guy doesn't shove shit up his nose."

"He plays righteous bass whatever he does. He must smoke a fuck of a lot if he wants a couple of ounces; how long are they here for, a week?"

"I guess he likes to party."

"Yeah, with Candy and maybe a few of her friends," Steve said and laughed.

Kiwi Paul was surprised and more than a little amused by their foray into 'the harder stuff' as he put it, but willingly came up with the goods. £125 for a quarter ounce of coke sounded about right, although they had no real experience of the market. £20 each for the ounces of grass seemed a little steep considering they were paying £100 for 16 ounces of hash when they bought their usual ten weights at a time. Paul assured them market forces prevailed whoever the ultimate customer. So the dope was secured the day before the concert and Candy informed. The band was apparently overjoyed.

Candy knew they would be attending the concert, along with most of London's hip elite, so they agreed to bring the gear with them. It was wild to think they were about to meet a contemporary rock legend on his first tour to Britain, together with one of the original members of the Byrds. They decided that, bugger market forces, they'd let them have the whole deal at cost.

The Rainbow was packed out. All manner of sartorial splendour was in evidence along with beads, headbands and bangles galore. The impression was of an enormous children's party where a thousand dress-up boxes had been ransacked. A motley collection of pirates, Indians (both North American and sub-continental), cowboys, expatriate Russian princesses, wizards, warlocks, damosels and the like, all convened to celebrate the first overseas appearance of a guitar hero since the break-up of the super-group he'd been a part of. Jonno dug out his purple crushed velvet loon pants even though they were really a little too tight in the crotch. They made his legs feel electric, like some exotic animal from the hidden forests of Venus in a Philip K. Dick novel. Through a thin blue tee-shirt he luxuriated in the fur lining of his open white Afghan coat. He turned the collar up, so that his hair was pushed forward on either side of his head, falling down to his breast.

They tossed a coin back at the flat to see who should deliver the gear, and Steve won, or lost, depending on the outcome. His jeans were tucked inside hand-crafted cowboy boots with silver toe caps, down which the small packet of white powder was stuffed. The grass was in the pockets of his denim shirt, over which he was wearing his fringed and beaded leather waistcoat. As Jonno looked around at the four thousand odd people crowded into the hall, the whole evening felt wild, like some coming together of the tribes.

For all the signs prohibiting smoking, as soon as the lights went down it seemed as if they were immediately thrown back up again as more than a thousand lighters lit over a thousand joints. Security guards, waving their arms in the air helplessly, scampered about until, overwhelmed by the numbers, they scurried away.

With a roar like a giant wave breaking on a tropical shore the band was welcomed onstage and then the music began. Shortly a man came down the aisle alongside them and tapped Steve on the shoulder, at which he stood and followed him back up the steps. This was it, Jonno thought, either the deal was about to be done, or the whole thing would turn out to be a set-up and Steve would not be coming back. Unlike the rest of the crowd Jonno was cheered when, after only three numbers, the band started trooping off the stage. Sensing the crowd's disappointment the guitarist leaned into the microphone and stated they just needed to take a short break to sort something out and would be back straightaway. Jonno pictured them all backstage snorting lines through rolled-up bank-notes or skinning up the grass. While they were still offstage Steve returned and regained his seat, muttering as he did so,

"Arrogant fucking prick."

"What happened?"

"They took me to this limo round the back where this Yank fucker was sitting. He took the grass then licked his finger and stuck it straight in the coke before rubbing it around on his gums. Then he said it was shit and he wasn't having any. I bet he feels like a complete tool now. Like Paul said, it's really pure gear. I reckon he was just missing the usual impurities. By now his whole mouth must be frozen fucking solid. Serve him right if they all kick the shit out of him."

As Steve was relaying this the members of the band began trickling back onto the stage and shortly the concert resumed. While the rhythm section, the bassist and drummer, looked happy enough and began to drive the others forward, all in all it was a fairly lack-lustre performance, and not up to the standard achieved on the double album back at their flat. While the members of the music-press attending in droves would in subsequent days write scathing, or at best limp reviews, Jonno and Steve were the only people outside the inner circle who knew the reason why.

When they got back home Jonno got the shaving mirror from the bathroom and Steve laid out four lines on it with his bank card, as Paul showed them when he delivered the coke. They each took a ten-pound note from the wooden box where they kept their money, rolled them into tight tubes and then took turns to snort up a line each. It didn't sting, as Jonno at first feared, but after a few minutes there was the mildly unpleasant sensation of a mass of acrid mucus sliding down the back of his throat. Beyond that he found the high that it gave him to be pleasant enough but really nothing spectacular, and he wondered what all the fuss was about. It wasn't too dissimilar from the high that hash gave him, beyond rendering him more active while experiencing it. Steve brought his guitar from his room and began to play in the lounge while Jonno fetched their scales from the kitchen and placed them on the coffee table.

He very carefully measured the remains of the little packet into one of the pans, which registered that there was a little under seven grams left.

"If we sell it for £20 a gram, we make our money back plus a little bit for the bother. We know at least seven people who would want to give it a try. That way we could be rid of it really quickly," Jonno said.

"We shouldn't sell all of it," Steve replied.

"Why not? You said yourself, it's really dangerous. I don't want to get busted with this stuff lying about the place."

"You worry too much; we're not going to get busted."

"Oh yeh? Famous last words."

"Besides which, it's fucking nice. I can see now why so many guitarists get right into it. It makes your playing seem effortless or something. And the sound is, I don't know, clearer somehow, more precise, like the instrument is singing. I bet Carlos Santana snorts a shit-load."

"Yeh well, he can afford it. I mean ok, it feels good, I'm feeling good, but it's nothing really special, is it?" He pointed at the powder in the stainless-steel pan, "I mean for the price of that, which might last the pair of us a fortnight if we were careful, we could buy enough hash to get us stoned constantly for six months or so. It's not worth it."

"Ok, you're right, it's expensive, but I want to give it a go. You smoked most of that opium remember, now it's my turn."

"Fair enough. Paul charged us twenty for that opium, so you have a gram of this and we'll sell the rest. Starting tomorrow. It's supposed to be really addictive, so I want to get rid of it as soon as possible, before you get hooked."

"Man, you worry too much. You're not my mother, you know."

"I'm aware of that. But we've got a good thing going here Steve, and drugs have already fucked up one of my friendships. I don't want it happening again."

"Yeah, yeah, yeah."

As Steve played on Jonno had to admit that it did sound good. He put this down to the superior quality of the new guitar, however, rather than any innate power bestowed by the cocaine. He knew, from his own literary endeavours, how easy it was to convince yourself that drugs were a necessary aid to creation. He busied himself with measuring out the white powder into seven equal deals, which he folded into neat squares of paper, before pushing one of them across the table towards Steve.

~ 23 ~

1972

Susie's flat was on the top floor of a five-story mansion block on Prince of Wales Drive. It being a Sunday the boys were all home, Hamish and Angus lying on a couple of couches, with Duncan sprawled on the floor. Going by the smell, they had been sampling Hamish's recently purchased weight of Pakistan's finest.

"Ah excellent. Just in time to put on a brew," said Duncan, I'm dry as dry but I don't think I can stand up. Hi Jonno, I hope you enjoyed the show."

"The music was brilliant. The rest was a little...unexpected."

"You're still together though, eh?" Hamish shot a quizzical look to Jonno, "After that wee shock to the system. I thought you were...never mind."

"We are. Just for a little while, as it turns out," Jonno answered him.

"That's what we need to talk to you about," Susie said, and went on to describe the break-in. When they brought the gear around the previous afternoon neither of them had mentioned Steve lurking around Highgate Cemetery, trying to find out where it was stashed. Now she enlightened them.

"The thing is we don't know what he's going to do next. He's obviously desperate. He didn't phone and he didn't come round to ask about it. He didn't find it at the cemetery, and last night he didn't find it in the flat. So next time it might be strong-arm stuff. It feels like it might be getting dangerous. So I want Jonno to come and stay with me for a little while. Would that be alright with you three?"

"Until you go away?" Hamish asked, to which Susie nodded.

"Can you cook?" Angus enquired.

"I have been known to whip up a mean curry."

"In that case," Angus said, "you're in as far as I'm concerned."

The other two nodded in affirmation.

"Is that all of your stuff?" Duncan asked him.

"I'm leaving everything else behind. I'm cutting and running. No, I'm making a fresh start. Yet another one. I feel like a snake, every now and again I have to shed my old skin. The alchemists believed it made them stronger, hopefully it works for me too. Steve is welcome to whatever I left behind. He took most of my records yesterday, he might as well have the rest, my desk, and whatever else he fancies. If he'd left an address there wouldn't be any need for all of this shit. I'd have just sent him his cut. Maybe not now though. The bastard took my stash again too. I've still got a bit left but I'll need to get some more from your office Hamish."

"No rush, man, there's plenty here just now. It's my day off tomorrow so it will have to wait until Tuesday."

"Fine. I've had an idea about where I can offload it all. If it checks out then maybe I can take it all off your hands on Tuesday."

"Nae bother."

Taking Jonno's hand Susie led him off towards her room. As they were going through the door Angus shouted after them "Just one thing Susie, no fucking screaming, ok? I'm jealous enough as it is."

Duncan and Angus collapsed into giggles, but Hamish frowned at them. Jonno glanced quickly at Susie's face to see if she was embarrassed but instead of blushing Susie shouted back at him, "Just for that you can make your own bloody tea. We're going out for a walk once we've dumped Jonno's stuff."

When they closed the door on them Susie said, "Bloody drummers, just can't help themselves being crude, can they?"

"I wouldn't know," Jonno replied as he looked around. It was a plain room with white painted walls and a grey fitted carpet upon which lay a double mattress. The high ceiling was painted in an eggshell blue which stretched down to a contrasting picture rail picked out in fire-engine red. A large sash window flooded the room with early afternoon sunlight and gave a view across the wide street to a lower mansion block opposite. He was pleased to see she was a tidy person. Before leaving to go to work on the Friday she must have straightened out the quilt on her bed and plumped up the pillows. There were no clothes scattered around, so they must have been either hung up in the white painted wardrobe, folded into the matching chest of drawers or else tidied away into the cane basket beside it. By the bed an orange crate lay on its side, on which stood a lamp with a chiffon scarf draped over its shade, and which housed three books. Jonno couldn't help himself from dropping to his knees to see what they were. He laughed when he saw that there were library copies of *Le Morte D'Arthur* and a slim volume of the poems of John Keats, next to the much thicker book of Grimm's Fairy Tales. This was not from a library, but of such an age that it looked to have been in her possession for a number of years.

"Childhood present?" He enquired.

"No. Charing Cross Road, second hand. I did have a copy at home which I loved so much that I just had to replace it. The others were homework."

"Homework?"

"Well I needed to check up on you, didn't I? Find out what I was getting myself into."

She cleared a couple of trinket boxes to one side on the top of the chest of drawers. Jonno picked up a framed photograph of a wild sea crashing against rocks before a flaming sunset breaking through a lowering sky.

"Home?" he asked.

"Not anymore," she replied. "You can put your typewriter on here and later I'll shift some clothes about so that you've got some drawer space. I loved coming round to your place, but this is even better. Makes the room complete." She held him by the hips and lifted her face for a kiss. Then, breaking away, she said "Come on, we've got to get to the launderette or I won't have anything to wear for work tomorrow. I'll show you *my* park while it's doing."

Having loaded her clothes into a machine they made their way into Battersea Park. Although it was the middle of November it was still a fine sunny afternoon and there were plenty of warmly dressed people about, some walking in family groups, perambulating around the ponds to allow their offspring to throw pieces of broken bread for the ducks. Some sat on benches reading the Sunday papers. Couples lay side by side kissing, or just idly running fingers through their partner's hair while they talked of whatever it is that young lovers do. Jonno and Susie joined them once they found a suitable spot in the shade of an ancient elm. With her fair complexion Susie had to be careful not to expose herself to too much sun.

"You are going to find that difficult in Australia," Jonno said once this was explained to him.

"Oh I'm going to be getting around in big hats and wearing plenty of cheesecloth clothing," she laughed. She was lying with her head on his right thigh, looking up into the branches above them. Suddenly she turned her head to look into his eyes. "Can we not talk about Australia, please? I know you don't want me to go and right now I don't want to either, but I *am* going to. I want to enjoy what little time we have left. It will all be spoilt if I constantly think you are trying to talk me out of it."

"Fair enough. I'll attempt to banish all thought of it. We will just be two young lovers who have recently met, enjoying the pleasure of each other's company. An idyll of Tristram and Iseult, where there is nothing but the present moment and no one except each other."

"Is this another story?"

"It's in your book about King Arthur."

"Oh, I'm only about a quarter of the way through it so far. At the moment it's mostly it's about Sir Launcelot. So tell me."

"Another time perhaps, it's too sad for such a lovely day. Tristram was a Cornish knight who fell in love with an Irish princess and it didn't end well. You should read it for yourself, one day when you are far away." So saying he bent down and kissed her lips. "But while they were together, they knew a kind of bliss," he said on pulling away. "Like us," he added before tasting her lips once more.

The afternoon passed in similar fashion before they returned to the launderette to dry and then take her washing home. She packed it all away and at the same time made room for some of Jonno's clothes. The rest he transferred to her now empty suitcase which they placed on what they decided was to be his side of the bed. Then they lay down on it while Susie rolled the pair of them a joint.

Jonno couldn't get the image of Tristram and Iseult out of his head, although not daring to mention it again. He had been given an old Victorian copy of *The Legends of King Arthur* when he was a child, which contained illustrations. One of them was of Tristram and Iseult in her cabin on the boat ferrying them back to Cornwall. It was an etching very much in the Pre-Raphaelite style, with Tristram looking enraptured as he held the flask containing a love potion, while she was lifting a beaker of it to her lips. Beneath, the caption read, 'By the time they had finished drinking they loved each other so well that their love never more might leave them.'

Since he was Cornish himself, this story had a more profound effect on him than all the other stories in the book. Now, as they lay side by side on the mattress on the floor, with the light fading as the sun set beyond the window, passing the joint from hand to hand, and from lip to lip, Jonno pictured them lying on a boat, journeying he knew not where. When Susie turned to stub out the roach in the ashtray on top of the orange crate, he reached for her and buried his face in her hair, then lifted it aside in order to kiss her slender neck.

Later, eschewing the company of others, they went out to find themselves a meal before, replete, they returned to spend their first night together in what Jonno thought of as an enchanted room.

~ 24 ~

1972

Unfortunately the incident at the Rainbow was not the last time the boys would find themselves mixed up with cocaine. Jonno wanted to unload it as quickly as possible, but once Steve got through the gram they had agreed upon, he demanded they keep back another, and then again another. Jonno could see this process being repeated for as long as any was left, so after much heated argument he finally insisted, and a few of their customers were more than happy to score a gram of what was, in their circles, an exotic substance.

When it was gone Jonno was relieved at its absence. So he was dismayed at the news Steve brought back from a delivery run to his friends in Brighton. Norman, one of their number, had flown out to Kenya after graduating, where his father worked in one of Her Majesty's embassies. Having settled down after the violence of the Mau-Mau riots ten years previously, the whole East African region was being plunged into turmoil again by Idi Amin, the president of Uganda. This so-called 'Butcher of Africa' was reputed to enjoy eating the livers of his enemies.

At some point during Norman's travels around such a hazardous and unstable area, this scion of an upper middle class, politically-involved English family, had connected with a gang of heavy-duty smugglers. They informed him they could lay their hands on unlimited amounts of the fabled South American marching powder, their border being so much more porous than that of his mother country. Norman proposed a shipment of ten kilos of cocaine to be shared between various members of their clique in Brighton, including two for Steve, who was known to have numerous contacts in London.

"No fucking way," was Jonno's response when Steve put the idea to him, "You have got to be joking. Who is this bloody idiot?"

"Hey, Norman's a good mate of ours. His father's in the foreign office."

"Oh, so he's another of the Hooray Henry's you knocked about with at Sussex, is he?"

"Why are you so antagonistic?"

"Because he's out of his fucking mind. For a start the amount of cash he wants for it. Jesus, if we wanted a few kilos of cocaine, we could buy it for about the same amount from Kiwi Paul, without the risk of smuggling it in."

"Yeh well, I agree with you there, he's in Africa, he doesn't know current market values, does he? It's a figure he's pulled out of the air, we're not tied to it. Once we'd got the stuff, we could pay him whatever's a reasonable amount. It would be win/win."

"Win bloody lose if we got caught. He's not taking any risks, is he? If it all goes belly up, he loses the small amount he's paid for it. Big bloody deal. We lose what? Several years of freedom. No bloody thank you."

"Sure, it's a bit of a gamble I'll give you, but the benefits if it pays off..."

"Steve, you're not thinking straight. You just want to get your hands on some more coke for nothing."

"That's not true."

"Isn't it? Think about it. This mate of yours, this Norman, is he a professional smuggler? No, he's an amateur, with no fucking idea. Frying his brains swanning around a country right on the equator, out of his gourd smoking top quality African grass and snorting copious amounts of this gang's product de jour. Is he smart enough to devise a way of getting it to us without raising custom's suspicions?"

"Trev reckons he'll pack it into some kind of tourist souvenir stuff and post it."

"Exactly. Stuff it into African drums or something equally as obvious. Might just as well stick a label on the parcel saying 'contraband included.' They're not stupid, customs people, they spend their whole lives intercepting drugs and God knows what else. You reckon Norman's up to fooling them?"

"Yeh, well, maybe not. He never was the smartest cookie, and when he got stoned, he was..." Steve trailed off, remembering numerous occasions their little gang of undergraduate mates had restrained Norman from some dangerous prank, such as attempting to scale one of the onion domes of Brighton Pavilion. After a few moments he continued with, "So what do you think we should we do?"

"Stop him, for Christ's sake. As quickly as possible. Do we have his address?"

"No. I guess the embassy in Nairobi might know where he is."

"Jesus. Ok, we send a telegram care of the embassy telling him we don't want it. And you ring Trev down in Brighton, tell him we don't want a bar of it and he shouldn't touch it either. And try to find out how far along the whole thing is."

Sending the telegram was easy enough. Jonno was reading a collection of stories by Ernest Hemingway. The title of one of them seemed to express perfectly what he wanted to say without implicating either the sender or the recipient in anything nefarious. The phone call was not so clear cut. As Steve related it, Trev seemed to think it was too late, that not much could be done to avoid whatever was likely to happen. He didn't even seem to be bothered, Steve said, expressing the feeling that Jonno, whom he never met, was being overly anxious. This made Jonno even more worried.

"Why the hell can't these people see it?" he asked Steve. "Are they so strung out, or are they so convinced of their privileged positions they can't imagine anything touching them?"

Either way, as day followed day with no news, Jonno's fears grew until they reached such a crescendo, he felt he had to confide in someone. The next time Kiwi Paul rang he told him the whole story.

"Move," was Paul's immediate advice. "If you reckon he's going to send it to your address then all you can do is split. Quickly. And make sure you cover your tracks. If they don't know where you are then they can't bust you for anything. Tell you what, I've been thinking it might be time for me to move again. I've been here for over a year now. But there's no connection they can have between you and me. Why don't you guys move in here?"

"We don't know where you are."

"That's the beauty of it, hardly anyone does. Tell you what, at 7 pm tomorrow be standing outside the Albert Hall. I'll pick you up and bring you round so you can see if you want it. I don't know about your partner Steve, but you're a pretty savvy bloke. Start thinking of some way of passing your place on to someone who'll let you know if anything happens, but won't give you away if something does."

Steve was sceptical about the need for such a change, but was prepared to go along with the attempt to distance them from what Jonno was insisting was a looming disaster. His initial response was one of amusement, similar to his mates down in Brighton. Once Paul picked them up and drove them around to his flat in West Kensington, his attitude underwent a radical shift. Suddenly he was in favour of moving, being instantly enamoured of the new flat. They both were.

It was not just because of its location, although they both considered its proximity to the centre of town to be a great plus. They both liked that although it was attached to the back of a tall tenement building, it was totally self-contained, with its own private side entrance from the tiny garden sequestered behind a high wall with an impenetrable, solid garden gate. There was another doorway in the living room which connected it to the hallway of the main building, leading to a front door framed by Victorian coloured glass panels.

The flat was so new and fresh, as if Paul had been the only tenant since the concrete pad was poured. It was smaller than their place at Archway, but compact, with nothing superfluous to their needs.

"It's furnished, so everything stays," Paul stated.

"Even that?" Steve enquired, indicating the coffee table sitting between the sofa and the solitary armchair. It was not a proper coffee table but rather a thick sheet of mirror glass with its edges ground smooth, resting on breeze-blocks at either end over which bits of carpet were placed.

"I confess it was my own construction, but I'll leave it if you like. It didn't cost me anything and I won't need it where I'm going. Maybe you'd like to try it out?"

"Would I ever," Steve said, knowing there was only be one reason for Paul to have a mirrored table.

"So are you going to take the place?" Paul asked. Jonno and Steve looked at each other and nodded.

"In that case we'll have a little celebration." Paul tipped some white powder onto the table-top and began shaping it into six lines with the use of his bankcard.

Once back home Jonno started ringing around his list of contacts, asking if anyone knew of someone wanting a flat. Not surprisingly lots of people did, but most dropped out at the first hurdle he erected, the stipulation that they be straight, or pretty much so.

Bea, from the Putney house, put him in touch with Sheila, another croupier at their gaming club, whose brother was looking for a place. As an intern at St Thomas' Hospital Richie didn't smoke dope himself, because of the serious nature of his work and the extremely long hours involved, but Sheila assured Jonno that he harboured no moral objections to his sister or anyone else doing so. Apparently, he and a couple of mates had been looking for a decent place for quite a while. Jonno met him in the hospital canteen and explained the situation.

It happened really quickly. The next weekend Richie and the other two medical students started to move their stuff in, half an hour after Jonno and Steve finished carrying theirs out.

Jonno and Steve not only took over Paul's flat, but also his way of doing business. They would no longer have people dropping round to score whenever they felt like it, but rather told their contacts they would phone when they had anything, and deliver if required. They kept their change of address from everyone, and only gave their new phone number to Doctor Richie, as they called him.

Shortly after the move another event occurred which almost drove the pair of them out of the business altogether. This was engineered by Kiwi Paul, who must have known it was a scam all along when he put them in touch with a big, dark-haired man called Pierre, another of his customers. In their world it was very definitely 'buyer beware.' Maybe Paul was testing out their nerve, while trying to help out a mate who was stuck with a worthless deal. This, they realised in retrospect, was the reason why the transaction needed to be done at eight o'clock in the morning. It also explained Pierre's macho posturing, his coming on all hard-man with his display of assorted coshes and so-called 'self-protection' devices. Jonno immediately christened him 'Powerful Pierre' after a villainous but dumb cartoon character. Kiwi Paul came on like a mate, Pierre came on like a violent criminal. The nick-name eased Jonno's sense of intimidation a little.

They hadn't been happy about driving to a strange flat to meet an unknown man at eight o'clock but if they wanted ten weights of Moroccan at a bargain price this was what they had to do. The story from Pierre was that the heat was coming down at any moment and the stuff needed to be moved on fast. Go now or forever miss their chance.

Terrified of an accident or a breakdown on the way home, Jonno sweated with the bag stashed under his seat while Steve navigated his little min-van round Trafalgar Square, shot through the Admiralty arch, raced down the Mall towards the Palace with its ceremonial sentries, sling-shotted round the Victoria Memorial towards Hyde Park, crawled through Knightsbridge and up Kensington High Street, passed by the artists' houses on Talgarth Road before finally reaching the safety of their little park and home.

The relief was short lived, however.

By lunchtime their heads were clear enough to realise the shit was useless. Steve reckoned it must have come by the Contiki route; been driven across Europe in badly insulated bus tyres the whole way from Morocco, with all of its goodness being gradually cooked out of it. It looked right, smelt right, it even tasted right. It just didn't fucking get you off. Since arriving home they had drunk two cups of tea each and virtually chain-smoked joints, desperately trying to get some sort of hit off of it. Failing, miserably.

They spent an hour agonising over their next step. Had Pierre given them a taste of something else? It would be easy enough. But that would have been a total rip-off. No, you get a couple of mugs up really early, when they're still out of it from the night before. You intimidate them so they're confused, and then you let them sample the actual product. If they're too stoned or stupid to notice then it's their own fault and not your problem.

Eventually they decided there was really no choice, they had to front up to Pierre, however 'powerful' he might be. After all, effete, intellectual grammar-school boys though they may be, at least there were two of them. And they were good customers of Paul's, who hopefully wouldn't be too happy if they were badly beaten up. They couldn't afford to take the hit. Not on ten weights. A thousand pounds was the limit of their capital. They had to return the gear and try to recover their money.

'Powerful', for all his initial bluster, proved a paper tiger. They were polite, respectful, explaining they were just in no position to help him get rid of *his* problem. They had tried hard to shift it but no one was interested. Here was the gear back again and they would be most grateful for the return of their cash. He grumbled but short of physical violence there was little he could do – after all they knew where he lived. Like the cold war being waged by governments all around them, the whole scene was balanced by the possibility of mutual destruction. Grassing someone up was as simple as pushing a button.

Jonno was still a bit pissed off with Kiwi Paul but thankful the situation was resolved reasonably amicably. There was bound to be a little residual ill-feeling but hopefully it would pass and the whole thing shortly turn into one of those amusing anecdotes for the equivalent, in their world, of the dinner table. War stories regaled between dealers interspersed by the licking of Rizlas, the shredding of cigarettes and the heating of lumps of hash until that intoxicating curlicue of lazy blue smoke peels off and it becomes soft enough to crumble between calloused finger and thumb. As with religions the wide world over, ritual is everything. Boom Shankar.

Relief at its successful conclusion made Jonno ignore his previous worries, so that when Kiwi Paul rang, wondering if they wanted ten weights of Afghani, the pair of them were more than enthusiastic. Reputedly collected by men in leather aprons running through fields of ripe plants growing high in mountain foothills, Afghani was Jonno's favourite dope. He knew the story was probably apocryphal, but liked to think of turban-wearing farmers scraping thick layers of accumulated resin off their aprons as he settled back, rolled a joint and imbibed the produce of their labours.

While delivering to a couple of guys in Stoke Newington, Jonno met a young Scottish woman called Susie. She was sitting in their flat awaiting his arrival, so that she could buy an ounce from them for her cousin Hamish. Jonno hadn't been with anyone on a regular basis since his short-lived intimacy with Kate, only enjoying an occasional one-night-stand, with a woman who sporadically travelled down from one of the northern universities to pick up supplies.

Susie seemed not at all impressed by his façade of big-city hip sensibility. This meant he was able to drop the mask he felt constrained to adopt in front of his customers. Having delivered his package he didn't make his usual swift exit. While the guys in the kitchen were getting on with weighing and cutting it up, he sank into a couch in the corner of the front room to converse with the auburn-haired beauty who reminded him a little of the portrait of Lizzie Siddal, and who conversed in the softest, most lyrical voice he had ever heard.

He started to feel increasingly connected in her presence, as if there were an electrical charge flowing between them. By the time he left to return to West Kensington he found he had been sitting and talking with her for a couple of hours. Not only that but, surprisingly for him, having ascertained she was not romantically involved with either of the flatmates she was visiting, he'd asked her whether she'd accompany him to a Titus Groans concert the following week.

The few relationships he had enjoyed over the years were either as a result of proximity, as in the case with Kate, or because of sharing common experiences, such as with Harriet after their adventure in Grosvenor Square. To ask a strange woman out on a date was a new experience for him, one he would normally have been far too shy to contemplate. There was just something about Susie, an attraction he felt so strongly that he knew he would forever regret not trying to see her again. It appeared she felt something of the same, for she said 'yes' with such alacrity, that before Jonno knew it they had arranged a time and place to meet for the concert at the coming weekend.

$$\sim 25 \sim$$

1972

Jonno awoke in the middle of stretching his legs, which gave him a twinge of cramp in a calf muscle. At first, he didn't know where he was, but having moved several times in the last few years, this was nothing new. It was when he saw Susie trying to slip out from beneath the other side of the quilt that the strange surroundings came back to him. He reached for her. She turned and apologised for waking him.

"What, and deprive me of the sight of my beautiful girl-friend naked in the morning? How could you be so cruel?"

"You are such a smooth talker."

"Isn't it still dark? I don't believe you have to go yet. Surely, it's still the middle of the night."

"For those who deal with dreams perhaps, but for those whose lives are run by clocks, it is past the time for ele-vation. I am just a simple working girl who has an office to get to."

"God woman, there is nothing simple about you. Are you sure you have to go in to work today?"

"Of course, today and every day. But don't you worry, if you go back to sleep, I'll be back before you know it." So saying she freed herself from his grasp and threw a cotton dressing gown around her shoulders. Even this seemed to him exotic, a sort of Japanese kimono affair, with birds of paradise perched on creepers which ran up and down its length. As she left the room he snuggled back down and pulled the quilt up over his ears while he thought about how to spend his day.

As he had said to Hamish the previous afternoon, he'd thought of somewhere he might be able to unload the stash. However much the Scotsman was convinced there was no danger to him from hiding it at his work, Jonno still felt responsible for his new friend's safety. Accidents can always happen, and he knew the discovery of a large amount of hash in the Borough Council's offices would lead to immediate dismissal, swiftly followed by a period of imprisonment. He couldn't let that happen.

There was no point in paying a visit this early in the morning so, having enjoyed watching Susie dress and then been kissed goodbye, he fell back asleep. Hamish was in the kitchen when he finally arose and they sat at the table together drinking cups of tea and sharing a joint.

"Got any plans for today?" Hamish asked him.

"Visiting a friend of a friend. Why?"

"I was thinking it might be a good idea for us to have a bit of a talk."

"You're not going to come on all protective big brother again, are you?"

"Nae man, nothing like that. Well, mebee a little, but nothing, you know, unpleasant. Just a wee bit of advice really. Something I was thinking of, and I was wondering whether you had."

"Sounds intriguing. I won't be long, just need to check something out."

As Jonno walked towards the nearest tube station he wondered what was on Hamish's mind. It seemed the guy liked him, and had no problem with his relationship with his cousin. Nevertheless he was uneasy. He knew that if Hamish considered these last few weeks posed some sort of threat to Susie's happiness, then he would have no compunction in asking him to leave. And if he was honest, he wondered if the whole arrangement was such a good thing himself. He really enjoyed waking up beside her that morning, and could see from her face that she did too. The prospect of a further two or three weeks was immensely appealing, but he knew it was going to make their eventual parting all the more gut-wrenching for the pair of them. He wondered if this is what Hamish wished to talk about.

He found the street with no difficulty, and recognised the lilac front door. He pushed the bell and waited apprehensively as he heard footsteps approaching. He hoped he wasn't making a mistake. Often what seemed like a good idea in the middle of the night, next morning turned out not to have been. While unsure of his welcome, the one thing he was certain of was that of all their contacts Steve would not have visited this one to check up on him.

The door opened to reveal Powerful Pierre who scowled at him when he realised who was standing on his doorstep.

"What the fuck do you want?" he asked.

"Nothing. I've got a proposal, that's all. Something you should like, can I come in and tell you about it?"

Grudgingly Pierre stood to one side, allowed Jonno to step into his hall, and then preceded him down it into the dingy, stale-smelling room at the back of his house. The curtains were still drawn. Pierre switched on the light before sinking into an overstuffed armchair and looking up at his visitor inquisitively. Jonno stood beside a wooden coffee table strewn with half-empty coffee mugs, over-filled ash-trays, well-thumbed Freak Brothers comics alongside cigarette packets with bits ripped off them and packets of Rizlas with their covers similarly butchered.

"Ok, what's the big deal?"

"I know we didn't part on particularly good terms last time, but I was impressed by how gentlemanly you were about returning our money."

"Didn't have any choice, did I? I lost a lot on that deal. If you've just come to gloat..."

"No, nothing like that. Mind if I sit down?"

Pierre nodded without replying. Jonno took up a position on the threadbare couch, pulled out a square of silver paper from one of his socks, reached for one of the packets of Rizlas and started to roll a joint. When it was done, he handed it to Pierre to light.

"The Moroccan of yours had all the goodness cooked out of it. This is top quality Paki Gold Seal with all of its goodness still inside, agreed?"

Having taken a few tokes before handing the joint back over the table Pierre nodded his head reluctantly, before blowing out a huge lungful of smoke.

"Yeh, so what?"

"Well, I don't know if you've heard from Kiwi Paul recently, but Steve and I are having a bit of trouble from the forces of law and order, and I have decided on withdrawing from the business altogether."

"I did hear a whisper."

"Oh yes, from...?"

"Paul of course."

"No one else? Good. Well my problem is that I've still got six- and three-quarter weights of this delightful substance in my possession. I could shift it on in the usual way but it could take me a couple of weeks. With the heat bearing down I want to move it in one go. So I decided to offer it as a job lot to one of the dealers we know. Since you took such a hit on the Moroccan I thought, by way of recompense, I'd give you first option. Interested?"

"How much?"

"Bought it from Paul at a hundred per. We were shifting it at one twenty. Its beautiful stuff, as I think you can appreciate."

They were still passing the joint backwards and forwards across the table.

"So I could buy it from Paul at one hundred."

"If he's got any left, then yes, you could. I'll give it to you at ninety."

"Eighty."

"Eighty-five and you have to take it tomorrow. Can you get the bread?"

"Say five hundred and fifty all up to make it a round figure."

"Five seventy bottom line. Is it a deal?"

Pierre stubbed the roach out into the least full of the ash-trays and they shook hands. "Can you leave...?"

"A taster, sure." Jonno picked up a penknife from the table and cut a few joints worth off the remainder of his quarter ounce, handing it to Pierre as he re-wrapped the rest in its silver paper.

"Do you need time to raise the cash?"

"No, I've got it in the bank."

Jonno smiled and said he'd be back with the gear at seven o'clock the next day. They shook hands again and Pierre escorted him to the front door. Satisfied, so far, with this encounter, but not convinced the transaction would go without a hitch, Jonno walked back to the tube station.

It hadn't been their fault that Pierre lost money over the Moroccan deal, but Jonno remembered him trying to scare them into not demanding their money back. If not for Kiwi Paul's protection Jonno was sure Pierre would have come on much more forcefully, told them it was their problem and to go and get fucked. If he really was going to retreat from the whole business then that protection would evaporate, maybe already had. After all what was in it for Paul? Everyone this high up the scale might seem friendly enough, but Jonno realised it was all just business, and a cut-throat one at that. Five hundred and seventy pounds was a sizable sum of money. One some people would be prepared to fight over. People such as Pierre.

"Now for Hamish," he thought as he gazed around the carriage. Although everything seemed to be progressing satisfactorily, he was still trying to keep an eye out for anyone who might be tagging along. It wasn't until he signed his name for the last time in the cop shop ledger, and hopefully had his confiscated possessions returned to him, that he would feel able to give up this constantly looking over his shoulder, this watching reflections in shop windows.

Hamish was lying on the couch in the living room, his long legs hanging over one end, with his head resting on a cushion at the other, listening to Nick Drake's *Pink Moon* album.

"Did things go well?" he asked, as Jonno sank into one of the armchairs.

"Oh man, I am so pissed off with all of it. Business. Money. Negotiating deals. Assessing risks. Second-guessing peoples' intentions. It's not who I meant to become and it sickens me to realise it's what I've turned into. Stay small Hamish, friendly. When you're just the little local dealer helping out your mates it's cool, it stays at the level of fun. And it can still feel like you're making a political statement, throwing blows against the empire. Get any bigger and the system just sucks you right in."

"Aye, well I think I can avoid that. The fact is I really enjoy my job, so I've nae reason to try to make money from the odd bit o'dealing. Like you say, I just do it to keep me and my mates in supplies."

"If it all works out, I'll be free of it tomorrow night. Just one more deal and then finish. But it could turn a little tricky. I was wondering if you would give me a bit of help tomorrow evening. Wearing your kilt."

"You're anticipating trouble?"

"I hope not. I've already thought up a little plan so it shouldn't come to anything, but just in case. You're a very imposing figure Hamish, and in full dress uniform..."

"Including the socks?"

"You understand me so well."

"Nae problem."

"Great. I'll go and put the kettle on and then you can tell me what it was you wanted to say?"

"It's about wee Susie, as you've nae doubt guessed."

"I did have an inkling, but go for it, say what you want to say."

"It's just this, man," and the big fellow with the face buried behind a mass of ginger hair began to talk as he followed Jonno into the kitchen. He started by exalting the qualities of his cousin, the beauty not only of her face but more especially of her nature, her trustfulness, and her kindness. For Jonno there was no problem agreeing with all of Hamish's preamble before, as he'd suspected, he moved on to her vulnerability, her capacity for hurt, and her unfortunate history of relationships. When it came to his summing up however, it was not as expected. Hamish was not telling him it would be best for his cousin if Jonno left. On the contrary.

"She's in love with you man, any fool can see that. She would never have found the strength to stand up in a club full of strangers and tell you if it wasnae true. So what you have to decide is what you are going to do about it."

"What can I do about it?"

"Obvious man. Go with her."

"What!? Go to Australia? Why the hell would I want to do...?"

"Because you're in love with her too. Aren't you? Why not? That's all I'm saying. I mean, what *are* you going to do now?"

"I haven't thought about it."

"Well, now's the time, isn't it? You say you're giving up the dealing."

"Oh yes. I'll have to. I'm going to get on with some serious writing."

"Well, you can do that anywhere, can you not?"

"I guess so."

"And you do love ma cousin, don't you? It's been pretty bloody clear to all of us right frae the beginning. And you are just what she needs, the poor wee thing. She has had such a hard time this last few years, it's been like watching the sun come out after a hail-storm these last weeks. I dinnae want tae see it going in again."

"Yes, but, Australia?"

"It's not necessarily what you think, you know. It's not all like that Barry McKenzie cartoon in Private Eye, all drunken louts spewing up in gutters down the Earl's Court Road. Has she told you anything about where she's going?"

"We've avoided talking about it."

"It's in the countryside. The bush they call it, near the coast in northern New South Wales. Her friend Mandy told us about it before she went back there. It's all hippie communes and people like you trying to create an alternative society. The Age of Aquarius and all that. People building their own shacks in the rain-forest out of mud-bricks and so forth. Land is dirt cheap as long as you're prepared to put the work in. It's not like this country, all building regulations and council approvals and miles and miles of red tape. Here only those whose ancestors were pals of William the bloody Conqueror can do whatever the fuck they want. It's not like that there. And forget about Rolf

Harris and his bloody wobbly board too. You need to think Richard Neville and Oz magazine, the bloke who designed the *Disraeli Gears* cover and that amazing Bob Dylan poster. Sure, there's probably lots of folk still living back in the nineteen-fifties but there are plenty of others who are right out there on the edge. You'd fit right in."

"Maybe."

"Aye, mebee, so why don't you go and find out?"

"It would be bloody ironic if I went."

"How d'ye mean?"

"One of my ancestors was a bit of a crim. Got sent out there, back in the good old transportation days."

"You're kiddin?" Hamish laughed.

"No. William Langbridge, one of my great-great-grandfathers. Sentenced to death for stealing a handkerchief or a leg of lamb or something. Commuted to transportation for the term of his natural to Van Diemen's Land sometime back in the 1830s. My mother got into tracing the family tree at one point."

"So you're partly Australian?"

"No, no. His wife had already born him a son, who was my great grandfather. She could remarry afterwards because in law William was considered to be dead."

"But you're a chip off the old family block. Hey, you might have relatives out there."

"Mum didn't get that far. She found out he married again, to some female convict relocated from Norfolk Island, so yes, I suppose I could have."

"There you are, you could go and find out. Christ, Susie would be over the moon if you…"

"Don't say a word! Not yet. I promise you I'll think about it. It's just such a bloody long way."

"Ok. I'll keep quiet. But if it was me, I'd be going. Especially with a woman I loved. You do, don't you?"

"Well, yes of course I do, *now*, but I only met her four weeks ago. How do I know if it'll last? She might want me now because she's about to go off into the unknown, and it's scary. But once we're there, she might change her mind. Maybe I won't be so attractive when I'm not a dealer anymore."

"She's nae that shallow."

"No, she's not, I know. But even so, Australia. It's such a big leap. I know nothing about the place except there's a bloody great big rock in the middle and they have a flying doctor service. Oh, and snakes and sharks and poisonous spiders, of course. Kangaroos, koala bears, Sydney harbour bridge and the opera house. That's the sum of my knowledge, none of which tells me what it's really like."

"Aye, and warm weather, lots of blue skies and sunshine. Great beaches. An outdoors kind of life, not cooped up like us here in the darkness, sheltering from the rain. Go. It'll be an adventure. If you don't like it, you can always come back."

"Jesus, you should get a job in their tourism department. I'll think about it, alright? I can't plan anything until I find out how I stand with the cops. And for Christ's sake don't mention anything to Susie. If she thinks I'm considering it she'll get her hopes up. And then if I decide against it, well, you know…"

So that was how they left it. Hamish with a barely suppressed grin on his face, as if he knew Jonno would ultimately have no choice but to accompany his new-found lover to the other side of the planet. He also appeared to be eagerly anticipating his part in the plan Jonno laid out for the following evening. Jonno was left with a huge decision to agonise over. His last truly life-changing choice had led to him standing by the side of the road just outside the campus of Sussex University, remembering his father telling him, "You don't want to be a drifter all of your life," and him thinking, "Yes I do."

It seemed everything he'd lived through since that day had just happened, with no conscious volition on his part. He'd drifted into and through it all. Now he stood at another cross-roads, having to make a choice which would dramatically affect his whole life. He was older now and had absorbed a plethora of different lessons. He knew that he must not fuck this one up.

~ 26 ~

1972

At the weekend the phone call came. Jonno woke that morning with a feeling of elation, remembering he was seeing Susie later. He hadn't stopped thinking about her. Her name was so often on his lips that Steve became bored hearing how good-looking she was, how her long auburn hair fell in ringlets over her breast and about the mellifluous quality of her voice. So he decided to deliver the two weights of Paki black earmarked for Trev down in Brighton a couple of days early, and drove off.

Jonno knew it was Doctor Ritchie as soon as he picked up, he could hear the clunking of coins falling in a phone box, which they had stipulated he must use.

"News?" he enquired as soon as they were connected.

"They've been. No problems though."

"How soon can you get there?"

"Take me about an hour."

"See you then."

He decided to walk to their pre-arranged meeting place since it was such a pleasant day, and it would take Ritchie a fair while to get down from Archway, or across from St. Thomas' Hospital. The High Street was crowded with shoppers, hippies of all description pouring in and out of Kensington Market, stocking up on clothes and all manner of ethnic jewellery in which to display themselves for the weekend. Records too, clutched under arms, maps of Middle Earth and rolled-up psychedelic posters destined for the walls of bed-sits, where Che Guevara might rub up alongside Gandalf, or Jimi Hendrix tearing off a mind-bending riff. Jonno could smell the patchouli oil from the other side of the road. He'd bought his purple velvet loon pants in there. He no longer wore them, except on very special occasions, such as to the recent Steve Stills concert. Mostly he had worn them while tripping, and he had happily long given that away.

On his side of the road young women were coming out of Biba, mulberry ostrich feather boas draped round their necks, or faces half hidden beneath giant, floppy purple hats, carrying bags displaying the iconic art nouveau emblem. He thought of the supposed Angry Brigade members on trial, and the bomb they were accused of letting off in the fashion store's stock room the previous year. He was amused by the deliberately misquoted Dylan line in their Communique 8 when it was published in International Times: "If you're not busy being born you're busy buying." They were protesting about the starvation wages paid to workers in Asian sweat-shops, as well as the exploitation of their own female sales assistants. The Communique ended with an unequivocal statement of beliefs which were shared by most members of the alternative society: "You can't reform profit capitalism and inhumanity," followed by a clear statement of their program; "Just kick it till it breaks."

The crowd thinned and he turned off into Kensington Gardens and headed for the statue of Peter Pan. There the polished figure stood, playing his pipe with carefree abandon as bronze rabbits, squirrels and fairies climbed up towards him, called as inexorably as Ratty and Mole to the Piper at the Gates of Dawn. As Jonno arrived a startled heron quitted its own statuesque pose atop a wooden mooring post, lazily flapping away from the Long Water to investigate the possibility of quieter fishing from the banks of the Serpentine. Finding an unoccupied bench Jonno withdrew a slim volume of Apollinaire's verse from his coat pocket and settled down to wait.

Soon a tall figure, dressed in jeans and a herring-bone sports jacket slid into the seat next to him. Jonno could see some looped black tubing and a curlicue of shining steel denoting a stethoscope protruding from one of his pockets.

"Thanks for coming, Ritchie. They turned up then."

"Oh yes, asking for Steve when they first knocked on the door. I told them he didn't live there any longer, and that we'd moved in a couple of weeks ago. They came in anyway. A man called Robert grilled us for hours while the rest of his people really turned the place over. He wanted to know your name, having worked out that two people lived there before us. I had to give it to him, sorry, but he was very insistent. He asked how we came to get the flat in the first place. I told him we answered an advert posted on the notice-board at work. Mark was brilliant. When I'd initially told him what might happen, he'd typed up a mock one on a work typewriter, complete with your old phone number. They came across it in one of his drawers, so that was cool. Eventually they began to realise that we were a complete dead end and it really upset them."

"Sorry about the hassle."

"Don't be, please, it was really most amusing. Mark's another medical student but Trevor's doing pharmacology, so he had all these pills in his room, all sorts in his pockets and his desk drawers. Their little eyes lit up like the cartoon pigs in the *Fritz the Cat* film. They thought they'd hit the jackpot until he explained what each one was. Never seen people so disappointed. They took some away for analysis but I imagine it was only to save face. They're all completely legal, and I'm damn sure they knew it. The funniest thing was when they opened the long boxes Mark and I have stored in the living room. They reached in and pulled up our skeletons. Honestly, I thought they'd wet themselves for a moment, all those arms and leg bones dancing about in the air like a couple of marionettes. I swear one of them turned green. God it was funny. They thought they'd found a couple of serial killers for a moment. Finally they all buggered off, none the wiser. They asked Chris down in the shop a few questions but he didn't know anything. So, I don't think they'll be back. They're really after you though, they were so bloody angry when they left. Good job I hid your new number at work, just in case."

"Thanks Ritchie. Apologise to the boys for me, ok?"

"It was fine. It's not as if we weren't expecting it. I haven't enjoyed so much free entertainment since the start of med school. And the flat is just perfect. The three of us were looking for weeks. Friends of friends is the only way you can get a decent place in this town. Sheila explained there might be a bit of a complication at first, but as far as I'm concerned, a bit of cloak and dagger was just icing on the cake. Terribly amusing. To be honest we were more than happy to strike a blow for personal freedom."

"Good for you."

"These blasted Tories. Acting all the time as if they've got some sort of monopoly on the moral high ground. When they support the bloody Yanks in Vietnam, apartheid in South Africa, and whatever the hell's going on over in Northern Ireland. It's all just ...so wrong. Have you been following the Angry Brigade's trial?"

"Sure. Of course."

"It seems it's alright for the state to employ violence, but if anyone else does it's a hanging offence. Even when all they do is damage property."

"Property is theft?"

"I wouldn't go quite that far. But you can't bury your head in the sand and ignore what's happening in the world. You're either part of the problem or part of the solution. Simple." So saying he stood and shook Jonno's hand before walking away.

So now he knew. Norman had indeed sent them at least a kilo of cocaine through the post, which the customs people saw through straight away, and were now looking for him and Steve. He spent the time walking back to the flat in West Kensington trying to work out what they should do.

He thought he was safe, as the cops didn't know where they'd moved to. But he needed to warn Steve, and his mates down in Brighton, to clean up their act. He didn't know whether stuff had been sent to Trev's address, or whether they'd arranged a subterfuge for its delivery. All he did know was that his partner Steve was down there delivering two weights of dope, and it was incumbent upon him to at least warn him to be prepared for an impending visit from the cops.

The problem was that he didn't know Trev's phone number. As part of their efforts to have very little incriminating information around the place Jonno had encoded all the phone numbers in their address book by adding a double-digit number to the real ones. Trev's number was so familiar to Steve, he hadn't bothered to write it down. Nevertheless, as soon as Jonno got home he rang directory enquiries and got a number for the Sussex hall of residence where Brian lived. He was one of their gang who'd stayed on to do his Master's. Jonno rang the number as soon as he came across it, but it just rang and rang.

He decided to have his shower first and get ready to meet Susie.

When he rang back later a man answered. Jonno cajoled him into knocking on Brian's door, but he was out. Jonno begged him to hold on for a moment longer and write a message. With obvious bad grace the owner of the disembodied voice agreed and jotted down Jonno's name and phone number, with the request that Brian ring him as soon as possible. Jonno tried to impress on the messenger the need for the utmost secrecy. If at all possible, he should deliver it into Brian's hand or, if not, to shove it underneath his door.

Jonno rolled a number of small joints and placed them in his half empty cigarette packet, before firing one up and smoking it while listening to Pink Floyd's *More* album. It was still his favourite and he was hoping it would act like a good luck charm for the evening ahead. He left the flat that evening confident he had done as much as possible to alert Steve to any potential danger.

~ 27 ~

1972

Jonno needed to do something, to take his mind off decision making. Since he was in the kitchen, he started to prepare a curry for them all. He hadn't cooked such a large meal for ages and it reminded him of being under Margo's tutelage in the Putney commune. While the range of spices available here was more limited, he still managed to create something which was enthusiastically received by his new flatmates. Susie did notice his rather pre-occupied demeanour and asked if anything was wrong. He explained it away by telling her he was feeling nervous about the following evening, which was not too far from the truth. Having been informed of his plans she agreed that it was a good idea to take her large and imposing cousin with him.

"He's enough to put the fear of God into any Sassenach," she assured him.

"I'm hoping it won't come to that," he told her before they both fell asleep.

It did.

Pierre was expecting Jonno to go round at seven o'clock. With his trusty holdall slung across one shoulder, he arrived an hour early, hoping thereby to thwart any plan Pierre might have made to deprive him of the stash. He was to be disappointed. Having been greeted at the door, and ushered down the hall into the back room, he found someone else sitting there. Someone he did not like the look of at all.

"Jonno, I'd like you to meet a friend of mine, Michael, or Mick for short, since he's a paddy," Pierre laughed.

The seated figure did not stand up or offer Jonno a hand to shake, merely nodded and affected a twisted scowl which emphasised the three blue stars amateurishly tattooed over the cheekbone beneath his left eye. He looked to be some kind of ageing skinhead, about twenty-eight or thirty years old, wearing jeans turned way up to display a pair of army boots, and red braces over a checked shirt with its sleeves similarly rolled up, as if he were ready for action. Beside him, over the back of the couch, was a bleach splashed denim jacket.

"So, you're the bloke with the gear, are you?" the seated figure asked.

Jonno ignored him and turned to Pierre. "Have you got the money?" he enquired.

"You're early," said Pierre.

"If you haven't, I can always come back later."

At this Mick started to rise but Pierre signalled for him to stay where he was.

"Let's all sit down Jonno," Pierre said, sinking into the couch beside Mick and indicating Jonno should take the armchair. "We need to have a little chat. When you didn't take that Moroccan I lost a shit-load of cash. So I reckon that you owe me some of what you've got in that little bag. I'm not greedy, but I'm buggered if I'm going to give you five hundred and seventy quid for it. I reckon something more like a couple of hundred would be fairer. What do you say?"

"Are you sure? Seems rather a lot for a load of dirty clothes," Jonno said as he slipped the holdall from his shoulder.

"What?" shouted Mick as he lunged for it, ripped it out of Jonno's hands and tore open the zip to rummage through the contents.

"Feck!" he swore. "It's all smelly socks and dirty bloody underpants."

"What the fuck are you playing at?" Pierre asked, jumping up again.

Jonno, looked at the two of them bending over him and with as innocent an expression as he could muster said, "I'm on the way to the laundromat."

"So where the fuck...?"

At that moment the door-bell rang, much to Jonno's relief, as it looked like the apoplectic Mick was about to plant him one.

"Ah," said Jonno, "I believe that to be the delivery you are expecting."

"Stay there," Pierre instructed him as he went to answer the door. A couple of minutes later he returned followed by a towering hairy-faced Scotsman resplendent in full ceremonial gear, consisting of Argyll jacket, waistcoat, kilt, sporran and knee-length socks displaying garter flashes and topped on the right-hand side with the black handle of a sgian dubh; the short, stabbing knife often referred to by Englishmen as a dirk. Whatever nomenclature used everyone in the room appreciated its function only too well.

"Jasus!" the Irishman expostulated, "Who the feck are you? Robert the fecking Bruce?"

"A descendent." Hamish replied. "Christ, it's like a bad fucking joke in here. An Englishman, an Irishman and a Scotsman. And you, with a name like yours I suppose you're some kind of a Frenchman?"

"So what if I am?"

"So nothing. You've lost just about every fucking war you've ever fought in, and if it comes down to it, you're going to lose this one too. I've got the dope you want in this wee baggie." He crouched down and placed his small backpack on the floor between his feet. "You can try to take it if you want. Be my guest laddie. But the only way you'll get it is by paying up. What's it to be?" As he stood back up, he pulled the knife out of its sheath in his sock and pretended to use it to clean dirt out from under his fingernails. When he saw Mick's fingers beginning to curl up into fists he turned to him, "I don't know where you're from hen, but I grew up in the Gorbals, you ken?"

Pierre looked at Hamish, then at the knife and finally at Mick. The skinhead slumped back onto the couch and shrugged his shoulders in Pierre's direction. It was clear to Jonno he was familiar with the Glaswegian district reputed to have been the most violent part of Europe during the fifties and early sixties. Pierre shot his off-sider a withering look before crossing to a cupboard beside the kitchen doorway. He slapped a bundle of notes down onto the coffee-table. Jonno counted out his five-hundred and seventy pounds and nodded to Hamish, who withdrew a plastic bag from the backpack and dropped it onto the table.

"I believe we're done here gentlemen," he said as he ushered Jonno before him down the hallway and out of the door, all the while turning his head back to keep an eye on Pierre and his so-called 'friend'. On their way home they called into an off-licence and Jonno presented Hamish with the most expensive bottle of single malt the establishment stocked. On reaching home he celebrated his liberation from the stash by buying them all a slap-up meal at the local Indian restaurant. There was much laughter amongst the Scottish lads as Hamish described the incident. Susie was more subdued, as also was Jonno, although for a slightly different reason.

A few days later he faced his final challenge.

He recognised the desk sergeant as the same one he had reported to on his previous three visits. He was sure the sergeant recognised him too, but pretended not to, forcing Jonno into the embarrassment of having to state his business. The overweight and ruddy-faced man reached beneath the counter for his big black ledger and scanned the contents.

"Last time, I see. Sign your moniker while I go and get your stuff." Shortly he reappeared with a clear plastic bag, which he upended onto the counter having first extracted a printed list of its contents. He indicated that Jonno should tick each item off, as he stuffed them into the holdall he had brought with him. It felt good to have his passport back again; the notebooks and scraps of poetry he was indifferent over, as also he was towards to the coded address book. He expected the chillum to be missing, but so too was his little Japanese lacquered box. This saddened him but he dared not provoke any antagonism by requesting its return, minus its contents of course. The last item was the important one, the hinged wooden box with their money. The sergeant tipped the banknotes onto the counter, took the elastic bands off each of the five bundled hundreds, and counted each ten-pound note, one by one in front of him.

"Five hundred, right?" he asked.

Jonno could only nod.

"Was there some suggestion you might have been dealing?" the policeman, still clutching the pile of notes, enquired while fixing him with a piercing stare.

Jonno assumed the exact same innocent expression he had used at Pierre's flat and stared right back at him while saying, "Nobody mentioned it."

They both knew they were playing a game, but stood there looking into each other's eyes for what felt to Jonno like an eternity. Finally the sergeant averted his gaze, stuffed the money back into the box and pushed it across the counter. As Jonno was tucking it into the holdall he was told, "I'd put that in a bank if I was you, sunshine. Now bugger off, and don't bloody come back."

Jonno was finally free. To celebrate he walked back past the old flat, where he sat on the grass in the park for quite a while, turning things over in his mind. Finally he rose and rang the bell at the side of his old front door. There was no response.

"Ok, that's it then," he said to nobody, and walked away.

With what was in his bag plus Pierre's contribution he was now in possession of just over a thousand pounds. He knew he ought to split it, but after Steve's behaviour of the last couple of weeks he no longer felt quite so obliged. Besides, he didn't know where Steve was, just as Steve didn't know the whereabouts of Susie's flat. He decided to walk around to Dave's place to see whether he had heard from him at all. He also thought Susie might have called in with Mel after work.

She wasn't there, which gave Jonno the opportunity to talk over an idea that had occurred to him as he'd been sitting in the park. The one thing he was sure of was the need for some kind of celebration. A surprise picnic for the following Sunday, he'd thought. It would be cold, of course, but if they wrapped up warm...He wanted to show Susie one of his favourite places before she left. A place for her to remember him by. Both Dave and Mel greeted the idea with enthusiasm, and Jonno peeled off a bunch of notes for them to call into Harrods and purchase a luxurious pre-packed hamper.

He was exhausted by the time he got back to Battersea, and hanging out for a joint. Hamish, just returned from work, was more than willing to supply his need. Before he did, however, he went across to the stereo and put his copy of *More* on, which reminded Jonno of the first night he and Susie had slept together. On hearing his voice she ran in from the kitchen.

"So, are you a free man now?" she asked.

"So it would appear. Free and quite well off. Shall I take you out for a meal?"

"No. It's my turn to cook. You have yet to experience the dubious pleasure of my culinary skills, so tonight's the night. Besides which, just because you are a bit flush at the moment you can't keep throwing your money all around the place, you might need it."

Jonno turned to Hamish and enquired "So it's true what they say about the Scots then is it?"

"I think mebbe it's got more to do with being female, man, than any kind of racial stereotyping."

"Yes well, you two just be careful of the gender stereotyping or I'll put poison in your food," Susie interjected, before disappearing back into the kitchen. As soon as she'd left Jonno told Hamish of his plans for the picnic.

"Aye, well that's a great idea man. I'll let the others know when they get back, they'll keep it secret. We'll make a damn fine day of it, right enough. But have you thought any more about what we were discussing?"

"All the time. It's just hard."

"Dinnae leave it too long man, or you'll find her gone."

~ 28 ~

1972

Susie did think it a little odd that the flat was empty by the time the two of them set out on Sunday morning, for what Jonno promised her would be 'an adventure'. The others usually lay in bed for hours at the weekend, but since it was late once she and Jonno had made enthusiastic love on waking, then fallen back to sleep again, she didn't think too much about it.

She was on unfamiliar ground when they stepped off the train at Hampstead Heath and Jonno led her up the main road, before turning left into a narrow little street lined with trees. They stopped before a garden gate which boasted a sign embellished with the words Keats House. Jonno opened the gate and they passed into a garden in front of a nicely proportioned but reasonably modest house.

"Shall we sit on this bench?" Jonno asked her.

"Is this where your poet lived?" Susie asked as she sat down.

"For a little while, yes. He was only twenty-five when he died. But this is where he did his best work, and where he fell in love. The story is that he was sitting underneath one of these trees when he wrote the Ode to a Nightingale, my favourite poem."

"Who did he fall in love with?"

"Fanny Brawne, who lived next door. The house was split in two back then, they were separated by a wall. He and another poet on one side and the Brawne family on the other. But I think their bedrooms were next to each other. I like to imagine them tapping on the wall."

"They didn't get married?"

"They couldn't. He was too poor to start with, and then too sick. Life was so different back then. Unlike Keats, most of the poets we still know these days were independently wealthy, they would have earned even less from their works than poets do now. Those who weren't couldn't just hop into bed with each other, like we have."

"No birth control."

"And sickness. Back then something like a quarter of all Londoners died of tuberculosis. Keats' mother did, two of his brothers, and him. It was like that until they invented penicillin I guess."

"And women died in childbirth."

"Exactly. Life was precarious. Which is why we should be grateful, and make the most of what we have."

"Is that what we've been doing, hopping into bed?"

"Partly, I guess, because we can. Isn't that what you said? 'A few movies, a couple of concerts maybe, smoking a bit of dope, some uncomplicated sex and then...goodbye.' But it doesn't diminish our feelings, or at least not mine, and I don't think yours. For some people sure, it's just screwing, and for some it's just fun, and there's nothing wrong with that. But sometimes fun turns into something else. Something people from a previous age, however wound up and frustrated by their longings, would have described as love."

Susie averted her face and pretended to look around at the assorted shrubs and bushes.

"Bloody poets. Always have to complicate things. Say twenty words when only three are needed. Are you saying you love me?" She asked.

"Yes."

"I love you, too."

"Good. You've nearly got enough for your ticket, haven't you?"

"I'm short twenty quid."

"So you could go pretty soon?"

"A few weeks, I suppose. Can we not talk about it? This garden is sad enough already, and it's such a beautiful day."

"I'll give you the twenty quid."

"You want rid of me?"

"No, I'm coming too, if you'll have me, that is. Can you buy me..."

Before he'd finished, she gave a little cry and threw her arms around him, kissing him full on the lips. He reached an arm underneath her legs and lifted her onto his lap without breaking the embrace. They remained sitting like that on the bench in Keats' garden for a long while. Since they didn't talk and hardly moved it didn't take long before the song thrush, which had been hopping about the place when they first arrived, became accustomed to their presence, and flew down from its perch on one of the trees to resume its quartering of the lawn. Eventually Jonno consulted his watch.

"Come on," he said, "It's time for your adventure."

"This wasn't it?" she asked, incredulous.

"Oh no, this is just the beginning." He placed her feet on the ground, took her hand and led her out of the garden. Just up the hill they passed through some trees on the edge of Hampstead Heath to find the three Scotsmen with Dave and Mel sitting on a couple of tartan rugs beside a glassy surfaced pond. There was no breeze to ruffle the water so that the trees and buildings opposite were perfectly reflected, upside-down. To one side of the rugs was an enormous wicker picnic hamper as well as the cases of musical instruments. As the couple approached Mel looked at Susie's face and asked if she was alright.

Susie looked around into the uplifted faces of her cousins and her friends for a moment. Then, shyly, she said, "Jonno's coming with me." Mel leapt up and hugged her, Hamish stood and shook Jonno's hand and the other three broke out into whoops and shouts of glee. The hamper was opened, plates passed around, bottles of wine were uncorked, liquids poured, and glasses raised in toasts. Then they all fell on the food with gusto.

Sometime later, most of them having laid back on the grass to digest, Hamish extracted a ready rolled joint from his cigarette packet, lit it and passed it around. Dave unsnapped his guitar case, took it out and started to play. After a while Duncan joined in with his violin, the two of them not playing any recognisable tune, just tootling around, improvising, and running up and down the strings. Finally Angus removed his bodhran from its round case, stared at the Celtic design painted on its skin for a while before beginning to tap gently on its surface with his fingers. Gradually his beats became louder and more pronounced, and he started to provide a rhythm for the other two to weave around and to follow. Eventually Susie could hold herself back no longer. She stood and walked down to stand right at the water's edge humming along to what was being played. The Scotsmen moved their tune into one she knew, with Dave joining in as best as he could, and Susie raised up her voice in joy, to sing straight out across the water to the houses and trees on the opposite bank, as well as to their inversions in the pond.

Later, in bed that night, Jonno turned to her and said, "It'll be Christmas soon. Before we go, you'll have to come home with me, anyway. You know you'll have to meet my mother."

"Oh God, she'll hate me."

"She'll love you. You'll be the daughter she never had."

"But I'm taking her boy away from her."

"She'll be coming out to visit, don't you worry. She's always complaining that my father never takes her anywhere. Now he won't have an excuse."

The End.

Eddy Knight was born and raised in Britain's West Country. He dropped out of college at the age of nineteen and worked at a number of clerical jobs, before doing an adult apprenticeship to become a bench hand joiner.

He left Britain to avoid the depredations of Margaret Thatcher, worked in the Netherlands, travelled around South East Asia and spent some time in New Zealand before settling in South Australia.

He gained a first-class honours degree in Drama Studies from The University of Adelaide before undertaking the Director's course at the Drama Centre of Flinders University. For the next thirteen years he directed plays in Adelaide and Melbourne as well as being mentored by Howard Barker in the UK and John Bell in Sydney.

Eddy gained a PhD in Creative Writing from The University of Adelaide. He has had short plays produced, gained awards in literary competitions and his short stories have appeared in various anthologies. His collection *A Short Walk to the Sea* was published in 2020 by Truth Serum Press. *Almost a Remembrance* is his first novel.

He lives in Port Adelaide with his partner and a Siamese cat.